DRAGON DOMAIN
Book Two of the Dragon Clan Trilogy

DRAGON DOMAIN

Book Two of the Dragon Clan Trilogy

By

Theresa Chaze

ISBN 1-58961-463-1

Published by PageFree Publishing, Inc.
109 South Farmer Street
Otsego, Michigan 49078
1-866-GO-BOOKS
www.pagefreepublishing.com

Dedicated to
James, Ricki Blanchard and the
members of Women Wiccan Writers
Thanks for your help and support

CHAPTER ONE

The water splashed against the dark sides of the bowl. She knew they were working, she could feel it. The water rolled against the opposite side. Placing a bucket on the floor beside the table leg, she breathed deeply of the herb and dark soil scented air. This was no ordinary greenhouse. The natural floor kept it connected to Mother Earth, the solar powered heaters and light brought the Sun Gods fertility into the four walls even in the deepest winter. The combination gave her strength beyond herself.

Squatting, she rinsed her hands in the bucket and dried them on the legs of her jeans. Her fingerprints were still dark with the outlines of soil and the same dark outlines were around and under her fingernails. They were actually clean, only time and absence from working with the plants would remove the embedded particles, but that would never happen. Standing, she tossed her thick braid back over her shoulder; it swung down along the small of her back.

She crossed the room and turned off the lights. Picking up a silver candleholder, she returned to the table. Snapping her fingers, the wick of the white candle came to life. The glow created a circle on the table, enveloping the bowl with light. The clear image of the flame reflected off the surface of the now calm water. She dipped her hand in, scooping up a handful. Slowly it seeped through her fingers, dripping back into the bowl to create wavelets.

Taking a deep breath, she centered within herself. The power of the dragon rose within her. She felt the energy of her tail swish back and forth as her human boundaries expanded before dissolving. Lowering her hand beneath the surface of the water, her fingers mimicked the movement of her tail. The transparency darkened, reflecting the star decorated sky. She felt her spirit lift on the wings of the dragon. She was in the sky below the stars and above the greenhouse.

Hovering, her long neck arched from right to left, checking the eastern and southern boundaries. The swamp protected them from the n orth and most of the western side. She saw no sign of intruders.

Several lights appeared in the cabins. One or two of the inhabitants openly stood in the windows, searching the sky. They sensed the energy currents of her beating wings. They could feel the rhythm on their skin, even if their other senses could not perceive her.

Below in the greenhouse, her hand still stirred the water; her body programmed to do so until her spirit returned.

Off to the left, Dominic stood in the library window, looking up at her. He was biding his time.

She stretched her long neck down, positioning her dragon spirit between her and her vulnerable body. Startled, he stepped backward. Quickly regaining his composure, he folded his arms over his muscular chest. With a snap of his neck, he flipped his dark hair back over his shoulder. His sky-blue eyes darkened to the color of slate. He would not openly start a battle he could not win; instead he'd wait for his opportunity.

Her point made, Cheyenne gained altitude. In the distance, she saw the flames and smoke rising from Coyote Springs. Her sisters were there. Tucking her shorter arms closer to her chest, she flew south toward them. She was not going to help or encourage them in their meddling. But she wouldn't allow them to be unprotected either.

Since Reverend Marshal arrived, he had been trying to change the town's attitude about the farm. There had been a balance of power until the dragon spirit shed blood and Rachael Franklin publicly showed the power of the dragon. Now Marshal had credibility and the people had fear. Cheyenne felt threatened by the interloper.

Her sisters didn't understand, they thought her resentment of the newcomer was childish. But it wasn't a tantrum, nor was it her pride. Dragons of different clans simply didn't mingle and Coyote Springs was within the one hundred-mile radius of her den.

She circled once around the perimeter of activity. Dark smoke mixed with steam bellowed out the upstairs windows. The firefighters rushed in and out of the house like ants with a mission. The police kept the crowds at bay. It had always amazed Cheyenne how the misfortune of another brought out the voyeurism of the masses. Standing in crowds beneath the trees or huddled in the cars, they waited to see if the occupants survived or if their bodies would be carried out. *Was it an accident? Or was it the sixth murder?*

Celeste stood among the police cars. As always she stood straight and erect. The blue and red lights strobed, giving her momentary spotlights intertwined with shadow. Bent at the elbow, she held her arms up in front of her, palms facing away. The left was closest to her chest. The right pointed toward their other sister, Jane. Sitting on the front seat of a patrol car, her long legs were stretched out the open door. She stared out the windshield at the house. They were working as a team. Jane searched; Celeste acted as an antenna and power source. Before it had always been the three of them. But more and more, it'd become a duo and a solitary. Cheyenne didn't understand.

They were not sisters of the blood, but of the soul. They had chosen one another as family. Celeste was the eldest. In reality, she was closer to being the age of a mother. In her mid-fifties, she still remembered when being Indian, even of mixed blood, was a shameful heritage whose religion was scorned by the Great White Brother. Her Hopi blood gave her patience and tolerance. The Scottish gave her the temper that made grown men quake when she was pushed to far. Her skin was still smooth, except for the tiny lines around her eyes. Her strong shoulders remained square. Her dark hair hung passed them to dance at the top of her thighs. Magic potions from L'Oreal, kept the gray at bay. Those who hinted it was unseemly for a woman of her age to wear her hair that long received only the point of her chin and a splattering of her hair across their face as she turned her backside on them.

Cheyenne's first memories in life were of Celeste looking down at her. Her life before that moment remained a void. What she had experienced for the first four or five years of her life had been forever beaten from her. When she was healthy enough, Celeste had taken her away from the Mesa. They never returned, even for Celeste's mother's funeral. Cheyenne never understood why she kept them moving, she dreamed of settling down and creating a home; but it was the last thing Celeste wanted. Twenty-five years had passed; Celeste had become her mother and mentor. Together they traveled from coast to coast, using their healing and psychic talents to support themselves.

They had met Jane almost five years ago. Celeste and Cheyenne had been helping the police find a missing eight-year-old girl; Jane had been working as a reporter for a local television station. It was through the investigation they met and become friends. Tall and tawny haired with the legs of a dancer, Jane was a local celebrity. Her career was successful. She had friends and family. She had a lover she enjoyed, but didn't love. She had an apartment with all the luxuries; it was safe and comfortable, but it had never been home to her.

The girl was found alive and bonds had formed between the three of them. It was the first time Cheyenne felt as if she had found her niche and wanted to stay, Celeste had wanted to move on immediately. It was the second time they disagreed.

Though a series of coincidences, Cheyenne had found the farm. It had long been abandoned. With Jane's help and the generosity of the child's parents, the sale was arranged, only then did Cheyenne tell Celeste. Reluctantly Celeste relented and within a few months, Jane moved in. The restoration took almost two years of hard work and sacrifice, but through the work they became a family. Cheyenne finally had the home she had been praying for.

From above, Cheyenne watched the smoke reduced to mere wisps, which dissipated above the treetops. Activity increased as the fire department put away its equipment and the police started to move in. She continued to watch, doing her best to remain hidden from their special gifts.

Jane stood, closing the car door behind her. Scanning the sky, she spoke to Celeste but Cheyenne couldn't hear the words. Celeste looked skyward. Immediately, Cheyenne withdrew, returning to the greenhouse.

Concentrating, she snapped back into her body. For a moment, she stood, staring into the water, stunned by the rapid decent. Blinking rapidly, she tried to clear the dizziness. Her heart stuttered as it tried to harmonize the different beats. She leaned against the table, submerging her arm to the wrist. Her stomach growled, not with hunger but with nausea. Breathing in through her nose, she breathed out through her mouth. The extra oxygen slowly returned her strength. Pulling her hand from the bowl, she turned and leaned back against the table. Looking skyward, she searched the heavens for the Big Dipper and the security it always brought her. She found it above the main house. She imagined its energy pouring into her, refilling her. Tilting her head backward, she closed her eyes and breathed deeply.

"Cheyenne." The timid voice called from the doorway.

Her eyes snapped open. Slowly she looked over her shoulder at the child standing in the doorway. "Lisa," anger tinted her voice, "what are you doing here?"

"You told me to come." Her voice quivered. "When . . . when they came back. I'm scared. And you promised."

Slowly inhaling, she arched her back, lifting her heels off the floor. Then exhaled, forcing the stagnant air from the bottom of her lungs. She relaxed her muscles, returning her heels to the ground. Wiping her damp and wrinkled hand on her pant leg, Cheyenne looked at the other end of the greenhouse, trying to collect herself. The child was still frail, a budding talent that needed guidance and protection. *But why now?* 'Dominic' was the reply. She inhaled deeply and turned toward the child. Slowly exhaling, she forced a smile to her lips. "Okay. Where is the shadow?" She extended her hand.

Lisa ran across the room, attaching herself to Cheyenne's legs. "It was in the barn."

Looking down at the brown head, she freed her hand and planted both on her hips. "What were you doing in the barn at this time of night?"

The small round face tilted up. Her hazel eyes speckled with gold sought for understanding. "It called to me."

"And you went?"

"It was lonely."

"Don't you—"

Lisa shrank away.

Annoyed with herself for her harshness, Cheyenne glanced up at the dipper. She needed alone time. But now she was needed.

Tears welled up, threatening to spill down Lisa's round cheeks.

"Lisa," Cheyenne spoke calmly, but firmly, "you mustn't just follow anything. Lonely or not. Next time come get me."

Nodding, the little hand pried its way into Cheyenne's, the small fingers intertwining with the adult's. "I will. Promise. Let me show you."

"No." Scraping the tentacles from her fingers, Cheyenne cupped her chin in her palms. "It's late. I'll take you back to bed."

"What if it calls again?"

"Tell it to talk to me."

"What if?"

"No, *what ifs*" Cheyenne pulled her toward the door. "You know the rules."

Lisa pulled free, crossing her arms across her chest.

"Lisa!" Cheyenne snapped.

The girl jumped.

"You know the rules."

Looking at the floor, the child nodded. "I won't act like a brat."

"Good girl. I'll walk you to your cabin."

Shaking her head, she walked to the door. "We're sleeping at the big house tonight."

Oh, really? Cheyenne thought. *Another agreement broken.*

Slowly turning the knob, Lisa looked out the door window. "I wish I could live with Rachael."

"Why?"

"The shadows can't follow me there."

Cheyenne flinched.

The door opened and closed behind the child. Cheyenne walked to the window. It was only about fifty yards between the back door of the main house and the greenhouse. The night was quiet. The light came on as it sensed her movement. Opening the door, the child disappeared inside.

Lisa loved the farm, yet she continued to seek out Rachael Franklin, spending as much time as she was allowed in the other dragon's company. Cheyenne found it disturbing, but she didn't know why.

Tossing her braid back over her shoulder, she returned to the table. The candle had burned down into the holder. The water was clear. She picked the bowl up and emptied it into the irrigation channel. She debated with herself whether she should put out the candle or let it die naturally. The flame danced, sparked and hissed into darkness. Debate over.

She looked around the greenhouse. Her eyes adjusted to the lower light level, allowing her to distinguish the plants from the night. The peace of the moment washed over her.

No people. No games. Just the quiet and softness of the night. Smiling, she relaxed into the moment.

A barn owl flew overhead, casting an almost unperceivable shadow through the ceiling glass. Some thought owls were an omen of death. To Cheyenne, they reminded her of Athena, Goddess of Wisdom. It was not wise to choose one God or Goddess above another; they all had their strengths and beauty, but for Cheyenne, Athena was right up at the top.

She said a short unstructured prayer for the child. She and her sisters were good kids caught up in a bad situation. Her family didn't want to see the pain they were causing. They just wanted ownership. On the farm, Cheyenne was Lisa's port in the storm. However, Dominic took every opportunity to use the child to find a weakness in her to exploit. Lisa's nightmares and the shadows, which called her to isolated places, were becoming more frequent since she started helping in the greenhouse. Cheyenne was certain Dominic was the cause. But Jane and Celeste wouldn't believe her without tangible proof and she had none.

Turning on the sprinkler system, she left the greenhouse, closing the door behind her. The late spring night wrapped itself around her. This was the time of day she found peace. She listened as the crickets and frogs sang. In the distance a dog howled, and many of the dogs on the farm answered. Several horses in the corral snorted. The earth and manure mixed to create fertility for the vegetables to grow from. The scent offended most people but to Cheyenne, it was almost perfume.

Smiling, she headed for the barn in easy, even steps. A few yards from the tack room, she brought her guard up. So far no one else had seen Lisa's shadows, but that didn't mean they didn't exist.

Cally, named so because of her markings, stepped out of the shadows. Seeing Cheyenne at the door, she double-timed it to slip inside before the door closed. Meowing, she rubbed against the cabinet where the cat food was stored.

"Hungry, girl?"

The cat answered in a long sorrowful "Meow."

"*Meow*? Nobody says *meow* any more." She pulled the bag from the cabinet and filled the dish. The hard kernels hitting the plastic quickly brought three more furry bodies from the stable part of the barn. "Don't give me that. I filled this bowl already twice today. And I saw all of you eat."

Ignoring her, they continued to crunch away.

"You're welcome." Shaking her head, Cheyenne returned the bag and walked out of the tack room into the barn. She scanned from left to right. The starlight gave the doorways and open windows a slight outline.

A low warning growl came from the back corner. Startled, Cheyenne stopped, her shield coming to full strength. A horse whinnied. The growl became more insistent. Half turning toward the sound, she scanned the darkness. Morgan stood, protecting her pups. "What's the danger, Morgan?"

Her tail wagged once, acknowledging her presence, yet she didn't drop her guard.

Cheyenne followed the tip of the nose to the corral entrance. At first she saw nothing. Then he moved ever so slightly, distinguishing his body from the rest of the shadows. It was not a spirit, at least not yet. "Dominic," she called out, "you know the rules."

"I'm not in the barn." The arrogance dripped from his voice. Stepping into the center of the gateway, he perched his hands on his hips. "It's a stupid rule."

"What are you doing here?"

He shuffled his feet, but did not cross the threshold. "Lisa—"

Cheyenne cut him off. "Knew I would take care of it!"

"Didn't your father teach you to speak with respect to your elders!"

"You are older in age, but not in wisdom," she snapped back. "You broke the rules again! Celeste isn't home. Neither is Jane. What were you doing in the main house?"

He lurched forward, but caught himself before he crossed the threshold.

"Others are beginning to see you as I see you," she warned.

"I know who my friends are," he growled, his voice emanating from deep in his throat.

"They are not as many as you think!" Cheyenne snapped back, taking a step toward him. "The only one you are fooling is Celeste. She thinks you love her. But you just want the farm!"

"Lesbian bitch!"

"That's good. How long did it take your tiny mind to think of it!"

His fists clenched.

"Just because women find comfort and support among themselves doesn't mean they are lesbians. But of course you couldn't understand. You only think with the head between your legs."

He growled.

Morgan answered him in kind, positioning herself between him and her pups.

Reaching behind, he focused on Morgan. "Keep out of this!"

Morgan howled, but did not back down.

Immediately the other canines on the farm answered her.

Pulling his hand around, he crossed the threshold. "I said shut up!" The blade was barely visible in the darkness.

"Get out!" Cheyenne snapped, advancing toward him.

Two dark shapes jumped the corral fence. Within seconds they had crossed the distance. Large and teeth-bared, Jerry's Shepard and wolf hybrids, Jasmine and Walter squared off with Dominic.

"This isn't over," he hissed.

"Anything happens to Morgan or her pups. We blame you."

His eyes shone red in the dark. "We never hurt our own."

"What is the knife for?"

Morgan's teeth shone white in the darkness, a warning rumbled from her throat. The other two harmonized.

"I was just protecting myself." He slowly backed out the corral archway.

Jasmine and Walter followed.

"They don't believe you. Neither do I."

Stepping out of the barn, he spun on his toes and marched into the darkness.

Walter positioned himself within the shadows near the corral door. Jasmine backtracked, finding other shadows to blend into. They intended to stay.

Briefly, Morgan nuzzled the palm of her hand before returning to her pups.

"It's all right, girl. He won't be back tonight. And if I have my way, any other night." Mentally, she made a note to herself to call Jerry; he would need to know where Jasmine and Walter were. Hopefully, he would allow them to stay until morning.

Jerry had become so unpredictable since Selene took the kids and left. He had come home from the boatyard and they were gone. The only note she left simply told him not to look for her. He had come to her crying, wanting to know where they were. Cheyenne honestly didn't know. He hadn't believed her. There had been nothing she could say to change his mind. He withdrew from his old friends, accusing them of plotting against him. Instead Dominic became his new best drinking buddy. They were physical opposites; Where Dominic was tall and lean, Jerry was short and burly. Many nights they'd sit on Jerry's front porch, drinking themselves stupid. In the morning, Jerry would be sprawled out and Dominic would have disappeared.

Cheyenne missed his friendship. Their conversations were now limited to the work that needed doing on the farm and the common lineage of their dogs.

Stepping out into the night air, she looked up. The Big Dipper still hung in the sky. Closing her eyes, she enjoyed the peace of the moment, not knowing how long it would last. Bunched together at the far end of the corral, the horses stomped and snorted, several whinnied. Opening her eyes, Cheyenne sensed their fear. They would be happier in the stalls tonight, Cheyenne thought. Slowly walking toward them, she hummed nothing in particular. The horses began to calm.

CHAPTER TWO

Celeste leaned back into the shadows. She didn't like being left behind. But it was just as well. The smoke outside was more than enough for her to deal with. Nervously she swished her hair over her shoulder and began braiding. She didn't understand. Why had Jane received the images? Of the two she always had the clearer sight. But it was fading more every day. Each morning, her visions were cloudier, less accurate than the day before. At first she thought it was illness or overwork. She had taken time for herself, trying to restore her strength. It didn't help. If anything, the decline increased. She suspected it was the crossover time between the phases of life. Long past maidenhood, her mother phase spanned a great portion of time, if now she was to begin the crone time of her life . . . *No!* Part of her screamed in pain. *No, not yet.*

Two officers walked passed her toward the house. They broke stride long enough too visually verify her identity before continuing.

She felt their distrust and anger roll toward her in waves. She shook it off and forced herself to bless them. It would be so easy to reach out and open their minds. So easy, yet so self-destructive. They didn't try to understand. But to forcibly open their minds would do irreparable damage to their brains and her soul. Combing her fingers through the braid, she freed the long strands from the loose knots.

She felt useless. Jane no longer needed her to confirm her sight. Cheyenne no longer came to her for advice and comfort; she had found her own answers. Most of the people, who had come to her for wisdom, now went elsewhere. *When had she lost control?* She stopped the thought. Part of her knew the answer; it was too painful to face.

The strong breeze was finally clearing away the smoke tainted air. Closing her eyes, she breathed deeply, trying to clear her lungs. There was a new scent, familiar yet irritating. She sneezed, her nose stuffing. The tickle in her throat quickly became a dry cough that shook her body and hurt her chest.

A hand grabbed her shoulder. Frightened, Celeste jerked away from it, clumsily spinning around.

Startled, Jane stepped backward. "Celeste. What's the matter?" Are you okay?"

Celeste nodded.

"Did you sense something?"

"Yes," Celeste lied. She hadn't even sensed Jane; it had never happened before.

"What did you see?"

"I'm not sure what to make of it," Celeste stalled. "Tell me what you saw in the house."

Jane looked at the ground. Reluctantly, her gaze shifted to the upstairs bedroom window. "It was him."

"I know."

Jane's eyes snapped back to Celeste. "We have to catch him. He's getting more brutal."

"Why do you think it is a he?"

"He?"

"Before you always referred to the person as the attacker. Not he or she. What changed?"

"I don't know." Her head tilted forward, her hand reaching up to brush the tawny strands behind her ear. The fingertips stopped on the pulse point behind the lobe. Her eyelids half closed; the pupils moved rapidly beneath them.

Celeste had seen this reaction from her before. Sometimes the information came so fast that she didn't have time to consciously remember it; instead she just stored the details for later. By partially closing off her other senses, she could flip through the stored information. It could be mere moments to a long intermittent search, which took days.

She looked past Jane at the house. The front door had been smashed off the hinges. The second story windows were broken, some by the heat, others by the firefighters venting the smoke. A single wisp of smoke rose from the hole in the roof above the bedroom where the body had been found. Celeste had heard the firemen—persons, she corrected herself, speculating that is where the fire was ignited, then artificially spread throughout the house with an accelerant. She took it to mean arson. She snorted to herself; some people just had to make things more complicated than they were.

Maxie stood next to his partner, Sammy, just short of the corner of the house. Detective Maxwell O'Connell, bright, handsome, red-haired pagan man. Pagan true, but he had not yet come out of the broom closet. The door was kept firmly shut by the fear of losing credibility. He had worked hard and loved his job. His co-workers already teased him for allowing Jane to help. What would they say if they knew how he spent his full and new moons? How many promotions would disappear, especially now the House of Christ was putting on pressure?

His sister had brought him to an herb class to ease his concern over her choice of treatment. Her AIDS couldn't be cured, but Nancy decided to stress living well, instead of existing for as long as possible. At first he had been angry, vengeful in his attack of the treatment. It had been Cheyenne who had cornered him, forcing him to see the pain he was heaping on his sister. He had blown up; Cheyenne had returned fire. Celeste had never been so proud of her daughter. Maxie had stormed off and didn't return to the farm for nearly a month. Jane had found him wandering around the stream where Nancy had found peace. He had cried in her arm. Together they spread her ashes on the banks.

A fireman—person, she again corrected herself. She shook her head; she was too old to change her vocabulary to be politically correct. The fireperson walked between Maxie and Sammy, dragging the still dripping hose.

Detective Sammy Davies had a spiritual power about her. Yet, she was a non-believer. She could instinctively dig up the information she needed from a scene or witness. She just knew how to ask the right questions. Celeste had tried to tell her, to help her train her gifts. Haughtily the young woman had told her it wasn't necessary; she wasn't psychic, just an excellent detective. It had planted the seeds of dislike in Celeste. She was an Elder, deserving of respect. But what Celeste found more disturbing was her inability to read the younger woman, whose brown eyes with flecks of gold had forced her more than once to look away. The two of them were perfect team. From their body language, Celeste often wondered just how intimate the partnership was.

"Celeste?" Jane touched the older woman's shoulder. "I trust Maxie."

Caught off guard by her sudden ability to read her so easily, Celeste turned around. "Then why aren't you open and honest about your relationship? Why are you hiding it?"

Planting her fists on her hips, her eyebrows arched, forming an exclamation mark line in the middle of her forehead. "Not now." Jane hissed. "Why do you always bring it up at the most inappropriate times?"

Startled, Celeste crossed her arms across her chest as if to protect herself from the words. *How could they treat her like this?*

"Celeste." Jane's hand dropped to her sides. "Why didn't you tell me Cheyenne was watching over us?"

"She wasn't here."

Jane pointed to the area above the tallest sycamore tree. "I saw her." The blue eyes stared down at her, searching and probing. Angrily, she pivoted toward the house. "I have to talk to Maxie."

"Wait!" Celeste grabbed her forearm. "Why did you think it was a man?"

"I caught a glimpse of him in the mirror"

"She saw his face?"

Jane sighed. "No. She only saw a vague glance. Brown hair and a full beard."

"That's what I saw, too," Celeste added quickly. "I just didn't know where it fit in."

Again Jane's blue eyes centered on Celeste, the pupils widening then narrowing. The softness of her features tensed, giving her a hardness Celeste had never seen before. Celeste reached out, touching the younger woman's shoulder; using her empathy, she tried to search for the reason, the cause of the anger she was sensing.

"Don't!" Jane jerked away and crossed the yard.

Stunned, Celeste watched her. For the first time, she noticed the weight she had gained, but it only served to accentuate her feminine curves. Even angry, her body moved in a sensuous way that attracted the attention of the men she passed. No longer a size seven, but more of a size fourteen, Jane could still get the blood to rise in a man without trying.

Frustrated, Celeste turned away. Men used to look at her like that. They had found her desirable. *Now-now*, Celeste chided herself. *I'm not that old, just older, not dead. I'm still desirable.* Inhaling deeply she tried to center herself, to find a place of peace. It kept slipping away from her. The harder she reached, the faster it disappeared, leaving only emptiness.

A car door slammed. Her eyes snapped open. Dominic was walking up the sidewalk towards her. A woman officer intercepted him. He tried to push past her.

"Officer, wait!" Celeste shouted, trying to keep the situation from getting out of hand. "He is with us."

She stepped aside, keeping both of them in her line of sight. "Why didn't he say so?"

"Why didn't you ask?" Dominic snapped.

"Enough!" Celeste interceded. "I've been waiting for you," she lied. In the past, she had always believed lying brought nothing but trouble; she was rapidly changing her mind.

Glaring down at the officer as he passed her, Dominic marched across the distance. Leaning forward, he kissed her cheek.

His male scent made the heat rise within her. The pressure and warmth of his large hands on her back gave her a sense of protection. His back was strong, lifting her up onto her toes. The self-doubt pushed away. He tilted her head up to meet his eyes. They were as blue as the summer sky. Even as children, he had always understood her needs. She hadn't realized how much she had missed him until she found him on the front porch a little over six months ago.

"You needed me. I felt it." His voice deep and smooth stated a fact. Celeste nodded.

He pulled her closer. "They're working against you."

"I don't want to believe that." Celeste felt the tears well in her eyes. Cheyenne was the daughter the mother had not blessed her womb with. She had deserted her family to keep her. She had entrusted her with her grandmother's teachings and prophecies that no other outsider had been given. Even when Cheyenne choose the path of the Dragon, Celeste had loved her and tried to understand.

"Celeste," he whispered. "Leave the past behind you." He gently released her.

Her heels returned to the ground, but she remained close to him. "I don't want to forget."

"They have. You're an elder. They don't have the right to question your wisdom. Not them. Not anyone." He tucked the long strands back behind her ear.

The strong scent of manure drifted up. Backing away, Celeste looked downward. "Dominic, what's on your boots?"

"Lisa saw a shadow in the barn."

"Please tell me you didn't."

"No, but she tried taunting me into breaking my word."

Celeste looked up into the blue eyes. "I'm sorry. I wish the two of you could make peace."

"It's not your place to be sorry." He reached out and touched her forearm. "It's hers."

"Celeste?" Jane's voice held the tinge of anger.

Celeste turned toward her.

"What is he doing here?" Maxie and Sammy stood on either side of Jane. Her entire posture spoke of her anger.

Again a shiver ran through Celeste's body. There was something about the female detective that made her uneasy. It was her eyes, which seemed able to dissect a person, ripping through to their deepest secrets. Those eyes focused on her. Celeste stepped back behind Dominic, trying to elude them.

"This is a restricted area!" Maxie snapped. "You know that Celeste."

Energy passed freely between Maxie and Jane. The power of it nearly made it a visible force. The heat of their passion wasn't good for either of them. But Jane wouldn't listen to her warnings. He was spiritually gifted. He needed to be taught slowly by someone who had the experience that Jane lacked.

Celeste felt the gold eyes on the side of her face. "Dominic." She tried to ignore them, to again use Dominic's body to shield herself, but the gold eyes continued to find her. Anger rose within her; how dare they triple team her! "Jane," she demanded, "why are you doing this to me?"

"She's not doing anything," Maxie interceded. "They're our rules. Not hers."

"We're helping you." Celeste snapped, the anger rising in her voice. "And Dominic helps us.'

"I don't want his help." Jane interjected, the anger rising in her voice. "I told you before. He interferes—"

"Why don't you trust me anymore?" Dominic stepped closer. "Don't listen to Cheyenne. She doesn't like me. I don't know why. That's why she lies."

"Cheyenne has never lied to me."

"Are you saying I have?" Celeste countered angrily. A thin dark string wound its way around and into her heart. It told her dark thoughts of betrayal. She found a freedom with its message. "Jane, after all that we've shared . . . all I've taught you—"

Jane retreated behind the detectives. "Why must you always make me choose?" Her voice quivered. "I love you both. I trust you both!"

"Another time!" Maxie snapped.

"You trusted me before." The darkening blue eyes fixed on Jane. "What happened?"

"Get lost or get arrested!" Sammy marched forward, blocking Jane from Dominic.

Dominic shifted his focus. "What's the charge?"

"Impeding an investigation." Sammy's lips curled into a slight smile.

"You'll never make it stick."

"It'll be fun to try." The brown of her eyes receded, engulfed by the gold. "Sergeant!"

Celeste panicked. She couldn't lose her only ally. "Wait. We'll leave." She tucked her hand around Dominic's arm.

"Celeste." Jane reached for her. "You don't have to leave. We need you."

Celeste looked up at Dominic. "Take me home."

He nodded. Gently covering her hand with his, he led the way, pushing a path clear between the threesome.

Celeste kept her head down. She didn't want to see the hurt in Jane's eyes or her own reflections in the golden-brown mirrors of Sammy's. Part of her felt regret, but the new and growing part of her laughed with satisfaction. Caught between tears and a savage delight, she continued to allow Dominic to lead her. Peripherally she watched the activity slow to a halt as they walked passed. Some snickered. Dominic pulled her closer. His strength and his scent made her dizzy. Another dark string found its way into her heart, making her stronger. As they walked, her back straightened. Her gaze focused forward. They still stared. Talking just loud enough for her to hear their voices but not their words.

Dominic opened the pickup door and helped her into the seat, closing it behind her. He walked around the back to the driver's side.

Through the windshield, Celeste watched the activity resume. The lights flashed blue and red. Jane stood among the detectives, looking at her. In her mind, Celeste heard her ask "Why?" Celeste closed her eyes. A tear slipped from beneath the lids, quickly followed by others. She didn't bother to wipe them away. She didn't answer the question Jane continued to ask; she didn't have an answer.

The engine roared to life and the pickup shot backward. She didn't want to see, didn't want to know. Dominic drove in silence. The sounds of the city and smoothness of the road gave way to the roughness and quietness of the country. Celeste leaned back in the seat, her body stubbornly refusing to relax. Looking out the window into the darkness, she watched the view change. More trees and fields, fewer houses. A dog barked and ran partway down the drive as they passed his home. Combing her fingers through a handful of hair, she separated the strand into three sections and began loosely braiding them.

Dominic reached out and dried the dampness on her cheek. His touch was warm and comforting. Gently he traced her cheek. The callus of his large hands felt rough against her skin. Throughout decades she had known him, he had always been a working man and proud to be so. Let some take the charity of the white man, but this child of Mother Earth could earn his own way. She smiled at the memory. His palm slid down her shoulder, tracing her arm down to her hand. She released her hair and their fingers intertwined. It was more intimate than a kiss.

They rounded the bend and turned on to the dirt driveway. The pickup jumped and bounced among the potholes.

Dominic slowed down. "If you arrange for me to use the tractor, I'll grate the road."

"I'll ask Cheyenne."

"It's your equipment as well!"

"Please . . ."

"When," his finger tightened their grip, "will you start taking what belongs to you."

"I'm tired."

He stopped the truck. Throwing it into to neutral, He swiveled on the seat. "Make her leave. It's the only way."

"You don't understand. It's not possible."

"We'll make it possible." Anger tainted his voice. "Together we can do anything."

Celeste lifted the latch. "Good night."

He reached over her and pulled the door shut. "I'll drive you to the door." The back of his arm pressed against her chest, holding her in the seat. His eyes gleamed with the light from the dash.

She felt his warmth against her skin. Time regressed. She was sixteen again. Butterflies bumped against the inside of her stomach.

He licked his lips.

Bending her arm at the elbow, she reached up and lightly touched his arm. The pressure increased on her chest. His scent filled her nostrils. Her hand dropped to the inside of his thigh, sliding her hand upward in small circular motions. He was ready for her. She pulled the zipper down.

He grabbed her hand, kissed the back and gently placed it on her lap. He opened the window and threw the truck into gear. It lurched forward. For no apparent reason, he had rejected her.

Stunned, Celeste stared out the windshield. The house grew in size as they drove closer. Most of the windows were dark. The pickup followed the drive around to the back.

The greenhouse was dark, as was the barn. Cheyenne was about. Celeste didn't know where; her energy seemed to be everywhere. *So it was true*, Celeste thought, *she did take flight. Why didn't I sense* . . . the thought trailed off, quickly followed by an unreasoning sadness and growing anger. She suddenly wanted Cheyenne to leave. It was irrational. She knew it. But she couldn't stop the thought.

The pickup stopped. Her head bobbed forward, freeing her mind for a few moments.

"I have to get back to the kids." His fingers tapped against the wheel, the gold of his ring gleamed in the moonlight. "Meredith complains I leave them with sitters too much."

She reached up and traced the outline of his jaw. He jerked his head away. Sadly, she withdrew her hand and opened the door.

Dominic caught her arm. "It's not what you think." His voice was raspy and harsh in the peaceful setting.

"I don't know what to think." She slid off the seat.

For a moment, he held on to her arm. "You'll understand soon. I promise."

Celeste freed her arm and slammed the door. Pivoting on her heels, she marched inside. Suddenly her bones ached. She was soul tired. All she wanted was a cup of tea, a long, hot bath and her bed.

The ticking on the grandfather clock in the dining room echoed in the otherwise silent house. Moonlight streamed in the window giving the kitchen an irradiant glow. The message light flashed on the machine. Did she want to know? Three calls were listed on the caller ID. She pushed the arrow. Franklin, Beverly. *What could her sister want now?* The remaining two were anonymous. She pushed the button. There were some things Jane and Cheyenne didn't need to know.

The familiar voice filled the kitchen. "Celeste, I'm concerned about Rachael. I've had this feeling for a long time. She says she's all right. But I keep being pulled back to Coyote Springs . . . Are you okay?" Her voice trailed off for a moment, but continued in a more regretful tone. "Did we do the right thing? Celeste, I need to know. I'm afraid for her and I don't know why."

The fear in her sister's voice reawakened her own feelings of guilt, which she didn't understand. How could she or Dominic have known Cheyenne would have reacted so negatively? Coyote Springs did need the store.

"She is just as much a daughter to me as the ones I bore." Beverly continued. "I'm trusting you to take care of her." The message ended.

The next message was dead air, ending with a click of the receiver.

The third beep brought Jane's voice. "Celeste. I'm sorry." She hesitated. "Seeing Dominic surprised me." A muffled voice in the background distracted her for a moment. She continued, her voice at a slightly higher pitch than before. "I won't be back to the farm tonight. I'll be at Raven's if you need me." The message ended. The machine beeped and the tape began to rewind.

She's lying, Celeste thought. She's not at Raven's, but at Maxie's. Should she call and confront the lie or let her believe she'd gotten away with it?

"Are you going to call?"

Startled, Celeste jumped back against the counter. A squeak of a scream escaped her lips.

Cheyenne stood just inside the archway of the dining room. The moonlight framed her outline, but masked her features. "You could expose the lie. But there is that silly rule of what goes around comes around. Are you hiding something Celeste?" Her voice was like a purr with words.

Celeste inhaled sharply and squared her shoulders. "What are you doing here?"

Cheyenne sauntered closer, her fingers trailing along the buffet, her attention absorbed by the act as if it was the most fascinating action. "Why shouldn't I be here? It's my house."

"Cheyenne!" Celeste snapped, beginning to feel like a trapped mouse.

Her fingers stopped at the corner. Her elfish face slowly tilted upward to meet Celeste's gaze. "What did you and your sister do to bring Rachael Franklin here?"

"None of your business!" Celeste snapped back, no longer caring to deny her involvement.

"Did Jane know?" Her voice was soft, but it hurt her more than a screaming fight. "Did you follow the rules or are you claiming elder privilege again?"

"I've always done what I thought best."

"Elder Privilege. Just as I thought." Her hand dropping to her side, Cheyenne walked though the dining room into the kitchen. "They're your consequences." She continued toward the back door, but stopped at the threshold. "Dominic broke the rules again. Once more and he's gone."

"It wasn't his fault. You baited him—"

Without listening, Cheyenne walked out, allowing the door to slam shut behind her.

Frustrated, Celeste picked up the teakettle. Her first inclination was to throw it at the back door. Common sense took hold. It would just be another mess to clean up. She returned the pot to the stove with a clatter. Crossing the room, she flipped open the machine's lid and popped out the tape. Slipping her fingernail under the brown ribbon, she snagged and yanked it from its housing. She threw the remains in the trash. Problem temporarily solved. She took a new cassette from the drawer, slipped it into the machine and began recording a new message.

Tomorrow she'd visit Dragon's Den and begin making Rachael Franklin her new best friend. No one needed to know what she did or why. She'd just have to be careful what she said and to whom.

CHAPTER THREE

Jane slowly sat on Maxie's sofa, cradling her head in her hands. Her head hurt. Her face hurt. Her split ends hurt. It felt like one big throbbing weight attached to her neck, stretching the muscles into tight bands of pain. A glass of amber liquid appeared on her right. Lifting her head, she took it from the familiar hand briefly intertwining her fingers with his. She couldn't look up. The glass was cold in her hand. She rubbed it against her cheek.

The springs in the sofa squeaked as he sat down beside her. Placing his palm on her shoulder, he gently swiveled her around. Starting at the small of her back, he massaged upward, loosing the offended muscles. She flinched. He kissed the sore spot and lowered his hands, slowly working his way back upward.

She had lied to Celeste. Part of her knew it wouldn't be believed. The three of them had been so close. Jane didn't understand what happened. Cheyenne had suddenly become so distant. It had something to do with Rachael Franklin. But what? None of them had heard of her until she moved to town. The whole mess at the cottage just made the situation with the House of Christ that much worse.

"You're thinking, not drinking." Maxie leaned forward and kissed the back of her neck. "Not good."

With a quick gulp, she finished it. Setting the empty glass on the table, Jane leaned back, pulling his arm over her shoulder and kissing his palm. "Sorry."

"Move in with me. It'll solve everything."

"I can't." She tried to sit up.

He pulled her back. "I want you to marry me."

"I don't want to get married." Snuggling back into his arms, she was grateful for his warmth and his strength. She loved his smell—earthy, but not musky. Unlike some men, he didn't smell as if he was in perpetual heat. Tracing his forearm down to his hand, she felt the familiar Celtic design.

"The only way you're getting that ring is to marry me," he mused.

"It's too big anyway," she teased back. "You'd have to make me a new one. And it took you almost five years to finish that one."

"Say *yes*. And I'll use my vacation time."

"And what would we use for a honeymoon?" She turned her head slightly, blinking back the pain.

Mischief twinkled back from the blue eyes. "A weekend here with me would be a like a week in paradise."

"Methinks, your sister and brothers must be humble, for you got all the conceit."

Tossing back his head, he laughed. Wrinkles formed around his eyes, revealing the joyous life he had lived. "Caught."

"You bet you are." She tickled her finger under his chin.

Suddenly serious, he caught her hand and brought it to his lips. "Marry me. Or hand-fast." He nuzzled her open palm. "Give me a year and a day to convince you."

His goatee tickled her palm, as his tongue traced her love line. Despite the raging stress headache, she felt the heat rise within her. "Not fair. Using my own hormones against me."

"End justifies the means," he murmured.

The endorphins kicked in; between the natural pain relievers and the alcohol the pain dulled to an ache. She rolled over on top of him. Two could play at that game. Stretching up, she licked the outermost ridge of his ear down to the lobe. Smiling, she nipped.

"Now who isn't playing fair?"

"Who said the end justifies the means?"

Scooping her up, he gently flipped her on her back, pinning her to the sofa. Gently brushing her hair from her face, he grinned down at her. "Me." His hand slid down to her buttocks, pulling her closer. He kissed down the nape of her neck." You stopped protesting."

"Protest?" she whispered in his ear. "Why should I protest? I have you right where I want you."

"You've cast a spell on me. I've never loved anyone as much as I love you."

Slipping her hand under his arm, she reached around and scratched the small of his back. "Not I, kind sir. Any spell on you was cast by yourself."

"I knew someone had." He kissed her.

His scent was intoxicating, shutting down the thinking part of her brain, leaving only the primitive, sensual part to control the movements of her body. His energy sent shivers up her spine. He touched; she responded. She caressed; he sighed. Hot skin. Quick breath. Blood pulsing throughout their bodies to the extreme edges of their tingling nerves. She arched her back. He pulled her head back, licking the hollow at the base of her neck.

The phone rang. The moment froze. Maxie's chin dropped to his chest as he reached over her shoulder.

She tried to intercept. "Don't."

"I have to." He lifted the receiver to his ear. "O'Connell. And this better be good."

Jane flopped back against the sofa, her hormones screaming in protest. It wasn't fair. It was nearly two. How dare they interrupt? They should know. She snorted, laughing at herself. No one was supposed to know. It would hurt his career too much if they knew about the detective and the witch. Unable to stop herself, she leaned forward and nipped his nipple.

"Ow!" Recoiling in pain, he pushed her away and glared down at her. "Nothing." He spoke quickly into the phone. "What did the autopsy reveal?" His eyebrow arched. "I'll be right back in." He listened for a moment and snapped back. "Why would Jane be here? I have no interest in her or any of that witch crap. They're just kooks and troublemakers . . . Hey, even the FBI uses psychics . . . Yea, right. Whatever."

That was it. It wasn't so much the words, but the tone in his voice that hurt. She was going to Raven's. She pushed him back and tried to roll from beneath him.

He shifted his weight, pinning her down. "Fine. I'll be in." He listened for a moment. "It'll be about forty-five minutes . . . Fine." He hung up the phone. "What was that all about?" he demanded.

"Get off me!" she sniped back, her passion turning to anger. "If I'm such a kook, why do you want to marry me?" She shoved him back and rolled off the sofa onto the floor.

He grabbed her waist as she stood. "I love you."

"You're just ashamed of me." She pushed his hands away.

Entangling his fingers with hers, he stood. "That's not true. I just don't want them to know about me. It'd ruin my career."

"That wouldn't happen if we got married?" She tried spinning away from him.

He stopped her. Their fingers still intertwined; he pushed her arms around her back, drawing her closer. "You could pretend to convert. They'd never know the difference."

"But I would," she snapped back. "I won't deny who I am for anybody! I'm Wiccan and proud of it!"

He pulled her closer and whispered, "I love you." His lips brushed her cheek. "Let me prove it."

"You're wasting your time," she growled back. "Unless you intend to rape me like he did!" The knowledge came with the images like the cold touch of death. She entered the dream the woman was having, full of images and people Jane didn't understand. The woman hadn't been afraid then. A noise startled her awake. Her eyes snapped open. The bedroom was dark. A movement on the right caught her attention. She only caught a glimpse of his face. Dark short hair, a beard and mustache. Or were they only shadows? She had tried to scream. The bag covered her face, sending her into a panic. He was on top of her. He said something, but she was too frightened to listen. Shaking her head, Jane tried to clear herself from the victim's point of view, to step back and get a clearer image of the attacker. She couldn't. She felt the woman's nails bite into the attacker's soft flesh. He screamed. Pain shot through the woman's face. Then nothing. Mercifully for the woman, but frustrating for Jane, she never regained consciousness. She didn't have to feel the brutality of the attack. But there was also no more information to be had.

Shivering, Jane opened her eyes. She looked toward the floor, trying to fix her own boundaries. Slowly her gaze lifted to Maxie. "She scratched him."

He had stepped back. "How did you know? The results just came back positive for DNA under her nails."

Jane stooped and picked up her shoes. "I saw a flash of a face. Dark hair, ear length. Possibly a beard and mustache."

"Possibly?"

"It was only a flash. She was being raped and she was terrified." Jane returned fire. "It could have been facial hair or it could have been shadows. It was too fast to tell!"

"That's it?"

"I get what I get. I told you that before." Jane sat on the ottoman and untied the laces of her shoe. Her anger mutated into fury. He was ashamed of her, except when he wanted her body or her abilities. She slipped the left shoe on and tied the knot. Without hesitating, she picked up the right. It wasn't her fault she couldn't find the killer. She wasn't going to apologize. Fumbling with it only made the knot tighter. Anger rising within her, she jerked the lace pulling the shoe from her hand. It dangled from her other hand by the lace. "Damn it!"

"Problems?"

Jane cocked her head to the side. She could see him out of the corner of her eye. At this moment she didn't like him very much. "Go'ta hell!"

"Having a tantrum?" He smirked and shook his head. "Why bother, you're just going to take them off again."

She snapped the shoe into her hand like a yo-yo and threw it at him, hitting him in the stomach.

More startled than hurt, he stood looking down at the shoe. Pointing downward, he looked at her. "What did you do that for?"

"For a while!" Ripping off her other shoe, she threw it at him.

Furious, he caught it in midair and slammed it on the floor. "What's your problem?"

"Want the list? You're the top five." She jumped to her feet and ran toward the front door. Grabbing the knob, she turned and pulled. Painfully her hand slipped off, her nails scraping the metal. She unlocked it and tried again. The door opened.

Maxie leaped, slamming it shut and pinning her against it. "We're not finished."

Angrily she stared up into his blue eyes. "Get your hands off me!'

"Not until we finish!"

"We're finished!" she hissed.

"Fine," he released her and stepped back. "Do what you want. You always do."

"Isn't that what you said you liked best about me? My independence!" she snapped. "Yet you keep trying to control me!" Turning the knob, she crossed the threshold, slamming the door behind her. For a moment, she stood on the porch just breathing the cool night air. The wood felt cold beneath her feet. The thought crossed her mind she should retrieve her shoes. *No, not likely*, she thought. Mentally she put on a pair of tennis shoes. Smiling, she looked down at her feet visualizing the comfy pair from the back of her closet that had been her favorite, now saved from the trash only by sentimentality. It didn't matter they had holes in them. She was the only one who could see them and her feet felt warmer.

Crossing the porch, she marched down the front steps and crossed the lawn. Dew glistened in the glow of the street-lights. The faint scent of grass lingered in the air in front of the Victorian style house. Jane remembered it. The color scheme was unusual. Pink with turquoise and beige trim. To describe the combination, it wouldn't seem to work together. But in reality, it looked like a life-size dollhouse behind an iron spiral fence. She turned the corner on Eleventh Street, following the iron fence. The house was dark and quiet, as were most of them. Every now and again, a porch light glowed as a beacon, awaiting the resident or flicker of a television screen that revealed signs of life. Crossing on to Thirteenth Street, a dog barked at her, starting a barking chain that continued down the street and followed her onto the next block. She found their presence comforting. She sensed annoyance from several of the houses, who didn't like their rest disturbed. *Get over it*, she thought back to them. As her mind touched theirs, she felt them recoil. Shaking her head, she sadly smiled, no wonder the talent became a recessive trait. Crossing Sixteenth Street, she continued to the middle of the block, then turned down the alley. Coyote Springs was a strange town. Some of the streets still weren't paved, but most of the alleys were.

Raven's house was the second one in. Her Jeep was parked in the driveway. The garage door was open. Reaching up, she grabbed the hanging rope and pulled the door down. The squeak of the wheels echoed among the houses. She opened the gate, closing it behind her and walked around the garage to the house. The backlight was on and the kitchen light shone though the screen door. The oldies station announced the time as two thirty, before continuing its salute to Elvis.

Raven was singing with the King. Normally she had a good voice, but Elvis just wasn't within her vocal range.

Her parents named her Margarita Anne Lavis. Her friends outside the craft and her co-workers at the police station called her Greta. Her job there was senior dispatcher. But those who knew her well called her Raven, Lady of the Air, named so for the darkness of her hair and her ability to float about any situation. Her brown eyes were able to see both sides of any argument. She had a voluptuous side that Jane had seen appear and disappear with a flick of her lashes. She could arouse a man to ecstasy or cut him to the quick in the same sentence.

"Don't just stand out there. Come in." Raven appeared in the doorway, holding a steaming teapot. "Maxie called. I was going to look for you. Just in case you decided to do something silly like walking home. But I felt you a'coming and made tea instead." She opened the screen door. "So what did he do now that has you walking the night air? In your bare feet no less."

"Same old." Jane walked in, carefully wiping her feet on the rug. "And I was being a bitch."

"I told you."

"I know." Jane cut her off. "You going to just stand there holding the pot or can I have a cup?"

"Mint, lemon, chamomile?"

"Mint."

Raven nodded and returned to the counter. Two mugs were already set out. She poured hot water into them and returned the pot to the stove. "You need to find a good Wiccan Man."

"Maxie is."

"Is that why he wants you to hide who you are?" She turned and offered a mug to Jane. "You don't want to hear this."

Jane breathed in the mint flavored steam. Raven was right; in the past, she had turned a deaf ear when Raven and others had tried to warn her. But now she was willing to listen.

"But I'll say it again." Raven leaned back against the counter. "Maybe this time you'll hear me. Maxwell O'Connell is a wanna-be. Nothing more."

"He says he wants to marry me."

Raven's voice lightened to a teasing tone. "He makes your hormones dance a lively jig."

"Yes." Jane hesitated. "He's so persistent."

"But you can't commit to him."

"No," Jane stated flatly. "I don't know why."

"Maybe it's because he doesn't want you for you," Raven hesitated. "When you're not around, the Old Hag calls him her boy."

"Please don't call Celeste that. We're having enough problems at the farm without name-calling. Besides, they don't even get along."

Raven's mug froze in mid sip and lowered back down to waist level. "It's an act. Always has been. From the beginning."

Jane sputtered, the hot tea dribbling down her chin.

"He has been going to Celeste for private classes." Raven took a quick sip before continuing. "They didn't want you to know."

"She promised me she wouldn't interfere."

"She lied. Again."

"Don't!" Jane dropped in a chair. "I don't have the energy."

"For the truth. Not to your face. But to others, she has said she is teaching him sexual magic."

"She said it wasn't true," Jane whispered. She didn't want to believe it, but it would explain why he suddenly had become more aggressive and energetic making love.

"The conviction is gone from your voice my dear sister." Raven set the mug on the counter.

Pivoting in the chair, Jane rested her chin on the corner of the chair back. The tea mug rested on her lap. "Raven, she's my elder. High Priestess to our family."

Gently, Raven took the cup from her hand and placed it on the table. "That's why I remain a solitary. I love the farm. I really do. I was happy for Cheyenne when she was able to create her dream. She was one of the reasons I moved here."

"But you were Celeste's friend."

"I've known her the longest. But we're not exactly friends." Raven licked her lips. "Celeste can be a kind and generous person. But there is also another side to her." She patted the empty air between them to quiet Jane's protests. "She can also be vain, petty and selfish, when she wants something or someone. I've seen her complete destroy a family because she had the hots for a man."

"I've never seen that side of her," Jane whispered, finding herself unable to meet the deep brown eyes.

"Talk to Cheyenne. She's seen that side. For a long time she was able to stop Celeste."

"We've talked."

"No. You haven't." Raven reached up and touched Jane's chin, slightly turning her face so their eyes met. "Talk to her away from the house. Where Celeste can't hear. Find her in the barn or the greenhouse. Ask the hard questions. And this time listen."

"I don't want to know."

"Then my dear sister, I feel sorry for you."

Jane closed her eyes. It didn't block the message from her mind. The doubts echoed off one another, becoming tangled and mixed until she felt unsure of everyone, including herself.

"Sister?"

Jane felt the warmth of Raven's hand on her forearm. It radiated love and support, but none of the controlling that most of her life now seemed filled with. She didn't open her eyes, nor did she pull away.

"I'm going to bed. The spare room is already set up." The hand slowly slipped away, "See you in the morning." She clicked the radio off, footsteps retreating through the living room and down the hallway. The bubbling of the aquarium was the only remaining sound.

The hardness of the chair hurt her forehead. She lifted her head and reached for her tea mug. Its contents had already cooled, still the first couple of sips were welcome. But like many things, it quickly became bitter. She walked to the sink, rinsed it out and placed it on the counter. Turning, she leaned backward. What did she want? The truth. Sometimes it was a loaded gun that backfired, shooting the questioner. What was the truth anyway? As a reporter, she knew what that was; facts were cut and dried. But the more she examined her life, the more she realized life wasn't that simple. *No*, she corrected herself, *there were still some things that were clear cut—lines not to be crossed. A person may make a mistake, but if the motives were pure—aye, that be the rub.*

Only the heart knew for sure and it wrote on pages only it could read. Jane shook her head. Reading too much Shakespeare lately; it was warping her sense of reality. Pushing off the counter, she headed for the living room and the spare bedroom beyond. Tomorrow was nearly here and she had yet to start the reset on her bio-clock.

CHAPTER FOUR

The morning sun shone down brightly, the warmth bringing out the shoppers to crowd Front Street. They wore smiles and carried packages. Celeste sat in her car, watching them radiate the sunshine in waves of happiness. Leaning back on the seat, she felt cold inside. It was happening too quickly, too out of control. The spring in the woman's step as she disappeared into Dragon's Den annoyed her.

It had been open a little over a month and business seemed well. Already at midmorning the shop was half-full with people.

Celeste felt reluctant to go inside. She didn't know why. Through others, she learned the shop was genuine, not just trying to cash in on the spiritual phase middle America was going through.

A woman and a teenage girl walked down the sidewalk toward the center of town. The girl stopped to look in. The woman jerked her back, making the sign of the cross, and pulled her quickly away.

Celeste smiled. The woman simply didn't get it. She just made the girl more curious and the whole store more fascinating. The girl would come back at least once. The woman's actions insured at least one visit and one lie.

Reaching around, she unlocked the door and pulled the latch. The door opened and Celeste held it in place, looking through the open window at the shop across the street. A car drove past. She used it as an excuse for not getting out. Another was coming so she waited while it passed without incident. Tapping her nail against the metal of the handle, she waited. The street behind her became vacant of traffic for blocks. There was no longer any excuse not to swing open the door and march across the street. No reason, except the nagging feeling that by doing so she would be stripping herself naked. All of all her defenses, all her subtle discretionary truths would be ripped away. She would be exposed to the unrelenting, unblinking eyes that were hotter than the sun beating down on the roof of her car.

Lowering her eyes, she looked at the emerald stone set in the silver ring. The stone of truth combined with the metal of the Goddess. She didn't regret anything. The gray truths *I told were done from love, not manipulation*, she consoled herself. *I'm not*—the thought didn't complete itself; it was lost in the view of her hand. The skin was still smooth, but where did the dark spots come from? She had seen the same patches on her grandmother's hands first, then her mother as they walked the wheel of time. Her nails were well trimmed and painted, the same shade matched her lips. Her fingers were a long as always but now the knuckles were more prominent. She curled them into a loose fist. There was no pain. *Why did they look so old?* She closed her eyes and shook the image away, choosing to focus on the promise to her sister. She had given her word, it was time to open the door and cross the street. It was still clear. First one sandal, then the other hit the pavement; she slammed the door shut and continued across.

The door opened before her and two teenage boys walked out. The last held it for her.

"I can do it!" Celeste snapped. The hurt and confused expression on his face made her immediately regret her shortness. She half turned to apologize, but he and his friend had already distanced themselves from her. *Not good*, she thought, stepping further into the store and closing the door behind her. Quickly, she scanned the room.

Carmen stood behind the counter, her arms folded across her chest. "Having a bad day?"

Sometimes Celeste found Carmen's directness annoying. "Is this anyway to treat a customer?" She tried to put a humorous spin to her voice; it only made her sound more sarcastic. "And an old friend."

Carmen didn't move.

Frustrated, Celeste couldn't read her as she had so many times before. She searched the brown eyes for a clue to what was happening but found none. Defensively, she looked around the room, "So this is Dragon's Den."

"Has been for over a month. I expected you earlier. Everyone else from the farm has—"

"Even Cheyenne?"

"No one expected her."

"I'm here now." Celeste picked up a lapis Goddess statue. It radiated with a life force of its own, which made her hand tingle. Turning over the foot high statue, she carefully examined its markings. None of them were familiar. She traced one with her fingertip, trying to get an impression. Nothing came.

"It's Saxon."

"Of course." The *I knew that* hung in the air unsaid. "So where is this mysterious Rachael Franklin?"

"Having breakfast with Kevin."

"You're Kevin?"

"He is not my Kevin." Carmen spoke slowly, stressing each word.

Smiling, she moved to the glass case filled with silver jewelry. She felt Carmen watching her back. "Rumor has it, you want him back." Carmen's facade started to crumble. Celeste looked at the younger woman. "You're not going to let her take your first love?"

The brown eyes narrowed. Carmen shifted her weight forward. "Celeste, what are you trying to start?"

Annoyed, she tossed her head back, the long strands bobbing around her buttocks. "It was just a question."

Uncrossing her arms, Carmen planted her open palms firmly on her hips. "Straight out. I've been hearing things about you." Carmen's voice carried throughout the store. Heads turned. Eyes stared. Carmen didn't care; she continued without lowering her voice. "After this conversation, I'm more inclined to believe the complaints about you."

The words slapped Celeste in the face. She didn't know if she felt more hurt than angry. "Who? Tell me who!" she retorted. "No one has come to me . . . except Cheyenne. And she's just jealous of Dominic!"

"Cheyenne isn't the only one!" Carmen snapped forward, her palms slapping against the glass of the counter between them.

The door swung open. Rachael Franklin ran in, closely followed by Kevin Mitchellson. "What's going on?" she demanded. "I could hear the two of you down the block."

Celeste felt the room charge with the woman's energy, forcing her to take a step backward.

Rachael quarter turned toward Carmen, still keeping Celeste in view. "Carmen, what's going on?"

"I'd like to introduce Celeste." Carmen's hand unfurled, pointing at Celeste.

Gathering her energy around her, Celeste leveled her chin and squared her shoulders; this arrogant child of a woman was not going to corner her. "You forget. We have already met." Peripherally, she saw the shoppers back away from the trio. Even Kevin took a defense step backward.

The gold flecks in the younger woman's hazel eyes took on a luminous quality that charged the air around them. Celeste felt the buzzing on her skin more than hearing it in her ears. The room warmed. Sweat formed at the nape of her neck and above the heart chakra. She refused to show her discomfort by wiping it away. A shiver crept up her spine, springing forth goose pimples on her flesh. With great effort, she kept eye contact. They burrowed into her, searching—prodding. No, her mind screamed back, you will not know my secrets! Using most of her remaining strength, she threw a wall of flames between them and broke eye contact.

With a casual wave, Rachael put out the flames and crossed the distance between them. "Lady, Beverly trusts you. But to me you are just another person on the path. My home," her arms spread out like wings, indicating the store, "and Dragon's Den is my domain. I have two rules. Honor and respect yourself. Honor and respect others. Follow them and you are welcome. Otherwise, the door is that way." One hand dropped to her side, the other followed her line of vision as she twisted at the hips to point at the door. "No one will stop you."

Fury flared. Again, one almost young enough to be her child dared to chastise her. "Are you ordering me out?" She snapped back.

Carmen moved to answer. Rachael quickly motioned for her to be silent.

A couple crept along the wall and disappeared out the front door. Other shoppers hid among the displays or down the back hallway. Betty Williams appeared in the archway, but the older red head did not cross the threshold.

I will not back down, Celeste screamed within.

Rachael leaned forward and whispered in her ear. "I know what you did to bring me here. Beverly told me the truth. What you do at the farm is none of mine. You bring it to my doorstep and everyone will know." The blonde rocked her weight backward, focusing her gaze back on to Celeste.

Celeste's mouth went dry. *Why had Beverly told her?* Her anger flared. She felt her face grow hot.

No, not now. A dark voice inside her whispered, *Another time, another place.*

Forcing a smile to her lips, Celeste listened to the cooling tone of the voice and banked the flames of anger. "There must be a misunderstanding. I only wanted to invite you to our full moon celebration."

"How kind of you." Rachael responded in the same tone. "But I've already made my own arrangements."

"Just ask Carmen, we celebrate in grand fashion."

Carmen's head titled slightly to one side, her dark curls brushing along her shoulder. "In the past, it was a very loving joyful occasion." The message behind the words had more meaning than the words themselves.

Rachael sucked the front of her teeth. "I understand."

Celeste felt the sting, but forced the smile to remain on her lips. "I hear you have an excellent selection of incense."

"Yes. I have a friend," Rachael stressed the word *friend*, "who makes them. Carmen, show our guest to the incense.

Whatever she likes is my gift to her. Celeste, do indulge yourself. I freely give them to you."

The emphasis she put on the word "freely" more than made her point. There was nothing Celeste could take from the store that she could use against either it or those that worked there. Their belief that she was capable of black magic annoyed Celeste. She had never deliberately hurt anyone. Mistakes sometimes happened. She had regrets just like everyone else. Why had everyone's hobby suddenly become making her out to be a villain? Anger mixed with self-pity rose within her. The dark voice comforted her. She forced a smile. "You are very generous. I won't take advantage."

"I'm sure." Rachael waved Carmen from behind the counter.

Carmen leveled her gaze on Rachael, her eyes narrowing. Wordlessly they communicated.

Celeste watched the energy flow between them. Carmen's strengths and weakness she knew well. The other she knew nothing about except what others told her. The blonde was quiet like a cat stalking prey. The thought made Celeste shiver with fear. She would prefer not to have either one behind her without someone watching her back. She followed Carmen's lead to the section on the back.

Carmen stopped and elaborately unfurled her arm, pointing from one side to the other.

Amazed, Celeste scanned from the stick and cones to jars containing the ground, which could be bought in bulk. Everything neatly labeled and organized, occasionally interspersed with herbal books. The bulk was on shelves draped with ivy that grew from a pot at the very top. It spread out to cover the shelves and had started to climb the wall. "I'm impressed."

"If you need anything . . ." Keeping her words short and clipped, she spun on her toes toward the front of the store. There was no question how she felt.

Celeste said nothing. Complaining about the behavior would do no good. She will get hers, the dark voice whispered. Smiling, she turned her attention to the shelves. Starting at one end, she tried to remember what she needed. Most were common herbs. Some were not. Reaching for the clove, her hand stopped in midair. Cowslip? Her Grandmother had ground it for tea and burned it as incense. She said it had the capacity to keep the spirit strong in the body. She needed its help now. She needed to slow down the ticking of the clock, to feel young and strong. She licked her lips and looked over her shoulder. She didn't want them to know.

Rachael and Kevin had disappeared into the back. The other clerk served a customer at the jewelry case. Carmen dusted a shelf. Celeste noted that she watched her by using the animal shaped mirrors. She felt like a thief. For a moment, Carmen half-turned. A full reflection of her face bounced off the mirror. The expression in her eyes drove a shiver down Celeste's spine; it was so cold and angry. She didn't understand why Carmen had come to dislike her so much. She searched her memory, but could not find anything she could have done to hurt her. The other shoppers had returned their attention back to the business of shopping. She knew some of the faces. They had either taken classes at the farm or through others had become part of the extended farm family who visited freely. They had respected her. Many sought her advice. Now they looked away and pretended not to see her. She had shared her knowledge and wisdom; they owed her more then they could ever repay with money.

You don't need herbs, the Dark Voice whispered. *Let me show you how to find new strength.*

Suddenly energy flooded her from all around the room. It was multi-flavored—sweet and young, yet full bodied like an aged wine. She closed her eyes and savored. Smiling, she focused on Carmen's image. At first nothing, but slowly the energy seeped from the image.

"Rachael!" Carmen screamed.

The energy radically changed, becoming hot and dry. Celeste's eyes snapped open.

Carmen was on her knees; the mirrors scattered around her on the floor. Her face was pale. She angrily stared at Celeste.

Looking around, she realized that everyone was staring at her. Several leaned against the bookshelves. One woman lay on the floor, seemingly unconscious. "What are you looking at?" Her voice sounded shrill to her own ears. Dropping the incense, she backed toward the door; their eyes followed her. "I didn't do anything." Her cheeks warmed with embarrassment. Anger rose into a fury.

Rachael and Kevin appeared from the back. The hazel eyes fixed on her, pushing her backward toward the front door. "What are you doing?" The blonde demanded.

"Nothing!" Celeste snapped.

Leaving Rachael's side, Kevin knelt at the unconscious woman's side and checked her pulse. "She has a pulse. It's weak. Call 911."

"It didn't do it," Celeste continued. "Why are you accusing me?"

Immediately the woman behind the counter reached for the phone and dialed the number.

"You can't prove anything!" Celeste hissed. The voice was her's, but the words came from the darkness inside her. For a moment, it frightened her. The darkness curled around her heart like a warm blanket, sheltering her from their anger and her own responsibility. None of them mattered. Only the dark hunger could keep her safe from the hazel eyes. She pulled it tighter. Tossing back her head, she laughed. "You can't prove anything," she repeated. "Say I did and the slander laws will make me a rich woman." Squaring her shoulders, she slowly sauntered out the front door. Briefly scanning the street, she crossed and opened her car door. Sliding in, she fit the key in the ignition.

Her hands were different. The dark spots were gone. She gently touched the smooth, clear skin and smiled. Self-satisfied, she turned the key and the engine roared to life. She backed up and pulled out. Blowing its horn, a car skidded to a halt. Flipping him off, Celeste continued, without regret. Her hands were beautiful and young. She felt stronger and more alive than she had in a long time. Nothing else mattered.

She took the direct route home and quickly pulled into the garage; she cut the engine and ran inside. The answering machine flashed, but she didn't care. She was aware of voices echoing from the front of the house. She didn't want to speak to them. Taking the back stairway, she ran to her room, impatient to see if there were any other changes.

Slamming the door, she stripped and stood in front of the mirror. Her body was the same. Disappointed, she sagged onto the edge of her bed, closed her eyes, and cradled her head in her hands. Tears welled up and fell as her body shook. Her nose stuffed up. Reaching for a tissue, she found the box was empty. *Oh, great!* She thought, just perfect. Mucus dripped from her nose. She wiped it way with the comforter without noticing. None of this seemed real. *Why had everyone abandoned her?* She loved them with her whole heart; everything she had done was for their best interest. *Why didn't they see that?* With the tips of her fingers, she wiped away the tears.

Crawling across the bed, she stretched out, pulling part of the comforter over her. Closing her eyes, she pulled the pillow to her, fluffing it to cradle her head. Just a little sleep and everything will be better. Everyone has bad days; I've just had more than my share all at once, she consoled herself. With her eyes closed her body felt heavy against the bed. She sank into sleep, but her mind would not rest, instead insisting on reviewing the morning's events. Only now she could not move. She was frozen in front of the incense. The customers walked around her, picking off pieces of her and attaching them on their own bodies. Rachael stood in the inner doorway, watching; her arms sternly folded across her chest. Anger became fear as Celeste tried to ward off the attackers. Would they leave nothing of her behind? She tried to cry out, but no sound escaped her. Her Grandmother walked into the store. *Not possible,* Celeste's mind screamed, *you died!* The elderly woman strolled across the room; her graying hair held back in a long braid, which lay over her shoulder and across her breast. The long traditional skirt flowed around her legs with each step. All her actions seemed slow motion, deliberately giving Celeste the opportunity to follow her approach. She stopped a few feet from Celeste. Her shoulder slightly stooped with age, yet the pride within her kept the fire in her eyes. Celeste quickly looked away unable to withstand the scrutiny of the older brown eyes.

"What are you doing, daughter of my blood?" The accusation was a mere whisper, but echoed loudly within Celeste's soul. "Why do you dishonor all I have taught you?"

I haven't, Celeste wanted to protest; but instead she stood mutely looking at the woman whose respect and love she had always sought. Now the brown eyes only held sadness and disapproval. Again she was the disobedient child caught riffling through Grandmother's ceremonial pack. She had been holding the healing feather up to the light, watching the rays filter through it and off the gemstones hanging from it when Grandmother and Mother walked into the lodge. Mother gasped in disbelief. Grandmother calmly marched across the room and held out her hand. Celeste had wished they had beaten her. Instead for an entire year her chores were doubled and she was banished from all of Grandmother's teachings. When the elders came to tell stories and share advice, she was sent to the barn until they left. She thought the year would never end. But eventually it did and she was brought before the elders to explain what she had learned. She told them what they wanted to hear. It seemed to satisfy them, yet they always seemed to be watching her, examining her motives. She was allowed to rejoin the others, but she never caught up to her sister and cousins. The year of lessons was always lost to her.

Grandmother reached out. Celeste's eyes followed her hand to her own hands, which held the same healing feather. Grandmother slipped it from her fingers. Celeste screamed in rage.

Her own scream woke her. Trembling, she lay on the bed looking at the ceiling, trying to focus her eyes. Reaching up, she wiped the sweat mixed with tears off her upper lip. She closed her eyes and swallowed hard, trying to force the fear from her throat. She didn't want to look, but she knew she had to. Slowly she opened her eyes and turned her head, unaware of the breath caught in her chest. The healing feather hung above her altar. Her chest uncoiled and she breathed a sigh of relief. Licking her lips, she sat up, sliding her legs over the bed. She felt dizzy and nauseous. The room tilted once as she stood, but quickly righted itself. It was still there. She had followed their rules, she had earned it. It rightfully belonged to her and the dream was a dream, nothing more.

Crossing the room, she reached out to touch it, feeling it warm under her fingertips. The eagle feather turned to dust and the gemstones shards fell on the table, making off-key tickling sounds. In disbelief, she stared, the fury rising within her. It was more than a symbol of her power; it was the focal point she used to reconnect with her ancestors. They were the seat and soul of her ability to connect with the Great Spirit. She was alone and powerless. Fear overwhelmed her. Her chest ached and her head swam as thoughts swooped down on her from every direction. The room darkened. She reached out to support herself on the table, her fingertips catching the edge of her altar cloth. It seemed to shrink from her. No! Her mind screamed, grasping it tighter. The cloth and her ritual belongings jumped into the air. The urn, which held portions of her Grandmother's and Mother's ashes, smashed at her feet, their remains spilling onto the floor. Quickly she knelt, trying to collect the pieces. They slipped though her fingers.

The door opened and closed.

"Go away!" she screamed.

The heavy footsteps ignored her, drawing closer. A shadow drifted across her as he knelt beside her. Dominic reached around and brushed the ashes from her hands.

"Look what I have done," Celeste cried.

"You've freed yourself." He pulled her closer, his fingers combing through her hair.

She felt his bare chest against her cheek. His scent filled her with visions of dark passion. She was no longer an elder, but a maiden reaching for the forbidden fruit. She no longer found reason to seek the light. He reached for her; she responded. They came together among the ashes.

CHAPTER FIVE

Cheyenne stuck the pitchfork into the pile of manure. Wiping her forehead with the back of her hand, she gazed around the barn. It was quiet. The livestock were out in the pasture absorbing the energy of the sun and consuming the nutrients that would be tomorrow's manure. She hated keeping them in the barn at night. They didn't like missing the warm nights and it made more work for her. But since Dominic's arrival, it just wasn't safe for them to be out in the pasture after dark.

Celeste had known him from before, but she never would explain where or when. It had been one of the few secrets she kept. The questions had made her nervous and defensive.

There was something about Dominic that Cheyenne had never trusted. There was a shadow in the blue eyes, which set off her alarm bells. The animal mutilations started the first full moon after he arrived. At first some of the teenagers, who visited the farm, were suspected of dabbling in the Dark Arts. Most took the Goddess oath swearing they were uninvolved. The four, who were part of Dominic's circle, would not. Three of them had arrived with Dominic. The fourth, Stephan, was local. Cheyenne had cornered him. Fearfully he confessed, but just as quickly recanted, claiming Cheyenne had forced him to lie. Celeste accused her of being jealous of Dominic. Jane refused to take a stand without more proof. For the first time, Cheyenne invoked her ownership privilege. Dominic would be limited to certain parts of the farm and he not allowed in the main house unsupervised. It was good in theory, but the practice left much to be desired. She regretted not listening to her instincts and giving into Celeste plea to allow him to stay.

Stabbing the manure, she pushed the topic from her mind. It was idle chatter that changed nothing and wasted energy in useless anger.

"Who you mad at?"

Cheyenne spun around, swinging the fork in front of her like a staff.

"Whoo!" Carmen jumped back out of the barn. "Peace sister!" She held up two fingers.

"Sorry. I was thinking dark thoughts."

"So I see." Carmen stepped back into the coolness of the barn. "Anything you'd like to share?"

"Usual." She drove the fork into the remaining pile. "What's up?"

Hesitating, Carmen pushed the dark strands back over her forehead. "The problem is getting worse."

Cheyenne looked away. A crest of anger rose within her. *She was not Celeste's keeper; why did they always come to her?* "What did Celeste do now?" The bite in her voice forced Carmen to take a step backward. She instantly regretted her tone. "Sorry."

"I know you're frustrated and angry. But you're the closest one—"

"I was."

"She came to the Den this morning."

"That's what you wanted."

Squaring her shoulders, Carmen's head snapped up, her eyes directly meeting Cheyenne's. "She vampired off most of the people in the store. Including me. She put one woman in the hospital. She nearly died."

In disbelief, Cheyenne stared back, not knowing what to say. Celeste, even in the self-destructive state she was in, couldn't be that stupid.

Carmen's licked her lips and continued. "She walked in with an attitude of mistress of the manor."

"She's been doing that a lot lately."

"I wasn't that nice to her. I admit that." Carmen shifted her weight. "I—she tried—"

"She pushed the Kevin button again."

Carmen nodded. "I love Rachael. Her and I are becoming fast friends. Eventually maybe sisters. Kevin. I still do love him. That is true. But they have been so good for each other. She gives him a sense of peace that I could never give him. He has helped her to become more open and trusting. Rachael has this core of pain that she refuses to talk about. I think it has something to do with her childhood."

"So do you love them both enough to step out of the way?"

Nodding, Carmen again shifted her weight. "It's not always easy watching them be so happy."

"But Celeste tempts the dark part of you?" Cheyenne breathed in though her nose. The manure and hay scents intertwined. The combination always calmed her racing mind and grounded her thoughts. Slowly she breathed out though her mouth. "You know there is a dark haired man you will meet. He'll love and respect you. As you will him. If you don't follow the higher path . . ." Cheyenne fought to find the right words. "If you allow your jealousy and lust to rule your heart and spirit, you'll lose both him and you. He is a man of honor. He cannot love what he does not respect. And if you poach on your friends' relationship, how will you feel about yourself?"

"I know!" Carmen snapped. "I didn't drive out her to talk about me and my lust troubles. Celeste has to be stopped!"

"By ignoring the truth about yourself, you give her power to control you. She'd give you permission to be selfish—to hurt two people you care about and who care about you."

"Stop it!" Carmen wiped her face with the palms of her hands. "I just wanted you to know what she did. Rachael was able to stop her. She has been permanently banned."

"It is Rachael Franklin's right to choose who comes into her shop."

"That's the first time you mentioned her by name. Rachael is a good person. The two of you are much alike."

"Then why are you thinking about hurting her?" Cheyenne cut in.

"I'm not!" Carmen spun on her toes and half-marched, half-ran out of the barn.

Cheyenne closed her eyes and slowly shook her head. It was becoming overwhelming. There were no more tears to be shed; no more arguments to be fought. There was nothing she could do to keep Celeste off this self-destructive path. Her only concern now was for the farm. How this would affect all the people who depended on this place as a safe haven. Not only the people who lived in the cabins, but also the ones who visited to find peace within its forests. She leaned against one of the stalls. More and more she was regretting rejoining the human race emotionally. It caused her pain and fear. It took away her self-reliance and muddied the waters of Truth. Her childhood was a mystery she didn't wish to solve. Instead she moved forward from the memory of Celeste finding her. She created deep bonds not with people, but the life forces of nature, with the Deva and animal spirits. Celeste had raised her, but the Rhea, spirit of the planet, was her true mother. It was only since settling in Coyote Springs had Cheyenne allowed other people to see into her soul. She had shared her visions and found support.

Horse hooves trotted in. Cheyenne glanced up to see Nightshade standing in front of her. He stomped impatiently, his head turning from side to side. She reached out and scratched his brown head. "I promised you a ride."

Again the white-socked hoof hit the ground, sending up a puff of dust.

"I haven't finished cleaning the barn yet."

His neck stretched forward, grabbing the abdomen part of her T-shirt. He pulled her forward onto the tips of her toes.

"Getting pushy aren't you?"

He backed up toward the tack room, dragging her with him.

Shifting her weight backwards, Cheyenne set her heels and the forward motion temporarily stopped. "If I give in easily; you get the wrong idea. But I do need a break. The ride will do us both good." She pulled the material from between his teeth. "Compromise. Give me ten minutes to finish up here and go to the bathroom."

Nightshade snorted. Turning tail, he walked out of the barn.

It wasn't much of a compromise. He had gotten his way, just not as fast as he wanted. Pulling the pitchfork from the manure, she suddenly felt pressure and pain in the middle of her forehead as her third eye pulsed. Outside the horses whinnied and stomped, bumping and crashing into one other as they crowded into an ever-tightening circle. The dogs howled for miles in every direction. The first wave of darkness hit, knocking the fork from her hand. The base of her spine became fire, radiating out in an uneven pattern. Her second chakra sunk into itself as the power center in her abdomen flared up to combine with the energy of her spine to protect her sexuality. Gasping for breath, she dropped to her knees. She sensed the second wave; she quickly threw up her shield as the darkness enveloped her. The rapidly placed defenses gave her only inches of clear space between her and the fowl gray matter. She sensed another wave. The smell of rotting flesh seeped through. Cheyenne gagged, the third wave rolling over her. The shield wavered. The darkness overshadowed the indirect sunlight. Her hands and feet lost feeling as the darkness drew the life force from her. Her heart beat rapidly, pain filling every nerve ending. She started to lose consciousness. Choking; she tried to breathe but the air was filled with the soul eating darkness. Instinctively, using her last bit of strength, she thrust her hands into the manure and earth as her shields collapsed. She was exposed; but only for a moment. The living spirit of the earth reached up and touched her fingertips, radiating up her hands and arms to her heart. Like exploding suns, light burst from her chest and forehead. The darkness retreated. Radiating up through her, the flares followed the dark threads, rapidly consuming them. In the distance, glass broke. The screams of a woman and man intertwined.

Cheyenne awoke lying face down. The air was cool against her skin. Slowly she inhaled. The air was drier and heavily scented with desert flowers. *How? Why?* But her questions were quickly disbursed by her concern for the animals. Struggling to her knees, she rose even more slowly to her feet and staggered to the corral.

All was quiet-too quiet. Most of the horses and the cows were at the opposite end of the pasture. Only Nightshade remained in the corral. Seeing her, his ears flattened and he shakily shied away.

She didn't approach him. Instead she walked along the barn, leaning heavily on the wall to steady herself. She surveyed the yard. It seemed unnatural. It was too quiet. No birds sang. The chickens, normally scattered throughout the yard clucking and chattering, had vanished. Swallowing the rising bile, she began to search. She found the first one beneath the hay wagon. It was cold, lifeless to the touch as if it had been dead for hours. Four more sat dead in the center of the yard; their life force sucked from them so quickly they didn't have a chance to react. Two more lay by the barn; their beaks in the dirt, their feathered behinds in the air. Seven in all, but where were the rest? She opened the coop door and found the rest of the flock huddled in the corner. Instead of scattering, they tightened their ranks, climbing over one another to get away from her. She stopped and backed up.

Stepping back into the sunlight, she realized how cold she was, not only on the outside, but the chill came from within. Something was wrong. She knew it, but didn't know what or how to fix it. Everything changed soon after Carmen had left. But she didn't have the power or the morality to create that kind of negativity. At best speed she crossed the distance to the barn door. Standing outside, she charted the bodies of the dead and followed the route, which led her to the main house.

It seemed darker. In spite of the sunlight, several lights were on. Upstairs, both of Celeste's bedroom windows had cracked. They were no longer transparent, but had a smoky quality, which reflected the images of the sky and clouds.

Dominic stepped in front of the right window. He was naked. He looked down at her; at first surprised, a self-satisfied smirk quickly formed on his lips. His fingertips trailed down the pelt of his chest hair down to his groin. Gathering his penis in his palm, he stroked it toward her. From behind, Celeste reached around and massaged his chest. With his free hand, he guided her hand downward.

Cheyenne turned away and marched back to the barn. The mystery had been solved. Celeste had joined Dominic on the dark path, there was nothing she could do for her. The woman she loved and respected was dead. A tear slipped down her cheek. The only thing left to do was to sever ties completely and watch her self-destruct. She couldn't go to Jane; she hadn't believed her earlier, now would be no different. Jane would have to come to the truth on her own. Until that time, she would stand alone. Tears welled up in her eyes, silently spilling onto her cheeks. Her stomach constricted, forcing the contents upward. Dropping to her knees, she retched, the red and yellow contents of her stomach splattering on the dirt floor. Her throat burned. She hadn't felt like eating for days. The few pieces of fruit she had eaten that morning were mostly digested, leaving only stomach fluid. She didn't have time for this. The barn needed to be cleaned, the animals needed care—she didn't have time or patience for her own weakness. She spit one last time and struggled to her feet. She needed to get her act together. But first she needed to clean away the darkness, which had touched her.

Walking to the tack room, she gathered her medicine bag and ran out the back door. She'd walk to the healing place. It was unnecessary to inflict the negativity on any of the horses; they didn't deserve it. She crossed the field, avoiding the occupied pasture. She wiped at the sweat forming on her upper lip with the back of her hand. She picked up speed; only slowing down when she crossed into the forest. She continued until she could no longer see the buildings. Stopping, she breathed deeply; just those few yards into the forest gave the air a different scent. In the shadows of the trees, she felt protected. As she continued down the barely visible path, the branches reached out to her in comforting hugs. As soft as a caress, their leaves brushed against her cheek. A gray squirrel scurried across her path and up an oak. It disappeared into the upper canopy. Looking up the trunk, she searched her memory for the symbolism for seeing a squirrel. She remembered it meant something about storing and protecting your resources in preparation for the future. There was also something about keeping to the higher spiritual path. She shook her head and continued.

Breaking through the density of the forest, she stepped into the small clearing. This was her sanctuary, forbidden to everyone except a handful of others who like herself had been invited. Neither Jane nor Celeste had been called to the circle. Celeste had been furious, trying to force her way in. Branches were dropped on her, but that was only the beginning. After the coyote pack circled her and forced her retreat, she no longer denied the spirits will.

On the first solstice at the farm, Cheyenne had been drawn away from the gathering, across the fields and through the trees. The early summer evening had hung heavy with powerful magic. The leaves rustled in the warm breeze. The peach and pink sunset had cast mystical shadows throughout the forest. Birds sang, proclaiming the bounty of the season. Stepping into the circle, she had found herself in another realm.

Cain had already been there, standing beneath the willow tree. He had watched her approach. She was not surprised. It was as if she had known he'd be there. Without speaking they watched each other's faces. She saw his change as the memories from the past came forward. Faces and names from his lives before came back to her. They had been sometimes enemies, sometimes lovers, but always deeply connected. As he stood before her, he looked much like when they had first met eons before. His hair reached down to the middle of his back. In the twilight, it appeared chestnut in color; in daylight it was sable brown. His eyes reminded her of a cave, for they were indeed an opening to something deeper. In this lifetime he was a man; in the other time, the time when they had swore beneath the full of the moon to protect each other's back, he was a she-a sister warrior. She still didn't know what the phrase meant.

Neither had known what to say. It was an absurd and awkward moment. Cheyenne extended her hand. He pushed it away and embraced her, calling her "sister." She hadn't realized how cold she had become until his body warmed her. They stood together, bathed in moonlight with their arms around each other. It had been natural.

Chatting and laughing, Lilith and Selene had arrived together a few minutes later. They met among the trees. Each had started from opposite directions, but had come together when their paths had crossed. Lilith looked in her twenties but was actually in her thirties. The chocolate brown of her skin made the aqua green of her eyes more prominent. Cheyenne hadn't understood the images she received until after she had gotten to know her much better. She saw a sheath of wheat. Lilith was slender, but still shaped like a woman. That isn't where the image originated from, but her philosophy of life. She had released her will—the need to control her individual destiny for the betterment of the planet and the universe beyond. Like the wheat, she bowed to the wind and did not break; she was willing to sacrifice herself to help sustain others. The peacefulness within her radiated out onto those around her.

Selene could be her opposite. Blonde and fair skinned, she vibrated with energy. She talked quickly, in short choppy sentences. Only her eyes revealed that she and Lilith were sisters of the spirit. Selene had the same aqua green eyes. Cheyenne had not received an image of Selene. Instead, Selene had waggled her finger back and forth in front of Cheyenne's face, an elfish grin on her face. She warned her it wasn't polite to read ahead of everyone else. Her forthrightness surprised her, as did Selene's decision to stay in Coyote Springs. Lilith and Cain had returned to their lives, visiting only occasionally. Selene moved into one of the cabins. Working together, she came to know her as a sometimes rash, sometimes outspoken woman of many talents, who often disappeared without a word. When she met and fell in love with Jerry, Selene had surprised Cheyenne. Knowing both of them, she wondered how Selene would cope with Jerry's possessive nature.

But that was all in the past. Cheyenne walked toward the willow. She knew what needed to be done. Placing her bag beneath the tree, she quickly stripped, dropping her clothing into a pile. Opening the bag, she pulled out her athame, driving it into to the ground to the hilt. The ritual knife represented her need to be within the healing realm of the earth. Again she reached into the bag, pulling out an array of cotton pouches filled with herbs. Searching through them, she selected the bags marked basil, ginger and sage, returning the rest. She dropped the pouches on the ground and pulled out the small cast iron cauldron. She ran down to the stream and filled it with water. Returning more slowly, she picked up dry twigs and branches. Setting the cauldron down, she put the wood in the fire pit. Gathering dry grass and leaves from around the pit, she tucked them under the branches. She looked skyward. "May the Gods bless this ceremony with fire." She patted the round in front of her. "May the Goddess bless this ceremony with fire." She snapped her fingers above the fire pit. Within seconds, wisps of smoke rose from the center. For an instant, the infant of a flame wavered as if the slightest breeze would blow it out, but then the leaves caught and the flame ate its way to the wood. "Thank you." She watched the flames dance and ignite the larger twigs, waiting until she was satisfied the fire had a life of its own before adding the larger pieces.

The breeze blew the smoke and heat into her face. She coughed, but did not move. She had always been drawn to the cleansing of fire. Despite her birth element being air, she had felt a kinship with it. In her mind, air fed fire and fire's heat moved air. Jane thought it was just because she didn't like the cold. Placing the cauldron on the reddening coals, she picked up the pouches and removed the rest of the items she would need.

Standing, she looked at the basin. She hadn't even considered that it might not be available. A flag had not been set. She could use it.

The basin was the only change they had made. With shovels, the four of them dug out a hole big enough for six to ritually bath at the same time. It had been an equal amount of work and play. It had taken three days of digging and mud fights. Late on the third afternoon, it was at last finished. They had stood on the banks, waiting to break down the wall that divided it from the stream. Stalling, each in turn found reasons to put off the ceremony until, frustrated, Selene shouted to the forest, "We're not waiting any more!" And broke down the barrier. Quickly, the water filled it, creating whirlpools and eddies, at first only at the mouth, but the texture of the bottom quickly spread them throughout the basin. Out of the corner of her eye, she had seen a shadow retreat deeper into the trees. The memory brought a smile to Cheyenne's lips. Several other times since then, she would sense their presence, but they never approached. Obviously for some reason it wasn't time for the two others to join the group. Later that afternoon Lilith and Cain left, but only Lilith returned regularly. The sacred space invited others. Some were local, others were not. They would just be drawn to the circle and simply slipped into their spots like pieces of a puzzle.

Reaching down, she pulled her bandanna from the bag. It would be her flag, telling the others the basin had been used. The water recycled itself every forty-eight hours. Until it cleansed itself, it wouldn't be wise to use it. Squatting, she placed a handful of each of the herbs into the steaming water. Sitting back on her bottom, she watched the steam rise, the aroma scenting the air. Closing her eyes, she imagined the steam to be soft white light, which she drew in through her nostrils, allowing it to fill her entire being with its healing power. All the anger she felt earlier drained away it, leaving only the sad memory of her lost friend. A tear slipped down her cheek, but she made no attempt brush it away. Celeste's friendship had been too important to brush it aside casually. The salty drop fell from her chin and was gone. She sighed. Her throat hurt. She just wished the pain and the loss would be done. She wanted to move on. But move on to what? The farm had been her dream; Celeste had turned it into a dark place, a place where shadows ruled. But that was going to change.

Shaking her head, she opened her eyes, returning her attention to the present task. The surface had begun to roll. The dried herb pieces bobbed with the heating water's motion. Waiting for it to break the boiling point, she reached around to grab her shirt to use as a hot pad. The water boiled and she picked up the pot. Pulling the shears and the candles out of the bag, she walked toward the basin.

A breeze blew her hair across her face, tickling her cheek, but she ignored it. She thought it strange that she felt nothing now. There should be anger or guilt. But she felt nothing except determination to complete the task at hand. Someone once said, "What is best done, is best done quickly." She couldn't remember who said it or in what context; it didn't matter. She placed the cauldron on the bank and planted the candles in the sand, one for each direction. Without hesitating, she stopped at the eastern candle and lit it.

Looking skyward, she called out, "Moltra, great dragon of the East. Whose tail swirls the winds, whose breath warms the air, whose love keeps this planet's air breathable, I, your daughter, who you named Shawntal, asks you to attend to protect and guide me." For a moment the air stilled, then a gush of wind swirled around her and the basin. Cheyenne smiled. Closing her eyes, she could see the luminescent bronze of his scales reflecting the sunshine. All around her, the air became heavy with the scent of ozone. She breathed deeply. The energy charged air opened her third eye, and then jumping from synapse to synapse, reached the activation point at the base of her skull. Her eyes snapped open. It had begun.

Taking four steps forward, she lit the Southern candle. She faced the sun. "Great dragon of the South, Chun'sa-ta, you who keeps this planet inhabitable with your warmth, you grow our food, you bring us light and separate us from darkness. I, your daughter Shawntal, ask that you attend my healing, bringing your protection and wisdom." The air around her heated with the breath of Chun'sa-ta. Again she closed her eyes, the copper of Chun'sa-ta scales stood beside the bronze of Moltra's.

Continuing her journey, she jumped the mouth of the basin and continued to the Western candle. Stooping, she lit it and reached toward the sky. "Lovena, great dragon of the West, I, Shawntal ask that you share your life restoring waters to help to guide and heal me. Wash away the darkness that has been sent to steal my light." For a moment, stillness ruled. Puzzled, she looked around. Lovena had never failed to answer her call before. Closing her eyes, she tilted her head back. Breathing deeply, she centered herself in her faith, both in herself and the powers of light. The leaves on the treetops blew in the growing wind. The sound became louder. Her eyes opened. The trees around the clearing were being blown in a pattern she had never seen before. The wind did not come from one direction, but formed a circle around the clearing that did not have an entrance point. It was as if the force came from above to encompass the clearing. The scope began to widen; the grass of the field bent to the will of the wind. Cheyenne watched the phenomenon rush toward her. She was not afraid. It enveloped her, blowing and pulling her hair skyward, nearly drawing the breath from her lungs. Her eyes dried. Intuition told her to close them. Something else demanded they stay open. Using all her will, she kept watching and waiting. It moved through her, centering on the basin. The water swirled up into a spout, nearly emptying the pool. Electricity snapped around the suspended liquid. Lovena appeared next to her sisters; her gold scales reflecting the sun to create a shining circlet above the spout. Smiling, Cheyenne felt grateful for the blessings, which had been bestowed upon her. The circlet melted into the water, which gently returned to the basin with calming wind. Again the field became quiet.

Amazed, Cheyenne stood, staring at the reflective surface, nearly forgetting to call the last dragon. Taking a deep breath, she forced the air into her lungs and stepped to the northern candle. Blinking rapidly to restore the moisture to her eyes, she shakily extended her arms. "Tir'th, great dragon of the Earth, I, Shawntal, call you to bring your healing and protection to my circle. Let your grounding force guide me through my healing. Make me so secure the dark forces are unable to raise fear in me. Prevent them from having any influence on my destiny." She did not have long to wait. The air around her filled with the scent of hot, moist earth. Her silver scales reflected from the blades of grass and the bark of the trees as she rose up from the earth to manifest fully next to the three others.

Cheyenne knew it was time. Picking up the cauldron, she held it to the sky. The kettle swung in the breeze. Carefully she poured the contents into the basin and set the empty pot on the bank. Expecting the water to be cool, she stepped gingerly into it. It was warm, like a bath. Relieved, she lowered herself until the water tickled her chin. Holding her breath, she ducked beneath the surface. Her hair floated in an array around her head as the water lovingly cradled her. The water pressure on her ears echoed with her own heartbeat. Bringing forth the memory of the attack, she imagined it was happening again. Only now while she floated in the safety of the dragons' presence, she was protected by the loving strength of her guardians. The darkness was pulled away from her. Her energy was renewed as each pore was cleansed of the experience. She broke to the surface and pushed her hair back over her forehead. Floating toward the center she watched the reflections of the clouds distort in her wake. Turning over on her back, she floated, allowing the sunshine to warm her stomach and face. Her third eye and solar plexus began to throb as her drained batteries began to recharge. She dropped her barriers and just allowed. Her eyes began to droop. Paddling with her hands, she found the shore and propped her head on the bank, her butt resting on the bottom. The gentle current kept her legs afloat. She held the memories of the attack, but none of the fear and pain remained. She could now look on the experience objectively and decide her course.

Cheyenne still cherished the memories of Celeste. But she did not like the person Celeste had become. She no longer trusted her on any level. All the begging and pleading was over. There had been nothing she could do or say to stop Celeste from changing, it all came down to free will. Everyone had to choose their own path and take responsibility for their choices. Although, like a stone being dropped in a pond, the ripples widen to touch every shore, so each of our decisions affects others with the rebounding results. How each reacts to the influence creates new ripples and new consequences. Cheyenne was determined to stay on the path of light. She wouldn't allow the fear and anger to lead her to do damage that would cost her dearly later. Nor could she continue to give or allow Celeste to take energy from her or her land when she would most likely use it to harm others.

She knew what she must do. She scanned the bank for the scissors. It wasn't something she wanted to do. They gleamed in the afternoon sun. Swimming over she reached up and took them from the grass. Again surprised by her own calmness, Cheyenne held them up to the sky. "With love and sadness, I ask that my ties to my mother-sister, Celeste, be severed. We no longer walk the same path. I can no longer come to her with unconditional love and perfect trust. She has broken faith with me. And in her eyes, I have broken faith with her. I ask the Goddesses and Gods to continue to guide and protect both of us. But as separate people, going on separate paths." She flipped her hair over, combing the fingers of her free hand through the strands. She watched the ends float on top of the water. She didn't want to. She loved her hair, how it felt brushing and playing with it. But there was no other way. Gathering it into a bunch, she brought up the blades. "To me, Celeste, the woman I loved is now dead."

The first strands were severed. The sound was deafening. They slide into the water, at first disappearing under the weight, then resurfacing to float on the surface. For a moment, the memories forced her to stop. It was more than just hair she was cutting. It was enjoying the sunshine during walks. Their talks into the late night, questioning the universe and their place in it. Celeste was the first person who made Cheyenne feel needed and wanted.

She contracted her hand. The next group of strands hit the surface. Water ran from the severed ends like blood from a limb. Her resolve wavered, but only for an instant. Celeste was no longer the loving woman of light, who held her hand and made the nightmares go away. Her mere presence no longer brought joy and a sense of security. That woman was gone. Cheyenne didn't know if she would every return. It was more than just her union with a man, there had always been men in Celeste's life. It was Dominic. He had no honor or truth within him. He took what he wanted no matter whom he hurt. What he wanted was the land. The blades came together a final time. Cheyenne would never allow him to abuse this spiritual place. The farm had many special groves and fields, where the worlds intersected and people found peace.

She evened off the ends and flipped the remaining back. Where once the ends bounced around her waist, now they barely reached her shoulders. There was nothing left to do but allow the sun to dry her and the current to cleanse the water. Later, she would cry. Probably many times. But now with the sun on her back, she began making plans of how to rid herself of both of them.

CHAPTER SIX

For a moment, Jane remained in that in-between stage between sleep and wake. Before opening her eyes, she mentally checked her body for stress points. She wasn't looking for anything specific. It was more of a vague feeling of her energy being off. In the past, she had been able to ward off physical annoyances by just checking her energy before becoming fully conscious. Her left side seemed a bit numb, most likely from sleeping in the same position too long. She usually didn't move around much when she slept in a strange bed. It made Maxie crazy. He said it was like sleeping with a corpse. Thinking of him suddenly brought back the anger and sadness. Part of her loved him. Yet there was something that kept her from committing to him.

She drifted downward into her body. Opening her eyes, she stared at the orange and white striped sheets. An instant later, the pain hit. Starting at the base of her skull, it raced over the top of her head, grabbing her cheekbones, trying to flip them over. She moaned and rolled onto her back. Closing her eyes, she tried to force herself back into the upper realms, where she could balance whatever was out of kilter. The throbbing continued, preventing her from concentrating. *Don't fight it*, came the thought, *just allow it to pass through you.* Keeping her eyes closed, she breathed deeply in through her nose, allowing the pain to flow over her like a wave on the shore. The pain lessened, only to be followed by a second then a third. She rolled over, ducking her head beneath the pillow and holding it tight, trying to block the pain. Images appeared in her mind. She didn't understand. It was the farm. A thin dark mist hovered around it. It reached for her. She retreated. It followed. Lightning flashed up from the ground. The mist scattered and recollected itself around the house. Just as suddenly the pain dulled to a throb. Carefully she opened her eyes. Unsure of what she should do, she pushed the pillow away and slowly lifted herself to a kneeling position. She looked around. The room hadn't changed, yet it was different. It was the smell. Ozone. She was more confused than ever.

Sliding off the bed onto her feet, she put on the short robe Raven had left at the foot of the bed. She tied the belt and opened the door. Continuing down the hallway, she stopped at the archway.

Raven was lying on the couch, a cloth across her forehead and eyes. In spite of the warmth of the room she hugged her favorite comforter to her chest. She shivered beneath it.

The sun streamed into the room. From her perspective there wasn't a cloud in the sky. Raven shouldn't be having a sinus attack. Yet, Raven was having what she would describe as a four-alarm attack.

Creeping further into the room, she noticed the broken teacup on the kitchen floor. Its contents spilled among the shattered pieces.

"Good afternoon." The voice came from the couch.

"What happened?"

"Something blew through."

"What?"

"I don't know. I heard you scream once. Then I got hit."
Raven lifted one end of the cloth to look at her. "My shields
didn't hold."

"I set up temporary barriers myself last night."

Raven recovered her eye. "I know. It didn't help." Her
voice was a combination of bitterness and anger. "I got images of darkness around the farm."

Jane didn't know what to say.

"It was an evil I haven't experienced before." Raven
waited.

The unasked question hung between them, testing their
friendship. Jane swallowed hard, not wanting to hear what
was coming. Carefully she knelt and picked up the pieces of
the broken cup. "It was your favorite."

"Forget it!" Raven snapped. Her hands covered her face.
She moaned in pain.

"I'm sorry." Jane couldn't move. She felt responsible,
but she didn't know why. "I don't know what happened."

"Celeste happened."

"Why do you assume—"

"Because it's the truth!" Raven's voice quivered with
pain and anger. "Just like Cheyenne has been trying to tell
you."

"She doesn't have any proof."

"But she does."

"Why didn't she tell me?" Jane snapped back and instantly regretting it. The dull throb sharpened into to stabbing pain behind her eyes.

"She tried to." Raven stressed each word. "You wouldn't
listen."

If Raven was right, this was all her fault. Jane dropped the pieces. "She was just jealous . . . jealous because she didn't have a man in her life. That's all."

Using one arm, Raven lifted herself into a sitting position. "Both Cheyenne and I fully dedicated the Samhain after she got the farm. She has no interest in dating or mating. Her total focus is on her spiritual path. Just like me."

"I didn't know."

"There is a lot you don't know."

It wasn't possible, Jane thought. *She's just trying to bait me. Cheyenne would have told us. Such radical commitments were never made lightly.* "You don't know what you're talking about."

"Fine. Believe what you like." Raven tried to stand, but as quickly sat back down. "It's your rude awakening ."

"I thought you were my friend." Her voice sounded whiny, but Jane didn't care. Since she started on the investigation, they had spent many hours together not only talking about the case but their lives as well. Raven was the only one who knew about her relationship with Maxie. She had always been open and honest with her, yet Raven chose to keep the most important aspect of her spirituality a secret. It wasn't rational, but suddenly Jane felt betrayed.

"Could you put more cold water on this?" Raven held up the cloth. "And put the water on for tea."

Taking it, Jane silently walked into the kitchen, doubt rapidly growing within her. She ran the water and soaked the cloth. Wringing the excess off, she returned to the living room and gently covered the prone woman's eyes. Raven murmured something but Jane didn't understand what she had said. Briefly stroking the black mane, she turned and returned to the kitchen.

Could she have been wrong? Perhaps, but about whom? Celeste or Cheyenne? Which one was lying? The past few months they hadn't been as close, but all relationships change. Without growth there would be stagnation and death. She filled the kettle and put it on the stove. It just didn't make sense, but nothing did any more. Pulling down the herb jars; she placed them on the counter and took the mixing bowl from its place on the shelf. Taking a pinch from the spearmint and chamomile, she ground the leaves between her fingers, allowing the pieces to drop into the bowl, and resealed the jars. A year ago, they had been planning an expansion of the classes and greenhouse. The classes had remained very popular despite the House of Christ, and the few rented cottages supplemented the farm income. In fact, Jane was forced to admit, Cheyenne's herbs were the only stable income they had. How did they become so dependent on her?

Across the room, the kettle began to bubble. She filled the tea balls and put them in cups. Nine months ago she had taken a leave of absence from the TV station to help Celeste with the classes. They had started by building a small but professional looking web site. It was beautiful; with pictures of the farm and information about Dragon Herbs. All of them taught classes online; but Cheyenne was too busy with the greenhouse and herbs to do more than teach one class. They were busy, tired and happy—a true team, each using their own particular talents for the best of the whole. As she thought back, she realized that it had only been a month before Dominic had arrived.

The kettle whistled. Startled by the shrillness, she grabbed for it and turned off the burner. Filling the cups, she watched the steam rise, carrying the scent of the herbs. She inhaled deeply, and for a few moments, her mind quieted. She noticed the tree outside had a bird's nest safely tucked in one of the branches, but she couldn't see if it was inhabited. Elsewhere, birds sang. Traffic rolled to and fro on the street as people went about living their own lives. Were they happy, or sad? A bit of both, she thought. Did they feel what happened earlier? Or was it hidden from them like a rude surprise waiting to be sprung on them when it was too late to do anything? She returned the kettle to the stove, the contents still rumbling with the heat. Steam continued to rise from the cups and she found herself lost within the wispy tendrils. It was fascinating how the steam formed shapes and patterns. Sometimes, she just wondered why. She didn't expect an answer—It was just something to occupy her mind, to keep it from asking questions she didn't want answered. Dangling the tea balls by their chains, she watched the water color. It was such a simple thing. Judging the tea to be strong enough, she dropped the balls in the sink and picked up one of the cups.

Raven was still lying on the couch, the cloth over her upper face. With, her black curls fanned out on the pillow; she looked like she was posing for a centerfold. A chicken pox scar on her left temple was the only blemish on her otherwise smooth skin. How old she was, no one really knew. Somehow Raven had always been able to dodge the question. She seemed in her late twenties, early thirties. Several of her commits gave the impression and the ages of her two sons made her somewhere in her late forties. She had two sons by two different men. One she chose to marry, the other was a good friend who for one night became more. Now divorced, she had her own home, her own money, her own path to follow. Her children were a source of pride and pain. The eldest chose his father over her; the rules weren't as strict. She shared custody of her youngest, but his primary residence was with his father. She loved him enough not to bounce him back and forth between the two homes. Some on the farm thought less of her for not having her sons, that she wasn't maternal enough to worship the Goddess. Her attitude was "whatever", using the familiar hand gesture. It was something Jane had always admired about her.

Bending over, she placed the cup on a coaster and slid it within her reach. Raven didn't stir. Sometimes sleep is the best medicine.

Taking her own mug out the back door, she sat on the steps. The shadows kept the cement cool, but soon they would creep back toward the house with the turn of the day. Protected by only the thin robe, her butt and thighs quickly felt the cold. Standing, she walked down the path into the sunlight. It warmed the back of her head and brought a smile to her lips. Mentally, she thanked Ra for putting his loving arms around her. The cup was hot in her hands, but the steam no longer rose from the liquid. She took a sip. It was good; lemon would make it better. The scent made her nose tingle.

The shadow of a bird flew across the lawn and she looked up. It was a jay. Ever present, ever watching; no matter what the season. Some people didn't like them at their bird feeders. Jane liked their tenacity and their ability to adapt to whatever life presented to them. They were character traits she wished she possessed. Sometimes she felt as if she had no control over her life, that she was always reacting to someone else's agenda.

Looking back over her thirty-six years, Jane realized that most of her life she did what was expected of her. It was like she checking off chores on a list that someone else wrote for her. Her thirty-seventh birthday was nearly four months away and she still didn't know what she wanted to be when she grew up. She no longer had a clue how to fill the rapidly growing void in her. The television station gave her a purpose for a while, then it was helping Celeste and Cheyenne. She was tired of playing peacemaker between them, yet she wasn't brave enough to confront them.

She sipped the cooling tea and continued to walk down the path, taking the left fork toward the swing. Sitting, she swiveled, crossing her legs and tucking her robe down between her thighs. Pulling on the support post of the swing, she started the back and forth motion. Closing her eyes and leaning back, she allowed the rhythm to comfort her. It reminded her of how her mother rocked her as a child when the monster in the closet wouldn't let her sleep. Her mother had been dead for many years, but remembering her joyfully brought her back. A smile crossed her lips. She released the need to think beyond the motion. Alternating between shadow and sunshine, she enjoyed both. Her other senses filled in the blanks left by her voluntary relinquishing of her sight. She allowed the sensory information to pass though her without keeping note. Somewhere close by a vehicle drove up and parked. Moments later, the swing jolted to a halt, spilling the tea into her lap. Her eyes snapped open. Maxie stood in front of her. Angrily she jumped to her feet, the spilled tea running down the front of the robe to the ground. She tried brushing it off before more could soak in.

"I thought you heard me."

"Does it look like I heard you?" Jane snapped. "Look what you did to Raven's robe!"

"Sorry. Okay?" he snapped back.

"Will that get the stain out?" She allowed her anger to flare. It was how she felt—angry and much put upon.

"I'll buy her a new one. Just get off it."

"Get off it?" Her voice rose to a shriek, sending the birds that were resting in the trees, into flight. "I'll get off it, you, and the investigation!" She spun on the balls of her feet and headed toward the back door.

He grabbed her upper arm and yanked her toward him. "You listen—"

That was enough. She allowed him to spin her partially around. Using the momentum he provided, she flung her free arm around. The heel of her hand landed firmly on his chin. Stunned, he released her, staggering backward. Her robe slipped off her shoulder, opening at the front. She ignored it and stepped into a defensive stance.

Holding his chin, he glared down at her. "I could arrest you."

"Oh, really Officer, on what charge?" She no longer found him cute and cuddly, fun to talk to and make love with; he was just one more needy person. She met his eyes. They were angry and demanding. Last week, even yesterday, she would have given in and apologized. But not today. "On what charge?" she repeated.

"Striking an officer!"

"An officer who overstepped his bounds." She countered.

"Just get dressed. They expect us at the station."

"I quit." It wasn't a decision she consciously made. The words surprised her, yet at the same instant a heavy weight was lifted from her heart. She knew it was the right thing to do.

"We don't have time for this!"

"I do. What you do—I don't care." She spun and rapidly continued toward the house.

"You can't!"

Suddenly he was between her and the back door. "I won't let you ruin this!"

"Just what don't you want ruined? The investigation or your sex life?"

"Whatever bug flew up your ass last night—just get over it! Just get your clothes, we'll talk about it at home."

"I'm not going with you."

"Just do it!"

A breeze bellowed the robe open further. The sun warmed her breasts. He could arrest her for indecent exposure. "No!"

Taking a deep breath, he clenched and unclenched his fists. "I love you." His voice was calmer, but the anger boiled just beneath the surface.

"Sounds like it." The back door swung open and Raven stepped out. "Who could resist such loving words."

"It none of your business!" Maxie growled.

"It's my yard, my house, my guest, and my business." She matched his tone.

"Bitch-dike."

"How quick the bigotry rears its ugly head. Just yesterday we were good friends."

"Raven's not a—"

"Don't explain!" She walked down the steps. "Get lost or do I make a phone call to your supervisor? I'm sure she'd be real interested in this conversation."

"What about your secrets?"

"Secrets? I don't have any secrets. My life is an open book." Raven smiled nastily. "You are the one who broke the departmental policy."

"Jane doesn't work for—"

"But I do!" Raven firmly planted her fists on her hips. "You have invaded my privacy. You have made sexual comments."

"Jane, this isn't over!" Snapping around heal to toe, he marched back to his truck. The engine roared to life and leaped backward. The tires screeched and he was gone.

"Gee that was fun!" Raven reached out and closed the opening of Jane's robe. "You keep flashing my neighbors and poor, old Mr. Radcliff is going to have a heart attack and the brat boys next door will have accidents in their drawers."

Jane weakly smiled and tied the belt, keeping the front closed. "I'm sorry."

"Why? You didn't do it? He did." Slipping her arm around Jane, she propelled her toward the door. "Let's go in. They know enough of your business."

Nodding, Jane followed. She sat at the kitchen table, leaning against the wall. It was too overwhelming—too much, too fast to take in. Decisions had to be made after thinking out all the options, not as the words were coming out of your mouth.

The water filled the teapot and metal hit metal as Raven put the pot on the stove. Opening the refrigerator, she pulled out eggs and butter. "When you're ready."

"Sorry. I was thinking." Running her fingers though her hair, she realized the tangled mess it was. "Last night, I don't know. One moment he was talking about marriage, then he lied about me being there. We argued. He was ashamed of me. He never was before."

"So he finally showed his true self."

"I shouldn't have gotten involved." Lifting the empty cup from her lap, Jane set it on the table. "Cheyenne was right. Why did I let Celeste talk me into it?"

"She can be quite good at that."

"I quit the investigation. Could you—"

"I'll let the right people know." She cracked an egg, dumping the contents into a bowl. "They are going to insist on knowing why?" Palming another egg, she hit it against the bowl and added it to the first. "So what are you going to do now? Go back to the TV station?"

"I don't know." It was the truth. Jane had no idea what was in her future. An image came to mind. She closed her eyes, trying to focus. Something or someone was calling to her. Her answers were elsewhere. She had wanted to do a walk-about on South Manitou. "No," came the clear thought, "Go west. Follow the sun to the end. It is there you will find the answers."

"Jane?' Two more empty eggshells lay on the counter and Raven had begun to stir the mixture. "You drifted away."

"I must go west." The statement was as obvious as the sun rising in the east.

"Don't let him chase you away!"

"No. I'm not running. I have to find something."

Raven pulled a frying pan from the wall and placed it on the stove, lighting the burner. "What?"

"I don't know. But it's important."

The butter hit the pan and sizzled. "Okay. What do you need me to do?"

"Look after Cheyenne."

"Not after both of them?" Her eyebrow arched.

"I wouldn't do that to you."

Hesitating long enough to pour the eggs in the melted butter, Raven turned. "Really talk to Cheyenne before you leave. Away from the others, especially Celeste. This time listen. Objectively as a reporter, not as either one's friend." Using a spatula, she stirred the mixture into scrabbled eggs. "Promise me."

"I don't think Dominic will do as much damage as she thinks."

"He already has."

"How? He takes care of his nieces. He pays his rent. He does what work on the farm he can with the restrictions."

"How does he get his money?"

"He works."

"Where?"

"I don't know." Jane didn't know what to think. It had never occurred to her before.

Raven took two plates from the cabinet and divided the eggs between them. "But didn't he still spend so much time at the house that Cheyenne moved to the outmost cabin."

"She said his energy made her ill."

"It's her house. Her land. Why should she have had to move?"

The truth slapped her across the face. Jane looked away, too embarrassed to meet the brown eyes.

Raven set one of the plates on the table in front of her. "Eat. You need the protein."

Jane pushed it away. No one had pointed out the obvious truth to her before. It sat like a lead weight in her stomach.

Raven pushed it back. "When do you want to leave?"

"Tomorrow." Again the decision was made without fore thought.

The fork clattered against Raven's plate. "You serious?"

Jane nodded.

"Why?"

"Because I need to."

"Cheyenne needs you."

"Thanks for the eggs and the guilt trip. Care to give me a ride home."

"Certainly. Right after you clean your plate."

"I'm not hungry."

"It's nearly noon and you haven't eaten. Feed your body or walk home." Raven's voice was defiant. There would be no changing her mind.

Picking up the fork, she fluffed the rapidly cooling eggs. *Great*, she thought sarcastically, *just what I need someone else who thinks they know what I need.*

The teakettle whistled. Raven slowly stood and turned off the heat. "What kind of tea?"

"Mint."

A steaming cup appeared in front of her with a commercially produced bag inside. Taking a bite, Jane realized her friend had been right. Her body did want to be fed. It was her that was being stubborn. Not only did they taste good, but they also had a calming affect on her unstable emotions. "Thanks."

Raven smiled. "No problem."

CHAPTER SEVEN

Raven's jeep disappeared down the driveway, leaving Jane alone in the yard. She was grateful she hadn't accepted the invitation to stay. She had to tell Cheyenne and Celeste of her decision; she didn't expect it to be pretty.

The sun warmed the crown of her head. In the shadow of the house, the dirt beneath her bare feet felt cool, but in the direct sun it warmed her like a loving hug. Jane knew she was doing the right thing. It was something she felt down to her core. She just couldn't explain it. But it didn't matter. Her confidence rose.

This time of day Cheyenne would be in the barn; Celeste could be anywhere. She decided to tell Cheyenne first. Rounding the corner of the garage, she noticed for the first time how quiet the yard was. No dogs barked. The horses in the corral were silently huddled together. She didn't understand. Slowing her pace, she continued toward the barn. She looked around. Several chickens sat, unmoving in the backyard. The wind shifted, the immediate stench making her gag. It was a smell like no other she had experienced before. More than rotting flesh, it smelled like all that was darkness combined with all that was ugly. Instinct told her to run. But her concern for Cheyenne wouldn't let her retreat. Encasing herself in a shell of light, she quickened her pace.

Entering the coolness of the barn, she looked around. It was empty. Cheyenne was always here at this time of day.

Where was she? Panic began to rise. Walking out into the corral, she searched the pasture. The horses shied away, only the fence kept them from running.

Behind her the back door of the tack room opened and closed. Someone moved around, opening and closing drawers. Jane quickly crossed the distance and flung open the door. Dominic was riffling though Cheyenne's desk. The door banged against the back wall and he snapped around.

"What are you doing in here?"

He briefly tensed, then seeing her he relaxed. "Jane."

"The barn is off-limits."

"This is the tack room. Not the barn." He smiled, tilting his head to the side like a little boy caught with his hand in the cookie jar. Casually he leaned back against the desk, tucking his hands into his back pockets. "Celeste asked me to get something for her."

It was an obvious lie. Jane felt like a fool. Angrily she crossed the room and yanked the piece of paper, barely sticking out of his back pocket. She held it up. "Celeste's. Not likely."

He snatched it back. "She doesn't have the right to keep information from us! Celeste has every right to know what's going on!"

"Why?" Calmly Cheyenne stepped through the open doorway from the barn.

"She owns—"

"Nothing!" Cheyenne set her medicine bag on her desk. "It's mine. All of it. The farm. The Dragon Herbs. Everything."

"You lie!" Dominic bellowed.

"No. She isn't." Suddenly Jane understood his true motives. He did want to be lord of the manor. "Dominic," Jane surprised herself with calmness in her voice that she didn't feel inside. Cheyenne hadn't been jealous or exaggerating. "Celeste and I live here though Cheyenne's friendship. Nothing more."

"But the website said—" Dominic stammered briefly, but quickly regained his composure. "It doesn't matter. Celeste and I are getting married. The kids and I will be moving to the main house."

"No. You will all be leaving," Cheyenne hissed. "Today, tomorrow at the latest."

He shifted his weight onto his back foot, but didn't retreat from his domineering posture. "That isn't legal."

"Legal or not. It will happen."

"What will happen?" Celeste slammed open the door and marched in.

"Darling, I'm glad you're here. I told them our good news." Encircling her with one arm, he kissed her forehead. "They have been telling me terrible lies."

Celeste looked from one to another. "Jane. Cheyenne. I love him. We are getting married on Friday."

"Celeste, I loved you like a sister." Jane began slowly. "I trusted you."

"Be happy for us." Celeste smiled up at Dominic. "I love him. We're very good together. "Please," she pleaded, "get to know him better."

"She just did," Cheyenne snapped.

Celeste continued, ignoring her. "Spend some time with us. You'll see. It's all lies. He truly is a good man."

"It's all lies. But it's been Dominic lying to you and you lying to yourself—and to us." The foolishness Jane felt rapidly changed into anger.

"Just get to know him." Celeste begged. "You'll see he can make the farm more profitable."

"I believed you. I ignored everyone's warnings and I believed you!" Jane screamed. "We were happy! We were creating a place of beauty. Then he—," the emotions tripped the words as they tumbled out, "you let him destroy everything! How could you?"

"I won't give him up!" Celeste screamed back. "He's too important to me. Get used to it!"

"No!" Cheyenne and Jane shouted in unison.

Celeste roughly pushed past Jane and marched to within a step of Cheyenne. "Are you happy? Look what you've done to us." Not waiting for a response, Celeste continued. "I asked if you are happy? You could have accepted him. But no, you just had to—"

"Tell the truth!" Cheyenne's eyes moistened; she blinked once and any sign of tears vanished. "No. Your pain doesn't give me pleasure."

"They why do you hurt me?" Celeste demanded. "I've been nothing but kind and generous to you."

Cheyenne glanced away for an instant. Her resolved wavered, but only for an instant. "I love the person you were like a mother. You were a bright, beautiful soul." Her gaze focused back on Celeste. "However the person you've become is not loving or kind. Carmen was here earlier."

"She couldn't wait—" Celeste cut in.

"She told me what you did at Dragon's Den." Cheyenne ignored the interruption. "She said you vampired energy off the people in the store."

"That's a lie!" Celeste snapped back.

Jane thought for a moment her heart would burst from the pain.

Stepping up behind Celeste, Dominic embraced her from behind and kissed her cheek. "It doesn't matter, sweetie. We'll take your share and they'll never hurt you again."

"Her share?" Cheyenne choked back a laugh. "Celeste, tell him the truth. My name is on the title. Not yours."

"No! It's not true!" He growled. "I saw the agreement between the three of you, making you equals."

Slowly Celeste turned and looked up at him. "It's true. The agreement was only valid for making decisions."

His mouth moved, but no words came out.

"Honey, I'm sorry. I tried to tell you."

"He only wanted you for what he thought you had." Cheyenne sniped. "It was never you."

Violently pushing Celeste out of the way, he leaped at Cheyenne, pinning her to the wall. Pulling back his fist, he swung. Cheyenne ducked. He hit the wall. The crack of the wood echoed around the tack room and out into the barn. Cheyenne's open palm shot upward, hitting him in the chin. He staggered backward.

Instinct leading reason, Jane forced her way between them. She stared up at him. "Get out! Get out now. Or there won't be a place to hide!"

There was silence in the tack room. The wind swung its door on its hinges; it squeaked. In the distance, a dog barked and voices spoke. The tension rose, filling the room to overflowing like steam in a kettle. His eyes turned the color of slate. It was becoming harder for Jane to breathe. She forced the air into her lungs. It hurt. She couldn't move. The door squeaked back and forth, tapping the wall behind it. Jane didn't dare blink. The energy flowed between them. From Cheyenne, she felt an emotion akin to fear. Celeste and Dominic radiated darkness, the likes of which she had never sensed before. She tried to weave a web of protection between her and Cheyenne. Dominic's energy flared. Physically he hadn't moved, however he still isolated them. The door slid into the catch, threatening to close. Several horses stomped closer to the barn. One nickered. Jane couldn't tell how many; there were more than two, fewer than the herd. Closer to the barn a dog's bark mixed with the voices of children. It was Shawn, Lisa, and Melanie. They were talking about the chickens. Lisa started calling Cheyenne, her voice rapidly approaching the barn.

A smug smile slowly spread across his lips and he pulled his energy back.

Moments later, the girls burst in, led by Lisa.

"Cheyenne!" Lisa screamed. "The chickens—" Seeing Dominic, she stopped short, her sisters bumping into her. She slowly pointed at him. "Dominic?"

The smile broadened on Dominic's lips. "Are you going to break your promise to Lisa? If I leave so do they."

Jane flinched, her resolve wavering. She hadn't had the opportunity to think through the details.

"They can stay or go home to their mother." Cheyenne interceded. "Either way they will always be welcome."

"I go, we all go." He repeated sarcastically. "You'll be taking away the only safe home they've ever known."

Questioning, the children looked from one adult to another. Melanie stepped closer to Dominic, forcing her little hand into his. Gently his fingers folded around it, pulling her closer to him. "I'll never desert them. I don't break my promises."

"Neither do I." Cheyenne cut in. The anger in her voice had been replaced by forceful confidence. "Pack your bags. I'll call Meredith. She'll decide where the children go."

"Don't I have a voice?" Celeste whined. "You can't just take everything!"

"I'm not taking anything that isn't mine." Cheyenne countered. "It was you who made the changes in your life."

"I just wanted to be with the man I love."

"Love and lust are not the same."

"Like you know what either are?" Celeste snapped. "So virginal. So controlled. So perfect in your chaste tower. What do you know of passion?"

"Passion? You claim to love him. True love comes from the soul not from—"

"Stop it!" Jane shouted, cutting Cheyenne off. "We don't need to go there."

Dominic crouched down to the eye level of the children. "Cheyenne is throwing us off the farm. We have to sleep in the truck tonight because we have nowhere else to go."

For a moment, it was as if they didn't understand. Tears welled up in Lisa's eyes. She walked to Cheyenne. "You said you loved me. That you'd protect me. What if the shadows come?"

"I was going to give you this on Litha." Cheyenne opened the cabinet door and reached behind the herb filled jars, pulling out a leather pouch. Unwrapping the strings, she held it out in front of Lisa. "I made a promise to you. Now I ask you formally, do you wish to be my daughter of spirit, daughter to the Dragon Clan of Fire?"

"I will always be part of the clan?"

Cheyenne nodded.

Her eyes widened in amazement. The tears disappeared. "Could I wear it now?"

"Yes. If you agree to follow the path of the dragon." Cheyenne whispered.

"No! She doesn't" Dominic bellowed, grabbing at the child's arm. "She's too young."

Lisa scratched and hissed at him. Quickly ducking his second attempt, she slid closer to Cheyenne. "I accept you as my spirit mother. I will follow the path of honor and truth." She spun around and lifted her hair. "Mother, I will make you proud."

Celeste grabbed for the bag. "She can't possibly know—"

Cheyenne slapped the older woman's hand away. "Lisa, what does it mean to be a dragon?"

Lisa quarter turned and looked up at Cheyenne. She smiled. Returning her gaze to the others, she set her shoulders into a proud stance. "A dragon searches for truth and wisdom. We fight for justice even if it hurts. We believe there are many different little truths and many paths to take. But there is only one big truth."

"Which is?" Cheyenne injected.

Lisa licked her upper lip. "That we only bring three things into each life. Our ability to love. Everything we've learned in the past. And honor. How we acted in the past is what our honor is like. Some people call it karma."

Jane was impressed. If the child understood what she said, she was much wiser than her years. "Lisa, how do you know this?" Gently turning the child toward her, Jane crouched. "Who taught you?"

"Some Cheyenne taught me. Some she helped me remember."

"You remember from before?"

"Enough!" Dominic roared. "This is senseless."

Jane focused on the light in the child's eyes; it was deep and full of love. The wisdom went back many eons. She didn't need to see any more. The old soul before her was only just awakening. Even though she lacked in the ability to communicate the concepts correctly, she instinctively understood their wisdom. Jane looked up at Cheyenne and nodded.

Lisa smiled and hugged the crouching woman before looking to Cheyenne.

Cheyenne opened the neck strap and held the bag out in front of her. "Lisa, I accept you as my daughter and a member of the fire clan."

"No!" Dominic screamed, lunging at the child.

Jane intercepted long enough for Lisa to duck her head through the loop, slipping the bag around her neck. Dominic's hand hit Jane on the side of the head, knocking her into Lisa and sprawling her across the counter. Cheyenne caught the falling child and stepped in front of her.

Angrily Jane pushed off the counter and jumped in front of Cheyenne. Feeling betrayed by Celeste and foolish for her own naivety, Jane shoved him backward. "Get out!" The volume of her voice hurt her throat. She didn't care. "Get out now. You have one hour!"

"Legally you have to give me thirty days," he countered.

"Fine. You just attacked your niece," Cheyenne smugly added. "It's called child abuse."

"It was an accident," Celeste snapped. "It's your word against ours."

Cheyenne didn't back down. "But who will they believe? A drug addict, an alcoholic who's been convicted of arson, B&E's, shooting up a town, assault—"

"Who have you been talking to?" he roared.

"That was a long time ago!" Celeste screamed at the same time. "He's clean and sober."

Still watching Dominic, Cheyenne half turned to make eye contact with the older woman. "His live-in kicked him out. She told the police and her family she was tired of supporting his lazy ass. So he trashed her house. He was arrested. But not for long enough. Her entire family had to get PPOs. Two weeks before he showed up here, someone shot her. The Arizona State Police seemed very interested in his whereabouts: I called them a few minutes ago."

Wordlessly, he spun on the balls of his toes and marched out the door. The door banged against the frame and bounced back to slam against the wall behind it.

"Dominic!" Melanie shrieked, following him to the threshold. The wind caught the door and swung it back, closing it in her face. She pushed it open and ran out. She scanned the yard, still calling his name. Somewhere in the yard a vehicle started. She ran toward it, disappearing around the side of the barn.

"Look what you've done!" Celeste's voice raised an octave. "You could have come to me. I would have explained. She was just being vindictive."

"His story." Jane interjected. "You wanted me to get to know him. I just did."

"He made some mistakes. Everyone has." Sarcasm dripped from Celeste's voice. "Except you. You're perfect. Not weak like the rest of humanity."

Jane watched the pain rise in Cheyenne's eyes. She felt the anguish radiate from her and then as quickly disappeared behind the shield Cheyenne raised. Until this moment, Jane never realized how much emotion Cheyenne felt. She was always so calm and logical; nothing seemed to be able to knock her from her center. "You've said enough!'

"It's not enough!" Celeste turned to Jane. "She's humiliated the man I love. And for what? Mistakes in his past. They weren't his fault. He took the blame for his friends. He is a good and honorable man!"

"Who just happens to steal, take drugs—"

"He's clean!"

Cheyenne continued as if Celeste hadn't interrupted. "And have a problem with alcohol—"

"He only drinks beer!"

"Beer is alcohol!" Jane snapped.

"He doesn't drink that much!"

"And burn other people's property," Cheyenne continued.

"Shut up!" Celeste screamed, pulling the reluctant Shawna to her. "You don't understand. We were going to raise the children together. Make a home. I was going to be their mother."

"We have a mother." Lisa's voice was calm and level despite the chaos. She tried to pry her struggling sister from Celeste's grip. Suddenly Lisa stopped and looked up. "Let go of my sister." She waited a moment, then stomped on the Celeste's foot.

Celeste screamed in pain and lost her grip.

Lisa yanked her sister close and spun them both around behind Cheyenne. With one hand, Shawna grabbed hold of Lisa's striped shirt; the thumb on the other hand disappeared into her mouth.

Jane and Cheyenne bumped into each other, both imposing their bodies between Celeste and the children. For an instant they looked at one another. In another time and place, it would have been funny. But now, Jane felt only anger.

"Why have you turned against me?"

"You've turned against yourself." Cheyenne's voice had a raspy quality that hadn't been there before. "Ever since Dominic."

"I've been happy." Celeste countered. "He makes me feel loved. He takes care of me. I . . . we will be good parents. You know that Cheyenne. I was a good mother to you."

"You are not that person any more."

"Yes, I am."

"You've become manipulative and interfering." Uncomfortably, Jane shifted her weight. This wasn't the proper way to do an intervention, but there wasn't any time to prepare and this might be their last chance to reach her. "You have broken the creed—Do what you will, but harm none."

"I haven't hurt anybody."

"What about Dragon's Den?" Cheyenne countered. "You vampired off them."

"I didn't—"

"And you've been trying to create a conflict between Carmen and Rachael."

"Kevin belongs with Carmen."

Another surprise Jane wasn't expecting. "Kevin is happily involved with Rachael. Why would you want to interfere?"

"Carmen was mistaken."

"Why did Selene suddenly leave Jerry?"

Celeste's mouth moved; no words came out.

Clinging closer to her sister, Shawna whined. Jane realized they needed to be elsewhere. They were too young to understand. "Lisa, take your sister to Lady Margaret's cabin. Tell her, I'll explain everything when I come to get you." Instinctively she quickly added. "Don't go with anyone but Cheyenne, your mother or me. Tell Lady Margaret I said so."

The bravery had faded and she quickly nodded. Skirting Celeste, the twosome vanished out the back door.

"You didn't have to do that." Celeste snapped. "I wouldn't have stolen them."

The anger in Celeste's voice confirmed that her instincts had been correct.

"Celeste, you are no longer welcome here." Cheyenne stated coldly. "I want you to leave."

The tack room became silent, a backdrop for the growing tension between the women. Jane wanted to say something, anything to break the silence. She could find nothing, not even a trivial remark. Celeste blinked; the whites of her eyes darkened. A stench seeped into the room seemingly from every possible entrance.

"By the Divine light, I banish you!" Cheyenne hissed.

The darkness in Celeste's eyes faded and vanished. She rapidly blinked, a wry smile crossing her lips. "I want what is mine."

Cheyenne nodded. "The three of us will divide what we jointly own."

"What about the money I've contributed to the farm?"

Cheyenne crossed her arm. "Consider it rent."

Celeste eyes narrowed. "I see." She spun around, her hair making an arch in her wake. The door slammed and she was gone.

Jane placed her hand on the younger woman's shoulder, half-turning her around. "Better late than never."

Sobbing, Cheyenne toppled toward her, her body shaking. Surprised, Jane caught her, encircling her arms around the nearly hysterical woman. Jane had never seen Cheyenne lose control. She didn't know what to do. For someone else, she would have known what to say. But what do you say when the strongest person you know falls to pieces? She just held her until the sobs lessened into hiccups. Taking a half step backward, she tilted the younger woman's face toward her own and wiped the tears away.

"I'm sorry." Cheyenne hiccupped again. "I try not to cry in front of other people. It makes them so uncomfortable."

Jane brushed the smooth cheek. "Silly. It's what sisters are for." For the first time, Jane really saw her, not as a spiritual being but as a woman with strengths and weaknesses. It was something that had never occurred to her before. She was always just Cheyenne. She was always there when she was needed. Jane never speculated where she got her strength or how she knew what was needed. It was something she had grown to take for granted. Gently she brushed down the brown strands. They ended at the shoulder. Startled, Jane spun her around. "What did you do?" she demanded.

"What I had to." Cheyenne's shoulders had begun to square as the moment passed. "I need you to help me gather Celeste's things."

"But your beautiful hair."

"It needed to be done. I'm mourning the death of one of my best friends."

"She didn't even notice. I'm sorry."

Cheyenne sadly smiled. "It doesn't matter."

"It does." Jane tried to slide her arms around the younger woman, but Cheyenne stepped backward. "You can't just keep it all locked up inside."

"Right now there are more important things. We have to go from room to room. Everything. Even the littlest thing has to be gone."

"Why?" Jane didn't understand.

Cheyenne shook her head, the newly cut ends swaying at her shoulders. "I don't know. It's just a feeling."

"How did you know about Dominic's past?"

Cheyenne hesitated for a moment. "I contacted a few people from the past who gave me names of others. I never knew why Celeste forbid me to contact her family . . . until I started asking questions." She again hesitated. "I learned more than I wanted to." Turning away she started closing drawers and straightening the cabinet unnecessarily. "I thought Celeste always walked the path of light."

Silently Jane waited, afraid to interrupt. She needed to know the whole story.

"I talked to her sister, Beverly. She wouldn't tell me anything until I told her Dominic was here. She was furious." Cheyenne turned around. There were lines around her eyes that hadn't been there just moments before. "She told me some of what Celeste had been hiding. The dark path called to Celeste early in life. When she was young she was controllable. After she met Dominic . . ." her voice trailed off. Taking a deep breath, she continued. "They met when they were about eleven or twelve. Dominic's parents returned to the Rez and they sought the help of Celeste's Grandmother, Running Doe. She was a very powerful medicine woman. Dominic had already turned to the dark path. They wanted Running Doe to take the dark spirits from their son. That is how Celeste met him. They became an evil team. Drugs. Stealing. Animal sacrifices. Separately they were somewhat controllable. Together they were unstoppable. Running Doe looked into their histories. She saw them together many times before—hurting others and themselves."

"Celeste would never—"

"Beverly and others told me, Celeste doesn't have a conscious when she is with him. When Celeste was sixteen, she was diagnosed with cancer. Her family took her off the Rez to get the intensive treatments. While she was away, Dominic was arrested for possession with intent to sell. Her family told her he had died of an overdose. His family told him the cancer killed her. The lies worked. Celeste was healed. When she returned home, she married the first man who asked her. He beat her. Her Grandmother convinced her to leave and forced her husband to leave her alone. She got involved with more abusive men. Each time she was rescued."

Jane didn't know what to say. It was so unlike the person she knew.

"Celeste had an affair with another medicine woman's husband. The woman learned of the affair and cursed her with barrenness. Soon after, the woman disappeared. Her daughter was catatonic for months. There is more, but no one would talk about it or why Celeste went back to her family tradition. She followed all the rules. Running Doe finally consented to allowing her to join their medicine circle. Celeste seemed to find peace. Two years later she found me in the desert. You know most of the rest."

The pull to go west increased the more Cheyenne talked. But how could she leave Cheyenne alone? "I came down to the barn for a reason." She blurted out. She couldn't stop the words at her lips. "I need to leave for a while. I don't know where or for how long."

"But it's important," Cheyenne cut in. "Do you have traveling money? Transportation?"

"I haven't thought it through yet." Startled by Cheyenne's easy acceptance, Jane stared at her. "It's like you knew."

Cheyenne sighed. "I suspected. When I looked ahead, I didn't see you."

"I'm sorry. You'll be alone."

Cheyenne closed the drawer Dominic had been snooping in. It barely made a sound. "None of us are truly alone. As for me, I'm never alone."

"Cheyenne . . ."

"Everything is fuzzy. I don't understand much of what I see. Disjointed snapshots with no point of reference. But I know by helping you, I help myself."

"How?"

"Take the Dodge. It's old, but reliable. We'll put on the topper and you can represent Dragon Eye Herbs. You can expand our customer base. The farm will need the added income."

Shocked, Jane didn't know what to say. Cheyenne had just made the trip possible. As Cheyenne continued talking, Jane cut her off. "I want to talk to the same people you talked to about Celeste."

"I don't know if they'll talk to you. They would only talk to me after Beverly assured them."

"I want to try. If I'm there they might tell me more."

"Are you sure you want to do that? It was more than implied it wasn't safe."

"What about you? If it isn't safe for me, what about you? They're here."

Cheyenne hesitated, scanning from the floor to the cabinet, her gaze coming to rest on the view outside the window. Her pupils dilated and narrowed, as if waves of information were flowing out of them to another destination.

Jane could sense the spiritual touch of others as they flowed past her to Cheyenne. They were loving and comforting. She realized Cheyenne had a support system totally and exclusively her own. She was jealous. She wanted to be part of the stream of unconditional love surrounding the younger woman, which wrapped itself around her like a warm coat.

Cheyenne smiled. "I'll be more than all right."

"Who was that?"

"Who was what?" Cheyenne countered.

Shaking, sadness crept up on Jane. Within moments the support system she had cherished had vanished almost as if it had never existed. The two women she loved the most in life were becoming strangers. *Why? What had she done to deserve such punishment?*

Not punishment, an inner voice told her, *a chance to make amends.*

Jane closed her eyes. Being alone and feeling unlovable were two challenges she had yet to conquer. She didn't feel strong enough to confront them now. It was too hard. She wanted to rewind time, to change the way events unfolded so they would have never been brought to this moment. If Dominic had never come or if she had listened and helped Cheyenne make him leave—but that was not their reality. Dominic did come. She had stood with Celeste. Their beautiful dream changed into a waking nightmare and it was equally her fault as it was Celeste's.

Cheyenne gently rubbed Jane's shoulder. "You will be fine."

Opening her eyes, Jane walked out of Cheyenne's reach. "How do you know?" Her confusion and fear reflected in her voice as anger. "Everything has changed!"

"It always does."

It was the truth, but Jane found no comfort. "I don't want to go. But I have to."

"When?"

"Anxious to get rid of me?"

"Don't do this." Cheyenne's voice remained level and quiet. "Not to me or yourself. We're both emotionally raw. We know what we must do. Will questioning make it any easier?"

Amused and frustrated at the logic, Jane snorted. "I have to pack. Contact a few friends. I will also help you pack away Celeste things. There is so much it will take both of us." She hesitated. "Will you move back to the main house?"

"I haven't decided yet."

"Please do. I don't want you out here alone. I'll call Raven. Ask her to move out for a while."

Cheyenne nodded.

"Do you want me to help you tell the others?"

She shook her head. "You won't have time for that."

Jane really wanted to hug her; it didn't feel appropriate. "I have calls to make."

"The Dodge will be ready when you need it."

Jane nodded and walked out the side door, gently closing it behind her. Their relationship was not over, just changing and growing.

CHAPTER EIGHT

Cheyenne cut up the beef liver and mixed it with the dog food. She deliberately kept her mind blank. Splitting the contents into equal parts, she dumped it into the smaller dishes. She just stood for a moment, looking out the window. Thoughts whirled around; she refused to be caught up by them. Other people's thoughts and emotions blew around the cabin like leaves in the fall wind, only her shields kept them from permeating her safe haven and disturbing her already thin sense of peace. Aries and Mercury sat patiently at her feet, waiting for their dinner. Littermates, the half-Wolf, half-Shepard pair had more patience and intelligence than most people she knew. Picking up the dishes, she placed them on the floor in front of them. Neither animal moved. Gliding her open hand downward from her forehead to her stomach, she signaled for them to eat. Simultaneously, they attacked their dinner.

Leaning against the counter, she folded her arms across her chest. She should eat something. The feast was still hours away. She planned to tell everyone after dinner. Most of the celebration would be over and there would be little left for her news to spoil.

During New Moon, problems were shared and solutions sought, the Full Moons were always joyous occasions of singing, dancing and sharing blessings. Tonight would be a mixture of both. Everyone was going to miss Jane. Cheyenne was especially going to feel the void. But in her heart she understood. An image came into her mind. Jane was walking westward into the sunset, only it was more than a sunset it was also a sunrise. Without breaking stride, Jane was joined by others. Together they were transformed into beings of light, which filled the horizon with golden brightness. The light from their hearts poured out and encased them. Where there were once three, there was one. Closing her eyes, Cheyenne allowed the peacefulness to wash away some of her confusion. Jane would be safe. But would the farm?

Yes, came the reply. *The others will come.*

Opening her eyes, she ran her fingers through her hair. She'd have Jenny even the ends tomorrow, hopefully without too many questions. There was so much that needed to be done. All she wanted to do was sleep, to drift off into the dreamless void of total separateness. But it was not to be, at least not today; and tomorrow wasn't looking good either.

Aries finished his dinner first and sat back on his haunches. Mercury licked his dish clean; the pressure of his tongue slid it across the tiles, bumping it against the counter. Realizing there was no more to be had, he also sat back and waited for the signal. Smiling, Cheyenne reached forward and scratched them between the ears. Their tails wagged. There were some places the darkness would never be able to penetrate for the love shone too brightly. With the wave of her hand, the duo raced out the open back door. She followed more slowly, stopping at the archway. Each dog took their familiar direction, inspecting their fenced-in turf and lifting a leg to mark it. As always they crossed in the center of the yard beneath the red maple, continuing in the direction the other had just come. Completing the circle, Mercury crawled into the hammock, stretching out so his head hung over the side. Aries lay down beneath the lilac bush, its drooping branches nearly hiding his presence. He was on alert. Later in the afternoon, the roles would be reversed and Mercury would guard the home turf. She didn't teach them; it was a routine they independently developed as pups. She had learned to trust their instincts. If they allowed a person to approach without too much fuss, they were allowed to enter. If they verbally told her they didn't trust the person, the closest they got was the bottom step of the porch.

She leaned on the doorway. In the mist of the sunshine and sweet summer breeze, she felt drained of hope for the future. It was not a safe place to be emotionally; it could be easily turned and used against her. Her dry eyes burned for the lack of tears.

A robin landed on the fence and called to another. It was considered the bird of hope and new beginnings. She saw only a dark path in front of her. It continued to sing. Cheyenne looked down at the wooden floor of the porch. She wished she could cry and get it out of her system. A creeping numbness spread up from her feet, quickly racing past her knees. She leaned more heavily against the frame, slowly sliding downward. She landed knees first with a thump. The vibration, closely followed by pain, radiated up her torso. She knelt half in, half out the doorway. She no longer had the energy to stand.

Aries barked and wagged his tail. Mercury lifted his head and half barked. Neither moved from their position.

A few minutes later, a chocolate colored hand reached down and lifted her to her feet. Her weight rested primarily on the other. She was led to the living room and draped over the sofa. Gently her feet were lifted, pillows propped under her knees and her feet placed on the softness of the sofa. Her eyes drifted upward.

Lilith sadly smiled down at her; her aquamarine eyes shone with love.

Cheyenne tried to explain.

A dark finger crossed Cheyenne's lips. "Shush. Sleep. We'll talk later." The finger moved from her lips to the brow between her eyes. The room spun around her. Her eyes closed, taking her into the darkness of the protected sleep.

She didn't understand. The dragons had cleansed her of the darkness. Why was she suddenly so weak? There was no logic behind what was happening to her. Everything was done properly. Her thoughts tilted and swirled. Opening her eyes only made it worse.

"Don't fight it." Lilith gently commanded. "Let go. I will catch you."

Again she felt the pressure between her eyes, only this time sleep quickly took her to a place of rest.

Slowly she awoke. Time had no meaning. Her body felt stiff from the lack of movement. She shifted her weight. It helped a little.

The floorboards creaked. Dishes clicked against one another. Footsteps approached the sofa. "Cheyenne . . ." Lilith whispered. "Wake up. You need to eat."

"No." She murmured.

"Don't be stubborn. You need nutrition." Her voice was gentle but firm, leaving no room for doubt that she would have her own way.

Cheyenne opened her eyes and tried to sit up. Her arms felt heavy and numb.

"Open your mouth."

Without question Cheyenne did as she was told. A spoonful of warm tomato soup passed her lips and slid down her throat. Wordlessly one spoonful followed another until the bowl was empty. Lilith took the bowl back to the kitchen. Moments later, she returned with two dishtowels. She rolled up the first into a tube and slid it around the back of Cheyenne's neck. The other she folded and draped across he eyes and forehead.

The towels felt cold and damp against her skin. For the first few moments, it was uncomfortable, but quickly the discomfort became a cooling kiss, which banished the fever she hadn't known was there.

"Sleep little sister. You're safe now."

Cheyenne wanted to thank her. As she formed the words, her body relaxed and she drifted back into sleep. The sounds around her faded away, becoming muffled and distant. She didn't know if she was moving away or if everything else was. Quickly she chided herself, of course everything else was standing still, she was moving into the land of sleep and dreams. She tried to control her path to dreams, sometimes she could, and sometimes she couldn't. Either way she felt no fear. She directed her imagination to conjure a scene from the tropics with hot, sandy beaches, lapping waves and dolphins swimming offshore. For as long as she could remember, she had wanted to swim with dolphins. No images came. Instead she drifted in the serene darkness within the embrace of a warm, soft pillow. No visions. No visitations from the beyond. Just quiet, peaceful rest. Her expectations melted into acceptance. Releasing control, she found herself floating on dark waters, knowing she was completely safe and protected. Sighing, she sank deeper into sleep; she knew no more until her eyes fluttered open with a will of their own.

The sun had followed its path across the sky. It now shone through the cracks in the curtains of the western windows. Cheyenne guessed that it was close to six. The stiffness in her body told her she hadn't moved much in her sleep. There had been more than tomatoes in the Lilith's soup. Scanning the room, she found her sitting in a chair across the room, reading a book. "What did you give me?"

The corners of her full lips curled upward. "It was just a little something I cooked up to teach little angels of light that they need to stop and care for themselves." She closed the book. "How do you feel?"

"Stiff. But emotionally better."

"Why didn't you call me sooner?"

"What time is it?"

"Almost six-thirty."

As quickly as her numbed mind and body would allow, Cheyenne sat up, trying to remember what still needed to be done.

"You'll regret that."

She was right. Pain flashed between her eyes, spreading across her forehead. She lowered herself back on the pillows. "There are about a hundred twenty people headed this way, expecting food, drink and entertainment. Almost nothing is done."

"Not your problem."

"I always—"

"Not this time. I found your notes on the desk and called the main house and told, someone-I think her name was Jane-that you couldn't do it." Leaning forward she looked directly into Cheyenne's eyes. "You took a heavy hit, little sister. Why didn't you call?" Her hand chopped through the air between them, stressing her point. "Not only can't you do it on your own; but you don't have to."

"I've done it before." Cheyenne refused to admit weakness, not even to herself. "Besides, who could I call?"

"Me! Raven, Selene—"

"Selene's gone."

"Not far. But that's not the point." Lilith sat back in the chair, dropping the book on the floor. "You never ask for help. It's going to stop."

Slowly Cheyenne slide to a sitting position. "You do what you have to."

Lilith right eyebrow arched. "So what happened?"

"The shit hit the fan."

"Obviously."

"I really don't feel like talking about it. Can't we pretend everything is ok?'

"We can. But it won't change anything." Lilith crossed her legs and settled into the chair. "And the elephant in the living room will still be there whether we talk about it or not."

Tears welled up in Cheyenne's eyes, threatening to spill over. "It hurts too much."

"That's good. You didn't shut yourself down again."

"Oh great! Some accomplishment." Cheyenne wiped away the falling tear and snuffled. "It doesn't solve anything and clouds the issues."

"Which are?"

Shaking her head back, Cheyenne brushed the hair from her face. Its length still surprised her. "I told Celeste and Dominic to leave. They both crossed the line. There'll be a problem separating Celeste's possessions from ours."

"Fighting over trinkets is silly."

"I don't care what little stuff she takes as long as she takes everything she brought into the house. I don't want there to be reason one for her to come back."

"It's a big change."

"Too much has happened."

Lilith nodded. "What else?"

"Jane is leaving."

"Did you ask her to?"

Cheyenne shook her head. "It's something she feels she needs to do. She doesn't know where or how long."

"It'll be two against one." Lilith leaned on the arm of the chair, resting her chin in her palm.

"Basically."

"Wrong." The aquamarine eyes twinkled. "It's two against all of us. It's a big house with many empty bedrooms. I want an eastern view."

"What about your house? Your clients?"

"I'm an accountant. My computer is my office. The house is rented." A sly smile crossed her lips. "Besides, there is someone I want you to meet. I'll bring her to the gathering tonight."

"But you said—"

"I've changed my mind." A long finger waggled in front of her face. "I'm genetically entitled."

Cheyenne was confused. Lilith had long proclaimed she wanted nothing to do with the rest of the members of the farm. "Why?"

"Never mind." Lilith paused. "If you're lucky, you'll understand by the end of the night."

Cheyenne weakly smiled. "More of your secrets?"

The sparkle in her eyes shouted the humor she was unable to hide. "It's what keeps me interesting."

"No, my dear sister. It's your zest for life and your ability to make a story out of a plain white wall."

"Nothing is ever plain or white. Everything is just shades of gray." The corners of her mouth curled upward, revealing almost unnaturally white teeth. In many ways she was a series of contrasts. Nothing ever seemed to disturb her. Tension was eased with a joke or a diversion. Yet, there was still an underlying current of focus and intensity.

Cheyenne's mind detoured on its own tangent. It occurred to her that most older people on the spiritual path seemed younger than their actual years. The children were still children, yet they had an understanding and maturity level beyond their age. She remembered reading somewhere that in Nirvana everyone was thirty. She wondered if it was true.

"Enterprise to Cheyenne. Enterprise to Cheyenne." Lilith waved her open palm in front of Cheyenne's face. "Do you read me?"

Rapidly blinking, Cheyenne snapped back. Smiling, she snatched the hand and kissed the palm. She put on her best Scottish accent. "'aye Cap'n. I hear 'ya. Beam me back."

"Did you find any intelligent life?"

"Aye. I did. But they'd be too involved with their own lives and with a helpin' others to be givin' much information."

Cheyenne gazed into the smiling eyes. The love in them reached out and embraced her, making everything all right. Her hand came up, gently tracing Cheyenne's cheek. Lilith leaned forward and kissed her forehead as a mother would a child. Cheyenne did feel like a small child who had just woke up from a nightmare only to find a loving protector already chasing away the bad dreams. It was love without strings or conditions. It was still a new experience for her. For a moment, Cheyenne became part of Lilith and together they became part of all living things. The birds sang. The squirrels chattered. All of life swirled around them and in them. Slowly their energy separated. The moment ended. Once again they were individuals.

Standing, Lilith shook back her hair. "I should say something." She hesitated. "But I can't think of a thing."

Words had deserted Cheyenne as well. The energy that passed between them was more intimate than sex, yet they had not touched. What she felt was more spiritual than physical. It was almost as if they had reinforced their own womanhood. Cheyenne had been taught true bonds were only possible between men and women. But she suddenly realized that women, who are strong within themselves and their femininity, were bonded first with all women. That is how it was meant to be. In primitive societies, all the women celebrated their moon time at the same time every month. It was this commitment to one another that made them strong. It was only when the commitment was sacrificed to men did women become weak and dependent. It was knowledge that came from her soul. She knew it to be true. Licking her lips, Cheyenne wanted to share the information, but she didn't know how. It just didn't seem the correct time to be speaking of philosophical insights.

Lilith smiled and nodded.

Outside, Aries and Mercury started barking. By the tone and volume, the arrival was not welcome. Standing, Cheyenne turned toward the door.

Lilith grabbed her arm. "Let me."

"Why?"

"Let me be your protector." She pinched the younger woman's chin. "Just watch and learn." Spinning on the balls of her feet, she marched to the front door.

Cheyenne followed a few paces behind.

With great flourish, Lilith opened the screen door, deliberately closing it behind her. She walked to the edge of the front porch and waited.

Cheyenne stayed within the confines of the cottage, protected from sight by the curtains of the inner door and Lilith's presence. The shadow strolled around the fence, becoming an overconfident Dominic. She felt her stomach tighten, preparing for another confrontation.

Seeing Lilith, Dominic stopped short of the porch. He stared at her.

"You needn't try to read me." Lilith continued down the porch, squaring off with the taller man. "I'll save you the effort. I'm your worse nightmare."

He sneered at her. "An overused cliché."

"A cliché it may be. But true." Her head bobbed slightly side to side. Her hand flipped up, the palm pointing at him. "In the past your darkness kept you from reaping what you sowed," elegantly her palm flipped over in a wave motion, "but your harvest time has come. And I'm the one at the handle end of the sickle whose business end is going to cut you down."

"Where's Cheyenne!" He demanded.

"In my cradle." Lilith's voice became stronger, her presence larger.

Dominic stepped backward. "What are you?"

"I am, the I am. I am the seer of all things. I know who you are and what you have done."

"Shut up! Where's Cheyenne?"

Lilith turned at the waist, extending her hand to Cheyenne. The whites of her eyes glowed.

Cheyenne stepped through the doorway and out onto the porch, stopping at the top step. Reaching out, her fingertips touched Lilith's. The power surged within her and she joined Lilith at the edge of the porch.

The color drained from Dominic's face.

Lilith returned her attention to him. "There is nothing you can do that cannot be undone and turned back on you."

Tossing the loose strands back over his shoulder, he balanced his weight equally on both feet and smiled. "I'm not finished yet."

"You have attacked twice. Twice it failed. Undo the damage you have done. You may still be granted grace." The words came from Lilith's mouth, but the voice was from a source much older and wiser.

His fists clenched. Setting his jaw, he recollected himself. "You can't frighten me. I know." He pointed at Cheyenne. "I know how to hurt you!" His anger flared. "You and all those others who forsake the male energy of the Gods." He stepped forward on an angle, putting himself in direct line of vision with Cheyenne. "She can't always be with you. One time when you take flight . . ." The threat remained unfinished. A hawk dived from nowhere; its extended talons scraping his forehead and scalp. He screamed in pain, beating the vacant air trying to ward off an attacker who had already disappeared.

"I'm everywhere." Lilith waved her hand. A gust of wind blew dirt into his face. "I am not limited by time or energy. And there is another cliché." Her voice lightened to resemble Lilith's. "You have to sleep sometime." She looked over her shoulder and winked. The glow had begun to fade in her eyes.

Furious, he rushed her. She spun around ducking and bringing up her leg. Her knee collided with his abdomen, doubling him over. Combining the strength and mass of both her hands into a fist, she slammed it down on the back of his neck.

He hit the ground with a grunt, immediately rolling out of her reach. Jumping into a crouch, he growled, revealing his growing canine teeth.

Immediately Aries and Mercury leaped at their side of the fence, growling and barking. Leaves rained down on him from the squirrels dashing and jumping between branches. From the left, the bushes rustled. A black and white body scurried from it. Its long striped tail erect. As quickly as its little legs could waddle, it crossed the distance, spun around and squirted a cloud of protective scent. Dominic didn't have the opportunity to dodge. The direct stream soaked his face; the cloud enveloped him.

Aries and Mercury leaped back, disappearing around the back of the house.

Laughing, Lilith covered her nose and ran up the steps.

Cheyenne's mouth dropped open, but she immediately closed it and followed.

With a flick of its tail, the skunk returned to the bushes.

Dominic rolled in the dirt and the tall grass. His eyes watered. Curses were flung at everyone and no one in particular. Stripping off his shirt, he tried to clean his face. Stumbling, he ran towards the main house.

Both women returned inside, closing the both doors behind them against the odor.

"At least his cologne matches his personality."

Cheyenne snickered. "No doubt about it. But we'd better close the windows or the inside will smell as bad as the outside."

"I'll do it. You go bring in your fur-kids. I don't think they like the outside anymore."

"Good idea." Cheyenne walked through the house to the back door. She didn't have to call them. They were at the screen door waiting. She opened it and they bumped into each other running in. She gave them each a good scratch and a treat before returning to the living room. "About your eyes. What was or should I say who was that?" For the first time since Cheyenne had known her, Lilith looked uncomfortable. "If you can't tell me, I'll understand."

Lilith returned to the chair. "It's not that I don't want to . . . but I can't. They are older than man's memory. They have no names; only visual energy signatures. They were here eons before man learned to walk upright. Their job is to keep order. It's only when someone brings disorder or when they are invited can they interfere."

A shiver went through Cheyenne. Was the problem larger than she suspected or was Lilith over dramatizing? "But you called them?"

Lilith nodded. "I needed them."

"Can't they stop—"

"No. They can only react. The law of free will binds them as well as frees us. They can only act indirectly. If someone wanted to commit suicide, they couldn't stop them. But they could influence people to be concerned."

Kneeling in front of Lilith, she looked up. "If we ask, could they help Celeste become herself again?"

Reaching down, she gently cupped the younger woman's chin. "Celeste is being herself. She used her free will to make decisions. No one can change that." She continued with a little more hope in her voice. "However they can and will send help to you and the others. I've already asked."

Cheyenne sat, leaning against the side of the chair. "She was an important part of my life for a long time. She saved me."

"It's different."

Sadly Cheyenne nodded. "My head knows. My heart remembers."

"That is your test. You must let go of your anger and your guilt. None of what she's done is your fault. As long as you feel responsible for her, she will have power over you." Sliding out of the chair, Lilith knelt beside her. "Guard your heart. Cherish the memories. But the person you loved doesn't exist any more. Mourn her loss and move on. The person she's become is no friend."

"I understand."

"Not yet. But you are beginning to." Lilith stood. "I'm getting to old to be sitting on the floor. What time do things start?"

"Dinner usually starts about 8:30."

She quickly looked at her watch. "We'll be late. I have to go. Don't leave the house without me."

"I'll be fine. Just meet me—"

"No!" Lilith stated firmly, but continued more calmly. "Stay here. Magic is afoot. You'll just get in the way. And before you ask, I'm not going to tell you." Quickly she patted the dogs' heads and disappeared out the back door.

Snickering to herself, she pushed on the back door. It wouldn't move. The front door wasn't a pleasant alternative. "Just swell!" The sarcasm in her voice brought the dogs to their feet. "No. No. Momma sorry. Nothing's wrong. She's just getting a dose of her own medicine and she doesn't like the taste."

Mercury shoved his nose beneath her hand. She scratched his ears. It was going to be an interesting night and she didn't have to be a psychic to know it.

CHAPTER NINE

Cheyenne added another name to the list of stores and towns. She had no idea which direction Jane would be taking. She listed her known contacts by direction, supplementing the list from ads from magazines. The list totaled fifty-two. It would be a good start. Jane is creative; she will be able to make other opportunities. Dropping the pencil on the desk, she swiveled in the chair, brushing her bangs back over her forehead. The new length was going to take some getting used to.

Lilith had been gone for over an hour. Don't leave. Wait for me. She had said.

Waiting wasn't one of Cheyenne's strongest virtues. She had read somewhere the best way to build patience was to do something else while you were developing it. She had showered and changed. She was all primped and as ready as she was going to be for the party. No Lilith. She went through her source magazines, starting the list. She had finished the primary and started on the secondary. She had paced for a while before starting the list of health food stores. Still no Lilith. She finished all she could do without using the computer at the main house.

Why did they have to go together? It's not like she didn't know how to get to the fire circle. She'd leave a note, telling her she had waited as long as she could, to just meet her there. Tucking a stray hair back behind her ear, she quickly wrote the message.

"Aries! Mercury! Potty time!" She jumped to her feet, note in hand. She'd put it on the back gate. The dogs followed closely behind her to the back door. Turning the door handle, she walked into the door. Startled she stepped back and just stared. She had forgotten about the door.

Aries nuzzled between her and the wall, popping the door open with his nose. His disappeared into the backyard, followed by Mercury, the door closing behind them.

Hum? She thought. She reached out and pushed. The door didn't budge. Biting her lower lip, she cocked her head to one side and planted her fists on her hips. Magic was afoot and she didn't do it. Someone has been messing with Momma Bear's den and she didn't like it.

In harmony, Aries and Mercury ran barking toward the back gate. Their tone was mixed. It was someone they recognized and liked, yet there was a stranger.

Frustrated, Cheyenne leaned against the doorframe, folding her arms across her chest. She felt like a prisoner in her own home. A breeze blew through the screen, freeing the short strands; they dangled in front of her eyes. She combed them back with her fingers. It was becoming a nasty trend.

Led by Mercury, Lilith appeared, carrying a bag in each hand. She was moving fast along the path. Looking over her shoulder, she stumbled but quickly regained her footing.

It suddenly made sense. Shifting her weight, she stood in full view, her open palms pushing against the frame. "I'd help," she called to the approaching figure, "but I seem to be trapped."

Lilith stopped and smiled. "Open-says-me."

The door popped open without assistance and Cheyenne stepped out on the porch.

"I have someone with me." Lilith sounded winded as she walked up the steps. "Aries won't let her in the yard."

Mercury sat at her feet. Cheyenne reached down and scratched his ears. "Aries!" She called. "Guide to me."

Aries howled a response.

"Follow him. But stick to the path." She yelled to the unseen visitor.

"Her name is April." Smiling, Lilith leaned against the railing, her breath returning to normal. "We met about five years ago at a Ren-fair."

Leaning forward and resting her palms on the railing, Cheyenne brought herself to eye level with the older woman. "How were you able to put a lock on my house?"

Sheepishly, Lilith shrugged.

"The 'ooh so innocent my hand really isn't in the cookie jar' look doesn't suit you."

Puckering her lips into a fake pout, she held the bags closer. "Keeping talking like that and I'll keep your Yule gift."

"You'll have forgotten all this by the end of December." Cheyenne countered.

A woman screamed. Aries growled. Both women snapped to attention. With one leap Mercury was off the porch, running across the lawn. Quickly both women followed.

A petite woman stood a few feet off the path, sword held defensively in front of her. Aries stood his ground in front of her growling. The fur on his back was raised, giving him a larger than normal appearance. Mercury had taken a position forty-five degrees to Aries's left; his teeth bared. His growl harmonized with his partner's. The sword waved back and forth menacingly.

"Aries! Mercury! Come!" Cheyenne commanded.

Neither moved. Their muscles were tensed, ready to spring in either direction. Cheyenne tried walking around Aries. He shifted, blocking her path.

"Cheyenne, they've never attacked—"

"Yes they have, but only when they sense a threat."

"April's cool. I've known her for a long time."

"Call them off!" The stranger commanded. "I'll do what I have to."

Cheyenne didn't like the threat. "Did you leave the path?"

"I dropped a bag." Slowly April swung the blade from right to left. She was petite to the point of being thin, but her arms strongly held the blade in front of her. She and it were not strangers. Her brown hair was tightly braided back in dual strands on each side of her head with three small beaded braids hanging on the left; it gave her face an angular appearance. Her light colored eyes seemed to focus on the entire scene. There was not anger or hatred within them, but a fierce defiance. She would not be bullied, by them or anyone. Behind her several bags lay on the ground, their contents strewn among the vegetation.

Cheyenne didn't understand. She didn't sense any darkness or evil from this woman. But why were her protectors reacting to her?

"Make them stand down. I will gather my things and go in peace." April addressed Cheyenne. "I don't stay where I'm not wanted."

"It just a misunderstanding. With everything that's been going on, he probably thought you were attacking. He defended me. You defended yourself. And it escalated. Sheath your sword."

"It's back down the path." April growled. "I did nothing—"

"Then flip it over and offer it to him." Lilith interjected.

"I won't leave myself open!" April snapped.

Aries growled, his lips folding back to expose his teeth.

Cheyenne grabbed his collar. "I have him."

"Like you could stop him."

"Think about it." Lilith calmed the tone of her voice. "All his actions have been defensive. At the gate, he was wary but not aggressive. Play it back. When did he get aggressive?"

"When I left the path."

"What did you do?"

"I pulled my sword."

"And he reacted?"

"Yes."

April thought for a moment. The blade of the sword dropped to the ground. She held it before her like a cross. "Lilith, I trust you."

Aries stared at the stranger's change in posture. He watched. April relaxed. The hair on his back flattened. She didn't move. Slowly, Cheyenne released her grip, yet remained prepared to intercede if necessary. Aries circled, sniffing the air. Mercury held back, more relaxed yet prepared. Aries's demeanor became calmer with every paw movement. Only April's eyes moved. He smelled her feet and legs up to her groin. Satisfied, he returned to Cheyenne and sat at her feet.

Embarrassed, Cheyenne looked down at him. "That's it? All the fuss, and that's it?"

Aries looked up at her. He blinked several times, looked at April and returned his attention to Cheyenne.

In her head, Cheyenne heard, "I'm just doing my job Mom. Just like you expect of me." She found it hard to be angry. He was following his training. There would be no punishment. Yet she felt the other woman's eyes on her expectantly waiting for her judgment. Trustingly he looked up at her. She turned to the newcomer. "April, I'm sorry he frightened you. He saw you actions as a threat and treated you as such."

"I don't like it." April shifted her weight from one foot to another. "But I understand."

"It's partially my fault. I should have come out to meet you." Quickly striding past the two women, Cheyenne bent down and began picking up the clothing. "It doesn't look like anything was damaged." She held up a leather vest. "What's this for?"

"Effect." Lilith smiled. "I promised you a surprised." She held up a pair of cropped leather pants. "Green is your color."

"I'm not wearing those."

"Yes, you are."

"No, I'm not."

"This could be entertaining." April cut in. "But aren't we late?" She pointed at Aries. "I'm going in the house. Don't bite me."

He gave her his sweetest, most innocent, 'little ole' me?' look.

"Not even on sale do I buy that." April marched toward the house. "Who pissed off the skunk?"

"She's very direct."

Lilith shrugged. "She always has been."

"It can be a time-saver."

Lilith picked up the last piece. "Or it can be bloody annoying."

Without fuss, April disappeared inside.

Feeling both annoyed and confused, Cheyenne watched the door close behind the stranger. Normally she maintained tight control over her turf. But Lilith was able to lock her in and a complete stranger was able to evade her defenses as if they didn't exist. She turned to Lilith. "Is there an open house sign on my house that I don't know about?"

Lilith's eyebrow arched, but she said nothing. Instead she followed the path to the back door and disappeared inside.

There was something tugging at her memory strings. Walking toward the house, Cheyenne tried to understand why she automatically respected this woman. April was not much older than herself, yet she inspired the respect of an elder. An old yearning awakened within Cheyenne; she didn't understand. Opening the back door, Cheyenne crossed the threshold. The dogs curled up on the porch.

April had laid out the clothing in sets. There were three. One was black with silver stitching. The second was also black, but it had gold designs. The third was green on green. It also had the same elaborate symbols, yet the colors blended so closely you needed to look closely to see them. Scanning the room, April's eyes met Cheyenne's. "It's nice. Comfortable."

Despite herself, warm satisfaction flooded Cheyenne.

Crossing the room, April reached out and pulled some of Cheyenne's hair through two fingers. Over Cheyenne's shoulder, she spoke to Lilith. "She cut how much off?"

"About ten inches." Lilith answered. "Will you be able to fix it and still be able to do the traditional pattern?"

April shrugged. "I'll do my best. No guarantee."

"What pattern?" Cheyenne cut in.

"Pattern of rank." April spun her around and propelled her toward the kitchen. "You sit down, I'll explain." She pointed at Lilith, "You go change."

"Sounds like a plan to me!" Lilith gathered the silver accented leather and walked into the bathroom, closing the door behind her.

"Sit." April commanded, pulling a hard case out of one of the bags. "And you. What made you hack off your hair?"

"It's a symbol of mourning."

"Who died?"

"A dear friendship." The sadness welled up in her throat and she sat in the closest chair.

"Would a dear friend hurt you?" April's hands deftly moved around her head, measuring and cutting. "No." She answered herself. "A friend," she emphasized the word, "is someone who loves and protects you. Who is loving and supportive even at times when it's inconvenient. They're there when you need them. Even when you don't want them. Friends are equals. Share and share alike. Sometimes one will have more than another, true, but it always changes and balances out. Which means little sister," April stepped around and tilted Cheyenne's head up, "you don't allow another to live off you financially, emotionally or just out-and-out steal your energy." She checked the length of the front hairs. "You are a loving, caring child of light. It is good to be generous. But friends you have to buy aren't worth anything." April combed her fingers through the hair at Cheyenne's brow and started braiding, adding in four wooden beads with the same design cut into them. "You've allowed certain people in your life to practically drain you dry. They have shown who they truly are. They have made their choices. The consequences are theirs not yours." She paused for a moment and started the second braid on the left side. To this braid she added four different colored beads. "Your challenge is to let go. Starting the first braid on the right side, she paused. "Repeat after me. None of my business."

"Why?"

"Just do it." She slipped on a red bead.

"None of my business."

"Not my problem."

"Not my problem." Cheyenne repeated.

"Go away. You're no longer a part of my life."

"What if she changes?"

"A person can't change their true nature." April quipped back.

At that moment, Cheyenne was angry with the newcomer. "You don't know them, I do."

April leaned over, looking her straight in the eyes. "You need to be honest with yourself."

The bathroom door flung open, banging against the wall behind it. Lilith stepped out. "Ta-da!" She shouted with flourish. Stepping into the kitchen, Lilith rotated from side to side, modeling the vest and knee length pants. The vest tapered down, ending just above her belly button. The pants began just below. The fit emphasized her arm muscles and flatness of her stomach, ignoring the fullness of her hips. "What do you think?" She beamed. "I still do good work."

"Magnificent as always." April chimed in. "If you'll finish her hair. I'll change."

"As good as done." Lilith stepped behind Cheyenne and measured out a hand full of hair. "You didn't make this easy."

April walked into the bathroom, carrying the other black set.

"Ok." Cheyenne tried to control the growing anger. "What the hell is going on?"

"I'm braiding your hair."

Cheyenne tried to stand, but the pain in her scalp kept her in her seat. "Ow!"

"Let me finish." Lilith kept her voice calm. "I know this is weird. I wish I could explain. But I can't. You have to remember, just like we did."

"Just tell me."

Slowly Lilith shook her head. "I can tell you about the braids. Nothing more. The ones on the right are the accomplishments. The wooden beads on the left tell of your family. Our mother's symbol is carved in. Her name was A'nona. You were her fourth child. You died without having a child so there is only one. If you had, their names would be inscribed on smaller beads."

"How did you know this?"

Lilith smiled and continued. "On the right side, you have four beads. Red, brown, orange, and green. April has already put the red. I will be putting the brown and green . . . and orange. You earned it but—"

"I died before it could be made official." Cheyenne blurted out, without knowing how she knew.

Lilith nodded. "Red is for warrior. Brown for hunter. Green is for healer."

"The orange was for the animal wisdom. I died because of a horse."

Lilith slowly nodded.

I mages flooded her mind. There were seven all together, including two brothers that lived in the village. She was a middle child, born nine months after the fertility ritual. Her name had been Tyr'gana. She was considered the daughter of the Horned God. Mother had been proud of her hunting skills. It was how she had won the horse. Her younger sister, Shan'na, had been jealous. Her father had brought the horses as gifts for the tribe council. Karr, elder councilwoman of the tribe, had declined and the horse was offered as a prize. Claiming the horse as a gift from her father, Shan'na tried to steal it. She was caught and punished. A cold shiver ran through her body. Her sister had caused them to be killed. Cheyenne met the aquamarine eyes. "Our sister killed us."

"What else do your remember?"

Cheyenne wiped the tear from her cheek. "She was jealous, because I was given the horse."

"Not given. Earned."

"My name was Tyr'gana. You were called Shalamar."

"Yes." Lilith kept her tone neutral.

"I need to know more."

"Finishing the last braid, the brown hands gently touched Cheyenne's shoulder. "I'm sorry little sister."

Reaching up, Cheyenne picked up her hand. Turning, she kissed her fingers. "Tell me."

Lilith shook her head. "Now is not the time." Forcing humor into her voice, she tried to lighten the mood. "Go change. We have a party to crash."

"It's my party."

"But we," Lilith pointed to the closed bathroom door then to herself, "are going to make it unforgettable."

The door opened. April stepped out. The vest corralled her ample breasts and revealed the well defined muscles of her arms. The breeches were longer than Lilith's, reaching down to mid-calf.

"And if the timing isn't right, it won't work." Lilith grabbed her by the forearms and pulled her out of the chair. "Get changed. And before you start whining, I designed it after your favorite. Don't think. Just let your fingers guide you and you'll know how to lace it."

Her legs wobbled. She caught the table to steady herself. "You haven't won."

April sat in the chair and crossed her legs. "Me first."

"Age before beauty."

"Maybe so, but I still look magnificent."

"Modest as always." Lilith freed the first braid. Adding the wooden beads, she started braiding.

"One thing I always found annoying."

"Just one?" Lilith quipped.

April smirked. "You always have good hair. Thick, long."

"Good genes."

Cheyenne realized she was either forgotten or being ignored. Reluctantly she retrieved the clothing and walked into the bathroom, closing the door behind her. Turning to the mirror, she examined her reflection. The hairstyle looked odd. She was more comfortable with it worn down, covering her neck. She felt different. Closing her eyes, she breathed deeply. Snatches of memories, picture post cards of a life long ago flashed before her inner eye too quickly for her to capture in her conscious memory.

Someone banged on the door. "Get dressed!" Lilith yelled.

Annoyed, she opened her eyes. The show stopped. Unbuttoning her shirt and slipping out of her jeans, she stood naked before the mirror. She reached for the pants. Opening the laces, she stepped into them. They felt stiff and awkward.

With difficulty she laced up the right side. The left was easier. They rested on her hips and fell to her knees. Squatting into a deep knee bend, she stretched them out; they gave easily. Standing, she realized the inverted triangle, reaching from her hips to her groin, was made of heavier leather. Something was missing. Her dagger. It hung tethered across her stomach and tied to her left thigh. Pleased with the memory, she slipped on the vest and laced up the front, adjusting the side laces for comfort. She traced the stitching down from her breasts until her fingertips came together at her navel. The workmanship was impeccable. The leather smelled different. She looked in the mirror. The memories flooded back. Her hair had had been dark, almost black, as been her mother's and most of her sisters'.

Banging on the other side of the door again snapped her back to the present. "Hurry up!" April demanded.

Taking a deep breath and slowly exhaling, she quickly checked the laces and opened the door. She stepped out, giving the other women a full view. She waited.

Lilith whistled her approval.

April shrugged. 'You never dressed yourself before?"

Her matter-of-factness was reassuring. Some things never changed. "I was remembering."

April reached over and straightened Cheyenne's vest. "Don't get lost there. The past is a good place to start looking for answers. But don't try to live there. It's done. It's over."

Confused, Cheyenne leaned against the doorframe. It was so much, so fast.

April reached forward, sliding her palm around the back of Cheyenne's neck. Gently she directed the younger woman's gaze to meet her own. "It's a cliché. But what goes around, comes around. And not just for the bad, but for the good to. We will all be together again. When we are, all of us, justice will be done. Understand?" April pulled her close, resting her head on her own shoulder. "It's a lot to take in. Your world has just gone boom. Friends you thought you could trust betrayed you. Now the past has started to come back."

Cheyenne pulled away and walked to the other end of the room. There was a memory crawling its way up from the deep recess of her soul. She turned to the window, searching for the familiar. Biting her lip, she forced the memories back downward. Right now she didn't want to know. She didn't want to remember. A turkey walked out of the underbrush. The Native Americans called them the give away bird. She licked her lips and turned toward April. "Why are you here? Why now?"

"You needed us." April didn't blink. "We are all linked. If not here, you would have been drawn to us some other place." Sadness crept into her voice. "This area is so much like our valley."

"When we met," Lilith pointed at April, "we clicked right away. Once we started comparing memories, the pieces started to make a picture. We did a lot of talking and crying."

"And yelling." April's hand sought and found the darker one. "We blamed each other."

"We forgave each other."

"Looking back, we saw the mistakes we made."

"Hopefully learning from them." Lilith brought April's hand to her lips, kissing the knuckles. "We all made mistakes."

"Our sister betrayed us!" Cheyenne blurted out.

"Yes." April agreed. "But we made mistakes as well. What chards of memories you now have are just that, pieces. In the stone decisions can't be made on such little information."

"Besides," releasing April's hand, Lilith crossed the room, "as April said. Now is not the time."

"I need to know one thing. Is-was Celeste our sister, Shan'na?"

"No." They answered in unison.

"Are you sure?"

"Yes." April answered. "I met her once in California. She was working at a New Age shop. I looked into her eyes and saw her. If she recognized me, she said nothing."

Cheyenne's eyebrow arched. The story sounded familiar, but she couldn't place it.

"Time to leave." Lilith walked toward the door. "Dogs in or out?"

"In." Walking to the back door, Cheyenne whistled. Both dogs ran to the back door, stopping only long enough for her to open the screen door. "I'll get them fresh water and meet you at the back gate."

Nodding, April picked up her sword and disappeared outside. Smiling, Lilith tweaked her cheek and followed.

Kneeling, Cheyenne patted the floor. Both dogs sat before her. "Momma will be gone for a little while. No one is to come in." She scratched their ears and stood. Centering her energy within her heart and focusing it out her palms, she spoke. "I call upon the Guardians of Light, the spirits and guardians of air, fire, water and earth to surround my home in an interlacing shield of light and love to protect my children, Aries and Mercury, my home, my car and all my possessions. From above and below and from all four directions,

I encircle us all in an impenetrable shield of an alternating energy which reflects back all negativity, both the seen and the unseen-the direct and the indirect, back to it source. May all who wish harm be guided elsewhere, finding nothing but confusion when attempting to find us. And so it is." With a final scratch, she walked out the door, locking it behind her.

They had waited for her outside the gate at Lilith's car. Both women were preoccupied by the contents of the trunk when Cheyenne walked up beside them.

Looking over her shoulder, April held out a knife, dangling by the straps of its sheath. "If you remember how to wear it, it's yours."

"Do I get a matching sword?" Cheyenne glibly asked.

"Only if you know how to make one." Cocking an eyebrow, April shifted her weight on to her left foot.

"Where did you get yours?"

"I made it. Do you want the dagger or not?"

Reaching for the dangling weapon, she centered the blade on her stomach, tying one set of straps around her waist and anchoring the bottom on her thigh. "Like this?" She asked with exaggerated innocence.

Grunting, April stepped forward and gently cuffed her behind the head. "Just like that."

"Hey!" Cheyenne rubbed the back of her head.

Snickering, Lilith pretended to be involved with the contents of the trunk.

With her opposite hand, April slapped back, hitting Lilith on the buttocks.

"Ow!" Lilith snapped up, catching the trunk with her hand before she hit the underside. "What was that for?"

"For a while." April snickered.

Rubbing her left cheek, Lilith narrowed her eyes and jutted out her chin. "Lame reason."

"It's all you're going to get."

"Love the comedy routine." Cheyenne cut in. "But aren't we late?"

Lilith blew April a kiss and closed the trunk. She wore a dagger on her right side; on the left hug a broadsword, the hilt matching that of the dagger. Following Cheyenne's gaze, Lilith smirked and re-adjusted the sword. "You're too short to have one."

"Where did you get that? I know you didn't make it. You're not that talented."

"Giving credit where credit is due—I have a very talented friend who is a true artisan."

"You're welcome." April cut in. "Let's go. Don't forget the drums. An artisan can't do manual labor."

"And I'm too short." Snickering, Cheyenne followed April down the path, leaving Lilith to carry both canvas bags herself.

Frustrated, Lilith slapped the trunk with her open palm. "Get back here!"

Giggling, her companions dashed down the path, stopping just out of her sight. Ducking behind a bush, Cheyenne allowed the playfulness of the moment to overtake her. Biting her lip to keep from giggling, she leaned over to look at April hiding behind a bush on the other side of the path. She looked silly. A grown woman, waiting to jump out and scare a friend.

"C'mon you guys." Lilith called from beyond their site. "I can't do it by myself."

Cheyenne giggled.

A finger immediately went to April's lips.

Cheyenne nodded, shifting her weight backward so the bush again concealed her. In spite of the joyful moment, thoughts of Celeste and Dominic crept into her mind. She dismissed them both and pushed them aside, instead keeping focus on the present.

The sounds of the drums banging together preceded Lilith. She slowly walked up the path, carrying the smaller bag in one hand and nearly dragging the larger one in the right. "Not funny guys." She muttered. Stopping short of their position, she dropped the bags. "If you don't come back and help—I'll leave 'em! I swear I will." She shouted up the path.

Cheyenne leaned to the left. April held up three fingers. Slowly she lowered them one by one. As the last curled to meet her palm, they jumped up and screamed. Lilith chimed in and jumped back. Recovering her composure, Lilith swung the large bag, hitting April in the buttocks. The "burroom" of the drum echoed among the trees. For an instant, the absurdity left them speechless. Lilith covered her mouth in a failed attempt not to laugh. The corners of her lips curled upward as a snorting sound rasped through her nose. April rubbed her hinny, laughing openly. Cheyenne watched them, tears of laughter welling up and spilling over her cheeks. Her laughter started as a sputter, which quickly became a full belly-laugh. Lilith dropped the bags; the drums bellowed their protest as they unceremoniously hit the ground. Grabbing her stomach with one hand while still rubbing her behind with the other, April's laughter was interspersed with hiccups.

Dropping to her knees, Cheyenne looked away, giving herself a few moments to catch her breath. Her ribs hurt. Her stomach ached. But she hadn't laughed with such free abandon since . . . her mind snapped back to better times. Sitting back on her heels, she realized what happened before wasn't so different than the present. Last time, it cost them their land, their family and their lives. They were so much stronger then; battle trained warriors who knew how to fight together, but now, this time, they were all strangers with only fragmented memories.

April crouched beside her. "What's the matter?"

"How can we possibly win?"

"Not now." The warning in April's voice was tempered with love.

"It's happening again." The panic grew inside Cheyenne stomach, pushing up on her diaphragm, making it hard for her to breathe. "We were seasoned warriors and we couldn't protect ourselves or our land."

A taunt smile crossed April's face, narrowing her lips. "You made the connection quickly. It's to your credit and your detriment."

"There are so few of us."

"More than you think." Lilith knelt opposite April.

"Yes, now is very close to what happened. But it's not the same. This time, they cannot use surprise or our own trusting nature against us. Through many cycles of lives, we've learned. The allies, who arrived too late last time, have already started to join us. We will all be forced to take an accounting of our lives. The same challenges will be presented. Either grace will be given or the full weight of the past will be carried."

"Who will make those decisions?"

"Someone higher on the spiritual food chain than us." The smile disappeared from April's face. "Just remember to keep in the present. Occupying your mind with things you can't change only wastes energy and delays the inevitable."

"It's like a hamster in a wheel. Running and running, but getting nowhere." Lilith gently brushed her cheek. "We all went through it."

"I understand." Cheyenne didn't really, but it was what they wanted to hear. "What if I remember more?"

"We're counting on it." Standing, April offered her hand to Lilith. "You were an excellent drummer and I'm going to need help awakening the old beat."

"There are others here." Lilith picked up the large bag. "Some from our tribe. Some from others. When the time comes, everyone will remember." Smiling, she offered her hand to Cheyenne. "You don't really understand, but you will."

April and Lilith made eye contact; nonverbal communication passed between the older siblings. Simultaneously they reached down and pulled Cheyenne to her feet.

"Hey! Hey!" Cheyenne screamed. "Child abuse."

"Not child, just abuse." Lilith quipped back. "Let's go or we'll lose our edge."

April picked up the smaller bag and headed down the path.

"You mean your actually going to help? Amazing!" Lilith continued in the same forced light tone. "You're going to help the poor, overburdened slave girl. This has to be a Kodak moment . . . and me without a camera!"

Stopping, April looked over her shoulder. "Keep it up. See what happens."

Shaking her head, a finger snapped to Lilith lips.

Arching an eyebrow, April continued down the path.

Smiling, Lilith followed more slowly.

Cheyenne watched them for a moment. If they were trying to make her feel better, it was having the opposite effect. There was a closeness between them she envied; it was something she had been searching her whole life for. A little voice inside reminded her that she too was part of that puzzle. Soon she would fit into place and be part of the whole. Taking a deep breath, she ran to catch up.

CHAPTER TEN

Snapping another table leg into place, Jane straightened and surveyed the progress. It was nearly seven. The food wasn't ready. The tables and chairs weren't set. She had no idea what Cheyenne had planned for ceremony, nor did she have a clue what to substitute it with. Cheyenne had always done most of the organizing. How did she do it? Contacting everyone took almost an hour. Jerry was collecting the wood for the fire pit and would light it later. Everyone else was making a dish to pass. Reaching for and snapping up the fourth leg, she flipped over the table and leveled it off. Continuing to the next, her mind swung between topics.

Celeste and Dominic had disappeared. She didn't have to be a sensitive to know they were going to try to ruin the evening. What of the ceremony? Who would lead? What did they have to be grateful for? Combing her fingers though her hair, she looked across the field toward Cheyenne's cabin. What would she say if Cheyenne didn't come? Was she all right? Who was the woman who called? All her attempts to reach out mentally to her sister were gently, yet firmly reflected back by a source Jane didn't recognize.

The back door opened and closed. Looking over her shoulder, Jane watched Raven cross the lawn, carrying an armload of linen.

Surveying the situation, Raven set the table clothes on one of the tables and picked up where Jane left off. "Though you could use some help. Any word from Cheyenne?

Jane shook her head.

"Meredith picked up the girls yet?"

"Not yet. Lisa is watching Shawna. Melanie's gone."

"Again? She'll turn up. She always does."

"Did you tell them?"

"Only Cheyenne."

"And?"

"She's loaning me the Dodge. I'll represent Dragon Eye Herbs on my trek across country." Taking the top tablecloth, Jane bellowed it out over the table closest to her.

"So you going to tell me what happened?"

"The truth hit me square in the face." The wind blew up one corner of the material. Jane smoothed it back down. "I found Dominic going through Cheyenne's files. He acted like lord of the manor. Entitled to know all of our business."

"You're kidding right?"

Jane shook her head. "He and Celeste are engaged."

"So? She's stupid."

"He was under the impression that gave him rights to the profits from Cheyenne's business and the land." The anger again rose with Jane. "We were in the process of telling him who owned what, when Celeste walked in."

"And it went from bad to worse."

"Celeste went from bullying to pleading to playing the misunderstood victim all in the same breath." Jane tapped the side of her head with her left hand. "I finally got it. Cheyenne wanted him gone tonight."

"Do you think Celeste will go with him?"

"At this point, I don't care. Cheyenne told her to leave."

Raven placed the last table. "What is everyone else going to do?"

"I don't know. Jerry has gotten really close to Dominic. I don't trust him any more. David and Janet," Jane shrugged. "We could always depend on him until they got engaged. She is trying to convert him. The only reason they haven't left is the cheap rent."

"What about Sandra and the kids?"

"She doesn't want to bring her kids into a war zone."

"Can you blame her? She's having enough trouble with her ex trying to take custody." Raven snorted. "It's amazing they let crack addicts and abusers keep custody of their kids, but a well balanced, loving pagan parent always has to be afraid."

"I don't know how many will come tonight. Lady Margaret and her daughter will be here for sure." Jane hesitated. "I don't know if you heard." Reluctant to say the words, she looked toward the field, hoping for a reason not to continue. She found none. Part of her didn't want to believe Celeste had crossed that dark line. Slowly she continued. "Celeste went to Dragon's Den this morning. Cheyenne told me. I didn't want to believe her . . . I made a few calls."

"Now what did she do?"

"I would have never thought she'd do it."

Frustration brought an edge to Raven's voice. "Just tell me!"

"I talked to both Jasmine and Leo. They were there. Celeste vampired. They felt her do it. According to Leo, she did it at random. She didn't care who she hurt."

Slowly pivoting on her toes, Raven made a quarter turn away from Jane. Her pupils narrowed, drawing out the thin green line around the outer edges to more prominence. Her lids drooped as she focused on a point beyond the yard. "Of all the things she's done," her voice trailed off, continuing with an added quiver. "I never would have thought it."

"It's Dominic's fault." Jane snapped. "She would have never . . ." Her voice trailed off, leaving the rest unsaid. She knew the statement was untrue. We are each responsible for ourselves. Others may influence us, but ultimately, we are the authors of our own destiny. "How can I leave Cheyenne alone with them?"

Her full lips curled into a cat-like smile. "Don't worry. She won't be alone."

Turning to follow Raven's line of sight, she saw three women crest the hill. She couldn't see their faces, but by the gate of the shorter one she recognized Cheyenne. The other two walked on either side of her, each carrying a bag. As they approached, Jane focused on the newcomers. One was fair skinned with brown hair, worn braided back on the top, while the lower half hung down in long, tight braids. The fading sunlight reflected off the colored beads. Her forehead was high with a very distinctive widow's peak. Her frame was petite, yet her aura was that of a larger woman with an almost manly stride. Her black vest and breeches accented her slender curves, but the dagger at her hip and hilt of her sword belabored the point that she was a defenseless female. The second woman was of African-American descent. Her hair was also braided, but the braids were thicker, less extreme. Her facial features were soft and feminine, yet her posture was of a warrior. She also wore black, but a broadsword hung naturally at her side.

Focusing between them, Jane saw the changes in Cheyenne for the first time. Her hair had been braided, giving her features harsher angles. She was different. Was it the braids or her attitude, Jane questioned. Something had changed in the short span of time and Jane had been left behind.

The threesome walked around the barn toward the backyard. Cheyenne was pointing and talking. Stopping on the other side of the backyard, Cheyenne stopped and surveyed the area.

Biting her low lip, Jane felt like a failure. She slipped around Raven and walked to meet them. "I'm sorry. We did our best with short notice. We didn't know what you had planned."

"Those plans were scrapped this afternoon." Cheyenne pointed to the fair-haired woman. "This is April. An old and new friend." Her hand crossed to the other woman. "And this is Lilith."

Lilith waggled her fingers at Raven. "Hiya sister! What's happening?"

"That's it?" Raven demanded, planting her fists on her hips. "No hug?"

The casual, teasing manor between them left Jane feeling like an outsider in her own home.

Quickly crossing the distance, Raven grabbed Lilith in a hug of familiarity. Releasing her, she tweaked one of Cheyenne's braids. "Why didn't you tell me she was coming? Wait a minute," she again turned her attention to Lilith, "didn't you say—"

"Never mind." Lilith cut her off. "Hell didn't freeze over."

"Just checking. And who is this?"

April held out her hand. "April."

The women clasped forearms. Their eyes met. The understanding was instantaneous. Electricity flowed between them.

Jane didn't feel a connection to any of them, not even Cheyenne. For the first time since she met Cheyenne, she stood totally alone. She turned away from them, choking back the emptiness. The evening breeze blew cool against her skin. The remaining rays of the sun shone bleakly, casting long shadows. This was no longer her home.

"Jane?"

She didn't turn. "Margaret is organizing the food. We decided on a potluck. We've already taken care of the fire. I don't know who'll be here."

"Jane." Cheyenne place her open palm on her shoulder.

Her hand was warm even with the material of her shirt between them. Jane sniffled back her feelings and turned around. "I didn't plan any ceremony."

"It's okay." Cheyenne smiled. "We have. Please join us."

"Why wouldn't I?" The words echoed within the emptiness that filled Jane. She thought she knew Cheyenne so well, but she was so wrong. Cheyenne had a life and a support system that she had known nothing about. Why had she kept so many secrets? Why couldn't she share as she always had with her?

"We eat here." Cheyenne pointed toward the left. "But we gather at the fire pit."

April nodded. "We'll wait for you there. I'm sure Jane has a few questions."

"I'll take you." Raven volunteered. "It'll be a good chance to catch up with an old friend and get to know a new."

The threesome walked away, talking among themselves.

Slowly Cheyenne turned and looked at her. The difference went far beyond the hair and the clothes. Jane no longer felt any connection to her, as if a wall had suddenly been thrown up between them. The silence between them made her uncomfortable.

Cocking her head to one side, Cheyenne sighed, briefly looking at the ground before making eye contact again. "I don't know where to begin."

"I'm sorry." It was all Jane could think of to say. "It's lame, but I am."

"I don't know what's going to happen." Cheyenne reached out and touched her cheek. "But there will always be room in my life for you."

"I don't want to lose you."

Cheyenne sadly smiled. "Just for tonight, let's enjoy the evening. Who know how many more we'll have?"

Jane licked her lips; tears filled her eyes. "I don't want to leave you alone. Ask me to stay and I will."

Cheyenne reached out and rubbed her arm. "I can't do it."

The warmth of her touch both comforted and sent the tears streaming down her cheeks. "I know."

Cheyenne glanced over her shoulder. "April and Lilith will be staying with me. Lilith has already met Dominic. He came out to the cabin." A self-satisfied smile crossed her lips. "You might say she made a lasting impression on him."

Her tone didn't accuse her, but the words were like acid on Jane's ears. They had protected her when she hid behind her objectivity. "Will you be moving back to the house?"

"Yes. It's safer. I'll have to put up another fence around the backyard for the guys."

"We should have never torn down the original."

"The pieces are in the barn. It'll just take a day or so."

"Both Lilith and April are moving in." Cheyenne thought for a moment. "I'll have to decide which rooms to give them."

"One of them can use mine."

"No. You'll need it when you come back."

Jane felt numb, yet strangely relieved. At least for a while, she still had a home. "We'd better join the circle. Everyone will be nervous."

"We have to explain."

"Do you think they'll come?"

"Depends on how much tomato juice Dominic can find." Laughing, Cheyenne held out her hand.

Confused, Jane took it. "What do you mean?"

"Long story." Over the hill, the drums started beating. "Come on!' Cheyenne pulled her toward the fire pit.

Jane released her hand. "Go ahead. I'll catch up."

With a spring in her step, Cheyenne dashed up the hill and disappeared on the opposite side.

Slowly climbing the incline, Jane realized how wrong she had been about so many things. She no longer trusted her judgment or intuition. She had trusted Celeste over Cheyenne, yet it was Cheyenne who had told the truth. Why hadn't see seen it?

The drumming became louder the closer she came; it reached for her soul, trying to awaken old memories. She pushed it away. Reaching the crest, she saw Cheyenne and Lilith with several other women playing drums of different sizes. One drum sat silently on the ground. Slowly April circled the fire, her feet matching the rhythm. One by one other women joined her dance. Young and old alike were pulled in. Jason and Alex tried to join; they were not so subtly pushed back. From the shadows of the field beyond the firelight, Lisa joined them, sitting at the vacant drum. She quickly took up the beat.

Jane felt herself drifting into a dream state. She shook her head, trying to focus. Jane felt unable to move forward or go backward. All the men and some of the women also appeared to be held in place. She dropped to her hands and knees. Through the tall grass, she saw the others struggling to stand. The air became hot, almost unbreathable.

Lilith altered the pattern; the others quickly harmonized to the change of movement. The air began to shimmer like a paved road on a hot summer afternoon. Subtly the dancer's movements became more individualized. One by one they took their turn jumping the flames. Starting on opposite sides, April and Raven jumped; meeting each other in the center, they locked arms, propelling each other in a one-eighty turn to the other side. Spontaneously other pairs followed suite. The cone of energy rose even faster as the women flew over the flames. April tossed a pouch into the fire, turning the flames amethyst. The drums stopped and the drummers joined the circle. The energy hung around them, pulsing and growing. It shimmered in the darkness. Reaching up to the sky, it didn't seem to lose any of its intensity. Extending their arms until their palms touched, their head tilted back, looking skyward. The light of the full moon drifted across the field. It connected with the cone. The women screamed, not in fury of fear, but shear ecstasy. The energy dispersed, sending shock waves in every direction.

It radiated through Jane, knocking the breath from her. It wasn't pain, but an intense awareness of her oneness with all women. It felt alien to her. Never before had she considered developing that kind of intimacy with a woman. It wasn't physical or sexual bonding but an emotional connection, creating a connection of total loyalty without reservation. Closing her eyes, she fought back the idea; she didn't want to change her beliefs. She liked the balance of male and female energy in her life. She pushed away the feminine and clung to the masculine. Behind her eyes, the pain began as a dull ache, rapidly becoming a shooting pain radiating through her entire face. It hurt to breathe. Swallowing hard, she fought back the nausea. Flattening herself against the contours of the hill, she dug her fingers into the dirt trying to dispel the energy. Instead of releasing, another power source surged upward, combining with the original. She tried to break the circuit by rolling. She was able to prop herself on her elbows before she was pulled flat. Crying, she prayed for help. She didn't want to change. No one had the right to force her. Free will! Her mind screamed. It was her last thought before all went dark.

She was no longer on the hill, but standing alone on a prairie. The waist high grass blew gently in the warm breeze. The sun shone brightly in the clear sky. Beyond the prairie, rolling hills reached up to the mountains. Misty clouds hung suspended around the peaks. She spun around trying to get her bearings. Behind her in the far distance, sparsely placed trees quickly became a dense forest.

Casually blown by the wind, the grass tapped against her. She took hold of a blade. Falling free of the shaft, the seeds fell into her hand, prickling her palm. She didn't want them. Flipping her hand over, she shook it. They wouldn't fall. Holding her hand out, she flattened her fingers, trying to get the wind to blow them off. They stubbornly remained. Frustrated she tried scraping them off with the fingers of her right hand. Immediately the seeds took root disappearing under her fingernails and into her palm. Panic filled her.

She felt the roots growing, weaving themselves through her nervous system and reaching up into her brain. They grew into stems and leaves becoming a rainbow of wildflowers. She was no longer an individual or human but a part of the prairie. Stubbornly she fought to keep her individuality. The harder she pushed, the faster she lost her sense of self. Deeper and deeper she sank until her separateness was a mere dream. No longer struggling, she allowed her boundaries to gently disperse until she was part of the nurturing whole. Her roots intertwined with the others, who interlaced with still others until the entire field was interconnected. Their leaves and flowers gentle caressed one another. No one knew the sadness of being alone. The sunlight and the rain were equally shared. Within the tiny light of what had been called Jane, there was contentment. The spark brightened, to find its place among the other stars. The stars swiveled and spun, lining their points to match with their neighbors. The light, which had been Jane, slowly turned. She felt herself reaching out to touch others like herself. Only by reaching to them and becoming part of the whole did she once again become separate onto herself.

Her eyes snapped open. She was face down in the dirt. Turning her head, she took a deep breath and raised herself on her elbows. Below, the dancers sat in meditative postures. The drums were silent. Two of the women, who had remained with the men, also sat cross-legged. The others lay in various positions on the ground.

Testing her equilibrium, she slowly sat. She felt light-headed but not dizzy. Deepening her breath, she brought the strength back to her limbs. Concentrating, she breathed in through her nose, held it for two counts, and slowly exhaled through her mouth. Her abdomen swelled and contracted.

Her fingers and toes tingled. Her face warmed. The air around her had cooled.

The fire below had mellowed to embers. The women around it slowly stood and stretched. Someone threw more wood into the pit. They smoldered and burst into flame, again giving dimensions to the figures around it. The two separate women joined the group. The others disappeared into the shadows.

Jane knew they wouldn't be back. Everything they built, all the dreams they had for the future, had just ended before her eyes. Was that why she felt the need to leave? Did she sense this and was unable to consciously deal with the message? She didn't understand. Frustrated, she slowly stood and reversed her path toward the house.

Tomorrow, she'd find Cheyenne and finalize the travel plans. Mentally she listed what she wanted to take with her. It occurred to her to put the rest into storage; she didn't know if she'd ever be back. She couldn't take everything with her, but there were things she couldn't part with either. Was she overreacting? Of course, she'd be back; she would have Cheyenne's truck and almost everything she owned will still be here.

Walking across the lawn, she tried to absorb and store every sensation. She couldn't-wouldn't believe it had all been a lie. It wasn't an illusion, but a great story she had read, but now the novel was over and it was time to return to reality. The motion sensor turned on the backlight. Stepping into the elliptical bright spots, she stopped short. The tables were broken and strewn around the yard.

The backdoor opened. Dominic loomed as a silhouette.

Startled, Jane took half a step backward.

"We want to talk to you." He shoved the door, slamming it against the outside of the house. His change in stance revealed the pelt of hair beneath his open shirt. The lights from the spotlights gave his eyes a luminance quality, which washed out the color. Cold rage radiated from him. "Now!"

Jane shivered. Ironically her only thought was all the sarcastic comments she made about the girls in the horror movies who couldn't save themselves. She laughed at herself.

He bolted down the stairs.

Jane screamed.

He stopped short.

Cheyenne and her two companions stepped into the light. Drawing her sword, Lilith took a confrontational stance between Jane and Dominic. "We meet again. You still stink!" The blade shone in the light. With the ease of a well practiced motion, Lilith traced the point from his Adam's apple to his belt buckle; a thin red line followed closely behind. "Still want to play?"

Fury rose, threatening to spill over and drown his common sense. "Celeste and I just want to talk to her."

"Splendid idea." April's mock friendliness was more than clear.

"Who are you?" He demanded, forcing himself not to advance forward. "You don't belong here."

"Neither do you!" Cheyenne snapped. "Lilith, you're right. He does still stink."

"What are you dressed for? Halloween isn't for months."

"What were you doing in my house?" Cheyenne countered. "You were told to pack and leave."

"Bitch!" He pushed away the blade.

With a twist of the wrist, the flat of the blade hit his palm and slide back toward his elbow, the point slicing through the skin to flay a pouch the width of the blade from his wrist four inches up his forearm. In a fluid motion Lilith pulled her sword free.

Stunned, he grabbed his injured arm. Blood oozed from between his fingers.

"Dominic!" Celeste screamed from the doorway. Again the door slammed open and she ran to him, protecting him with her own body. She tried to examine his injury; he pulled away. Angrily she turned on the other women. "Isn't it enough your making him homeless? To steal the only stable home the children have ever known. How can he work now?"

"Did he ever?" Cheyenne quipped back. "What are you doing here?"

"I live here!" Celeste snapped. "Everything I own is in this house. I won't let you steal it from me too."

"We didn't steal anything from you!" Resentment rose in Jane. How dare she try turning this back on them. It was Celeste and Dominic who lied. They had manipulated. Celeste was the one who kept him here. Jane pushed past Cheyenne and squared off with Celeste. "You did this. All of it. It's your fault! You ruined everything!"

Pulling Jane back, April interceded both physically and verbally. "You must be this Celeste I've heard so much about."

"Who are you? What are you doing here?"

"Defending my sister." April casually unfurled to point at Cheyenne.

"Cheyenne doesn't have any family. Just me" Celeste hissed. "And I've disowned her!"

"You can't hurt me any more." Cheyenne stated without emotion. "Not anymore. The woman I loved is dead. Get off my property. I'll have your belongs delivered to you. Come back and I'll have you arrested."

Celeste squared her shoulder and pointed at Dominic's arm. "We'll have you arrested!"

"Go for it." Lilith purred. "From the angle and placement of the wound it is quite evident I was defending myself."

Dominic had tied his shirt around his arm as a makeshift bandage. The blood was already beginning to seep through. He turned and searched their faces. He met April's eyes. She flinched and reached for the hilt of her dagger. Dominic blinked and focused on Jane's eyes. His pupils had deepened to a slate blue almost gray, yet the fire in them burned her across the distance between them. The pain in her eyes radiated to the back of her skull. She couldn't turn away. She couldn't cry out. The pain became hot and throbbing, ever increasing like waves against the shore before an approaching storm. She felt the ground coming up to meet her. Someone caught her before she hit the ground. Cheyenne called her name. She reached out, but found only air.

There was a scuffle. Dominic swore and grunted. Celeste called his name. Metal scraped metal. His voice became an animalistic growl. April's and Lilith's voices spread out; Cheyenne's remained close to her.

Suddenly above a dragon spirit manifested in the physical realm. It hovered above them. It shimmered in a rainbow of colors but the eyes swirled a multitude of shades of blue. With each wing beat, currents of energy radiated downward, soothing her like a cool glass of water on a hot summer afternoon. She's beautiful, Jane thought, I wonder if that is what Cheyenne looks like.

"I banish you!" Celeste's voice echoed from everywhere.

For an instant, it backed off, but for only that moment. It swooped down, extending the talons on its long legs. Celeste shrieked as a dragon claw scrapped her shoulder. The growling intensified. Dominic leaped at it. With a casual flip of the tail, he was knocked backward. Holding her shoulder, Celeste scampered into the shadows. Dominic rolled into the darkness and followed her.

Stretching its neck forward it looked at them, focusing briefly on Cheyenne before turning its attention to April. The two communicated wordlessly. April nodded. With a whip of its tail and a flip of its torso, it arched its neck and flew upward, disappearing into the night.

"That's pretty fancy flying." Lilith quipped. "Who was that?"

"Help me get Jane inside." April spoke from Jane's right. "I felt him probing. If I had known she was so vulnerable, I'd have protected her."

"April, really who was that? Cheyenne do you know?"

"I've got an idea." Anger tinged Cheyenne's voice as she stared in the direction of the departing dragon.

"Don't get your panties in a bunch." April snapped. "I called for help. We needed it. She came."

"Dragons of different clans don't mix." Cheyenne snapped.

"Oh really? We mixed well. I'm from the water clan. You are from the air clan." April matched her tone. "She is from the fire clan. All we need is an Earth for a quorum."

"That hasn't been done for centuries!'

"Ladies, the debate is wonderful." Lilith's voice dripped with sarcasm. "But aren't you forgetting someone?"

"Jane." Cheyenne whispered. "I'm sorry."

"Me too."

"The two of you carry her. I'll get the door." Lilith's voice trailed away.

Jane felt herself being lifted and carried. She teetered on the brink of consciousness, not knowing which way she would tip. So much had happened. Self-doubt again rose. She hadn't the strength to push it down. She wanted to cry; there weren't any tears left. There was nothing to do but accept the reality of what was and could not be changed. The door closed behind them. The kitchen light came on.

"Lilith, help April take her upstairs. I'm going to call Margaret. She lives in one of the cabins."

"Is she a doctor?" Lilith asked switching positions with Cheyenne.

"Midwife and nurse-practitioner."

"Which room?" April asked.

"Third on the right."

The tones of the phone were Jane's last memory as she faded into unconsciousness. She no longer fought; she no longer had a reason to stay in the battle.

CHAPTER ELEVEN

The sun shone in the window. It looked like midmorning. Jane rolled over. She didn't want to see it. Her body ached in places she didn't know existed. Physically and emotionally, she was exhausted. Common sense told her to stay in bed. Yet something told her she was running out of time. She didn't understand. But every time she didn't listen to her inner voice, she regretted it.

The night before was a dark memory that haunted her. Shivering, she had returned to consciousness in her own bed. Margaret left the blood pressure cup attached and offered her some tea. Jane had refused, Margaret had insisted. It was a blend she had never tasted before. The tea made her relax, spreading a tingling feeling throughout her entire body. Gently she brushed Jane's check with her fingertips. The warmth of her touch comforted her.

"You've had a shock," she had said. "Sweetie, can't go to sleep until your vitals stabilize. You have to talk to me."

Jane turned her head away.

Gently, Margaret turned her head back to face her. "Cheyenne tells me you're leaving us for a while. Where are you going?"

Jane didn't want to talk. She wanted to sleep. Her body felt heavy and cold. It would be so easy to drift away and just keep going. She closed her eyes.

Margaret gently shook her until she opened her eyes. "Talk to me." She insisted. "Where are you going?"

"Just away." Jane had mumbled.

"Tell me why?"

"No. I want to sleep."

"You can't sweetie."

Again Jane felt pressure around her arm as her blood pressure was checked. "Just let me go."

"I can't do that sweetie." The pressure released with a low hiss. "What do you want to take with you? What clothes?"

Slowly, subtly Margaret kept her talking. Every few minutes she would check her pulse and blood pressure. Time passed. Jane had no idea of how long. The shivering stopped. Jane felt tired, but clearheaded. The blood pressure cup had been removed. Looking tired, Margaret kissed her forehead and told her to get some sleep. She would be back in the morning to check on her. Jane had turned over and immediately fallen asleep. But it was filled with horrid dreams of torture and death. She had been frightened awake several times. The sun was now shining and the birds singing. But not in her heart. Her stomach growled, reminding her it been along time since she'd eaten. Mentally she made a list of things she wanted to accomplish this morning before she left. She was leaving today. That was not how she planned it. But it was true. Some time between falling asleep and waking, her plans had changed. She needed to be on the road before two, but first she needed to eat. Tossing back the blanket, she slowly sat up. Her feet found the floor. Standing, she crossed the room and opened the window. Everything appeared normal. The tables had been put away. The fire pit had been cleared and reset for next time. Would there be a next time? The horses followed their normal routine in the pasture. The chickens scratched the ground. The scene gave her a sense of peace. Whistling, she called up a breeze. Gently it obeyed her call. It drifted through the screen to cool her bare skin. Closing her eyes, she stood for a moment. The breeze smelled of the coming of summer. A single tear fell. It was the scent of home or what was home. Her stomach growled. Sadly she smiled. Walking away from the window, she stopped to slip on a t-shirt and a pair of boxers before continuing downstairs. She reminded herself to ask Cheyenne to water the plants in her bedroom.

Making her way to the kitchen, Jane was surprised to find Cheyenne at the stove, making pancakes. "What are you doing here this time of day?"

"I just got back." Cheyenne poured steaming water into a cup. The scent of rosehips rose on the steam. "On my way up the drive, I saw you at the window."

"It was stuffy."

I'm not surprised." Cheyenne offered her the cup. "I have bad news."

"More?" Gratefully, Jane accepted the cup, bracing herself for whatever. She had gotten to the point that no matter what it was, it'd just be one more thing.

"I went to the bank," Cheyenne shifted her weight from one foot to the other. "April suggested I protect the household accounts." Turning off the heat, she flipped the cooked pancakes off the griddle and on to a plate.

"And?" Jane cut in.

"Celeste and Dominic beat me there by a half-hour." Bitterness flooded Cheyenne's obviously forced calm, putting an edge on every word. "They took everything. I have fifty-seven dollars and twenty cents to pay all the bills and to meet this week's payroll."

"When did you put her on your business account?"

"I didn't!" Cheyenne snapped. "They produced two checks. They had a third but there wasn't enough in the account to cover it."

"She wouldn't!" Jane was wrong; there was something that could still shock her.

"But she did. The bank manager called the police. I filed a report. The bank filed a report. The teller was a friend of Dominic's. He was fired."

"You'll get your money back? Right?"

"It could take up to ninety days." Cheyenne sank into the straight back chair. "The process has already started."

"Are you sure it was Celeste?" The look on Cheyenne's face instantly made Jane regret asking. "I'm sorry. It's just when I think she's hit bottom, she proves me wrong."

Cheyenne leaned forward, resting her forearms on her thighs. She wouldn't meet Jane's eyes. "I've taken out a loan to cover the household expenses and Dragon's Eye. I can get the business money back. But everything in the household account is gone. Her name was on the account."

"But it was all our money!"

"We'd have to take her to court and prove it. It could take months. By that time, who knows how much would be left?"

"So you're just giving up!'

Cheyenne lifted her head to meet Jane's gaze. Her eyes were cold and angry.

Jane shivered. Without saying a word, Cheyenne had accused her. "I'm sorry." She whispered. "I keep saying it but it doesn't seem to help." Silence hung in the room. Jane stood and walked to the stove. Turning on the heat, she poured more batter on the griddle. Suddenly she wasn't hungry, but she needed to do something. "I have some money in my accounts and my 401k from the TV station. It's yours."

"No." Cheyenne whispered. "You'll need it for your journey."

Jane couldn't turn around. "Are you asking me not to come back?"

"That's not what I said." Cheyenne's voice was flat. "You'll need to contact your bank. The bank manager called to warn them. But you'll have to go in person to change the accounts. It's the only way to protect them."

"I hadn't thought of that." The bubbles formed in the batter and she carefully flipped them over. "Could I just call?"

"I'm just passing on what I was told." Cheyenne stood and walked to the window. She looked out at the cabins. "Things will have to change around here. No one is going to like it."

"What can I do? Just tell me. Please."

"Go on your quest."

"Let me help you."

"You have to leave." Cheyenne turned around. "She has taken all she is going to. I have cut myself free. You have not. As long as you are here, she will use you against me."

Smoke billowed from the griddle. Angrily turning off the burner, she scraped off the pancakes and tossed them into the sink. They hissed. "I can't believe this is happening! You're kicking me out!"

"No."

"But that's what you said."

"You are not safe here or in town until you free yourself from Celeste. No one who cares about you is safe. I'm their primary target. They can't get at me directly. So they'll use you."

"Because I'm weak!"

"Because you still care! You're still trying to save her. But you can't. She doesn't want to be saved. The sooner you realize it . . ." Cheyenne's voice trailed off.

Shaking, Jane leaned against the counter, tears streaming down her cheeks. She simply couldn't absorb any more. She didn't want to leave. She wanted to stay home. But she didn't have a home. Not any more. She didn't fit anywhere. No one would catch her if she fell. No one would worry if she were late. There was no longer any safe haven to hide. She was alone.

The floor squeaked as Cheyenne crossed the room. Her arms encircled Jane. She felt warm, but Jane found no comfort. She felt empty and alone, like when her mother died. They hadn't been close for years, but when the breast cancer won the battle, Jane felt a sadness that reached into her core. There was nothing else like it. She was no longer connected to anyone. Her father still lived, yet Jane felt like an orphan. The alcohol had separated those years before. He had never tried to make a connection and Jane had given up trying.

"You need to eat."

Jane shook her head.

"I had some fruit earlier. The pancakes were for you."

Jane's stomach growled. She allowed herself to be led to the table. Cheyenne pulled the chair out and Jane sat down. Moments later, the pancakes appeared on a plate in front of her, complete with butter and syrup. A glass of cold milk followed.

"They're a little cool." Cheyenne apologized.

"It doesn't matter." Jane ate. The plate and the glass were emptied. She hadn't tasted any of it. Licking the white mustache off, Jane looked up at Cheyenne. "When do you want me out?"

Leaning against the counter, Cheyenne shook her head. "I don't want you out. I want you to stay. But it isn't safe. Last night proved it."

"I need to go to the bank and tell a few friends." Jane knew she was right. She had been the most vulnerable. If she stayed, she would be an open target. If she left others would be safe, but where would she go? "Could the truck be ready by noon or one o'clock?"

"The oil was changed last week. It'll need gas. It'll only take a few minutes to load the incense and herbs."

"Ok. I'll leave my car here."

"I'll take good care of it."

"I still have to pack." Jane snuffled. "Then I'll be ready."

"Where will you go?"

"West." Jane answered simply. Standing, she turned and walked through the dining room and up to her bedroom. Quickly showering and dressing, she grabbed her purse and keys. Taking the stairs two steps at a time, she ran down the stairs and out the front door. The garage door was already open, Celeste's car parked in its normal spot. Seeing it, Jane felt her anger flare, but she reminded herself to keep on track. Getting behind the wheel, she backed out, focusing on what she needed to do. The bank would be first. Then Sammy at the police station. With any luck Raven would be there and Maxie wouldn't. There were several other friends she would like to say good-bye to, but there simply wasn't time. She'd write them from the road and explain.

She pulled out on the road and rolled down the window. Pushing down on the accelerator, she sped toward town.

Her mind relaxed into neutral as the miles cruised beneath the wheels. She knew these roads so well. The ones that stretched out before her later that day were mere lines on a map. Where they would lead her Jane didn't know. But the open road called to her, begging her to hurry to meet her destiny. She needed to go for more than just reasons of safety. There was something or someone waiting for her. She didn't understand the feeling, but she didn't have to. There were times in her life when she didn't heed her intuition. One time it nearly cost her a dear friend, the other brought her to the brink of death. She had made a promise to herself and the Divine, while waiting for the rescue team to free her from the smoldering wreck that had once been her car, to always listen when her inner voice spoke. Her life since then had not been sorrow free, but the gentle guidance had softened the pain. She hadn't been able to stop her Grandmother from dying, however she was able to be at her bedside during the final hours before she crossed over. It had brought them both peace. Entering the city limits, Jane questioned why she hadn't been warned about Dominic. Or had she, but hadn't understood. Maybe Cheyenne was the voice her intuition had used.

Shaking her head, she pulled into the bank parking lot. It no longer mattered. Everything was out in the open. Finding a spot, she pulled in and turned off the ignition. She opened the door and reached for her purse. A familiar face appeared in the passenger window. Startled, Jane snapped backward, scraping her head along the ceiling of the car. "OW! DAMN! Sammy!" Straightening, she stepped backward out of the car. Rubbing the top of her head, she looked at the other woman on the opposite side.

"That's what you get for running out on us." Sammy walked around the back of the car. "Maxie said you were quitting."

Jane's hand dropped to her hip. "I'm leaving town for a while."

"In the middle of an investigation? What did he do?"

"It's not just him."

"He's my partner. I know he can be an ass." Sammy shook her head. "He can also be a good man."

"You wouldn't understand."

"Try me?" Sammy asked gently.

Licking her lips, Jane glanced skyward before settling her gaze on the gold flecked eyes. "We had some problems at the farm."

"I heard about the bank accounts this morning. Dixie is the officer in charge. She asked me what I knew. I couldn't tell her much. If it helps, warrants have been issued for both of them."

"Good. I have a favor to ask."

"Can't you stay? Please." Sammy folded her arms across her chest. "I didn't believe you when you started. But you made me a believer."

Jane shook her head. "It isn't possible."

"Maxie said he wanted to marry you." It wasn't an accusation.

"Yes. But he wants to change who I am." Jane hesitated. "I can't—won't live a lie."

Focusing on Jane, the gold specks expanded in the tawny eyes. Slowly Sammy nodded and the tawny coloring again became dominant. "I understand. What is your favor?"

"Look after Cheyenne and Raven."

"Who is Raven?"

Under normal circumstances, Jane would never out another, yet this was not normal and the taboo would have to be broken for Raven's safety. "Margarita Lavis."

"Greta? She's . . ." Sammy's voice trailed off.

"We've been friends for a long time.

"What a minute! Is that how you knew so much about the investigation!"

A man in a suit stopped to stare.

"Mind your own business!" Sammy snapped.

"Lower your voice and the rest of the world will." He yelled back and continued across the parking lot and into the bank.

"That was clever!"

Jane felt like an idiot. This wasn't the way she wanted to leave things. But lately what did go smoothly? "Raven didn't give me information, if that is what you are asking. It's not the way you think. I would ask her questions. She would find information for me."

"Like what?"

"The women's birthdays. Did you know they all were born on either the eleven or twelfth of the month? Three on November 11. Two on December 12. One on January 11."

"So?"

"It's important. I don't know why."

"What else?"

"I asked about where they shopped, where they worked, where they went to church . . ."

"We check all that. They all worked within the downtown area."

"It's obvious."

"What?" Anger tainted Sammy's voice.

"It's downtown."

"That's a lot of help."

"I'm sorry. I did my best." Jane refused to give into her own anger. She needed Sammy to protect them. "Believe me or not, Dominic will do his best to hurt Cheyenne and Raven. They are my friends. I thought you were too."

Sammy's facial features slightly softened. "What do you want me to do?"

"Just be more aware. Send more patrol cars past the farm. Don't let Raven walk to her car alone. He's vindictive. She is Cheyenne's friend and she stood up to him."

"A double reason." Sammy hesitated. "Ok. I'll do my best. But we're stretched thin."

"I understand."

"What about Maxie?"

Not knowing how she would react, Jane stated it flat-out. "It's over."

"Honest. Refreshingly honest." Sammy slowly started walking toward her car, but stopped in midstep. "By the way, one of Dominic's nieces is missing."

"Melanie disappears regularly. She'll turn up."

"It's Lisa."

"Lisa? Oh, try Dragon's Den or Rachael Franklin's house. When we couldn't find her around the farm, that's where she'd be. She wants to live there."

"Oh really? Does her mother know?" Sammy shifted her weight away from Jane.

"Yes. It's one reason they don't get along." Jane closed her car door.

"But she's six?"

"Long story."

"Whatever. I'll pass along the information." Sammy continued to her car.

For a moment, Jane watched her, mentally crossing one item off her list. Looking toward the building, she prepared herself for the next step. She crossed the lot and opened the door. The air-conditioning curled all around her, making her shiver. Walking further inside, she scanned the faces, hoping to see Celeste; yet dreading the possibility. There were only a few people waiting for service. She debated with herself whether she should wait in line for a counter clerk or go to the Accounts department. Deciding against the counter, she crossed the room and knocked on the room divider, which separated the department from the rest of the bank.

"Just a sec." She continued to type at her terminal. 'Anna-Lyn Bradley' was printed in bold lettering on the nameplate. Beneath, in smaller print, was written 'Accounts Manager'. Her dark hair was pulled back into a French twist. She left it full enough around her face to pull one's gaze upward toward her cheekbones and eyes, away from the fullness under her chin that some women develop in their late thirties. Pivoting in her chair, Anna-Lyn looked up and smiled. "May I help you?"

"I'm Jane Easton. I have a checking and savings account here. There may be a problem."

She motioned for Jane to sit down in the chair in front of her desk. "I got a call this morning. I need your ID and the account numbers."

Sitting down, Jane reached in her purse, pulling out her checkbook and passbook. She set them on the desk. "She was a friend and I trusted her."

Anna-Lyn arched one eyebrow, but said nothing. Instead she turned to her terminal and typed in the information. Nodding, she returned her attention to Jane. "The last check you wrote according to your registrar was 2788 on the fourteenth.

It cleared on the fifteenth. Your balance is six cents off from ours. Very good by the way." She pushed a couple of buttons and the screen changed. "For the savings, except for the interest accrued, the balances are exact. Did you want to close the accounts and open new ones?"

"If that's what it takes. I will be making a large withdrawal today." Uncomfortably Jane shifted in the chair. "The friend already stole checks and cashed them from another friend. The police have been notified. Could we put a notation that the police are to be called if someone tries to use the original account?"

"I can do it. But it won't help unless he or she tries to cash them at the bank."

"When they used Cheyenne's checks, they went to the bank. They may or may not do it again."

"If they're smart, they won't." Anna-Lyn pulled out several sheets of paper and placed them on the desk in front of Jane with a pen. 'Fill these out. I'll start the new accounts. You'll have to destroy all your old checks. I'll give you a starter book. It'll take at least two weeks for the new checks to arrive."

So much for the cute fairy designer checks, Jane thought. "Fine. I'll need two thousand in traveler's checks and five hundred in cash."

"Out of what accounts?"

"Take the five hundred from the checking."

"And the rest out of the savings. Do you want your banking information sent to the same address?"

"I don't know." Celeste was gone, but she still had access to the house and the mailbox. Quickly writing down Raven's address, she slid the piece of paper across the desk. "For now send it here." She'd tell Raven when she saw her.

Right before you confess that you outed her, she sniped at herself.

Anna-Lyn entered the information and stood. "I'll get your traveler checks and cash." Walking around the desk, she disappeared into the inner sanctum of the tellers.

Jane people watched without focusing on one person or space. It was nearly eleven. She still needed to talk to Raven. But where was she? What are the odds she'd just walk into the bank? Unlikely, she answered herself. Plus she still had to pack. She decided to call and leave a message if she wasn't at home. It wasn't what she wanted but it would have to do.

Anna Lyn returned and placed a receipt in front of her to sign. "You didn't specify the denominations."

"It doesn't matter." Jane signed and accepted the offered envelope. "Thank you."

"My pleasure."

Jane smiled and walked toward the door. Stunned by the brightness and the heat, she stopped just outside. For a moment, she felt someone watching her. Shading her eyes, she looked around. There weren't many people on the street or cars parked along the site. Whoever it was radiated anger and frustration. Her eyes still hadn't adjusted to the light level. They watered, making it difficult to see. A car on the right screeched away from the curb. The muffler rumbled. It was yellow and dirty. The sun reflecting off the glass made it impossible to see who was inside. It raced down the street and disappeared around the corner. The feeling went away. Startled, Jane tried to dispel the ugly sensations.

Returning to her car, she unlocked the door. The interior was stiflingly hot. Opening both the passenger and driver windows, she slipped into the seat and closed the door. The digital thermometer on the bank read ninety-two degrees. It wasn't even noon yet.

Pulling out into traffic, she retraced her path back to the farm. It was ten after eleven when she walked back into the kitchen. The table was set for four and pots were on the stove. She lifted the lids. In one pot, fresh asparagus had been steamed with herbs. The others contained fried potatoes and sausage. Cheyenne had made her favorite foods. But where was she? She walked through the dining room. "Cheyenne!"

Footsteps ran down the upstairs hall and April appeared at the balcony railing. "She's in the barn. One of the cows decided to calf early and is having a difficult time. Lilith is helping, but it's too yucky for me."

"Oh." Jane felt disappointed. She had been counting on a having a few minutes alone with Cheyenne before she left.

"Cheyenne wasn't happy about it either." April walked down the stairs. "She gave me the list of people for you to contact. I hope you don't mind. I added a few and made some calls. Their addresses are on a separate sheet. They would be happy for you to stay with them for a few days. It'll help the budget." She shrugged. "Cheyenne told me what Celeste and Dominic did."

"Thanks." Sadly Jane smiled. "I have to pack yet."

"Need help?"

Jane shook her head.

"Lunch is ready when you are." Maternally April slipped her arms around Jane. "Don't worry. We're ok. You're ok. And you'll be back before you know it." Patting Jane's back, she released her and walked around the corner.

Jane stood at the bottom of the stairs, staring at the empty air where April had been standing. She liked the woman, yet was suspicious at the same time. Or better said; she was uncertain of her own perceptions of her. Shaking her head, she slowly climbed the stairs and walked into her bedroom.

The late morning sun had begun to find its way through the windows. It felt cold and empty. Mechanically she pulled her suitcases from the back of her closet and opened them on the bed. Starting at the mirrored dresser; she opened drawers, pulling out undergarments and nightshirts. She took enough for two weeks. There was no logical reason why. It just seemed like a good number. Moving on to other drawers, she filled the first suitcase and the smaller second. Necessities from the bathroom filled the overnight case. She looked at her altar. She wanted to take it. There were many things she couldn't replace. She looked at the suitcases. They were already overfilled. If she took some of the more fragile statues and shells, they could be easily broken by the pressure of the clothing. A tear slipped down her cheek. She would just have to trust and have faith. Closing the suitcases, she stacked them by the door.

It was quarter to twelve. Time to be leaving. Biting her tongue, she quickly picked up the phone and dialed Raven's number. After four rings, her machine picked up. Not listening to the familiar message, Jane waited for the louder beep before starting her message. "Raven. Jane. I'm sorry. I'm leaving earlier than expected. We've had more problems. I'm having my banking stuff sent to your address. Celeste cleaned out the household account and stole Cheyenne's . . . but you probably know that. Take care of her for me. I'll be in touch." She started to hang up the phone. "Raven, I'm sorry. I asked Sammy to watch out for both of you. I-I-I outed you. I'll explain when I can." Hanging up the receiver she felt like a total coward.

Rapidly crossing the room, she picked up her suitcases and walked out, leaving the door open. Walking down the stairs, she left her suitcases in the front hallway before continuing into the kitchen. April had placed steaming bowls of potatoes, asparagus, and sausage on the table. The aroma awakened Jane's stomach. It growled in anticipation. "It smells good."

"Good. Eat." April ordered, pulling out a chair. "Take ten minutes and eat. Make me happy, your stomach happy, and Cheyenne . . ."

"Everyone keeps telling me to eat."

"Maybe you should listen." April sat down in a chair on the opposite side of the table. She spooned out large portions of asparagus and put the tips on two plates, placing one in front of Jane. "If you can eat and talk at the same time, I need to ask some questions about the cabins."

Jane forked a small piece of sausage and put it on her plate. "I don't know much. Celeste took care of the household accounts."

Her eyebrow arched. "Why am I not surprised?"

The bitterness in her voice caught Jane off guard. "Why do you say it like that?"

"Her boyfriend and several other tenants haven't paid rent in months. Dominic not at all."

The fork clattered against Jane's plate. "This just keeps getting better and better."

"Ok. Then that wasn't the agreement?"

"No."

"Fine. Some people are in for a rude surprise. Cheyenne has asked me to go through the books."

"I see." Jane took a bite of the asparagus; it was a little tough, but it was to be expected so late in the season. She swallowed. "I also haven't paid rent in along time."

"Yes, but you also contributed to the household account." April put a piece of sausage on her plate. "The household credit cards have been canceled and the phone number will be changed to an unlisted. I've given you both mine and Lilith's cell-phone numbers with the other information. I didn't know if you had one, but you can use my calling card. Don't worry about the bill, we'll settle up when you get back. Call one of us in a couple of days, we should have the new phone number by then."

"You're very organized." Jane didn't know if she felt relieved or offended.

"I'll talk. You eat. If I have the wrong information you can tell me."

Reluctantly Jane nodded and cut off a piece of sausage. She chewed, but didn't really taste it.

"Ok. There are ten cabins that are available to be rented."

"Nine. One is Cheyenne's."

"She's moving back to the house, so it'll be available."

Jane shrugged. "I'm glad. She'll be safer."

Again her eyebrow rose. "Ok. Right now three are vacant. Out of the six which are rented, three aren't paying rent. Of the three which are paying rent, one is a month behind . . . you're not eating."

"You're telling me this now and you're surprised I'm not eating?" The fork clattered against the china. "I don't know you or Lilith. But I'm forced to trust you, because my presence endangers Cheyenne. A woman who I thought was a dear friend has betrayed my trust and love." Anger replaced her hunger. "Cheyenne and I helped so many people, yet we have to depend on strangers when we need help." She hesitated for a moment, pushing down the rising fury. "I was happy with Celeste and Cheyenne. We were family. We had plans and dreams for the future."

"Then Dominic came."

Jane nodded. "And Rachael Franklin moved into town. Suddenly Cheyenne acted like we betrayed her. I didn't understand. We didn't have anything to do with it. All these things started happening. Animals disappeared. Rumors of dark rituals. Celeste said one thing. Cheyenne another. I didn't know who to believe. Dominic was pushing me to move in with Maxie. Maxie started pressuring me to marry him."

"The pot boiled over and no one knew how to turn off the heat."

"What?"

"It was a saying my mother had." April set her fork across her plate. "The rest was, sometimes all you can do is clean up the burner. What or why doesn't matter. All that matters is there is a mess to clean up before you can cook again, otherwise you're really going to stink up the house."

It made sense to Jane; it was wisdom without trying to point a finger. "You're mother seems like a wise woman."

"Sometimes." April picked up her fork and stabbed an asparagus spear. "I wasn't trying to force you out. Just provide solutions."

Jane stood. "I'm sorry I snapped."

April shrugged. "Maybe it's too early to start cleaning up?"

"The pot is still boiling over." Jane finished her thought. The Grandfather clock chimed noon. "Oh great! I wanted to be on the road by now."

"Finish your lunch." April ordered. "I promised Cheyenne."

"I'll be late."

"For what?"

"I don't know. But if I'm not gone in like now, I'm going to miss something important."

For a moment, April looked like she was going to give her an argument. Instead she shook her head and reached across the table for a manila colored envelope. "Here are the lists. Without pushing it, you can make Toledo by this evening." She pulled a sheet of paper out and pointed to a name. "Lady Bridget is expecting you. Call her if the spirit moves you to another direction."

Gratefully, Jane accepted the envelope. "Thanks. Tell Cheyenne . . . tell her I love her. I'll keep in touch . . . and I promise to eat."

"I'll do that." April stood. "Let me help you with your luggage. The pickup is loaded and the keys are inside."

"I saw it." Jane grabbed the last bite of sausage and followed April.

The two women collected Jane's suitcases and loaded them into the back end of the pickup. Jane didn't stop to count the boxes of incense and oil. They were clearly labeled. When she got the chance, she'd go through them.

Closing the topper's lid, April turned to Jane. "I almost forgot. Lilith put her Visa card in the envelope with my phone card. Use them sparingly. We canceled all the house charge cards."

"Including the MasterCard?"

"We didn't know there was one."

"Maybe it's just Celeste's. I saw a statement in the second drawer of the desk last week. She wasn't too happy about it."

"I'll look for it."

Walking toward the door, Jane stopped. "I'd have all the locks changed and another set of bolts put on the doors. The cabins too. It's better safe than sorry."

"It's on the afternoon list."

Jane opened the door and slide onto the seat. "Tell Raven, I'm sorry and I'll explain when I call."

"I will. You'll need to gas up on the way out. We didn't have time."

"Gas for the car. Caffeine for me." Jane slipped the shoulder strap around her and snapped the clasp.

April closed the door. "Safe journey."

"Keep Cheyenne safe." Jane started the engine.

Stepping back, April nodded.

Jane put it into gear and drove down the driveway. Watching the house in the rearview mirror, she nearly didn't stop at the road. Chiding herself, she waited for the car to pass and pulled out. Driving back into town, she started to get the feel of the truck. It handled differently than her car. It was bigger and bulkier, with the impression of being followed. Eventually she would get used to it.

Pulling into the station, she parked at an empty pump and got out. She twisted off the cap and inserted the nozzle. She missed the days when you could wash your windows while the gas pumped automatically.

"You're Jane Easton."

Startled, Jane stepped back, spilling gas on the pavement. Quickly she loosened her grip and the stream stopped.

Rachael jumped back from the puddle. "Sorry."

"My fault. I'm a bit jumpy." She reinserted the nozzle and continued to fill the tank. "You're Rachael Franklin."

"I've seen you in my store. But we've never really met."

The pump clicked off and Jane returned the nozzle to the pump. "You have a nice shop." She replaced the cap and closed the cover.

"I was hoping you'd come in." Rachael hesitated. "There are a few things you should know."

"I heard what Celeste did." Annoyed, Jane started walking toward the building. "I'm not responsible for what she did or does."

Rachael followed. "You don't know it all."

"And I don't want to."

Rachael grabbed her arm, preventing her from going inside. "She arranged with my mentor, her sister, Beverly to bring me here."

"So? Why are you and Cheyenne making a federal case of it? We needed a good spiritual store."

Tucking the long strands behind her ear, Rachael pulled them away from the entrance, allowing a man to exit. "You don't understand. I belong to the an Elemental Dragon Clan."

"So does Cheyenne."

"A different clan." Rachael bit her lower lip and released her grip. "Clans don't mix. Unless there are very special circumstances, we can injure or kill one another accidentally. Bev told Celeste. Celeste told her there wasn't a problem. So they arranged for me to move here. I thought it was fate."

Shading her eyes with her palm, Jane looked away. It explained why Cheyenne was so upset. "Why—"

"Bev didn't understand either." Rachael hesitated and continued. "I called her and told what's been happening. She got real upset when I described Dominic."

"Do you think she would talk to me?" Jane asked, hopefully. "I need to know more about him."

"Why?" Suspicion grew in her voice.

Jane shifted her weight. "Since he came to the farm, we've had nothing but conflicts. Animals have been ritually killed. Some of the children have been tormented by nightmares. By the way; have you seen Meredith's daughter, Lisa? She's missing."

"She's at my house. She told me her mother knew."

Jane shook her head. "She reported her missing."

"Swell." Rachael shook her head. "I'll call Meredith."

"Lisa was called to by shadows. No one else saw them." Jane added quickly. "But Cheyenne believes Dominic was using Lisa against her. Cheyenne adopted Lisa as an apprentice. Wasn't Lisa going to stay with you when her mother lost custody? Doesn't that give you and Cheyenne something in common?"

Rachael rested her palms on her hips. "She's a good kid. Ok, I'll talk to Bev and call you."

"I'll have to call you." Jane pointed to the pickup. "I'm on my way out of town. It's a long story." The car behind the pickup beeped. "Trust me." She felt the hazel eyes specked with gold on her, searching and probing; she did nothing to prevent it.

Nodding, Rachael took a pen and a scrap of paper from her purse. She wrote a name and number. "Here is Bev's number." She held out the slip of paper. "Just so you know. Dragon's may be very clannish. We stick to our own. But anyone, who threatens a dragon, threatens us all. The Hell's

Angels said it best, 'All on one.' Your dragon might not like it, but if Dominic tries anything again, he'll find himself with more dragon than he knows what to do with."

Startled, Jane connected the events of the night before. "It was you."

A slow smile crossed Rachael's lips. "I admit and deny nothing. I'll tell Bev to expect your call." With a flip of her hair, Rachael sauntered to her car.

Jane watched her drive away. If she had been just a few minutes later she would have lost the opportunity to make an ally. The car blew its horn again. Jane waved and walked toward the door.

CHAPTER TWELVE

Wiping her damp hand on the towel, Cheyenne watched the pickup drive down the lane and out on to the road. If she had run, she could have stopped her long enough to say good-bye. Lilith had watched her and the clock. The minutes had ticked by. The calf had been delivered and accepted by his mother. It had been a difficult delivery, but in the end he would be a fine, strong bull. The dust had already begun to settle back on the lane. Cheyenne wadded up the paper and tossed it into the trash as she walked back into the tack room.

"Why didn't you go?"

"I don't know." Exhausted, Cheyenne sat on the stool and leaned back against the counter. She nodded toward the barn interior. "What do you want to name him?"

"Clever dodge of topic."

Cheyenne stared at the partially closed door. "I just want to sleep for a week and wake up someplace else."

"What do you expect me to say to that?" Lilith folded her arms across her chest. "Go ahead. Take a long cruise on the river denial."

Sadly smiling at the absurdities of the situation, Cheyenne stood and stretched. "Sounds wonderful. Where do I book passage?"

"It's far from over."

"I know." Cheyenne sighed. Combing her fingers through her hair, she stopped at the ends, holding them out before her. "I can't believe I did it."

"It'll grow back." Taking the strands, Lilith gave them a gentle tug. "No more split ends."

Cheyenne twirled her right index finger in a circle. "Yippee."

"You forgot to add the enthusiasm."

"Don't have any." Cheyenne close the door leading into the barn and walked toward the outside door. "I need food."

"Excellent idea, little sister."

Cheyenne felt her right eyebrow arch; she never did like being physically or verbally patted on the head. Slowly following Lilith back to the house, she scanned the empty corral, it looked long deserted. The horses were safely in the back pasture. She wondered if it was a premonition or just a projection of her mood on the environment.

The back door closed behind Lilith as she walked inside the main house. Cheyenne stopped in the middle of the yard. On most days the main house and yard would be alive with activity, but not any longer.

Except for Marc coming to the barn, she hadn't seen any of the tenants. He had come during the birthing. Refusing to enter, he stood at the corral entrance, shifting his weight from foot to foot as he told her they were leaving at the end of the week. He didn't say why, but she knew and understood why he and Marie didn't want their daughters to be part of the whole ugly mess. He had double-timed it out of sight before she could ask any questions. His appearance had explained why Debra and Lynne didn't come to the barn that morning to help feed the animals. It was so unlike them to miss a morning. They had braved blizzards to make sure the animals had food and water. Today they hadn't even called. She couldn't blame them. What could they say? To whom should they be loyal? How could they make sense out of a senseless situation?

The back door squeaked open. "Get in here and quit sulking!" April yelled.

Snapping her attention back outward, Cheyenne waved, continuing slowly toward the house. Her mind refused to get off the topic of what-ifs and maybe-onlys. She opened the door and was greeted by the scent of cooking sausage. Her mind cleared. Her mouth watered. Her stomach growled.

"Wash you hands and sit at the table." April continued in the same authoritative tone.

"Yes, mother." Cheyenne had meant it to be funny, however it sounded more snide than humorous.

"Don't give me that! Someone has to be the adult around here." April poured the steaming water into three cups. The rising steam smelled of raspberry.

"Hey!" Lilith cut in. "Don't forget about me!"

"The statement stands." April placed one cup on the table in front of her. "But the comment was more toward the three who lived here."

Cheyenne washed her hands in the kitchen sink and dried them on a dishtowel. "We were doing all right."

"Really?" April perched her fist on her hips. "You had a really good idea. This is wonderful land—fertile and strong. Healthy animals. The blessings of the Goddesses and Gods. And what did the three of you do? Wasted it!"

"We didn't!" Cheyenne protested.

"Didn't you?" April countered. "You limited whom you would allow to live here. People need safe, inexpensive homes. You had empty houses. And the ones who you did choose, you allowed to use you. They didn't do the agreed work. Didn't pay their rent on time. And that one cabin, she allowed her kids to make a wreck of it. That's why Dominic was able to move it. The darkness is more than willing to fill any empty places."

Cheyenne had known this. She just never realized it applied to them. "I didn't see."

April sat in an empty chair on Cheyenne's left. "I'm going to tell you my story. Don't interrupt. And I don't want your pity. I did it to myself."

Cheyenne simply nodded.

Lilith sipped her tea and looked out the window.

"Growing up I was a rebel. Except I didn't have the discipline to fight for or against anything. I just wanted to be different. My parents loved me dearly. They pulled me out of one situation after another. I got pregnant. We got married. I dropped out of high school. I had a son. We got divorced. I took drugs. Drank excessively. Why? Because I didn't know what else to do. I was so concerned with fitting in that I didn't see I was an emptying my soul. My parents took my son. I left town to be free. I hooked for a while. Moved around. Had no need of a home. I got pregnant again. But the drugs aborted it. I tried to settle down. Got a job. Fell in love. We wanted a child. So I got pregnant. But he was more interested in being able to father a child than to be a dad. He deserted us before she was born. I had a beautiful baby girl. I met another man, who I thought was the love of my life—again! He was a little younger, wilder. He liked his pot and his beer. But he said he loved me. So it didn't matter that he didn't like to work. I did-sometimes. My grandmother died and left me a little money. We put a down payment on a house. Only he didn't want to get a job to support it. What I made didn't cover the utilities."

April paused. She looked away and brushed a tear from the corner of her eyes. Swallowing, she returned her gaze to Cheyenne. "We had parties. A couple of friends came up with the idea to plant some homegrown on the back of the property. Just a little to sell to friends. I didn't stop him. He wasn't smart. We got caught. We went to jail. His friends forgot we existed. We lost our home. My son's wife refused to allow him or her son to be involved with us. Social services took my daughter and placed her in foster care. By then my parents had died."

April's tone flattened into a lifeless shadow of itself. "At first she fought to stay with me. But her foster parents introduced her to a life of not having to worry about money, drunken parties or not having enough food. They pushed her to do better in school. They refused to accept her excuses. She graduated at the top of her class. She's in college now, studying veterinary medicine."

April cupped her face in her hands; her fingertips pushed upward on the corners of her eyes, trying to prevent the tears from spilling over. "Where was I when my daughter needed me? Getting drunk or high. I had three miscarriages. But I couldn't go to the hospital. We were too smart to work full-time at jobs with insurance." Sarcasm crept into her voice and anger danced in her eyes. "I learned about witchcraft. We had magic so we didn't need to work. The Goddess will provide. That's what I thought. Have a bill, don't get a job—burn a candle." She cocked her head to one side. "Wrong answer. The Christians do have one thing right. Goddess does help those who help themselves. We stopped trying. She stopped helping and took back all her blessings." Shaking her head, April exhaled. "It took me three years of living on the street and many shit jobs before I started to understand how much damage I've done. My daughter hates me. She calls her foster mother, "mom". My son has disowned me. My beautiful grandson thinks I'm dead. All because I couldn't find the strength to fill myself from the inside."

She wiped her nose on a paper napkin and snuffled. "So you see the morals of my story are," April hesitated, a measured calmness coming to her voice. She lifted one finger. "To be grateful for what you are given." She lifted a second finger. "To share openly what you are given. "Third," another finger joined the two, "take responsibility for what you do or don't do. But never take on what doesn't belong to you. You can help others, but they have to be willing to do for themselves. You can't and shouldn't fix others' problems. We can only fix our own. And you can never-ever save a person from themselves."

Lilith's chair scraped against the tile as she slid it away from the table. Wordlessly she walked around and knelt beside April, encircling her arms around the slight woman.

Half turning, April sadly smiled and patted one of the dark hands. "Everything has changed for me in the past six years. I stopped feeling sorry for myself and took responsibility for my life. I went back to school and got my diploma, not just a GED. I went to college even though I didn't know what I wanted. By the end of the first year I did. I love the workings of the legal system."

"You're a lawyer?" Hope rose in Cheyenne; they were going to need one to deal with Celeste, but she had no idea how to choose one.

April shook her head. "Paralegal. It is what I studied to make a living. But what I fell in love with was," she paused and smiled, "blacksmithing."

"You're a blacksmith?" Cheyenne choked.

"Just how else could I make the swords." Amusement twinkled in her eyes.

"But? But? You're so small"

"Size doesn't matter."

"So men keep telling us." Lilith chuckled. She held up her left hand, the thumb and index finger forming a three inch arch. "And this is six inches."

April looked over shoulder. "I'm trying to be serious here."

Gently biting the tip of her tongue, Lilith shrugged and returned to her seat. "You started it."

April continued. "If it's ok with you I'll take care of the minor legal stuff with the tenants. Dealing with the back rent and keeping them current. I can also find new tenants. But the banking and the money issues, I won't touch."

"I learned that hard one already." Cheyenne cut in. "I allowed Celeste to take care of the household accounts."

"You trusted her." Lilith consoled.

"Yes I did and look where it got me." Cheyenne didn't wait for a response. "In a big financial hole."

"I found the leases in the desk and information about another credit card." April continued. "Jane gave me the heads up and I looked for it. It was listed for Dragon Eye Herbs. You need to cancel it immediately."

"Oh great! How many more?"

"A credit report will tell you. Also you can put a warning on your credit history to watch for fraud. I can get the paperwork if you like."

"Thanks, April. Yes, please we need to rent all the cabins, including mine ASAP."

"According to the leases, every adult is suppose to put ten hours of work on the farm a week as part of the lower rent. Has anyone?"

"Lady Margarita and her daughter are the only ones who helped freely. The others showed up only when I got nasty about it. And even then only for a short time."

"Good." April smiled. "We have just cause to ask them to leave."

"And find tenants who will pay their rent." Lilith interjected.

"Agreed." April nodded. "I've got a month vacation. My boss is a very good lawyer. I recommend her. Be it her or another, you will definitely need a lawyer."

"That was going to be one of my questions. But first," Cheyenne looked over her shoulder at the stove, "can we eat?"

"Works for me!" Lilith jumped up and led the way.

Within a few minutes, all three had full plates and were back at the table eating. The food renewed Cheyenne's strength and resolve. There were things that needed to be done immediately. Mentally she made a list and prioritized it. With the plates nearly empty and full stomachs, Cheyenne looked up at the two other women and smiled. "Thank you."

"We haven't done anything yet." Lilith quipped back. "But you're welcome."

"Ok." April wiped her lips with a napkin. "We have to make a plan."

"First thing. I need to do the financial stuff." Cheyenne began. "But I also want all of Celeste and Dominic things off the property."

"Their private spaces should also be cleaned, cleansed and changed so they can't visualize their way back." Lilith laid her fork across her plate. "It would be best to lease storage, put it all in there—"

"And give the code to the police." April interjected. "Cheyenne do you know if anyone who could get a message to Celeste, letting her know where her things are and how to get them?"

"Yes, several, and one lives here. I like the idea about the police, it'll serve a dual purpose."

"Yes. The police idea is great. But I don't like the idea of them having an ally on the property." Lilith continued. "It's not safe or wise."

"Agreed. Who is it?"

"Jerry." Cheyenne answered. "But he was here before Dominic came. Lilith, you probably remember Selene talking about him."

"It's Selene's Jerry?" Lilith shook her head. "I've always had mixed feelings about him. From things she's said, he isn't too stable."

"Since Dominic showed up, he is even less so."

"Great!" April set her fork over her plate and pushed it towards the center of the table. "If memory serves me, he hasn't paid rent in two months almost three."

"So we can evict him?" Lilith asked.

"Him and most of the others."

"Margaret and her daughter stay." Cheyenne interjected.

"I agree. She is the only one who has never been late with her rent." A confused expression crossed April's face. "I'm surprised Celeste didn't try to hide the missing or late payments."

"I never asked to look at the house books." Cheyenne felt like kicking herself. If she hadn't been so trusting, most of this wouldn't have happened. "Wasn't I just the smart one?"

Beneath the table, Lilith kicked Cheyenne in the shin.

"Owe! What was that for?" Cheyenne demanded.

"Didn't you just ask to be kicked?"

"No!"

"Gee, I thought I heard you asking to be abused." Lilith shrugged. "My mistake."

"Excuse me." April injected. "Back to the list. It'll be easy to get Dominic's stuff out of his cottage and Celeste's out of her room. But I'm sure she has things scattered around the house."

"I'll have to go room to room." Cheyenne stood and walked to the refrigerator, pulling off several sheets of the attached notepad and taking the pen out of its holder. She returned to the table.

"Good idea." April leaned forward. "Add changing the locks to the list."

"We're not going to be able to do all this ourselves." Lilith shifted in the chair.

"Do all what? Knock, knock." Raven stood outside the screen door with a suitcase in her hand. Without waiting for an invitation, she walked in. "Well, you said I could stay anytime." She leaned over and looked into the empty pots. "No lunch left. Hmm?"

Startled and grateful, Cheyenne stood. "How did you know?"

"Jane called. She wouldn't have left so quickly if she had a choice." Dropping her bag by the counter, she walked to the table. "Ok, fill me in."

"We're making a list of what needs to be done and dividing the labor." April pointed to herself. "I'm temporarily responsible for the cabins. It might not be too late to put an ad in the paper for tomorrow's edition."

"You're listing the cabins?" Raven slipped into an empty chair. "Won't that make it more difficult to screen people?"

"We're no longer exclusively Wiccan." Cheyenne mimed quotation marks around Wiccan.

"And," April sat back in the chair, "you should raise the rents to match the area. They are about two hundred too low."

"We had decided to keep it affordable."

"Nice sentiment. But your low rent got you low rent people who didn't like to pay rent."

Cheyenne didn't have anything to say; she was right. "Ok. Rent goes up. But I want to be the one to tell them."

"What do you need me to do?" Raven asked. "You have me for two days. I took personal time."

"Good. Would you like to help me clean out Dominic's cabin?" Lilith leaned towards her. "We're moving everything into storage and giving the combination to the cops."

Raven choked back a laugh. "That's good. I like it."

"It was April's idea." Lilith continued.

Raven held out her had to April. "You're a genius."

Shaking the dark hand, she smiled. "Thank you very much." She released it and patted the back. "Now back to the list. I'll go into town. Get the new locks. Rent the storage and get the U-haul."

Cheyenne cut in. "I've got an account with one of the hardware stores. I'll call so you can charge the locks. He also rents U-hauls."

"Great, a two-fer. But I'll place the ad first. I'll say something along the lines of quiet, country cabins for rent. Several available for immediate occupancy."

"They come unfurnished." Cheyenne clarified. "The furniture in Dominic's cabin actually belongs to me."

"Are you sure want it back?" Lilith asked.

"No." Cheyenne shook her head. "I thought we'd donate it."

"Or burn it. Why inflect that ick on anyone else?"

"Let's wait to see what we find before we build that pyre." Lilith stood. "Speaking of which, let's get to it."

Raven stood. "If you're serious about renting to anyone. Sammy at the station is looking for a new place. I can vouch for her."

"Sammy who?" For some reason, she knew the name but couldn't place a face to it.

"Detective Samantha Davies. Jane probably talked about her."

"Ok." Cheyenne nodded. "She respected her. Tell her about the cabins and invite her out. Just so you know. The boys and I are moving back to the main house."

"Good! Thank you!' Raven hugged her. "I was going to suggest it."

"But," Lilith injected, "we shouldn't show it for at least a week. Or at least until the skunk smell is gone."

Raven's eyebrow arched. "One of the guys have an oops?"

Lilith chuckled. "No. Dominic came for a visit and pissed off Mother Nature."

"Oh." Raven chucked. "That what you were talking about last night. Aren't skunks usually nocturnal?"

"I admit and deny nothing." Lilith smirked.

"You never do." April quipped back. "Raven, Jane said something about using you as a contact person. So you'll need to keep checking you machine."

"I can do that by remote."

"Good."

"I'll start making phone calls and going through the desk." Cheyenne stood.

"We're off to assess the damage in his cabin." Lilith chimed in.

"I'm off to town." April stacked the plates and carried them to the sink. Rinsing them off, she looked over her shoulder. "Raven, do you want a sandwich or something?"

"I'll raid the frig after we check the damage."

"April, you might as well get the largest truck. Celeste has a lot of stuff. After I get the calls made, I'm going to start separating her stuff out from Jane's and mine."

April rinsed off the dishes. "We still have to get you moved in."

"Right now. I'll move just what I need."

The women separated. Cheyenne walked through the dining room and into the office. Through the window, she saw April drive away. It was all starting to come together. She watched until the dust had begun to settle.

Pictures of happier times hung on the wall next to the window. She took one off. It was of the three of them, painting the living room. Cheyenne didn't remember who took the picture. It didn't matter. None of it mattered anymore. She dropped the picture in the trash and sat behind the desk.

CHAPTER THIRTEEN

Celeste opened the back porch door, allowing it to bang shut behind her. She needed to be alone. Dominic's friend Steve and his wife, Nancy, had made her welcome, but only because of Dominic. Their house was small even for the couple and three children. Dominic had promised her it would only be for a day or two, until they could make other arrangements. Stepping out into the cool evening air, she brushed back her hair. It felt damp and sticky. Her whole body did, in spite of the breeze. She knew it was happening again. Something inside her was changing. She couldn't stop it; part of her welcomed the reawakening. Gently she slid her open palms along her face, wiping away the forming sweat. The tips of her fingers touched her trembling lips. Pushing them against her teeth, she tried to make them stop. Slowly she walked a few steps across the porch to the swing set. All her joints began to ache at once. Sitting down, she wasn't sure if she would be able to stand without help. The pain welled up from the arches of her feet, burning upward through her ankles and centering on her knees. She bit her lip to keep from crying out.

Rubbing her knees, she looked out at the backyard. It had been carefully and lovingly fenced in to protect the children. Money was tight, but not when it came to the care of the children. Steve had built a playhouse that was more of a medieval castle, complete with drawbridge and towers. He

207

taught all three of his children, including his daughter Sarah, how to fence. First with wooden swords, then later with the real thing. They belonged to the local chapter of the SCA. As the children got older, they to started to participate in the events. Nancy was the one who had initiated the children's events at their gatherings. Looking around the yard at the scattered toys and clothesline, envy grew in Celeste. Nancy had everything she had always wanted, yet she just accepted it as her due. She wasn't grateful for her husband and children. Celeste choked back a sob. *Why couldn't this be mine?* She asked herself. *It was all I ever wanted.*

Laughter drifted through the open window. The children had been sent to Nancy's mother to spend the night so their parents could have an adult night. Dominic had something planned for later, but he wouldn't share with her. He said it was a surprise. They had ordered pizza and popped in a movie. The three of them had cracked open a six pack. *The first of many,* Celeste thought. Dominic had promised he wouldn't drink any more and except for beer he had kept his word. He said he loved her and promised to take care of her, yet she caught his eyes drifting to Nancy's youthful body. He was her last chance for love; there wasn't anything she wouldn't do to keep him.

With the money they got from Cheyenne's and the farm accounts, they would buy their own home in the country; it wouldn't be as big, but it didn't matter. She would start teaching again. Dominic would work the farm as it should be done. They would sue for custody of his nieces and they would be a family. Dominic promised. For a moment, it bothered her to cash the checks, but he was right; Cheyenne did owe her. They all did. A breeze freed a few strands of her hair. They tickled her nose and she tucked them back behind her ear. *They weren't stealing,* she consoled herself. She had contributed to the household with the profits from her classes and by maintaining the household books. She never saw how Cheyenne had been taking advantage of her until Dominic pointed it out. He was right; she was entitled to more than they took. Maybe they should sue to get part of the farm. *No,* she answered herself. *It was best to make a clean break.* Dominic found a forty-acre farm that was available. Tomorrow they were going to talk to the owner, if they liked it they could make an offer.

The back door swung open and Dominic stepped out, carrying a bottle of beer. "What's wrong?"

Celeste shook her head. "I just needed some fresh air."

He crossed the yard and stopped the swing. "It'll be all right." He crouched beside her and lifted her chin. "I promised you."

"I know."

"Don't you love me?"

"Yes, but—"

"Then don't doubt me." He pulled her closer and kissed her.

Shivers radiated throughout her body, pushing the pain back down through the arches of her feet. He touched her and she felt younger. No one else had ever been able reach down inside her and awaken the fire that she had been forced to bank. "I believe you." She whispered.

He dropped the bottle on the ground. His hand slid up under her shirt and bra to caress her nipple. Unlike in her youth, they were slow to respond. He kissed her and a wave of energy radiated from him into her, making her feel like she did when she met him decades before. She traced his pelt of a chest down to his belt buckle. Tugging on his zipper, she slipped her hand inside to massage the hardening organ. It pulsed with growing energy.

"Are you ready?" He whispered. "Are you ready to start your new life?"

"Are they still awake?" Celeste attempted to pull her hand back.

He caught her. "They're joining us." He kissed her again. "Come with me." Pulling her to her feet, he pulled her back inside the house.

In the living room, Steve and Nancy talked in hushed voices. Nancy shook her head. Dominic pulled Celeste into the room. Nancy tried to run from the room; Steve yanked her back to the couch.

"I don't want to." Nancy stammered. "Steve, don't make me. Please"

"If you love me." He stood, towering above her. "You promised me."

She winced as the skin beneath his fingers turned white, but said nothing more.

Celeste's internal alarm bells went off. She hesitated. "Dominic?"

Anger flashed in the blue eyes. He blinked and it was gone. "Trust me." He whispered.

Licking her lips, the doubt grew. Dominic increased the pressure on her palm. It didn't hurt exactly, just brought her attention back to him. She wanted to focus on him, to block everything else out. "Help me."

He kissed her hand. "I will." Dominic held out his hand to Steve, who dropped something into his waiting palm. He held them out to Celeste. "Take them both."

"I need water." Celeste whispered.

Steve gave Dominic a half empty bottle of beer before turning his attention to Nancy.

Putting the pills in her mouth, Celeste washed them down with the beer. It was bitter and warm. She tried not to gag.

Across the room, Nancy also swallowed tablets. Celeste assumed they were the same kind.

Celeste looked up into Dominic's eyes. The pupils reflected the light that was beyond the lights of the room. He kissed her forehead. She didn't think about consequences; they didn't matter any more. Nothing mattered beyond Dominic.

His arm slid around her waist and guided her toward the center of the room to a small, long coffee table. Candles of all sizes and shapes had been lit. Dominic turned out the light closest to him. Steve turned out the other. Nancy stood on the opposite side of the table, looking at Celeste. The fear in her eyes was rapidly being replaced by an out-of-focus haze. Steve stepped beside her and pushed her to the floor.

Dominic grabbed Celeste from behind, forcing her downward. She tried to remain standing. "Give into me." He growled in her ear. She tried to protest; it came out as an unintelligible mumble. Her will slid from her. Shaking, she lowered herself to the floor. Steve and Nancy had already removed their clothing. Dominic stripped, tossing his clothes into the shadows. Steve crawled around the table and helped remove Celeste's clothing. She could do nothing to stop him. Kneeling beside her, he cupped her breasts in his hands. Acting as a human bra, he returned the hanging flesh back to it's original position and kissed them. She shuttered. He smiled and released them, returning to Nancy's side.

Dominic was behind her. She couldn't see him, but she felt his presence.

His voice came from the darkness beyond the light of the candles. "Do you give yourselves freely to the Dark Lord?"

"We do." Steve answered.

Sitting on his thigh and slumping back against Steve's bare chest, Nancy nodded slowly. She stared at the floor. Her arms hung limply at her sides.

"What do you offer in return for the Dark Lord's gifts?" Dominic continued.

Steve cleared his throat. "All that he asks." He continued, sounding more rehearsed. "Nancy and I offer our youth, our strength, and our fertility." He blinked rapidly. "In exchange for the power over the elements and others."

"If you forgo all that came before, say the prayer."

Steve recited what sounded like gibberish until he ended with "Nema."

Celeste realized it was the Lord's Prayer backward.

Dominic reached over her and placed a gold platter on the table. "What offerings do you bring?"

Pulling a knife from beneath the couch behind him, Steve cut a lock of his own sandy blonde hair and dropped it on the platter. Grabbing some of Nancy's hair, he cut and dropped it on top of his own. "We offer our hair, which is a symbol of our loyalty." Turning over his wrist, he cut. The blood welled up. He held his wrist over the platter. The droplets splattered as they hit the metal. He waited until there was a puddle about a silver dollar size. He reached for Nancy's wrist. She tried to pull away. Roughly he yanked her arm and held it over the platter. He sliced. She whimpered. A thin red line formed, becoming a bloody stream, which mixed with his own on the metal. He released her arm. She snapped it back, smearing blood on her stomach. "We offer our blood to symbolize our souls. All that we have been. All that we are. All that we shall be." Placing the knife on the floor, he picked up a baggie and dumped the contents on the spreading blood. "Our fingernails. Representing our strength and energy." Dropping the baggy on the floor, he pulled two knotted cords from beneath the couch. "Our measure." His hand opened. The cords fell, splattering the blood against the sides. "We offer ourselves in totality."

Smiling, Dominic reached and dipped his hand in the blood. "The Dark Lord accepts your offerings." Licking his palm, a low growl emanated from deep in his throat. Tilting his head back, the blood trickled down either side of his chin. He breathed deeply. The younger couple shuddered. Nancy cried out. Dominic laughed. Dipping his fingertips back in the blood, he brought them to Celeste's lips. Before she could turn her face, he had wiped his fingers clean, using her lower teeth to scrap it from his skin. She tried not to swallow. The blood mixed with her salvia. Some dribble out of the corner of her mouth. But against her will, the rest slide down her throat. Three more times he brought his fingers to her lips. Each time it tasted better. The fourth time she sucked his fingers clean. Her mind suddenly cleared. All the doubt and guilt were gone. She felt the power rising within her, making her feel stronger than she had ever felt before.

Laughing, he kissed her temple and reached for the cords. Snapping them open, he pushed the table out of the way and sat beside Celeste. Blood oozed from Nancy's arm as Dominic grabbed her arm and pulled her to him. He looped the cord around her wrists. "I bind you to me. You are mine, whenever, for whatever I wish." Snapping her wrists to her ankles, he wrapped the cord around them. "You can never escape me. I own you, your soul, and all your loins produce." Reaching over the prone body, he retrieved the other cord and offered it to Celeste.

Without hesitation, she took it and smiled. She grabbed Steve's wrists. Surprised, he tried to pull back. Her nails dug into his flesh. He gasped in pain. It pleased her. She wounded the cord around his wrists and pulled. "I bind you to me. You are mine."

"Dominic?" He protested.

She snapped the cord down with a strength she had thought long gone and wound it around his hairy ankles. "You are mine whenever, for whatever I wish. You can never escape me. I own you, your soul and all your loins produce." Smiling, she snapped the cord, yanking out the leg hair it entangled.

Steve screamed in pain.

Dominic laughed and kissed her cheek. "Good girl. You learned fast."

"This isn't what we agreed to!" Steve sputtered. "You promised!"

"I lied." Dominic laughed. "Now." He pulled the cord holding Nancy's wrists and ankles. "We make it official." He released the cord and grabbed Nancy's wrist; pulling her away from Steve, he stood before her. "Please me, girl."

Kneeling before him, she looked up, crying. "No. Please."

The slap was heard more than seen. Nancy sprawled on the floor. Steve reacted. Celeste yanked the cord. He was thrown off balance as the cord snaked up his leg, ripping hair and cutting flesh.

"None of your business. She belongs to him. You are mine."

He looked up at her, understanding appearing in his eyes. He watched Dominic flip Nancy on her back and cover her with his own body. Nancy screamed. He tried to move. Celeste held him tight with one hand. With the other, she laced her fingers in his hair and yanked his head back. His eyes snapped open. The horror in his eyes gave her pleasure. "Please me." She demanded. "Please me." She repeated, grabbing his penis. Her body tingled not with sexual pleasure but with the anticipation of his youthful energy filling her body. She could feel the beating of his heart through his scalp; it excited her. It felt like her heart beating in her chest, pumping her blood into her capillaries. His life surged into her, making her younger with each beat. Steve quivered beneath her hand. She pulled his hair just for pleasure. He whimpered, growing more limp.

Dominic pried her fingers from his hair, freeing him from her grasp. Steve collapsed unconscious on the floor. "Careful, dearest. You'll kill him. And we need him to get others."

"I didn't know it could be like this." She whispered.

"It's only the beginning." He kissed her deeply.

She felt the desire rising within her. Her no longer sagging breasts responded as they did in her youth. She looked down at them with pride. Smiling, she returned her gaze to meet his slate blue eyes. "I want more."

"Tomorrow." Wrapping his arms around her, he gently laid her backward. Using Steve as her pillow, Dominic helped her recapture her long lost passion.

CHAPTER FOURTEEN

Celeste awoke slowly, not knowing where she was. She sat up. The room spun around her. Closing her eyes, she rested her forehead on her knees, trying to clear the dizziness. The night before was a hazy memory. She didn't know how she got into the twin bed. The last thing she remembered was falling asleep on the living room floor. She had made love with Dominic. Steve and Nancy were there. Why? The memories crept back in snapshots. The ecstasy and the cruelty crept around her conscience. Pushing her hair back over her forehead, she flung back the sheet. Her knees and ankles were no longer swollen. The age spots on her arms and hands had disappeared. Although her breasts still sagged, it was from weight not age. Caressing her face, she slowly traced her cheeks until she was combing back her hair with her fingers. Tilting her head back, she breathed deeply. Nothing hurt. It was real, not a drug induced fantasy. Laughing she jumped out of bed. For a moment, the dizziness returned. She grabbed the headboard to steady herself. She saw herself in the mirror on the dresser. The woman she remembered on her fortieth birthday stared back at her. Tossing back her hair, she laughed and pirouetted. It truly was her reflection. Slipping on the robe that was left at the foot of the bed, she ran out of the room, looking for Dominic.

Voices came from the kitchen. She followed them. Nancy was hunched over the stove, her attention on the frying pan in front of her. Steve and Dominic sat at the table. Dominic talked. Steve nodded on cue.

"Good morning!" Celeste announced. "I feel wonderful!"

The spatula clattered against the pan.

Smiling, Dominic quickly rose and embraced her. "You look wonderful." He pulled a chair out for her. "Nancy, more eggs and bacon." He ordered. "Your mistress is hungry."

Without turning, she reached for two more eggs and broke them in the frying pan.

Dominic returned to the table, angling his chair so he could face Celeste. "I'm going to give you something you've always wanted."

"A gift." Celeste stretched, testing her new body. "I love gifts."

"This one will be very special." He grabbed the younger man by the shoulder, making him wince. "You haven't greeted your mistress properly."

Steve didn't move.

With a casual back hand, Dominic knocked him from the chair. "Do it!"

Steve tried to stand. Dominic pushed him face down on the tile. "You haven't earned the right to walk. Crawl on your belly."

Celeste remembered the surge of energy. She wanted more. Smiling she crooked her finger.

Even as he shook his head, his body crawled to her. His movements were slow and labored.

Reaching down, she grabbed him by the hair and yanked his head to table level. "Who do you belong to?"

Steve hesitated.

Celeste curled her fingers.

Tears ran down his cheeks. "To you. I belong to you."

Celeste smiled. "Please me."

"No." Dominic warned. "He's too weak." Reaching back, he grabbed Nancy by the back of her shorts; the frying pan spun off the stove. "Here. You are new to the blood. You must feed frequently. But just a taste. She's my surprise." He pushed the trembling women toward her and she stumbled over her husband. "Please her." He commanded.

Nancy hesitated.

Dominic grabbed her, snapping her head up. "I own you. Do it!" He shoved her toward Celeste. "Steve, finish making breakfast. We're still hungry."

Looking down at Nancy's bruised face and arms, she found herself strangely excited. Last night she had taken from Steve without really knowing how she did it. "How do I do it?"

Dominic smiled. "Kiss her."

"On the mouth. She's a woman." It wasn't that she was homophobic, but it wasn't anything she had wanted to do. Shrugging, she grabbed the front of Nancy's shirt and pulled her closer, kissing her on the mouth. As their lips touched, the circuit was completed. The youthful energy flowed into her. It was sweet and fresh. She slipped her arm around the younger woman's waist, pulling her closer.

Dominic pulled the limp woman away from her and dropped her on the floor. He waggled his finger in front of Celeste's face. "You must learn self-control."

She kissed his moving finger. "But I like it."

"I know you do." He kissed her forehead. "That's why we need them to bring us more disciples. They'll have time to recover between feedings." He turned to the prone woman. "Go rest. Later we start making the child."

The pan clattered against the stove, but Steve said nothing.

"What child?" The spark of jealousy ignited in Celeste.

My gift to you." Dominic kissed her fingertips. "You have always wanted a child. I'm going to give you one." Two steaming plates appeared in front of them. Dominic looked up. "Go lie down. Not with Nancy. In one of the kids' rooms."

Steve nodded and shuffled his way down the hall.

"I don't like it. I want to have your child." Celeste protested.

"You're jealous!" He laughed.

"Don't laugh." Celeste pushed the chair away from the table.

"Think about it." Dominic knelt beside her. "It will be ours. We are one. She will just be the carrier. Nothing more. You are the one I love. The only one."

Celeste felt her face flush as the sexual energy raced within her.

"If you were pregnant you couldn't feel what you're feeling now. This way you get that feeling over and over . . . and still get the child you want.

"I want more." She whispered. "I'm hungry."

He kissed her fingers and sat back in the chair. Pushing one plate closer, he picked up his fork. "It'll help."

She took a bite. "It's burned."

"Don't pout. You drained him." He took a bite of egg and made a face. "You're right. But we still need food. Later, after he's rested, I'll send him to the store."

'I'll go." Celeste offered.

Dominic shook his head. "Not until you get control of yourself." In large mouthfuls, he quickly finished the eggs, washing them down with milk. "I was thinking we need someone on the police force to protect us. No doubt they've started telling lies about us."

Celeste smiled. "And I have just the person."

Dominic spread his hand out in front of him, palms up. "Don't keep it to yourself."

"Detective Maxwell Conner."

"Why him? He doesn't have much power."

"He's a link to Jane. She still has feelings for him that we could tap into if we had control of him. I have been teaching him without Jane's knowledge. I convinced him that it would be best if she didn't know." Celeste smiled. "I'll tell him I can teach him how to get her back."

"Through him we could control her, then Cheyenne." Dominic clicked his tongue on his teeth. "I like it."

"But, my dear one. You'll have to teach me how. There is no way he'll agree to do what we did last night."

He brought her hand to his lips. "There are other ways."

"I'm a quick study."

"That you are."

Celeste combed her free hand through her hair, pausing a moment to look at the back of her hand. She liked feeling young and strong. "How long will it last?"

"As long as you continue to feed." He chucked.

"I can do that." She licked her lips. "Speaking of which. I have to find Maxie. Could you have Steve or Nancy call the station while I shower and change? I just need to know where he is. Maybe they can claim to be an informant or something."

"You're learning." He stood and leaned over to kiss her on the forehead.

For a moment, the world spun around her. As her mind cleared, she knew how to make Maxie her own. She smiled up at him. "Thank you. It'll be easy."

He winked and straightened. "I'll have Steve make the call. I need to plant some seeds to grow that child you want." He half turned. "And leave me some hot water."

She watched him walk down the hallway. Stopping briefly at the first doorway, he ordered Steve to make the phone call. He continued down the hall and disappeared into the master bedroom. Moments later Nancy cried out. Suddenly Celeste's stomach churned. She wanted a child desperately. Dominic was going to give her one. But it wouldn't really be her child. It would be Dominic's and the woman he was making love to. She walked down the hall, stopping outside the door. Nancy was crying. Dominic was working himself into a frenzy.

"*Not love,*" an inner voice told her. "*Sex. Reproductive sex. No more.*"

Celeste inhaled sharply. Placing her hand on the door, she shivered. Behind her a door opened. Steve peaked out. "Mind your own business." She snapped. The door closed. She continued down the hall to the bathroom. She closed the door and her mind. Stripping off the robe, she turned on the water. The steam filled the room. Looking in the mirror, she turned one way, then the other. Her dimensions hadn't changed, yet there were subtle differences—with only more to come, she thought. Pushing the door further open, she stepped into the hot stream, closing it behind her. Her Grandmother's image came to mind. She pushed it away and lathered. Celeste felt alive, more alive than she had in a very long time. Her skin tingled. Her Grandmother's image appeared in the steam. Startled, Celeste stepped back, but the new darkness in her heart caught her, feeding her new strength. "Go away old woman. You're dead!" Violently she wiped the steam off the door; the image vanished. Shaking her head, the ends of her hair slapped her back and thighs. Washing and rinsing, she turned off the water and stepped out.

Dominic stood in front of the toilet, relieving himself. "What was that all about?" Droplets of blood ran down his inner thigh.

"An old woman trying to interfere." Celeste grabbed a towel and wrapped it around most of her hair. The dripping ends hung out the bottom.

His eyebrow arched, but he didn't pursue the topic. "Maxie has taken a couple of personal days. They think he is at home."

"Good, that will make it easier." Celeste dried herself with a separate towel. "Do you think she has conceived?"

He shook the last droplets off and flushed. "To early to tell. It could take a while. She was on the pill. There are a couple of dresses in her closet that may fit. We also have to make arrangements to get our stuff."

Numbly, Celeste nodded. *It could take a while? How long, how many times would he be with her? How long could she endure?*

Taking the towel from her hand, he casually brushed the blood off and dropped the towel. Kissing her forehead on the way out the door, he called back. "Hurry up! The day's a wasting."

"I will." She answered automatically. Exchanging the wet towel around her head for a dry one, she walked down the hall to the bedroom. The door was ajar. She pushed it open.

Nancy was curled up on the bed in a near fetal position, clutching the blood splattered sheet. Celeste diverted her eyes. She didn't want to see. She didn't want to know. That wasn't a woman. It was a thing—an incubator for their child. Crossing the room, she scanned the hanging clothes. Three dresses had been separated. One by one she held them up, deciding on the pastel flowered. Slipping it over her head, she found it tight around her hips, but not so much that it was uncomfortable. The towel had fallen off. She left it on the floor. Walking out of the room, she shook her hair free and combed her fingers through it.

Steve sat in a chair, staring vacantly at the wall across the room. He shrunk back as she approached.

Totally nude, Dominic walked in from the kitchen, carrying a steaming cup of coffee. "You look beautiful darling. Where are you going to start looking for him?"

"At his house."

Happy hunting." He kissed her cheek. "And you don't have to worry about their brats. He called his mother and they will be staying there indefinitely."

"Good thinking." Celeste took the cup from his hand and drank from it. "We can play whenever we want."

"It wasn't supposta be like this." Steve murmured.

Dominic snickered. Taking the cup back, he walked down the hall.

"What did you expect?" Celeste snapped. "To be equals?"

"Please." He begged. "I'll do anything. But stop him from hurting her."

"He owns her, just like I own you." Celeste stepped toward the door and stopped. "Clean up the house. It's a mess."

He shuddered and sank into the chair.

His fear gave her pleasure. "I need your car. Where are the keys?"

He pointed to the top of the TV.

She crossed the room and snatched them up. On the way out the door, she decided if Dominic could enjoy himself, so could she. Steve wasn't anyone she could be attracted to, but Maxie was another story. It was very easy to see why he aroused Jane. Soon he would belong to her and she would use him as she pleased. Smiling, she walked out the door.

The car was old, but started easily. She backed out and pointed it across town. In the strange car, she felt invisible. Her car was still parked at the farm. Dominic's truck was hidden in Steve and Nancy's garage. If the police were looking for them, they were safe for now. After she turned Maxie, Jane and Cheyenne would have no alternative but to give her what she wanted. Part of her wanted the farm; not to live on, but to sell it so they couldn't have it either. It could never be home for her again. They had spoiled it.

Turning down the alley, she saw Maxie's car parked at an angle in his driveway. Suddenly she became nervous. *What if she forgot? What if she wasn't strong enough? No, if she forgot, she'd improvise. She would simply use his ego against him. His bigotry and anger made him vulnerable.* She parked the car and stepped out. Quickly crossing the lawn, she walked up the two steps and opened the back door. She looked around. The kitchen was empty. With her open palm, she pushed the door the rest of the way open and walked inside. Silently she closed it and locked it behind her. The house was dark and quiet. The only light came through the kitchen windows. She walked further in. Dirty dishes littered the counter, half filling the double sinks. She continued through the house. The living room drapes were pulled shut, making the room an eerie twilight. She stopped for a moment to allow her eyes to adjust.

He sat in the corner chair between two large potted plants. Shadows covered his facial features. He lifted the bottle to his lips and drank. Slowly the bottle floated its way back to his lap. "What d'ya want?" His voice was heavy and slurred.

Smiling, Celeste realized this was going to easier than she thought. She walked to the end of the counter that divided the living room and kitchen. "I was worried about you."

"Were you?" He took a long drink, wiping his lips with the back of his hand. "Did the bitch tell you?"

"No. Jane didn't tell me. But I heard," Celeste stepped into the shadows of the room, "that she hurt you."

"Hurt me?" Maxie snapped. "She couldn't hurt me! I just'ta used her. That's all."

Celeste knelt beside him. Taking the bottle from him, she licked up its neck and took a drink. The wine was sweet and cheap. She took a second drink. Wine dribbled from the corner of her mouth. Slowly she licked it away. "You loved her. Trusted her. She made you think she loved you."

"Whatever!" He snapped the bottle from her and brought it to his lips. In middrink he stopped and stared at her. "You look different."

"I am different.' She placed a hand on his knee, the other on the opposite thigh. She massaged upward toward his groin.

"Wha—" He tried pushing her hand away.

"Shush." Celeste quickly moved her hand from his knee to his lips. Seductively she brushed the outer edge of his upper lip. "I want to take your pain away."

"No!" He tried to slip from her grasp, but the alcohol and the pressure she placed on his thigh kept him in place. Her hand moved upward, fondling and gently pulling, rhythmically in time with her own breath, which she altered to match his own. She felt the swelling beneath the cotton material. She kissed his thigh. "Let me help you." She whispered.

"You can't." He mumbled.

Tilting her head to meet his eyes, she sent energy from her fingertip into his groin, traveling up his spinal column to his heart chakra. The suction cups attached, numbing his emotional center. "Doesn't it feel better?"

He groaned with pleasure.

"Accept me. Give yourself totally." She whispered. She sensed Jane; the light of her flaring up to protect him. It pulled at the tentacles she had spun around his heart.

Inhaling sharply, he pushed Celeste away. "I can't!" He cried. "I love her."

Undaunted, Celeste intertwined her fingers with his. Bringing them to her mouth, she alternated sucking and licking his fingertips. "I'll make you feel strong. Like a man. She treated you like a boy. A toy she picked up when it suited her." She straddled his thighs. She liked the way his muscles felt against her bare skin. "She gave you pain. I'll give you pleasure." Smelling her own heat rise to mix with his pheromones, she rolled forward, covering him with her body, and kissing him. Her free hand slid down the inside of his sweat pants, pulling the front down in the process.

A primordial groan emanated deep from with in him.

"Do you accept me?" She whispered in his ear.

He nodded.

"Say it. Say it out loud."

"Yes! I accept you." His breath came hard.

"Totally? Freely?" She pulled his sweat pants out of the way.

Wrapping his arms around her, he tried pulling her back on top of him.

She hovered above him; her hand massaging him, yet refusing to guide him in. "Give yourself totally to me." She hissed. "Say it or I'll take back the pleasure and return the pain."

He shuddered, hesitating only for an instant. "Yes, I accept' you totally."

She guided him inside. Her own energy entered him as he entered her. Pulsating, throbbing—intertwining itself around his nervous system. As his passion came to a climax so did he now belong to her. She didn't need his blood or his measure. She owned him just the same, him and that part of Jane that cared for him. Lifting herself off him, she sat back on his thighs. This one she would take better care off. He would do more than feed her; he would please her. Dominic was going to have Nancy to satisfy him. Maxie would do the same for her.

Maxie laid back. His eyes were closed. He had relaxed back into the chair. Sleep threatened to overtake him.

It was time he learned, she thought. Leaning forward, she kissed him, gently at first, but the kiss became a bite. Laughing she pulled way, licking his blood off her lips.

He screamed and stared at her. "Why—"

"Because I can." She licked the trickle of his lip. "You gave yourself to me."

"Get off!" He ordered.

"Make me." She daunted.

He reached for her.

She shoved him back. "I forbid you to move."

His body ceased to move. Panic filled his eyes.

"You see. I own you." Standing, she grabbed him by the hair and pulled him to his feet. She released him and he dropped limply to the floor. She rolled him on his back. "Try to fight me. Go ahead. Without my permission, you can't move, can't breathe." Her hand slide down to his now limp manhood. "This belongs to me." With a squeeze of her hand, she sent an energy pulse. The organ grew in her hand. "Whenever I want. For as long as I want."

"I didn't mean—I renounce you." He whispered.

She slapped him across the face. "Too late for that."

Blood oozed from his nose, mixing with that from his lip. "Why are you doing this to me? Didn't Jane hurt me enough?"

She leaned forward and licked the free flowing blood. "Because of you I will make her pay as well. Through you, I will take her." She smiled, knowing that once she had Jane, Cheyenne would be open and easy. She would have revenge on both of them and there was nothing they could do to stop her. Intertwining her fingers with his chest hair, she felt his heart beat, his blood coursing through his body. She sensed his life energy. Through him, she reached out and touched Jane. The image of Jane cowering in a chair appeared in her mind. She reached out and touched the outer edges of Jane's aura; her energy was sweet and strong. With a flash of searing white energy, the connection was broken. The energy was disorganized and unfamiliar. Jane hadn't been able to stop her, but someone else had. Celeste reached out again, seeking a weakness. Suddenly Dominic's energy joined with hers. Together they sought for a weakness to exploit only to be rebuffed again. It didn't matter. She wasn't strong enough to break through yet, but that would soon change. Returning her attention to the quivering man, she pulled the dress over her head. "You will make me feel like the most beautiful woman in the world."

He turned his face away.

Angrily, she slapped him. Grabbing his chin, she forced him to face her. "You want to please me."

"You are ugly—soul ugly!"

Pinching his chin, she reached down with her free hand and grabbed his testicles. Completing the circuit, she sent an energy pulse.

His hair rose on end. His mouth moved. No words came out. His body quivered. The shock waves shook his body. His palms bounced off the floor making a thumping sound as they hit the carpet.

She released him and he went limp beneath her. "Any time, any place. With you or not. I can do that and much, much more. Understand?"

His eyes slowly opened and he slightly nodded.

"Good boy." She patted his cheek. "You learn fast." She stood and sat in the chair he had vacated. "I'll give you a moment to collect yourself. Then you will make me feel like the most beautiful woman in the world."

Breathing hard, he stared at the ceiling. Tears spilled out of his eyes and onto the floor. He licked his lips. Tasting blood, he reached up and wiped it away, smearing it across his cheek. As his breathing slowed, becoming less labored he turned his head to look up at her.

I'm going to enjoy him, she thought, *as much as possible. Steve and others will feed me. Maxie will protect us and gratify me. Later, when I'm stronger, I'll take my revenge.* "I'm waiting."

Painfully he rolled onto his stomach and tried to stand. Smiling Celeste pointed to the floor. Swallowing hard, Maxie returned to his knees and crawled across the floor. Sitting back on his heels, he looked up at her.

CHAPTER FIFTEEN

Jane stood in front of the window, watching the rain blow nearly horizontally. The wind howled around the house, shaking the windowpanes. Lightning flashed. Second's later thunder cracked. It was the middle of the afternoon, yet it was as dark as night. The sensors turned on the streetlights and they bobbed like lonely beacons on the street awash with rain.

Lady Bridget and her daughter, Shelly, were in the kitchen making ice tea by candlelight. Lady Bridget wasn't exactly what she expected. But, then again, she hadn't known what to expect. But when the tall, full figured brunette answered the door, she was still surprised. Her long hair hung in a single braid down her back, disguising its true length. Her deep brown eyes shone brightly with the love of life and spirit. Shelly quickly joined her at the door. She was a slightly younger version of Bridget. There was no mistaking their common gene pool. Originally Jane had thought they were sisters. It wasn't until later during conversation, did she learn Bridget was twenty years her senior. The two of them had tittered about Jane's mistake, implying that it was a common error. They had greeted her openly with trust and love. During dinner, she learned more about April. Some of her past made Jane apprehensive, but the changes she had made in her path took great courage and strength; they were both qualities Jane admired. By the end of dinner, Jane was reassured.

That had been almost two days ago. Lady Bridget had insisted she stay until she was stronger. Gratefully she had agreed. Being pampered and mothered, she had slept and ate peacefully for the first time in months. The farm and all its problems were so far away, they no longer mattered. She was safe and protected. The urgency she had felt no longer prodded her to move on. Something had changed, but she didn't have a clue to what or how.

The power had been knocked out an hour or so ago. But she wasn't really sure how long it had been. Her sense of time had gone weird since she arrived in Toledo. They had been talking on the back porch watching the storm blow in. The wind picked up. Together they had gathered the lawn furniture and safely tucked it in the garage. Before they could reach the house, the rain came down without warning. It was a hot summer rain that made it necessary to close the windows but made the inside unbearably hot. They left a few windows open on the sheltered side of the house. It didn't help much. She felt her way to the chair and sat down. It was a comfy old chair that had already been softened by many other butts. Leaning back, she shifted her position so she'd still be able to look out the window.

Thunder rumbled. Lightning struck. The house shook. The room was ablaze like daylight. Suddenly Jane became uneasy. An electrical current surrounded her, making the air around her cold and rank. Its fingers reached for her heart. She screamed.

Lady Bridget and Shelly raced into the room, each carrying a candle. Bridget stopped short and shoved Shelly back out of the room. Quickly circling her left hand above the candle flame, she drew up an intense white ball of light. It grew to the size of a basketball. Angrily she shouted. "Dark One, who invades my domain, return whence you came." She threw the ball at Jane. It hit in front of her, exposing the dark shadow of a figure looming over her. It crackled and hissed.

For an instant, Jane saw Celeste's face. Horrified by the naked evil she saw in her eyes, she shrieked and covered her face.

The shadow folded into itself and disappeared through the window, cracking the pane. Another window cracked, echoing off the walls.

"Mother?" The younger woman's voice questioned, but revealed no fear.

"Protect Jane." Lady Bridget ordered.

Shelly nodded. Crossing the room, she stood behind Jane's chair. Using the candlestick, she drew a double pentacle in the air. "I surround Jane and myself in the protection of the Goddess." Stepping closer to the chair, she made a circle of light, which encompassed them both. "With this candle, I set up a barrier of light from each direction." She raised the candle. "And from above." She lowered the candle. "And below. This barrier is created from the will of the Goddess; it is seamless and impenetrable, unending as the Goddess's love. It reflects back to the sender all negativity both the seen and the unseen the direct and the indirect. So mote it be."

The air around them warmed. Jane felt like a child next to the younger woman. She looked up at her. Shelly was no longer a woman in her early twenties; she was a Priestess, knowledgeable in her craft and strong with the energy of the Goddess. "What about your mother?"

Shelly leaned around the chair, carefully keeping within the glow of the candle. "Mother is safe. She has battled worse before and sent him squealing with his tail between his legs. No matter what stay in the circle of light. She needs to concentrate on him. Not worry about us."

It made sense to Jane.

The younger woman sat on the arm of the chair, taking Jane's hand in her own. "We'll be ok. Mom called the others when we heard you scream. Her working partners are just minutes away. Besides," she proudly shook back her long wavy hair, "my mother can take care of it herself."

"Shush!" Lady Bridget hissed. The candle held high, she scanned the room. Her brown eyes darted from corner to corner. She walked toward the center of the room. The floor beneath her creaked. Lightning flashed, illuminating the room. For an instant, a dark form was revealed hovering within the folds of the drapes.

Jane's scream was cut short by Shelly's hand, becoming more of a muffled squeak.

"Shussh." Shelly whispered. "You're safe. Mom knows it's there."

"I know who it is." Jane whispered back.

"Later." The younger woman brought a single finger to her lips.

Nodding, Jane involuntary pulled her feet onto the cushions of the chair. Her stomach churned. She was out of her league, out of possibilities, and nearly out of courage. She was an intuitive who studied Wicca. But nothing she had learned had prepared her for this kind of experience.

Lady Bridget stood alone in the darkness of the room. Her attention totally focused.

Lightning flashed in sequence, giving the room a strobe effect. It was enough to give the shadow dimension and form. It was the size of a serving platter. Patches were nearly transparent. Other parts were too dense to see through. It pulsed in the rhythm of a heart beating; the general shape of the shadows changed with each beat.

Streams of pure white light came up from the floor and down from the ceiling, engulfing Lady Bridget. It folded around her as the streams met and combined. Holding the candle with both hands before her, she released it. Instead of falling, it was held suspended. Spreading her arm out palms up, she slowly pivoted her hands. Highly focused beams of silver shot out of her palms, combining in the flame of the candle, and shot across the room, hitting the shadow.

It squealed. Shrinking back, it tried to hide deeper in the folds of the curtains. The light followed, spreading out to cover the shadow in violet flames. The squeal increased in pitch until it went beyond what the human ear could register, yet the sound vibration could be felt on their skin like an itch scratching wouldn't cure. The windowpane rattled, threatening to break. Lightning flashed. Thunder cracked. Another flash revealed the presence of a second shadow. It joined with the first. The itch stopped. Together they disburse the flame, eating their way up the light to Lady Bridget.

Jane saw her weaken. She tugged on Shelly's sleeve. "Go help her." She whispered. "Never mind me."

"I can't" Shelly cried.

The front door burst open. Footsteps raced across the entranceway. Two men followed by a woman appeared in the archway. The younger man continued into the room; stepping behind Lady Bridget, he placed his open hands behind hers. Gold streams of light joined the silver, intertwining and reinforcing.

The shadows were forced back. Pushed, but not injured, both shadows escaped out the window. The storm continued. but for a moment the house was silent. The candle flickered out and fell to the floor with a clatter. The streams ceased. Only Shelly's candle remained; its light was the only illumination in the room.

"It's over." Lady Bridget collapsed against the man behind her.

"What the hell brought him back?" The elderly man demanded from the darkness.

"Is she ok?" The unknown woman beside him asked. "We need light." She continued. "Shelly drop your shield, its over. And start lighting the candles."

"Yes, Grandmother." Shelly licked her lips. "All is well. All is clear. Time for the shield to disappear." The candle flickered but did not go out. She quickly stood and circled the room, lighting every candle she could find. Within minutes the room was a maze of flickering candle shadows and intertwining circles of candlelight.

The younger man had carried Lady Bridget to the sofa and was kneeling on the floor beside her. His build and general appearance was that of the elderly man, only his hair was longer and age hadn't weighed down on his back. "You called Hon. I'll be the first to admit you were right. He did come back."

Taking one of the candles, the elderly woman quietly slipped from the room.

"Sometimes it would be good to be wrong." She dryly answered. "Shelly, are you and Jane ok?"

"Yes, Mom. Are you?"

Lady Bridget nodded. "He has found a companion and followers." She looked directly at the elderly man. "He's stronger than before." Her voice held the angry edge of an accusation.

"Is she one of them?" The elderly man demanded.

"No." Lady Bridge countered. "One of his intended victims. One of many that didn't need to be."

"Enough!" He growled. "I get your point."

Lady Bridget sat up and unfurled her hand in Jane's direction. "Jane Easton of Coyote Springs. A mutual friend sent her to me for protection. The Dark One went to her home when we drove him out. Within the last few months, he has destroyed the bonds she had with two other friends. It seems he knew one of them from childhood. They reconnected and she has become his companion . . . in everything."

"I saw her face in the first shadow." Jane nervously contributed. "I saw her, but there was so much ugliness. She wasn't like that before. She was a loving, kind woman."

"If she has become like him," the younger man cut her off, "the ugliness is all that's left of her."

"Jane, this is George Jr." Lady Bridget pointed to the younger man. "He is my working partner and confidant."

George Jr. bowed slightly at the waist, his deep brown eyes never leaving Jane's gaze. He smiled, revealing a small chip in his left canine giving it a sharper point. A dark ponytail hung just past his shoulders. His frame was lean, yet strong beneath the tee shirt and well-worn jeans. He was definably a physical person.

Feeling his raw sexual energy, Jane felt herself blush, but refused to look away. If he wanted to read her, fine—two could play at that game. Relaxing into herself, she looked at him with her special gift. The image she received was that of a hawk, flying high over a valley. She knew it was the guardian spirit of this place—protective, loyal, yet totally free. She didn't know if this applied to his spiritual path or to his relationship with Lady Bridget. He was very sexually attractive, but there was no way she would poach on her new friend's turf.

Her hand shifted to the older man. "As you can see by the likeness, this is George Sr."

Jane forced herself to shift her line of sight. She wanted to know more about the Junior. The Senior had left a first impression of being hard and controlling. George Sr. had the same stature; only age had curled the once square shoulders inward, giving him a slight hunch. Gray had invaded the nearly black hair. His eyes still had the same passion and fire, yet his conservative nature banked the heat into glowing embers. He extended his hand. She accepted it. The swollen knuckles made her wince from the pain she knew he must have been feeling. The images flashed. He was a Native American shaman protecting a small band of elders and children from the attacking white man. But he was also a captain of a ship, battling to keep his ship from being claimed by the sea. Yet again, he was a small child being cradled in his mother's arms while he slowly slipped from on life into the next. There was so much more, but the images faded. He was strong. He was weak. He was all this and more. Jane blinked rapidly and released his hand.

"Find what you were looking for?" He asked gently.

Embarrassed, Jane simply nodded.

He stepped back to his original position.

Amused, Lady Bridget smiled. She looked around the room for the older woman.

"Lady Jennifer took a candle. I think she went into the kitchen." Shelly contributed. "Do you want me to go find her?"

Lady Bridget brow furrowed. "Yes, please."

In the hallway, the light of the candle preceded her. Lady Jennifer walked into the room, carrying the candle in one hand and a glass of water in the other. "No need to send out a search party. I just went to get you a glass of water." She offered the glass to Lady Bridget and sat in a chair opposite her. "What did I miss?"

"I was making introductions." She took a drink from the glass. "Lady Jennifer, this is Jane Easton. Jane, Lady Jennifer."

"A pleasure dear." She smiled at Jane. Her hair had turned mostly gray, with only a hint of the auburn it had once had been. Age had not been able to bend her shoulders or her pride. She carried herself with strength and vigor, as if the graying and the wrinkles were an elaborate disguise to hide her true youth. Without waiting for a response she turned to the two Georges. "It seems we didn't take care of the problem properly the first time." Her voice took on an edge. "This time we'll do it our way."

The senior George winced under his wife's blue-green eyes. "I didn't think it was necessary—it was too dangerous. It still is."

"Now it's even more so!" She snapped. "I may be an old woman, but I can still do my part! The day I can't, I'll step down as High Priestess."

Setting the glass on the coffee table, Lady Bridget reached out and clasped the older woman's hand. "I—we all have faith in you. It would be risky no matter who called them."

Lady Jennifer squeezed her hand and continued. "So how far has he gotten?"

"We don't know yet." Lady Bridget answered.

Sitting on the opposite end of the couch, George Jr. casually propped his legs on the coffee table, crossing them at the ankle. "All we know is that he has set up housekeeping in Coyote Springs. He has taken a companion. We don't know how many he has connected to."

"Don't be subtle." His father snapped. "They're his slaves. He owns them body and soul."

"Dad, getting angry won't help." Uncrossing his legs and slipping them off the table, the younger man leaned forward. "But it's true. What every we send after him, he'll just farm out to one of his people. We drove him out by sticking together and cutting him off from his energy source. He won't fall for the same trick twice."

"They were able to follow the love strings attached to Jane's heart." Lady Bridget patted the back her hand and released it. "First order of business is to cut those strings."

"Cheyenne cut her hair to cut the ties."

"It was more complicated than that I'm sure." Lady Jennifer continued. "Who is Cheyenne?"

"Cel—"

"No names!" The older woman cut her off. "To use their names gives them the ability to listen in."

Startled at her own near mistake, Jane quickly nodded. She knew better, yet she nearly cost them dearly. She licked her lips, trying to find the right words. "The woman, who was my friend, found Cheyenne in the desert and raised her as her own daughter."

"So she knew the Dark One?" Shelly asked, sitting on the arm of the sofa next to her mother.

"No. From what I've been told. The Dark One and my friend were separated before she went on her vision quest in the desert. Cheyenne was the first to be aware of the changes in my friend. She warned us. But we-I didn't listen. I thought I was being open minded and fair." Her voice turned bitter. "But instead I was naive and foolish."

"Don't." George Jr. contradicted. "The Dark One can be very persuasive. He lives behind a facade of deceit. He doesn't let anyone see the whole person. Probably not even your friend truly understands what she's gotten herself into."

"Not our problem!" George Sr. crossed his arms across his chest.

"Agreed." Bridget and Jennifer replied in unison.

"So you can't help my friend?"

Lady Bridget shook her head. "The best we can do is stop them from hurting others. But first we have to remove her from your heart, mind, and soul. You need to stop caring. Stop the guilt, the anger—all emotions and thoughts of her must end. She has to become more than a stranger, but someone you actively banish from your universe."

"How can I do that?" Jane was confused. How could she just stop having feelings for someone who was important to her for so long?

"We will help you." Lady Bridget reassured. "But you will have to do the work yourself. You must reject them of your own free will and continually reinforce the rejection." She smiled. "You don't understand now. But you will."

"The darkness can't take over your spirit unless you invite it in or allow it to enter through another."

"Son, you're belaboring the point." The older man chuckled. "Don't know where you get it."

"Not from me." Lady Jennifer quipped back, lightening the mood.

Jane felt out of place within their easy familiarity. They had so much love and history between them. She had that once. But it was gone—stolen by a man who thought only of himself and a woman, who pretended to be a friend.

"Stop!" Lady Bridget snapped. "Don't go there. Anger only helps them."

"I'm trying." Jane knew her voice sounded whiney, but she couldn't stop. "Seeing you together only reminds me of what I lost. How can I not be angry?"

Smiling, George Sr. patted his son's shoulder and walked around the chair to Jane. "I don't want to talk down at you. I can't kneel down so you'll have to come up."

"No you can have my perch." Standing, Lady Bridget stood up and offered him the seat. "I'll find another place to land." She walked around the table and sat on the arm of the sofa next to George Jr.

Arching his eyebrow, he slowly lowered himself to a sitting position next to Jane. His eye level was still above Jane's, but he leaned forward to compensate. "I speak as an equal. One light worker to another. Never to dominate or be dominated by."

His words touched Jane deep inside, to the place where she had always found her truth. He flared a spark of a memory but like a dream quickly fades when awakened too quickly; the memory never materialized but remained waiting in the recesses of her subconscious for another time. He reached out and touched her chin. His fingertips were warm against her skin. The brownness of his eyes drew her into their circle of love.

Suddenly Jane was certain she was safe among them. There was no logic, just a deep instinctive belief.

"Love," he continued, "true love makes us stronger, not weaker. It doesn't dominate or make demands, reasonable or unreasonable. It supports without controlling. When you truly love someone, it transcends time and space. It brings trust and security—faith when none expect or ask for it. These days love is bandied around as if it was nothing. When you truly love someone, it's with your soul not your body. Sex is only one tiny part. It is the sprinkles on top of the frosting of the cake, which is love."

"Dad."

He looked over his shoulder toward the sofa.

George Jr. formed a T with his hands. "Didn't you just accuse me of belaboring the point?"

Again his eyebrow arched, but instead of answering, he turned back to Jane. "The point I'm trying to make—"

"The long, hard way." Jennifer chimed in.

Shelly giggled into her palm.

He grunted and continued. "If you truly love someone, love them enough to let them go. Everyone must face their own mistakes, to either learn from them or repeat them until they do."

"You're talking about karma?" Jane asked.

He nodded. "Yours and theirs. From what little I sensed, someone has been saving your friend for a long time. Not only she is not grateful, but she hasn't learned anything from it. You can't put yourself and everyone around you at risk to save someone who doesn't want to be saved."

"Part of me understands." Jane conceded. "But I still miss the person she was."

"That person doesn't exist any more." Lady Jennifer's voice was soft, but the truth of her words echoed deep within Jane.

"I know." Jane simple replied. "I saw that before I left home. Cheyenne ritually removed her by cutting her hair. I need to do the same."

"If you wish." Lady Bridget injected. "But there are other ways, which will be more effective for you. All you have to do is ask."

Jane licked her lips and squared her shoulders. "I want them removed from my head and heart. I want them gone from my life on every level."

"If I may?" Lady Jennifer shifted in her seat. "I would like to share a page from my past. When I was a young woman, a little older than Shelly, I became involved with a coven. We were uninformed, but talented. There wasn't the knowledge available like there is today. We abused our gifts. We channeled who we wanted, whenever we wanted without thought to the consequences. We woke some of the Old Ones, who were best left alone, and involved them in our tomfoolery. During one of our session I laughingly asked for the wisdom of all ages. Three days later, I was struck by lightning. I survived but nothing was ever the same. I finally saw what we were really doing. We were playing with powers and things that we didn't understand. I tried to explain to them, but they refused to stop. I couldn't do it any more. I walked away. For some reason they thought they needed me. I wanted a clean break. They didn't want to let go. They called. They came to my door; I refuse to answer. What they couldn't accomplish on a physical level, they tried on a spiritual. I was bombarded with their thoughts and demands. A friend kept clearing them from my aura. But because I missed them as friends, they always had a way back in. Finally George sat me down and forced me to make a choice. I chose the path of light. The next time they came calling, I busied my mind. I ran math tables. Mentally sang a "Hundred Bottles of Beer on the Wall", the theme to Gilligan's Island—anything to occupy my mind. One time I took those bottles off the wall and put them back on twice before they went away. The most important part was I refused to participate. I didn't play their game and they had no power over me. One by one they went away. What happened to them, I don't know. It's none of my business." She brought a fingertip to her upper lip and wiped away the moisture. "Which, by the way, became one of my mantras. None of my business. Not interested. Not my problem."

George leaned over and kissed his mother's cheek.

"I can help you." Jennifer continued. "But only if you are serious. You have to make the choice."

"And stick to it." George Sr. interjected.

Jane knew they were right. It was going to take discipline and self-control. The dark finger, which had touched her, whispered she wasn't strong enough. It was her fault. All of it. She should have protected Celeste. She had promised to be there for Celeste always, yet now she was deserting her. She had made a commitment. She couldn't break it. It was her betrayal. It was her fault.

A petite, aged hand slowly arched in front of her face, heat radiating from the open palm. "Dark One be gone. Take with you on all levels the lies and doubt you have sewn. Let them find only barren ground in this child's light. I call upon the spirit of this place called Earth to guide and protect this innocent from the darkness, which tries to impregnate her with its evil. I call upon the deities of the air, fire, water and earth to set up barriers around this child of light so no thought sent to her may influence her decision."

The voice became silent. Jane's mind became clear. As the tide washes the shore clean so the doubt and guilt withdrew from her mind. "I will not be party," she began slowly, "to black magic on any level. I will not share energy with anyone who uses magic to harm others."

"Is that your answer?" The elderly woman asked.

Jane nodded.

"Do you wish our help?"

"Yes."

"Very well. We come to you with open hearts and complete trust."

"And I receive you with an open heart and complete trust." Jane relaxed; finally, she understood what was happening. "What do you want me to do?"

Painfully standing George Sr. retrieved a candle from the mantle and placed it on the table in front of her. "While we prepare, you need to concentrate on the candle. Let nothing outside yourself distract you from the flame. Can you do that?"

"Yes." Her voice reflected the uncertainty she felt. "I will do my best." She amended.

"I appreciate your honesty. If your attention starts to waver, say 'Goddess of light protect me.' And start again. Do you understand?"

Jane nodded and made herself comfortable on the couch. Blinking rapidly, she turned her attention on the flickering flame.

He turned to Lady Bridget. "How are Shelly's studies advancing? Could she hold a field without endangering herself?"

"I can answer for myself." The younger woman hesitated, obviously debating with herself. Slowly she shook her head. "No. This is too important. I don't have the confidence, therefore I would be unreliable."

The elderly man smiled and slowly nodded. "I understand."

"But I will stay here and monitor Jane. If she gets into trouble, I'll support her—and call if I need help."

The flame flickered. Jane allowed herself to fall into the subtle shades of blue at its center. Their voices fell away, becoming muffled echoes which no longer had any importance. She blinked. The image remained in her mind. A fear of the future crept into her mind. She breathed deeply and centered her focus back on the flame. The fear remained, yet she did not acknowledge it. The flame became her whole world. The varying blueness became a protective egg, which she had crawled into like a fetus. Inside she was safe. Her physical boundaries expanded. The flames, like a womb, expanded to accommodate her. In the distance, she heard Celeste voice calling her, begging her to save her.

She sensed more than saw Shelly's arms spreading around behind her. The flames took on a new sheen, as the energy and love she sent reinforced Jane's resolve.

Celeste's voice suddenly stopped and was replace by Shelly's. "Give in to the Divine love." The voice echoed around her, sending ripples through the energy she floated in. She didn't fight the motion. Instead she rode the waves, allowing them to flow through her and around her. The rocking motion calmed her. Before her the candle continued to burn. Beyond it lay nothing.

A moment or an eternity later, Shelly reached down and took her hands. "Come with me."

Shakily she stood. Someone behind her steadied her. Together the three of them slowly walked out of the living room and down the hall. The fuzzy images around her had no importance. They took her into a room. It was dark, except for a circle of candlelight. In the center, Lady Jennifer and Lady Bridget sat on a mattress. They led her between them. She sat; her guides moved back into the shadows.

Lady Jennifer cupped her chin in her hand. "Child, have you seen the Great Mother's womb?"

"No." Jane whispered.

"I'm going to take you there. Lie down and put your head on my lap." Her hand dropped from her chin to her hand, gently pulling her closer.

Jane slowly turned and reclined backward. Her head reclined against the cotton material covering the soft thighs. Her body had begun to relax. Out of the corner of her eye, she saw Lady Bridget stand and walk behind them. She raised her hands. She spoke words, Jane didn't understand. They were lyrical; one passage flowed into another. From somewhere around her feet, George Jr. answered in the same language. It was a well rehearsed duet.

"Breathe in and out. Like waves on the sea." Lady Jennifer whispered. "The waves gently roll in, kiss the shore and then roll back. The sun is warm. There is a breeze. It blows your hair and tickles your nose."

Her nose did tickle. Moving it around satisfied the urge to scratch. The energy around them shimmered. The images changed. She was no longer in Lady Bridget's home, but alone on a beach. The blueness of the sky and the calmness the sea became reality. The cool mud squished between her toes. The next wave rolled to the shore covering her ankles. Her body was bare and tanned. Crouching down, she scooped up the water in her hands, only it wasn't water; it was liquid light. Sparkling and crackling it flowed through her fingers back to its source. Frightened by the raw, unbridled energy, she backed up on to dry land. "Where am I?" She yelled.

"Shush." Lady Jennifer whispered. "I'm here."

"Where? I can't see you." She spun around, scanning the beach and the cliff jutting up from the beach behind her.

"I am with you."

The voice came from the water. It was her mother's voice, yet her own. Jane stopped and slowly turned toward it. A jetty shot up several yards from the shore. It moved closer, changing into the most beautiful woman she had ever seen. Her soft brown hair hung in loose curls just past her shoulders. Her face was heart shaped with two glowing amber eyes. Light and love emitted from the oval orbs. Her skin was smooth, almost translucent. Beneath the teal garb, her body moved with the grace of maturity but without the stress of time. She stepped on the beach. The breeze bellowed out her translucent wings.

"You're an angel?" Jane whispered, unable to understand the contradiction. "But you're Pagan."

"All religions are the same if you don't get stuck in the small stuff." She tittered. "All have incarnated at one time or another in all religions and cultures. Humans are not the only ones who must learn and grow spiritually." She stretched; slowly turning, she allowed the breeze to caress all of her. A smaller set of wings fluttered between her shoulder blades. "It's been so long since I've taken my own form." She stretched her arms out and rolled her shoulders backward. "I don't get a chance very often."

"You have two sets of wings?"

"One bet," she perched her palms on her hip. "Lose one little bet," she pointed backward with her thumb, "and you end up with these. It was terribly rude. But," her arms returned to her sides, "that's not why we're here."

"I have so many questions."

"Now is not the time. We have much work to do."

"Are you the Goddess or an angel?" Jane had to know.

She patiently smiled. "There are many levels and kinds of divine beings. When this planet was created, the Life Carriers and the assistant Life Carriers brought together the proper elements and energies to create life as you know it. Another being became the Mother energy to nurture it and help it grow. Yet another became the Father energy to actively encourage growth and curiosity. Together they keep balance on all realms. But there are others with other responsibilities and talents, each working for a specific goal. Does that answer you question child?"

"I'm sorry, no. It confused me more."

"It will have do for now." She smiled and nodded. "I understand. You can call me Mother or Nasha. Whichever one you are comfortable with." She reached out her hand to Jane. "Take my hand child. Our time grows short."

Nasha's hand had a texture to it like that of a human hand, yet it made Jane's skin tingle. It wasn't unpleasant, yet it was impossible to ignore. They walked away from the water toward the cliff. Jane slowed her pace. The closer they came, more rapidly the energy rose. The tingle in her Jane's hand sent chills up her arm; she didn't want to go any closer. Nasha tightened her grip on Jane's hand and kept her moving forward.

"I don't want to." The fear rose in Jane.

"The darkness, which has touched you, is afraid. Don't allow it to stop you."

At the base of the cliff was a cave. The sea had found the ability to crawl across the short hump of sand. The liquid light washed in and out of the cave with each wave. On each side the banks were dry, as well as the small rocks on which they walked. The walls were cool and irregular to Jane's touch. The glow from the water became the sole source of light

"Quickly. You will be called back soon." Nasha increased her pace to a slow jog. The tunnel opened to a large cavern so filled with light there was no shadows. "This is where each species was conceived and created. All species accomplishments and failures are recorded here." She pointed to a section across the shining pool. "That is human history." Her arm arced ninety degrees to the right. "Over here, is the history and names of the original spirits of each animal and plant. When a new species is created, it has no individuality—no spirit or soul; whichever you prefer. But as it grows and learns, parts separate and develop their own-ness. Eventually it develops a personality and the ability to ascend. When it becomes separate onto itself, it is asked to choose a name. That name is written on the wall."

"Is my name written there?"

Nasha nodded. "To cleanse yourself of the darkness, you must return to who you really are."

Jane licked her lips. "I don't see a path around the water."

"You must walk though it."

Jane hesitated. The voice inside told her no; it would kill her with great pain. Suddenly she recognized the voice not as her own, but that of Celeste. Facing her fear, she walked toward the edge. She looked into the water. There was no bottom, only her reflection staring back up at her. The fear rose. She quashed it by stepping into the pool. The glow covered her ankle. The next step covered her knee. Her skin tingled. Inside her chest, a fire ignited around her heart. It smoldered and ignited. She grabbed her chest, but kept going. In the middle of the pool the water was shoulder level; she stopped. The pain threatened to overwhelm her. It was beyond anything she had ever felt before. Taking a trembling, deep breath, she submerged. The flame flared, reaching out through her blood stream to every cell in her body, leaving only ashes in its wake. Just as suddenly, it died down and out. Jane broke the surface and exhaled; quickly following it was a deep breath; it was deep and easy. She had forgotten how easy breathing could be. She finished crossing the pool and walked on to the opposite shore.

On the wall closest to her were markings in a language she didn't consciously understand. There were no pictures. Just rows and rows of writing. She traced the markings. It gave her a sense of peace, but it wasn't the one she was looking for. They were names. She didn't know how she knew, but she did. Scanning them, she looked for her own. She sidestepped further down. It was there. She knew it. Her hands glided over the carvings. They were cold and empty. Her pinky on her left hand found a warm spot. She reached for it with both hands, gently feeling her way. She remembered all of it. Her awakening. Why she chose her name. Every moment since then flooded back.

Suddenly Nasha was beside Jane. "It's time to go back."

"No." Jane backed away. "I want to remember. I have to know."

"The darkness had been replaced by the light of rebirth." Nasha's tone became firm. "It is now time to return."

The energy snapped and crackled around her. The sound of a thousand bees buzzing made her eyes snap open. She sharply inhaled.

They were all sitting around her, watching and waiting.

"I went through the pool." She spoke the words without knowing the meaning behind them. It seemed to satisfy them. Dizzily Jane sat up. "I don't remember."

"It's ok." Lady Jennifer reassured.

"Are we ready?" George Sr. asked crisply.

"Nothing to do it, but to do it." His son answered flippantly.

"Don't be cheeky." The older man snapped. "This isn't a game!"

"Stop the bickering." Lady Jennifer stood. "Get to your places."

Lady Jennifer and Lady Bridget stood opposite each other; the eldest stood at Jane's head, the youngest at her feet. The eldest George stood to her right; the youngest took his position on her left.

Shelly joined her on the mattress. "We have to stay here. Neither of us are strong enough to participate. We can watch, but don't leave the circle."

"Again?"

"This is very old magic. The words aren't as important as the vibrational level. We're very lucky. Usually they don't allow anyone to watch."

The dizziness was finally clearing from Jane's mind, only to be replaced by questions. Before she could ask, George Sr. began.

"Lords of light." His voice echoed throughout the room. "We call upon the Ancients whose names and numbers have been lost in time. You who reach back into our tribal memories. I call upon you to come and defend us from the darkness, which tries to steal our light."

Their breathing was the only sound Jane could hear. She looked around the sparsely furnished room, but neither saw nor felt anything out of place. The storm outside had quieted. A dim light shone through the window. Jane didn't know if it was the moon or the electricity had been restored to the streetlight.

Shelly took her hand. It was sweaty in her hand. Their eyes met. Embarrassed, she smiled and released her hand; wiping her own on the stomach of her shirt, she again took Jane's hand.

Jane smiled back, grateful for the younger woman's presence.

Lady Bridget began. The match flashed. She lit the candle at her feet. "We call Alecto. Eldest sister of the Bringers of Justice. We call to thee to come and bring justice to us and for us."

George Jr. lit the candle at his feet and straightened. "We call Tisiphone to come and bring justice to us and for us."

A match flared behind Jane. She turned in time to see Lady Jennifer light the candle. She straightened, but continued to look into the flame. "We call Megaera to come and bring justice to us and for us."

George Sr. lit the candle. "Nemesis, come and bring justice to us and for us." He cleared his throat and called out. "Alecto! Tisiphone! Megara! Nemesis! Join us! Alecto, Tisiphone, Megaera, Nemesis—join us"

The others harmonized with his chant. The glass in the window vibrated.

Lady Jennifer's voice rang strong and clear over them as she left the chant and began the incantation. "Let the veils part. May our voices and our intent be carried on the strength of our wills. Bring your wisdom of the ages back to this plane of existence to restore balance and justice."

From deep beneath them a rumble started, rushing upward, increasing in speed and deepening in tone.

It was beyond all Jane had been taught. Fear overwhelmed her. She tightened her grip on Shelly's hand. The younger woman gasped in pain. Jane force herself to release her grasp only to find the younger woman's grip had been as strong as hers.

The floor shook. The wood creaked with the vibration. The air became hot and humid.

Sweat trickled down her face and back. She dared not wipe it away. The sizzle and smell of wood burning filtered through the air. Energy crackled around them. It was too much. Jane closed her eyes. She didn't want to see. She didn't want to know. The odor of rotting flesh seeped up through the floor, permeating the room. Jane gagged.

"You have called. We have come." Four female voices spoke in unison.

"We called you by the old names to face an old enemy." Lady Jennifer continued. "We need your justice and protection."

"Open your eyes. But say nothing, even if they speak to you." Shelly whispered directly into her ear.

Jane opened her eyes, slowly scanning the room. Like ghostly apparitions, they floated about two feet off the candles, which were lit to summon them. The floor around them had darkened and smoldered with their power. With women's head and arms, they had bird like bodies, with wings attached to their backs and talons instead of feet. Their wings did not move. Their feathers shone silver in the candlelight.

Their talons were gold, except for the tips, which were black and red with blood. Only their delicate facial features implied femininity. Jane focused on the one in the eastern corner. Her features were innocent and beautiful. Her eyes were large and oval, only the red pupils belied the image. Its eyes widened. Tilting her head to one side, she returned her interest. It did not move, yet suddenly the face was just inches from Jane's. Jane flinched, but didn't turn away. The red eyes focused on her. Jane trembled. She couldn't control it. Just as rapidly, the face moved back.

"We have watched and waited. Unable to do more until asked." They began. "The Dark One intertwines with souls leading them off their path of knowledge."

"Is he an Old One?" George Jr. asked in amazement.

"No." The foursome replied. "He is a changeling. He and the other have joined together many times. Each time pain and sorrow follow them."

"The other?" Lady Bridget asked. "Who is the other?"

"She was the daughter of the one known as Cernonus and a human woman. The changeling came to her soon after she took her name. He wanted her birthright and all the protection that came from it. Her father warned her. She did not believe." Curling her talons into fists, the one on the left continued alone. Her voice was the deepest of the four. "She was warned by many. She did not listen. She did not learn. Many lifetimes they shared. Each time, she followed him, believing the lies he told her. Together they followed their selfish desires. Each time her birthright protected them both from the justice they had earned."

"No more." The southern one continued. "Her father has forsaken her. Her siblings no longer defend or excuse her. A forever beyond forever mother has turned her back on her."

"All that was needed," the eastern one continued the thought, "was for justice to be requested."

"For the harm done to ourselves and all the others, I ask for justice on all levels, in whatever means necessary to re-balance the scales." Bridget's voice was strong and confident as she looked from one being to the next.

"Granted." They answered in unison. They spread their wings, the tips touching to create a circle. Singing in a language older than humans, they harmonized. The pressure in the room suddenly increased. Immediately all four humans hit the floor. The varying tones of the thuds echoed off the walls. The younger man tried to force his way to his feet, but only succeeded in awkwardly arching his back before he was knocked on his side and pinned down. He continued to struggle. His face flushed from the effort. Sweat beaded and streamed down. Grunting, he again rolled on his stomach and tried to rise. He succeeding in rising a few inches, only to crash back. This time he remained still.

The pressure became heat then freezing cold. Jane's teeth chattered together. Steam formed as she exhaled. Through her hand, she felt Shelly shiver. Her teeth also clicked to-gether. Jane wanted to reach out, but already knew it was im-possible. The cold made breathing painful. She tried to hold her breath. Shivering made it impossible. She felt her body shutting down as the cold sent her body into shock. Unable to do more, Jane closed her eyes and surrendered.

Her eyes fluttered open. She was safely bundled under many layers of quilts and blankets. Sunshine filled the room. It was hard to focus. The light hurt her eyes. Pulling the top comforter closer, she covered her eyes.

"So you're finally awake!" George Jr. stood and crossed the room, pulling back the corner of the blanket. "Wakey, wakey!"

"No." Jane whined. The coolness of the room on her bare skin made her shiver.

"It's been two days. You need to get up." The teasing quickly disappeared from his voice.

"Two days?" Holding the covers to her, she sat up. Dizziness flooded over her, but she forced herself to stay in a sitting position. "What happened?"

"Later. You need to eat . . . and," his eyebrow arched, "bathe."

"Why is it so cold in here?"

"It's eighty-four outside and a little warmer in here."

"I have goose bumps."

"If the hot shower and moving around doesn't change that, we'll get you to a doctor." He walked toward the door. "Do you want me to send Bridget or Shelly up to help?"

Jane shook her head. Lifting the coverings, she realized that she wore nothing else. Smiling, she folded her arm over the top comforter, pinning it to her chest.

"Shy?" He snickered. "A shy witch? Isn't that an oxymoron?"

"Close the door behind you." Jane matched his teasing tone.

Clicking his tongue against his teeth and pointing his right index finger at her, he slowly backed out the door, closing it behind him.

After several attempts, she made it to the bathroom. Standing on quivering legs, she leaned against the sink to help support her weight. She looked at her reflection. The paleness of her skin made the dark circles under her eyes look like shiners. Her hair was greasy. Her teeth felt an inch thick. Moving around did help warm her, but it also awakened other bodily functions. She relieved herself and flushed. Waiting for the toilet to cycle, she picked up her brushed and started working through the tangles. Two days? She didn't remember dreaming, nor did she remember much beyond the candles being lit. She had so many questions, but they would wait. Turning the handles, she tested the water and compensated until she found a comfortable temperature. Switching the water from the spout to the shower, she stepped inside, pulling back the flowered curtain.

The water massaged her head and back. It felt wonderful! For a few moments, she just let the hot water massage the kinks out of her shoulders. Stepping back, she closed her eyes and let it run down from her head to her toes. The muscles in her legs ceased to tremble, becoming re-accustomed to her weight. Becoming drenched, her hair flattened. She picked up the shampoo and poured some in her palm. Massaging it into her hair, she gently scratched her scalp. The lather foamed up; some ran down her check, off her chin on to her chest, only to be washed away. Closing her eyes, she rinsed. Steam started to fill the shower, seeping around the curtain. Jane reached for the conditioner. Filling her palm, she returned the bottle to the soap shelf and mixed the conditioner in her hair. Breathing in the steam, she realized for the first time she felt totally different—lighter and stronger than she had in a long time. Reaching for the soap, she held it under the stream. The combination of the heat and water release the lavender scent. Bringing the bar to her nose, she inhaled the relaxing fragrance. Shelly had a natural instinct when it came to her soap craft. Not to little scent, yet not so strong that it overwhelmed the senses. Lathering the bar between her palms, she washed. Something radically had changed. Even the texture of her skin felt different to her own touch.

"You plan to empty my water heater." Lady Bridget quipped from the other side of the curtain.

Embarrassed, Jane peaked around the edge. "Sorry."

Lady Bridget stood in the archway with a steaming cup of something in her hand. "No problem."

Ducking back behind the curtain, Jane quickly rinsed and turned off the water. Pulling back the plastic, she accepted the towel Lady Bridget offered and wrapped it around her head. The second towel she dried off with and stepped on to the bath rug. "Sorry about the water."

"Don't worry about it." She set the steaming mug on the stacked shelves over the toilet. "My own blend of teas. It'll help with the chills."

"Thanks." Jane wrapped the damp towel around her, tucking the top end down between her breasts. "The shower and moving around warmed me." Reaching for her moisturize, she opened the jar and applied a dab to her forehead. "I feel different."

"Different? A good different or a bad different?"

"Good." Jane continued to spread the white lotion on her face. "I can't describe it. Everything feels different. Like new."

She chuckled. "Because you have been to the Great Mother's womb. You're again a child fresh born. All the negativity which has touched you from birth to two days ago is now gone. No one has ties to you or on you. You can now say your friend's name out loud. She no longer has any connection to you, nor will she again. It's like you have never met her."

For a moment, Jane couldn't remember who she was talking about. Then the name returned, but no image appeared with it. "Her name is Celeste. I can't remember what she looks like."

Lady Bridget nodded. "There will be many of the specifics you won't remember."

"Then how can I help?"

"You'll remember what is important." She shrugged. "The rest . . . Shelly is making you brunch."

"What about Cheyenne? I can remember her."

"We'll talk about it downstairs. You haven't eaten in a while."

"Funny. I don't feel hungry."

"Not hungry or did Georgie tell you about my daughter's cooking?"

"Georgie?"

"Georgie, that's his nickname. And when he is really annoying, I sing George of the Jungle." Lady Bridget turned and walked back into the bedroom.

Jane took her toothbrush out of the travel case and rinsed it. Adding the toothpaste she followed as far as the archway. "Are the two of you close?" Brushing her teeth, she watched and listened, not knowing why her answer was important.

"We're working partners if that's what you're asking." She stripped the bedding off and dumped into a pile. For a moment, her movements seemed awkward. "If you're asking if there is more. Sometimes yes. Sometimes no. I don't own him and he don't own me."

Jane leaned in, spitting into the sink and rinsing the brush. Leaning back into view, she watch Bridget take the pillow cases off and toss them on the pile; the brush and the foam, prevented Jane from speaking.

She stopped and turned toward Jane. "We have honesty, respect and love between us. No matter what else happens, that will never change."

Jane nodded and returned to the sink to finish brushing her teeth. She had mixed feelings about her answers. She didn't know why.

"We went through your suitcases. Ritually washed all you clothes, except the dress that needed to be dry-cleaned. It was sent to the cleaners and smudged with cedar and sage along with the rest of your things. Shelly and Georgie washed and did a cleansing of the pick-up yesterday. He found an icky thingy attached. But it's been taken care of."

Jane wasn't sure she was comfortable with them invading her privacy. "What kind of icky thingy?"

"I don't know what they are really called. It looks like a spindly ten-legged spider. They are attached to things so they can be traced. Just like a spider spins a web from its body's secretions, this thing leaves a trail its creator can follow. However, more often than not it eventually attacks the person it's following and kills them."

"I've never heard of such a thing."

"It was still very young and easy to kill. We want to give you a clean start all the way around." Lady Bridget answered her unspoken question.

Looking in the mirror, the color had returned to her cheeks and the circles had almost disappeared. Her body felt clean and light, yet there was a loneliness staring back in her eyes.

"What's the matter?" Lady Bridget stepped into the doorway.

"I just suddenly felt all alone."

Reaching across the distance between them, she rubbed Jane's shoulder. "That will change. Only now you are filled with the love of the Goddess herself."

The warmth on her shoulder comforted her. "Maybe Cheyenne and I can rebuild our friendship."

"Her and others." Lady Bridget smiled. "Get dressed."

Bobbing her head in a quick nod, Jane walked to her suitcase. Pulling the tee shirt and cutoffs out, she quickly put them on. Flipping the one towel over her shoulder and rubbing her hair with the other, she walked back to the bathroom. She hung the towels and quickly brushed out her hair. The ends still dripped, but it didn't matter. Walking quickly, she caught up with Lady Bridget at the top of the stairs. Together they walked down.

Halfway to the downstairs, the thought of food awakened her appetite. Her stomach growled.

In the kitchen, Shelly stirred the contents of something with a wooden spoon. She wore a light sundress and her hair in pigtails. Outside, Georgie and his parents sat in plastic chairs around a matching table. The large umbrella kept the late morning sun off them.

Jane followed Lady Bridget into the room. "Looks good."

"Thanks." Shelly poured pasta into the strainer. "I'm slowly learning."

"Georgie teases her that everything she cooks tastes like soap."

"Yes, but she makes very good soap." Jane slipped into a chair by the table. "What is it?"

"Vegetable pasta with baby shrimp." She poured the contents of the strainer into a larger bowl. Steam rose. "I use the steam to defrost the veggies. Normally, I'd use fresh, but

Lady Jennifer would prefer George didn't have fresh vegetable any more."

"It's an age thing." Lady Bridget explained, walking to the refrigerator and opening the door. "Would you like some lemonade?"

"The tea!" Jane suddenly remembered the cup. "I forgot it."

"Don't worry about it. Shelly?"

"Yes, please Mom." She had poured a light yellow mixture on top of the pasta and was mixing it in. "Could you also pull out the fruit dish? It's on the second shelf."

"No problem." She finished filling the third glass and returned the pitcher to the frig. She pulled out the large fruit filled glass bowl and set it on the counter. Before drinking from her glass, she put one the counter near Shelly and the other in front of Jane. "Did we decide if we're eating in or out?"

"Out. The muffins are already outside. We didn't know how much time Jane would need." Finishing, Shelly stuck the large spoon in the top of the dish. "Done."

Pulling another serving spoon out of the drawer, Lady Bridget slipped it under the plastic wrap and picked up the bowl. "I've got the fruit."

"I'll take the pasta."

"What do you want me to carry?"

"Get real. You can barely carry yourself!"

"Mom! That wasn't nice."

"But accurate." Jane conceded. She still felt a little wobbly. "Let me get the door."

"See." Bridget nodded in Jane's direction as she walked to the back door.

"I know." Shelly frowned disapprovingly at her mother. "It still wasn't nice."

Continuing their exchange, they walked passed Jane out the door. She followed a few paces behind. Despite the tone in their voices, the love between them was more than a bond of parent to child; it was one of respect between individuals. They rounded the corner of the house.

"Look the dead girl walking!" Georgie quipped.

"Like there are any girls around!" Lady Bridget set the bowl on the table.

"Ok. Fine. Dead woman walking. Give me food. I didn't have breakfast."

"You're such a cliché!" She teased.

"Maybe so," he reached for the bowl, "but I'm still cute."

"If you say so dear." Stifling her smile, Lady Jennifer patted the empty seat beside her. "Jane, come sit next to me. I'll protect you from the bad humor that is surely to follow." The older woman seemed almost sickly; whereas last night she was an ageless woman of power, today she seemed small and old.

"Are you implying I'm not cute?"

"I'm your mother dear. I have to think you're cute. It's in the rulebook."

"Shelly, you think I'm cute."

Shelly sat in an empty chair. "Keep me out of it."

George Sr. grunted. "Don't ask me. I don't even know you."

"Jane—Jane, you're a woman of the world."

"Don't even go there." Lady Bridget sat on the last empty chair. "She's had enough trauma."

"I'm crushed! I'm shattered! I'm totally traumatized!"

"You're overacting!" his mother teased back.

"Weren't you so starving you couldn't wait?" Lady Bridget cut in. "So eat already!"

He leaned towards her and puckered. "You can stop my mouth with a kiss."

She leaned in towards him. "Give up brushing your teeth again?"

He flicked his tongue out at her.

"Obviously he takes after Jennifer's family." George Sr. reached for the fruit bowl.

"More likely a throw back from one of you ancestors!" The older woman quipped back.

Uncomfortable, Jane sat back in the chair, trying to be invisible. On most occasions she would have joined in their easy humor, only today it only made her feel more alone. Her eyes filled with tears. Discreetly reaching up, she freed her hair from behind her ear, allowing it to cover one side of her face. She looked towards the fairy gardens on the other side of the yard. She didn't want them to see her tears. A small, brown bird landed on one of the many the foxglove. It chirped and continued to the ground, disappearing into the lush foliage. It reminded her of their front yard. Cheyenne and Selene had designed and created a maze of walkways and garden beds where one could walk to think or just enjoy the peacefulness of the beauty. Selene had been the primary caretaker. After she left, Cheyenne tried to maintain it, but there was only so much she could do.

"Jane?" Her hand trembling, Lady Jennifer reached out and tucked her hair back behind her ear. "They didn't mean—they just wanted—I don't know."

Jane brushed away the tear and looked back at them. "You've been so very kind. It's just me."

"I understand." Lady Bridget scooped some of the pasta salad on her plate and passed the bowl on. "We were going to wait until after lunch. But it may be best just to start."

Lady Jennifer took the bowl and put portions both on her plate and Jane's. "But only if you agree to eat." She stated firmly. "Your spirit has been restored. Now it is time to do the same for your body."

Jane slowly nodded and scooted her chair closer to the table. "I can listen and eat at the same time." She picked up the fork. "So what's happened in the last two days?"

Georgie opened his mouth but quickly closed it and picked up his fork.

"It's been quiet around here." Lady Jennifer began. "Both weather and energy wise. We've all been resting and researching."

"I also took the liberty of making a call," Lady Bridget began. "To Celeste's sister, Beverly. I found her number in your pick-up. I explained who I was and what had been happening."

Jane stopped chewing, waiting for her to finish.

"What I told her upset her a great deal. She had sensed something was wrong." She stopped and took a drink of her lemonade before continuing. "She told me a bit of their history. Their Grandmother was one of the keepers of the Old Wisdom. She once banished Celeste because of Dominic. She didn't tell me why. I wasn't comfortable asking. But she was able to talk their Grandmother back into again teaching her the old ways along with her sisters and cousins. Eventually Celeste was given one of the Sacred Feathers and was initiated into outer Elder Circle. She wouldn't say how, but Celeste again shamed herself." Lady Bridget shook her head.

"She did say it was enough to exclude her from ever reaching the inner circle."

"So she has a history of working with the dark energies." The older man pushed around the food on his plate. "So how bad is she?"

"The woman I first met and called friend," Jane began slowly, "was a kind and loving person. She was generous and kind. In all the years I knew her she never deliberately hurt anyone."

"But she changed when?" Shelly asked.

"Everything was going so well. The farm was becoming prosperous." Jane bit her lip. "It might be my fault. He found us by the website I created."

"Dominic?" Shelly picked up her glass, but didn't drink. "He seems to be the trigger."

"Agreed," her mother interjected.

"After Dominic, things started happening on the farm. People got sick. Animals went missing. When or if we found them, they were mutilated. Cheyenne accused Dominic. But Celeste defended him. Without proof, the rest of us did nothing." Again guilt rose in Jane and she felt her cheeks becoming warm. "I thought I was being objective."

Lady Jennifer took her hand within her own. "What changed your mind?"

"I caught him going through Cheyenne's business papers. He tried to claim the farm as his own." Jane took a deep breath. "The truth is the farm and everything on it belongs to Cheyenne. It is her hard work that pays the mortgage and gets the work done. She is and always will be the heart. Celeste and I . . ." Her voice trailed off.

"Okay. We can't do anything from here." Lady Bridget continued without waiting for anyone else. "Bev and her family are going to meet us in Coyote Springs. Her exact words were-'we take care of our own.' We have to be there. I don't know why. But last night in meditation I was told to prepare for the trip."

"All of us? Or just you?" Georgie reached across the table and took her hand.

Bridget smiled, but gently freed her hand. "Jane, Shelly and I will be the only ones going."

"Why am I excluded?" The older woman demanded. "I am still quite capable—"

"No, you're not." Bridget firmly cut her off. "If we could have dealt with him from a distance like before you could protect yourself. On the spiritual plane there aren't many stronger."

"You need me to represent the crone!"

"Jennifer, please!" Lady Bridget pleaded. "When push comes to shove, you are no longer physically capable of defending yourself. If we had to fight, you can't. It's a simple fact."

"What about me?" Georgie snapped. "I am quite capable of defend myself! And I'm very knowledgeable!"

Bridget stared at him.

Jumping to his feet, he knocked the chair backward and on to the ground. "A man can handle the energy!" Clenching and unclenching his fists, he stared back, unwilling to back down.

Not a word was said. Jane felt the air thicken. This was an old argument. She had no place in it, even if she did understand what it was about. In most covens, there was a balance of power between the feminine and masculine. Only in Dianic covens was the male energy excluded. From every

271

indication, they weren't women's only coven. Yet, the division was clearly down the gender lines.

Angrily, he turned. Kicking the chair out of his way, he stomped down the path, disappearing into the woods beyond the gardens.

Slowly, George stood, dropping his fork on his plate with a clatter. He pushed back the chair. "Since I am not needed, Jen, call when you want to come home."

"Bridget?" The older woman looked up at the younger. "We'll need to talk when you get back." She looked up at her husband. "I won't be staying. Take me home."

Slowly Bridget nodded. "George. I'm sorry."

"If we had done it right the first time . . ." He cut himself off, leaving the unfinished sentence hanging in the air. He extended his hand to his wife. She stood and joined him beside the table, looping her arm through his.

Shelly looked from her mother to the departing older couple. "Mother, go after them."

They walked through the garden gate and disappeared around the house. Without moving, Lady Bridget watched them leave. Shelly stood. Her mother grabbed her arm before she could leave the table. "Don't. It'll only make it worse. It was over the moment George made the decision for all of us. We just didn't know it until now."

"But, I love them."

"So do I." She encircled her arms around her daughter, pulling her close. "That's why it hurts so much."

"I don't understand." Jane looked from one to the other.

"You wouldn't." Lady Bridget kissed her daughter on the forehead and wiped away her tears. "Sweet one. Go inside and finish your lunch. I need to talk to Jane."

Slightly nodding, she picked up her nearly full plate and returned inside.

Sighing, Bridget sat back down and reluctantly starting eating. After a few mouthfuls, she returned her attention to Jane. "If we had taken care of the problem, you wouldn't have had to deal with him at all. He would have been stopped here. It would have been easier and safer. But George refused."

"Why?"

"He wouldn't let Jennifer be a participant with the Triple Goddess calling. At the best of times, it's very dangerous. But it is also very effective."

Jane blankly stared at her.

"It's a ritual that connects the different realms. If you are not strong enough or well trained, it shorts out the body's electrical—nervous system. Jennifer was willing. We didn't have to be in his presence to make it work so there was no physical threat." Lady Bridget shrugged. "George refused to allow her. Without the pure Goddess energy to give a clear pathway the best we could do was to chase him away. The ritual we did was mixed and balanced. Shelly, Jennifer and I were the maiden, mother, crone. Their grandson, Josh, Georgie and George are our youth, father, and elder. We all participated in order to complete the circuit. With the energy split six ways, no one was in danger. But is was also incapable of stopping him."

"Couldn't you do that now?

Bridget shook her head. "They are too strong. The only possibility is to create the Triple Goddess link through which the Old Ones may physically manifest in our dimension. But this time we will have to be physically near him for them to manifest. Without someone there to monitor the link, he could break it and kill us by remote by creating an energy feedback. I will be the crone. Shelly will still be the maiden. But you dear one, will be the mother."

"I don't know how." Jane began to panic. "I've never—"

"I know." She slowly shook her head. "But we don't have any other choice." Pushing Jane's plate closer to the edge of the table, she picked up the fork and held the handle out to Jane. "Eat. Afterwards class starts. We have about two weeks." Before she could ask, Bridget answered her question. "He is his most powerful during full moon. It's also when he is the most active. I think that is when he will attack your friend."

"But the moon is the Goddess's energy?"

"True. But he is an energy vampire. There is more energy available for him to feed off of." Bridget shook her head. "We may be stronger, but so will he. Only he'll have his followers to supply him while we will only have ourselves."

"If he was so strong before that you could barely deal with him." Jane took the fork. "Celeste could make him unbeatable?" She looked at her plate. She didn't feel hungry, but eating was necessary. She couldn't allow herself to become physically worn down.

"I know, but we have to try." Picking up her plate, she stood. "When you're done, come get me."

The door closed behind her and suddenly she was alone in the yard. Quickly eating, she found herself reluctant to go back in. Instead she wandered around the yard, taking time to smell the flowers and to touch the ornaments. She needed time to think. She found the spinning metal wind thingy; she didn't know what else to call it. The odd shape seemed to be made of copper. Hanging from a lower branch of the weeping willow, it twisted and turned at the whims of the breeze.

Its sheen reflected the sunlight around the yard. She reached out and spun it. It cast shadows and light on her face. It all didn't have to happen. They could still be happy together. If only . . . but only . . .

"It's beautiful."

Startled, Jane snapped around. "I thought you left in a huff."

Georgie walked up beside her. "I did." He stepped closer. "But I came back."

"Why?" She stepped around him and continued down the path to the fountain.

"You don't have to do it." He followed. "There are other ways."

Ignoring him, she continued to walk.

Reaching out, he spun her around. "You don't know what's involved. It's very dangerous!"

Brushing off his hand, she glared up at him. "Lady Bridget told me he could have been stopped here. But your father refused. Why?"

He didn't look away. "He had his reasons."

"Like what? Was he afraid?"

His eyes leveled on her and she flinched. "Yes, he was afraid. Afraid it would kill my mother! She isn't as strong as she pretends. Her heart—" He took a deep breath. "There are other ways of taking care of problems."

"But you didn't take care of the problem. You dumped it in our laps and because of it a good woman—"

"Made her own decision!" he growled back. "It isn't our fault."

It was true. Celeste made her decision and she alone would reap the results. Reluctantly she nodded. "Yes, but how many others have been harmed who didn't need to be because your family couldn't be honest?"

This time he flinched.

"What's the old saying—all evil needs to succeed is for good people to do nothing."

"We did something!"

"Yes, I guess you did." Spinning on her toes, she walked back into the house, slamming the door behind her.

CHAPTER SIXTEEN

Cheyenne stared out the window at the horses grazing in the field. The sight would have normally comforted her, but not today. She didn't think there was anything that could relax the nervous fluttering in her stomach. The bank fraud division at the bank claimed there was nothing they could do to return the household account. Celeste's name was on it; she was legally entitled to withdraw funds. As for the forged checks, paperwork had been filed. But it could take up to ninety days for the money to be returned. During that time the bank would still expect payments on the loan and the mortgage on time and in full. She didn't know where the money was going to come from. After all the betrayals and lies, she was quickly running out of tears and faith.

The New Moon had come and gone. No one felt like celebrating. Instead Cheyenne had done a private healing ritual. It was little more than a white candle and a prayer. But it was all she had the spirit for.

For a couple of weeks, she had heard rumors about Celeste and Dominic. But the rumor mill had been silent for days. She prayed they had left town. They hadn't. They wouldn't until they had taken revenge. Cheyenne knew she was at the top of their list. How many more, she had no way of knowing.

Half turning, she leaned against the window frame. The household accounts were in worse shape than she thought.

The financial arrangements had always been relaxed. But in the past couple of months, Margaret and her daughter were the only ones who actually still paid rent. Loans had been given to Jerry and Dominic from money set aside for the property taxes. So far none had been paid back. It was all going to change. How many would acknowledge their obligations and pay their debts or would she have to take them to court? Either way, with the exception of Margaret, they were all being evicted. April took care of the paperwork. It was all legal and final except for the notifications. That would happen in a matter of minutes.

April had listed the cabins, including her own, in the paper. Two of the empty cabins had already been rented. Both of the new tenants were women. One was a detective; Raven gave her a glowing recommendation. Carmen was the other. Her own move back into the main house would be permanent. It was either that or pay herself rent and that was just plain silly. It was her house. She should have never moved out in the first place. But she mistakenly tried to make peace; they took advantage. It was a hard lesson to learn. There was still much to be done. Her furniture and things needed to be moved. She had just moved the bare necessities. The fence had to be put back up around the backyard for the guys. They were very good, but she wasn't comfortable allowing them free run.

Much of the past weeks had been taken up with gathering Celeste's belongings. With Raven's help, she had gone from room to room—closet to closet—drawer to drawer sorting out and removing everything that belonged to Celeste. For the things they bought jointly, the decision was made by who used it the most. As for the appliances, they stayed. After all the household money she stole, it was little enough payment. Everything had been packed up and deposited in a rental space. She had made an agreement with the management to pay two months rent; after which, they should consider the property abandoned and take whatever steps they needed to. The police were given the combination. If Celeste and Dominic wanted their property, that is where they would have to go. Last night the four of them did cleansing rituals on Dominic's cabin and the main house.

There was a knock on the door, quickly followed by Lilith poking her head in. "Everybody's here."

"Thanks. I'll be right there. Is April ready?"

"She's more than ready."

"Good." Cheyenne combed back her hair and straightened her shoulders. "Let's go."

Together they walked down the hall and into the living room. April waited for them in the hallway just outside the living room. She smiled and held up the folder. With Cheyenne leading they walked across the threshold. Just inside, they stopped. Slowly Cheyenne scanned the room.

Sitting together like a nineteenth century portrait, Margaret and her daughter Kim sat on the settee. Wisps of gray had invaded the short brown curls of the older woman, but her face remained as smooth as her teenage daughter's. The twinkle in her gray-green eyes spoke her approval. Seeing Cheyenne, Kim tried to stand, but her mother restrained her; leaning over, she whispered into her ear. Kim nodded and sat back.

On the left, Karen stood, her arms folded over the ample bosom, which had nursed all five of her children. She briefly glared at Cheyenne, before diverting her gaze back out the window.

To the right, Janet smugly sat in the overstuffed chair that matched the settee. David stood behind her. She had wanted to move since David asked her to marry him. He had refused to move or change his religion. Many nights, their arguing had broken the peace of the farm. She had openly told many that if she could get him away from the evil influences, she would be able to convert him back to the one true God.

Well, Cheyenne thought, *she was finally going to get the chance to make good on the boast.*

His arm perched on the mantle; Jerry stood alone by the fireplace. His fingers impatiently tapped against the wood. Sweat matted down the hair on his chest and trickled down to dampen his too small tank top. Shifting his weight, he swayed a bit before using the mantel to steady himself.

Cheyenne wondered how much he had to drink already. Sadly she shook her head; he never used to be so self-destructive. But he wasn't her responsibility; none of them were. She cleared her throat and begun. "You're all aware of the changes. Jane has gone on a vision quest. She will be back. Celeste and Dominic are gone and are not welcome back for any reason."

"Controlling bitch," Jerry grumbled. "It's your fault."

"Think what you like." Cheyenne forced her voice to remain level. "It doesn't matter. Celeste made her decision. And so have I." Walking around the room, she met each one's gaze. "There are going to many changes. Most of you won't like them."

"We have leases," Jerry snapped.

"Which all but Lady Margaret and her daughter have broken," April cut in.

"Who are you and why do I care," Jerry answered in kind.

"She is my new House Manager." Cheyenne stopped in front of him. "She has been going over the books. It seems you haven't found it necessary to pay rent for two months."

"I paid Celeste . . . in cash."

"There's no record of it." April walked further into the room. "Not anywhere."

"I trusted her."

"Your mistake," Cheyenne continued, stopping in the middle of the room. "And except for Lady Margaret and her daughter, none of you have put in the required hours on the farm."

"I have five children!" Karen snapped. "I don't have time."

Cheyenne looked over her shoulder at the women by the window. "You are also close to two months behind."

"It's not my fault! Celeste knows! He hasn't been sending support checks!"

"Not our problem," Lilith entered the conversation. "You shouldn't have had so my kids if you couldn't support them. And my name is Lilith."

"And very good friend." Cheyenne added. "What Celeste did or didn't do is over. This has always been my property. I'm taking back control. Starting with getting rid of the deadweight." She reached out in April's direction; April deposited the folder in her waiting hand. "Jerry, Karen, and it'll make you happy Nancy—David," she pulled out three sheets of paper, "are now officially notified of your eviction."

David beat on the back of the chair with his fist. "We're only two weeks late. I have the canceled checks to prove it."

"Yes, but the last time you helped me on the farm was last fall when I badgered you. And even then it lasted one week."

"That clause isn't legal!"

"It's very legal and binding." Lilith countered. "You each have a week."

"A week!" Karen screeched.

"Technically, I only had to give you five days." Cheyenne countered. "And I've seen the condition of your cabin. Don't expect a deposit back."

"You can't do this! You can't! It's not my fault!" Karen's voice raised an octave.

"Having five kids isn't your fault—why?" Lilith pivoted to confront her. "Have you made any attempt to get a job? Any at all?"

"My children need me—"

"They need you to set a good example of a woman supporting herself."

Steadying himself against the mantle, Jerry rose to his full height. "You're just taking revenge on Celeste and Dominic's friends! It has nothing to do with the rents."

Anger and self-righteousness rose in Cheyenne. "They emptied the household accounts and forged checks to empty mine. If it wasn't for my good credit at the bank, the household couldn't buy a candy bar and a soda. So don't you defend those thieves to me! Summer taxes are coming due. I have a payroll to meet. Suppliers, utilities, and a mortgage to pay. With what? I had to take out a loan to cover expenses until the bank reimburses the money they stole from Dragon Herbs. I'm going to have to sue to get the rest back!"

"Until then," April stepped closer to Cheyenne, "the cabins will have to support the mortgage. Which means the rents will be increased to reflect the current market and the tenants will be expected to pay rent on time, in full."

Walking around the room, Cheyenne handed out the eviction notices to all but the women on the settee.

"What about them?" Jerry pointed at Lady Margaret and Kim.

Slowly Lady Margaret stood. "I've never been late and we've always done more than our share of work around here."

"You have only one child and she's grown." Karen countered.

"Most of the women I help through the birthing process have more than one child and a full-time job. You do what you have to do."

"I can't." Karen whined.

"Then you don't deserve the children. Not providing a safe home, food, clothing and emotional support is child abuse." Lady Margaret countered. "And before you blame the father—I'd like to point out you chose him."

"Wait a minute!' Janet stood up. "That's cruel!"

"But the truth!" Lady Margaret pivoted to face her. "I've known them both for over ten years. Billy never could hold a job and he's had a problem with alcohol since he was a teenager." She pointed at Karen. "And she knew it. Yet, she married him anyway."

"He said he'd change. He promised."

"Like that was worth a pile of beans on an iceberg." Lady Margaret snipped back.

"I don't know what that means." Karen marched across the room. "I'm just a common, ignorant woman. I'm not educated like you."

"Only because you choose to be." Lady Margaret faced off with the younger woman. "You chose to get pregnant and quit high school—and never go back."

"Enough!" Cheyenne intercede. "It doesn't matter."

"Cheyenne." Lady Margaret returned her attention to Cheyenne. "Just let me know what the new rent is."

Gratefully Cheyenne nodded.

Standing, Kim quickly hugged Cheyenne. "I'll do what I can to help out."

"Thanks, Kim. I appreciate it. Just don't neglect your studies."

"Like mom would let that happen." She winked at her mother.

Lady Margaret stood. "You don't need us here for this?"

"No." April interceded.

"Good." Lady Margaret cut her off. "We have things to do. Elsewhere." She strolled out of the room, quickly followed by Kim.

David looked over the notice. "We need at least to the end of the month to find a place."

"No, we can be out in a couple of days." Janet reached out and took his arm. "Mom and Dad still have the studio over the garage. They built it just for us, remember."

"It's not going to happen." He detangled her fingers from his arm. "I won't put myself in that position. You can move back with Mommy and Daddy Christian if you want. But if necessary I'll move in with my sister and her girlfriend until I can find a place."

Janet stepped back. "Fine. We'll talk about it at home." Turning on her heels, she walked out of the room, slamming the front door behind her.

"That was interesting." Lilith smiled. "Just so you know, tomorrow I'm filing for the unpaid rent in small claims court."

"I told you I paid!" Jerry balled up the sheet of paper and threw it at Cheyenne. "I don't owe you anything! And I'm not leaving!"

"You've been legally served. You don't have a choice." Lilith recovered the wad and pulled the edges, ripping it in her attempt to unfurl it. She again offered it to him. "It's the only notice you'll get.'

His hands clenched into fists, his knuckles turning white. "Bitch!'

"You say that like it's a bad thing." Lilith purred.

His fist snapped forward, hitting Lilith in the stomach; she flew backward, sprawling across the couch. April leaped at him, pushing him backward a few feet; his mass and the little room she had to work kept her from pushing him into the wall. He swung again, but found only vacant air. Frustrated he tried to back fist the smaller woman. She dodged and countered with a kick to the chest, knocking the air from him.

"Is this how you plan to run things now?" David demanded.

"I didn't want this!" Cheyenne snapped back. "I didn't cause it. But I'm the one who has to pickup the pieces!"

"Forget about the eviction. We'll be out of here today!" He headed for the door, but stopped at the archway. He half turned back toward Cheyenne, his finger pointing at her. "For the record. It's your fault. All of it!"

"I spoke the truth." Cheyenne growled, her temper threatening to burst loose. "No matter how many people agree to a lie, it's still a lie!"

"Says you!" Jerry shouted, his breath still coming hard. "You wanted to control everything. The stock. The planting. Every ritual had to be your way. You never listen to anyone. Celeste and Jane stuck up for you. The rest of us had to bite our tongues. Only Dominic didn't. He wouldn't shut up. That's why you hated him."

"I hated him for what he did and what he caused to happen!"

"He challenged your almighty authority over everyone," David snapped.

"If that's what you think," Cheyenne paused to catch her breath, "then you are both idiots!"

"I don't have to take this!" David stormed out the front door, leaving it to swing open behind him.

"This isn't over," Jerry growled. "You'll pay for it, I promise you." He marched toward the door.

"Jerry."

He paused at the archway.

"Tell Celeste and Dominic their things have been moved to storage. The police have all the information."

Without looking back, he continued out the front door, taking extra effort to slam it behind him.

"That went well." The sarcasm dripped from April's voice. "Least they didn't knock it off the hinges."

"What about me? Karen demanded, her voice raising in pitch. "We don't have anywhere else to go. We can't afford to move."

"Not our problem," April interceded.

"It is your fault!" She lunged at Cheyenne, pushing her backward. "Why couldn't you just keep quiet! What Dominic and Celeste did was none of your business!"

Angrily April grabbed Karen's arm and twisted it behind her back. "We've had enough. Call social services or the local charities." She bullied her out of the room and out the front door, making a point to quietly close it behind her. With great flourish, she locked it. Wiping her hands together, she walked back into the room. "That is that."

Cheyenne walked to the fireplace. "I have a really bad feeling."

"So do I." Lilith whined, rubbing her stomach.

April leaned over the back of the sofa. "See what happens when you let your guard down."

"Kiss my ass." Lilith matched April's tone.

"Grin and bare it."

"You'd die if I did."

"Try it and find out."

Suddenly Cheyenne felt old and empty. She was tired of the constant battles and bickering. She didn't even have the energy to produce tears. For many years, she thought most of these people were her friends. She had loved them as family. *How could she have been so wrong about them? They turned on her so quickly. Did she ever know them?* "They were good people." She whispered to no one in particular, but she needed to hear the words even if they weren't true.

"Fine nest of life suckers." April countered. "I didn't start to change until I was forced to see what I'd become. It didn't mean I liked it in the beginning. Matter of fact, for a long time I hated the woman who held up the mirror. But it wasn't her. It was me I hated."

"But you learned from it." Lilith cut in.

"Yes. But it took a long time." April licked her lips. "I'd be embarrassed to tell you how long."

"It doesn't matter." Lilith continued as she took April's hand in her own. "You learned and grew as a person. It's time to let it go."

Sadly smiling, April looked from Lilith to Cheyenne. "Thank you allowing me to even up some of my karma . . . for letting me take care of you."

"I do seem to need a lot of it." Joining them at the couch, Cheyenne sat down next to Lilith. "I'm so tired. But I'm afraid to blink."

With her free hand, Lilith reached out and took Cheyenne's, creating a link between all three women. "We're here. You can drop your guard a little. We'll take up the slack."

"It's better for us to do it." April picked up the thought. "We're not emotionally involved. We can be more objective."

"I found the old fencing in the barn," Lilith continued. "All the pieces are there. We just need to dig the holes. Go get your dogs. They shouldn't be spending the days by themselves. It's too dangerous for them to be alone. And you need them here. We'll take my car. It's bigger and we can bring some more of your stuff back."

"The sooner you clear it out, the faster I can show it and rent it." Releasing Lilith's hand, April stood. "Detective Sammy and her cats are moving into the two bedroom this afternoon. Do you know her?"

Cheyenne shook her head. "I've heard the name. But I don't have a face to go with it. I refused to get involved with that whole mess."

"Good for you." April walked to the door. "Let's all keep that sensible attitude and maybe our sanity will survive all this." She disappeared down the hallway.

Dropping Cheyenne's hand, Lilith jumped to her feet. "Let's go, daylight's a-wastin'."

Cheyenne cocked an eyebrow at the obviously fake southern accent. Under normal circumstances, she would have had a smart-ass remark, but right now she just didn't have the energy. There had to be a reason all of this was happening. Just because she didn't see it, didn't mean it wasn't there. Now was not the time to let her guard down. *They may be more objective, but they also didn't know Celeste and Dominic . . . and all the others,* she corrected herself, *wondering just how many there were.* Distracted, she stood and followed Lilith toward the door. Cheyenne wasn't sure if she was underestimating them or over. It had been five days since she filed the police report. She hadn't heard from them. According to the paper, there had been another murder. She could understand why that would take priority. In the same thought, she knew Celeste and Dominic hadn't just gone away.

"HEY!" Lilith pinched her arm. "Back to the present."

"Ow!" Cheyenne jumped back, rubbing her forearm. "That hurt!"

"It was supposed to." Lilith snorted and marched from the room. "Get a move on," she yelled from the hallway.

She had to run to keep up with the taller woman, barely catching up with her at the back door. Together they walked to Lilith's wagon and drove down the back path. Lilith sped down the two-track, quickly slowing down as they started to bounce and jump among the ruts.

Within a few minutes, they were parking outside her cabin. Mercury and Aries happily ran to the gate barking. Suddenly, Cheyenne felt part of the dark cloud lift. She jumped out and ran to them. She opened the gate and slipped in.

They had only been parted a couple of hours, but she still missed them. Kneeling and scratching their ears, she talked the familiar baby talk to them, telling them how much she loved them.

Lilith walked past them and to the back door. Quickly she returned, pointing at the door. "The door was unlocked."

Standing, Cheyenne and the dogs walked to meet her. "Maybe April—"

"She was with me all day."

'I didn't even come to the cabin this morning." Cheyenne was surprised by how rapidly she had disassociated the cabin with home. She had enjoyed the privacy. But now she was happy to be back "home" in the main house. It was like another piece of the puzzle falling into place. "I was late. So I fed them at the house and brought ice water for them in a jug. We came in the back gate and I only went as far as the tree line."

"I don't like it." Lilith stopped short.

"Neither do I." Cheyenne echoed.

Together they returned to the back porch. Opening the screen door, Lilith easily turned the knob and pushed on the door.

Cheyenne grabbed both dogs before they could push passed them. For some reason her little voice said, it wasn't safe for them inside. "Stay. Sit." She commanded.

Without question, both dogs sat and looked up at her.

She followed Lilith inside. It wasn't any one thing she could put her finger on, but the inside felt odd—different than it had the day before. Walking from room to room, she could find nothing out of place. "Lilith. Something is different."

"I feel it, too."

"What?"

"I don't know." The older woman stopped in the bathroom archway. "My first instinct is to throw everything out. Not the furniture. But it should be cleaned before it's used. But anything that will touch the skin or be eaten shouldn't be."

"All my clothes and personal stuff have already been moved." Cheyenne walked into the living room. "There wasn't much to take. The guys and I have only been here a couple of months. I hadn't built up much of a larder and the freezer was too small to keep much."

"Leave it," Lilith repeated with more emphasis. "Just leave it all. We'll toss it out."

Cheyenne backtracked and met her in the kitchen. There was a fresh bag of dog food she wanted to get and the guys' favorite toys. She reached for the bag, but an unseen hand pulled her back. From the outside, it appeared untouched, yet there was something wrong with it. She didn't know what. Sitting outside the door, they looked at her; their tails waging. She decided to leave it and buy fresh. She would come back later and throw it away after pouring ammonia on it. The smell would keep everything else from eating it.

"What?"

"I was going to take the food." Cheyenne picked up the bag to show her. "It's unopened. But it doesn't feel right."

"Don't. And their toys too." Crossing the room, Lilith reached out and touched it. "It feels hot."

"I'll buy them fresh this afternoon when I go into town." Cheyenne grabbed their leashes. Immediately they heated up in her hand and she dropped them. "They got hot!'

"Wash your hands!"

Doing as she was told, she ran the water, scrubbing her hands with generous amounts of soap. "Everything stays. We can come back with gloves and plastic bags. What can be burned will be. Everything else will be soaked in ammonia and tossed."

"Let's get out of here." Lilith walked toward the backdoor.

Cheyenne locked the door behind them. "We can walk back if you don't want muddy seats."

"Seats can be cleaned. Gray hair is harder to get rid of. And that's what I'll get along with a chewing out, if I let you walk back by yourself." Lilith led the way back to her car. "Besides, it's faster."

Cheyenne slapped her thigh. "Come." The dogs immediately followed her. She opened the door. "In." She pointed to the backseat and the dogs piled in. "Sit." They did as they were commanded. "Good boys." She closed the door and got into the front seat.

Lilith slid behind the wheel and started the engine. "Maybe we shouldn't rent the cabin right away."

"I was thinking the same thing." Cheyenne stared at the cabin. It had been a safe refuse. But right now she couldn't guarantee it still was. "I think it needs to be thoroughly cleaned and sanitized. We don't have time right now for such a large project."

Lilith backed the car up into the turn around and turned it back towards the main house. "It just seems to keep getting better and better." The sarcasm in her voice held a tint of sadness.

The return trip was silent. Cheyenne didn't want to believe Celeste would have any part in hurting Aries and Mercury; she claimed to love them and had promised to care for them if anything should happen to her. The car reached the crest of the lump that pretended to be a hill. April and Raven had already begun digging the holes for the posts.

"Maybe if we sneak around the front, they won't see us." Lilith mused.

"Nice idea. But the trail goes right past."

"We could smile and wave."

"Okay, you do that and I'll duck." Cheyenne tried to get into the teasing mood, but try as she might the feeling just wasn't there.

Lilith parked the car and opened the door. "Why don't you and the boys take a nap? You need the rest. We can take care of it."

April walked over, casually carrying her shovel. Aries barked once before his tail started wagging. "That's right, furball. You know me."

"Are the two of you ever going to make peace?" Cheyenne opened the door and climbed out. She pulled back the seat. "Okay, guys, out. Go tree."

Mercury cocked his head and sat down. Aries went to the nearest tree and lifted his leg.

"Are you sure? Nap time. Mercury, go potty tree."

Mercury looked up, his dark eyes reflecting her image.

"Okay. Don't want any whining later."

Raven dug the shovel into the ground and joined the group at the car. "I see why you wanted me to stay."

"Excuse me," April intercepted the comment. "Weren't you the one who was just saying how grateful she was?"

"Yes," Raven teased back. "But I didn't think I'd be put to manual labor so fast. It's bad enough Sammy has me helping her move."

"She's here already?" Lilith closed the car door. "Good. I was looking forward to meeting her."

"She just went back to town to get another load." April wiped the sweat off her upper lip. "Good vibes. Honest. Straightforward."

"Sounds like my kind of person." Walking around the car, she took the shovel from April. "The reinforcements are here."

"Good. It's harder than it looks." April grabbed the handle of the shovel. "But get your own. They're in the shed."

With her free hand, Lilith grabbed the handle above April's and winked at her.

April clicked her tongue, using her opposite hand she grabbed the wood above Lilith's hand. Giggling, their hands alternated up the handle until April's fingers covered the top. "I win. Go get your own."

Lilith stuck her tongue out and headed for the shed.

"You're such a child!"

"But that's why you love me!" Lilith called back.

Turning back to Cheyenne, April grimaced. "You look like hell."

"Of course, I'm covered in dirt and sweat," Raven interceded.

"And you stink too. But I wasn't going to mention it!" April looked over her shoulder at Raven and winked. Slowly turning her head back she faced Cheyenne. "You still here? You need a nap.."

"Why is everyone trying to put me to bed?" Cheyenne planted her fists on her hips. "I was going to take a nap, but—"

"Yep. Definitely needs a nap." Raven cut her off. "By the way, love the dark circle your sporting champ. But as a fashion statement, I don't think they'll catch on."

"Don't be petulant. Remember you promised to let us help you." April pinched her cheek. "Now go gather you kids and go take care of yourself."

Hating to admit it, Cheyenne briefly looked up at her bedroom window. She could be stubborn and end up digging or she could take care of herself and go nap. She slapped her thigh and both dogs ran to her. "Have fun." Walking away, she heard Raven question April about what magic she used. Snickering to herself, Cheyenne answered under her breath. "Common sense."

Without checking the mail on the hallway table, Cheyenne led the dogs upstairs to her new old room, closing the door behind them. Sitting on the edge of the bed, she slowly leaned back, her hair fanning out around her head. The layers of shadows from the curtains and the trees outside danced on the ceiling. The breeze brought the scent of green grass and the multitudes of flowers through the open window along with the buzzing of a bee on the outside of the screen. Rolling over, she brushed her hair from her face. The bee zig-zagged and disappeared in the direction of the roof.

Mercury had curled up beneath the window. Aries laid down in front of the door. They were going to have to get use to having people around full-time again. She didn't think there would be a problem. They were well socialized as pups. It would also be good to have their littermate Chester around. Jerry would no doubt take Jasmine and Walter with him. But Morgan had been Selene's; she and her pups would stay. Since he refused to care for them; he had no claims on them. But if Cheyenne had her way, he would leave alone. Something had changed within him. She didn't know what; she had a sneaking suspicion that in this case ignorance was not bless, but in fact, it could be dangerous.

She really didn't have time be just lollygagging around. There was still so much to get done. Resting her chin on her overlapping hands, she watched the curtain waver in the breeze. She did need the rest. Sadly, she smiled at the absurdity of her life. Slowly she stood and stripped. Sliding back across the bed, her body seemed to remember the uniqueness of the mattress. She shifted and found a comfortable position. Part of the bed had been warmed by the sun. She curled her legs, allowing her feet to nestle in the warm pocket. She watched the shadows on the ceiling, allowing her eyes to drift shut. She listened to the chickens and the livestock continue their day, not knowing or caring that this was anything other than a common summer day. Birds chirped and sang. In the distance, crows quarreled among themselves. Following the Zen concept of sleeping, she became one with the mattress, drifting into the peace beyond consciousness. Then there was nothing.

Harsh, angry voices with jumbled words pulled her back upward. Cheyenne fought to stay where thoughts and worries floated by to be left untouched. Her spirit rapidly descended and was unceremoniously thrown back into her body by the unseen hand of fate. Her eyes snapped open. She was face down; her body numb in places from the lack of activity. She couldn't have been asleep long. The shadows hadn't lengthened much. For a few moments, she remained motionless, collecting her senses.

Pushing up on her right arm, she half rolled, half sat up on the edge of the bed. Their voices were so loud, she expected to find a man and at least two women in the room with her. But she was alone with Aries and Mercury. Their silence worried her. Normally they would be in a barking frenzy. Mercury sat at the foot of the bed watching the window. Aries nervously paced the room. Cheyenne stood and slowly crossed the room. Mercury intercepted her. Murmuring soothing words, she scratched his ears and slid around him. Instinct told her to stay out of sight. Keeping close to the wall, she pulled the curtain back.

April and a woman Cheyenne didn't recognize were physically holding a disheveled man away from the house. His reddish hair shone in the sunlight, not from health but from the lack of care. He was well built, yet he gave the impression of gauntness to the point of starvation. His angular features seemed familiar, yet she couldn't place where she knew him. Normally she would have reached out with her other senses to try to place his piece within the puzzle of her life. Something told her to hold back, to be silent and still. Instead she focused on her hearing, trying to make out the individual words. At first she could only distinguish between the women and the man. The women's voices separated between April and the strange woman. The intonations of the male brought images of Jane's detective friend, whose name eluded her memory. Closing her eyes she completely focused on their words.

"Get out of my way, Sammy!" He snapped. "You shouldn't be here!"

That answers one question, Cheyenne thought.

"I saw the checks!" Sammy growled. "The signatures weren't even close."

"Celeste had a right to the household account. Part of it was part hers!"

"That's not what the warrant's for."

"Dominic and Celeste just want their stuff!"

"It's all gone!" April yelled. "We put it in storage."

"I don't believe you."

"It's true!" Sammy's voice lowered to a dead calm. "And they don't have the code. Only the Captain does."

"What?" His voice took on a hushed amazement.

"Maxie, what's wrong with you?"

"There's nothing wrong with me." He stammered.

"You look like hell."

"There's nothing wrong with me!" His voice rose to a shriek.

"Ya, right. And BO and stale beer is a real turn on." April sniped in.

"Shut up!" Sammy snapped. "Maxie, I know about you and Jane. She hurt you. But she'll be back. You could patch—"

"No!" he screeched.

"Okay, okay," Sammy's voice softened. "You'll find someone else."

"Why did she do this to me?" His voice quivered. "I didn't know. I didn't understand."

"I don't know why Jane—"

"NOT JANE!"

"Let me help you. I've been able to cover for you so far. But I'm running out of excuses. We've had another murder. You have to come back. We need you."

"No . . . No . . . Please don't make me." His words started to roll together into a low growl. "Get away from me . . ."

"Maxie, what's wrong?" Sammy's voice lost its certainty.

His voice lost all semblance of humanity.

Sammy screamed his name in fear. April screamed an incoherent phrase.

The unearthly sounds made Cheyenne's eyes snap open. She peaked around the curtain.

Sprawled on the ground, April struggled to free herself from his chokehold. Sammy jumped to her feet and leaped on him, knocking him off April. The two of them fought; rolling, kicking and punching. Holding her throat, April scampered backward. A knife arched up. April sprung forward, punching him in the kidney region. He screamed. The knife flashed down toward Sammy's chest. She rolled to the left. The knife bit more ground than flesh. Sammy kicked upward, ramming his teeth together. Wildly swiping with his backhand, he caught her in the knee, knocking it against its hinge. She screamed and staggered out of his reach.

April slammed him in the face, knocking him off balance. Taking several steps backward, he regained his balance and lunged forward. She swerved. The knife caught her upper arm. The blood rolled down her arm and dripped from her fingertips. She ignored it.

Smiling he brought the bloody blade to his mouth and licked it clean. "I own you now." His voice was clear. "I own you." He repeated.

In horror, Cheyenne watched his image shift and distort. His ash-gray flesh sagged loosely on his frame like an under inflated balloon. His eyes were empty sockets—black holes where his soul should be seen, yet was no longer there. He licked his lips. A pin size glow appeared in each of the black voids. His darkness extended out his fingers, reaching for April. She stared at him, unmoving.

Sammy tried to stand. Her knee buckled. She screamed to April.

It turned its head. A smile forming on the ghoulish face. "I haven't forgotten you." Returning his attention to April, he again reached out with the dark strings. They circled her, entering any break in her skin.

His skin inflated and the glow in his eyes became brighter. Hollywood made mockeries of them, telling tales of monsters that sleep by day and drink the blood of others by night. She knew it was not the blood he sought but her soul's life force.

Panicking, Cheyenne didn't know what to do. She had no experience with such creatures. If she took flight in dragon form, her body would be vulnerable. Aries and Mercury wouldn't be able to defend her. Mentally she screamed for help. Horrified, she watched the black sockets turn and look up at her.

It had heard her. Tossing its head back, a gargled sound of laughter echoed up towards her from both inside and outside.

Quickly she slammed the window shut and backed away. The windowpane cracked. In unison, the dogs howled in pain. Yanking their collars, she pulled them as close as she could get them and threw up a shield of fire.

A black string threaded its way through the crack and across the room, crackling and hissing as it touched her shield. Puffs of acrid smoke drifted up in a thin line as the string wound around her, seeking entrance. Mercury growled. The string focused on him. Cheyenne hushed him. The room took on a smoky hue. It seemed like hours, yet it had been mere minutes. She began to tire from the energy drain. More than once she lost track of the head of the string, only to find it trying to burrow its way behind her. She reinforced the spot, only to have it move on to find another weak area.

Outside, a woman screamed, only to have the voice suddenly cut off.

She began to sweat both from fear and exhaustion. The thread had loosely wrapped itself around them several times. If her shield collapsed, there would be no escape.

The energy level around her suddenly shifted. A second shield of fire sprung from the floor around the first ring. The flame shimmered silver. A flare grasped the string, burning its way across the room, continuing toward the source. Quickly the gargling laughter became a shriek of pain. The glass burst into pieces. A gust of wind blew the screen across the room; swirling around the room to create a vortex, which gathered the smoke into a small ball. White and gold flakes encased it and whisked it out the window. For an instant, the vacuum created an unnatural silence. The silver flames flared around her and vanished, taking with them her ability to maintain her own defenses. Cheyenne crumpled to the floor between the nearly unconscious dogs. Dizzily she fought her way to a half sitting position and crawled to the window. Defenseless and exhausted, there wasn't much she could do, but she wasn't going to be blind-sided. Pulling herself across the shards of glass, she looked out the window. Both April and Sammy looked like broken dolls tossed on the ground. There was no sign of Maxie. A movement in the sky caught her attention. She looked up. It was gone. All she left was an afterimage of silver and gold wings. Shaking her head, she carefully lowered herself back to the floor. Mercury whined. She didn't have the strength to help him.

Somewhere in the house a door slammed, followed by footsteps running up the stairs. Lilith burst in the door, stopping short of Aries tail. "Oh my Goddess!"

Unable to move, Cheyenne peaked from beneath her armpit. "April—Sammy . . . backyard." She whispered. "Need help. Help my kids."

On her way across the room, Lilith stopped at each dog, checking them for injury. She knelt beside Cheyenne, carefully lifting her on to the bed. "What happened?"

Cheyenne shook her head. The motion sent waves of pain radiating from her face to her neck. "I'm ok. Save my kids." She pleaded.

"Sure you are," Lilith retorted sarcastically. "What happened? Raven and I were out front. We heard the fight, but we couldn't get around to the back of house. There was a barrier—it smelled like death and felt freezing cold. Then I heard a scream. I thought it was you. We backtracked and came through the house."

Unable to speak, Cheyenne pointed toward the window.

Grabbing her hand in her own mocha colored, Lilith encircled it within her own. "Your hand is so cold. Raven went out back."

Looking over her shoulder, Lilith cocked her head to one side. "How did the window get broken?" Standing she crossed the room and pulled the curtain back. She gasped and picked up the phone.

Satisfied, Cheyenne lay on the bed watching the ceiling spin around her. At the foot of the bed, one of the dogs whined. She couldn't see them. But she needed to. Slowly rolling onto her stomach, she ignored the throbbing pain and crawled to the edge. Mercury looked up at her; his brown eyes were filled with pain and fear. She reached down and scratched his ears; he blinked and closed his eyes. She couldn't see Aries's face but his breathing was slow and labored. She could only reach his hindquarter. She gently rubbed. The muscles beneath her hand quivered. She stretched. The room spun. She slumped forward, her chin hitting the mattress.

A void surrounded her. She floated in nothingness; her body reduced to the electromagnetic vapor, which was her spirit. She looked around. Beside her, two clouds shimmered and sparkled. She recognized them by their feel, not their shape, as Mercury and Aries. Reaching out to them, she realized she also shimmered as they. Her need to be close drew them to her. She touched them and again she saw them as before. Aries licked her cheek. Mercury snuggled close, embedding his snout beneath her arm. They were together, that was all that mattered to her. The concept of time drifted away. They floated on the sea of serenity, unwilling to look back, unwilling to remember what they were leaving behind. Their energy bodies melded into her. Instead of three, they were one. She saw herself and the world through their eyes. They found her to be odd, sometimes frustrating, sometimes boring, yet the undercurrent was always unconditional love. Returning their love in kind, Cheyenne realized for as long as they were together, she didn't care if they ever went back. Farther and farther they drifted, floating on the waves of the universal energy, surrounded by the glow of divine peace and love. The cords tying them to their bodies became taut, stretched thin by the increasing distance. Cheyenne smiled, gently caressing her connection point at her abdomen. With ease she could pluck them all free.

From the left, ripples formed in the energy as if a stone had been dropped in a crystal clean pool. It echoed out, surrounding them, pulling them backward. Mercury began to slip away. His cord snapped. Desperately Cheyenne tried to grab him, refusing to leave him behind. His soul left the triad. His eyes registered only love for them both. She fought against the unseen hand, which pushed him further away.

"No!" She screamed. "We all go or none of us!" Mercury didn't fight; he merely watched. Angrily she grabbed both Aries and her cords. "All or none!" She repeated.

Their momentum slowed and stopped. She waited and watched, refusing to move her hands. A cascade of light rolled in from beyond her sight. She braced herself, preparing to snap the tethers. It arced around them, seeking Mercury. Streamlining itself, one end flowed up the cord and into him. The other end snaked downward intertwining with the other two, gradually pulling him back to Cheyenne. Tearfully she embraced him, while keeping a firm grip on Aries. Silently she nodded, allowing the force to take the three of them back.

Air burst back into her lungs. Coughing her eyes snapped open, but she saw only darkness. Blindly she felt for fur. Her hands only found empty air. Panicking, she screamed.

Warm hands immediately restrained her, cooing soothing sounds.

She wanted only Aries and Mercury. Arching her back and spinning around, she blindly fought against the hands, screaming their names.

Running feet on the wood floor ran toward her in the darkness. More hands restrained her until she could no more than wiggle beneath their pressure. A female voice shushed her. Cool liquid brushed against her lips. "They're fine." She whispered. "The vet's with them in my room. Quiet. They're hurting themselves trying to get to you."

The last sentence made sense to Cheyenne. She ceased to struggle and the pressure lifted. "I can't see." She whispered.

"You have bandages over your eyes." Becoming louder, the female voice became Lilith's. "There was glass everywhere inside and out. It was like the glass shattered."

"April? Sammy?"

"Cuts and bruises. Sammy went to the hospital. Her knee was dislocated. Being outside, they faired better. Do you want some water?"

"I want Aries and Mercury."

"It wouldn't be good for any of you. Drink this." Lilith ordered.

The glass touched her lower lip, she felt the warm water fill her mouth. She swallowed. For a moment, her stomach lurched. Belching, she forced the water to stay down.

"Lady Margaret was here. You don't have a concussion. You're out of shock. But you will be staying in bed for a few days to allow your body to regain its strength. You won't be blind. The bandages are to prevent infection and keep down the scarring. None of the cuts are deep enough for stitches."

Blindness hadn't even occurred to her. Instinctively, Cheyenne reached up to touch the gauze. It covered from the tip of her nose to the top of her forehead.

"And washing your hair won't be much fun for a while either."

"Who else is in the room?"

"Why do you think there is someone else?"

"Have you recently grown extra arms?"

Lilith chucked. "No."

"Who's here?" Cheyenne felt the mattress sink beside her. She reached out. "Lilith?"

"Yes, I'm here."

She felt a hand encircle her own. The warmth of her touch gave Cheyenne a sense of safety.

"I'm here too." April chimed in, from a further distance. "I just went in to talk to the vet."

"How are they?" Panic again started to rise. "Will they be okay?"

"They are in shock. I tried to explain what happened. I don't think he believed me until he saw you and the remains of your room."

"I told them which vet to call." Nancy cut in, adding quickly. "If you want me to leave, I'll understand. I just wanted to make sure you were ok."

"She's was able to calm Aries and Mercury. Without her, they might not have made it," April intervened.

"Thank you, Nancy."

"I didn't understand before." Nancy's voice trembled. "The kids and I found a place to live. We'll be packed and out at the end of the week."

Cheyenne didn't know what to say. Within moments, the silence became awkward. Nancy mumbled something about leaving.

Cheyenne waited until she could no longer hear Nancy's departing footsteps. "Who pulled us back?"

"Pulled you back?" Lilith increased the pressure on her hand. "What do you mean?"

With difficulty, Cheyenne swallowed. Her throat hurt. "We were drifting away. Someone grabbed us and Mercury was separated. I wouldn't leave without him." The room became silent. "I threatened to break our cords. They brought him back."

A gentle hand brushed along her chin. "You need rest. Relax. I'll wake you again in a little while."

Cheyenne felt herself drifting into sleep. The mattress rose next to her and she realized they hadn't answered her question. She reminded herself to ask it again later.

CHAPTER SEVENTEEN

Again Dominic's fist slammed into Maxie's mouth. Blood spurted from the third split. "Why didn't you do what I told you?" The large hand held fast to the front of the blood soaked shirt.

"I did." Maxie whispered, bubbles forming in the corner of his mouth.

"I said stay away from the main house!"

"Your cabin was empty." Maxie whimpered.

Angrily, Dominic shook him and tossed him against the wall like discarded trash. The impact sent vibration that radiated through the wall, knocking books off the shelf at the opposite end. Limply Maxie slid to the floor, his head leaving a thick streak of blood on the wall.

"You better not have killed him!" Celeste snapped, kneeling beside the prone man. "We still need him."

"Satisfy yourself elsewhere!" He growled back.

"He's still a police officer." She matched his tone. "He could get the codes."

"How? Your excess made him useless. I told you to control yourself."

"I tried." Celeste whined, her resolve waning. She had tried, but the hunger was stronger than she. In truth, it was her vanity. She had drained Steve to an empty shell, who curled up in the corner of the bedroom, waiting to die. His life force had restored a decade of youth for now. Mark was a weasel of a man, who never satisfied her. He did their errands and gathered information. With the warrants out, it was no longer safe for either of them to leave the house during the day; it limited her ability to find more young men to fill her need. She just would have to make do. Jerry had come to her willingly. He had been strong once but his self-abusive drinking had drained him physically and spiritually. In spite of his size, he wouldn't be more than a snack. She still enjoyed Maxie the most. He had been the toughest to tame and the most sexually excitable. Unfortunately, he had begun to burn out. She needed more. She needed to be young again to keep Dominic. He rarely came to her any more. Instead he found pleasure with the younger woman. He claimed it was for procreation. But Celeste knew he was attracted to her youth.

"Celeste!"

His anger snapped her attention back. "I'll try harder."

"It's too late for that. His partner saw him. She knows he is connected to us."

"We should leave town. We have enough money to start over."

"We can't." He sat on the sofa. Rubbing his hands over his face, he looked at the floor. "You don't understand. The full moon is coming up."

"In a couple of days." She knelt in front of him and tilted his head up. There was fear in his eyes. Only once when they were children and her grandmother caught them together, had she seen him actually afraid.

"I have to do ritual."

She kissed his cheek. "We can. Mark will get us a goat. There is plenty of secluded forest."

"The police have the knife." He growled, his anger again welling up.

"We'll get another." Celeste didn't understand. It was just a kitchen knife. Nothing special. Why would he obsess over something that could easily be replaced? "It'll be all right."

He grabbed her wrist with his trembling hand. "It wasn't just a knife. It was consecrated in blood." His eyes narrowed, turning the color of slate. "The night of my dedication. She was the daughter of a High Priestess, not yet of the cycle of blood. I took her innocence and the blade took her heart. If I don't bloody it every full moon, its blade will turn against me."

"Why?" Celeste's voice quivered with fear and uncertainty.

"Because that's the way it is!" he bellowed, shoving her backward. "You don't need to know why! It just needs to be done."

The police had the knife. With Maxie's obvious injuries he was of no use to them. Maybe she could seduce another officer? No, his partner would have made a report. But they couldn't possibly know or understand what they had. Maybe she could find someone young and inexperienced or a clerk working at the station. "Dom, Maxie isn't any use any more."

He glared at her; his eyes more gray than blue.

"But if I'm careful, I could get another."

"How? Neither of us can leave this shack." Standing, he walked around the room waving his arms. "We can't show our faces."

"They don't know about Maxie. And it was Maxie who attacked his partner."

"Are you willing to take the risk?" His question hung in the air like a dagger above both their heads. "With all the friends Cheyenne and Jane have. With everyone of them out to get you. And now that lady cop—who knows what she

309

knows or suspects." He started to pace. "I don't know what to do."

"We have two days."

"Two days or two weeks. It doesn't matter. We've trapped ourselves."

"There has to be another way. Could you rededicate?" Celeste was grabbing at straws. "On the Pagan path, we can when there is a major change in our lives or teachings. It is a way of integrating the new into the old. I'm your working partner. I'm new. We're joining our paths." As the words came out of her mouth, the ideas solidified in her mind. "You wouldn't actually need the original to consecrate the new knife in both our names."

"Yes," he began slowly. "But where could we find pure blood of power."

"Lisa." The name sprang from Celeste's lips before it formed in her mind.

"She's my niece!"

"Is she? She chose Cheyenne over you. She chose the dragon path over your teachings." Celeste watched the conflict in his eyes. "Think of it. Your bloodline is powerful. And Lisa chose Cheyenne's path. A dragonet. Innocent, virginal both to the blood and to heritage. Who could be more powerful?"

"She's my niece," he repeated with less enthusiasm. "Besides, the police will be watching Meredith and the kids. We couldn't get close."

"Probably." Celeste smiled. *She would have the child's soul; Lisa had rejected her offer of love, so now she'd know her hatred.* "But her sister could bring her to us."

"Melanie?"

Celeste crossed the room and sat beside him. Sliding her arms up under his shirt, she embraced him. She stretched to kiss his neck and whisper in his ear. "She'll do anything for you. Almost as much as me."

Sighing, he relaxed, melting around her. "It could work."

"Together nothing is beyond us," she whispered. Feeling secure, her hand drifted from the small of his back to his groin. It swelled under her touch. "I have a request."

"Anything." He licked the lobe of her ear and down her neck.

"Nancy. She is young." Celeste tilted his head to meet her gaze. "She is a threat to me."

"Why?" His hands groped downward, taking hold of both of her buttocks. "She is nothing but a broodmare for the child you want."

"Want me more." She squeezed; he gasped.

"What do you want me to do?"

"Nancy is inferior." She squeezed again. "You don't really need her. We can find another more worthy of your seed."

He shook his head.

"I'm hungry." She stated flatly, releasing her grip.

He blinked once and leaned backward, his arm pointing toward the bedroom. "I'll need some time and privacy to reach Melanie. I'll have her bring Lisa here tomorrow afternoon. By the time they start looking for her, it'll be all over and we'll be out of town."

Smiling, she kissed his lips and walked toward the bedroom door. *She'd have her man and her way. Nothing could be better, except taking down Cheyenne. Maxie had mumbled something about having reached her. How much damage did he do? Just how vulnerable was she? Was it possible to get more from them? They had close to ten thousand dollars, but that wouldn't last long. Both Cheyenne and Jane had some valuable jewelry. There were several pieces she had always wanted; the rest could be sold. Jane and Cheyenne owed her.*

Nancy lay sprawled across the bed. Other than the sheet covering her stomach, she was completely nude. Celeste walked to the foot of the bed. She stood, watching the late afternoon shadows from the curtains dance across the prone figure. The younger woman didn't seem to be aware of her. Celeste watched her shallow breath. Her lips were swollen and split. Deep black finger marks, made more prominent by the paleness of her skin, marked her throat, breasts, and thighs. Her wrists were bruised and raw from the belts around the bed frame he used to restrain her. A smile crossed Celeste lips. Dominic had been telling her the truth; she was nothing to him. Celeste pulled the sheet away, Nancy's eyes opened; she stared in terror at Celeste.

Sitting at the edge of the bed, Celeste trailed her fingers upward from the naked thighs. She didn't know what to do. With males, she had taken their life forces sexually. With a female, she wasn't sure. Her fingers reached the belly button and she sensed a different energy source. It was faint, but still distinct. Dominic's seeds had taken root. It was not yet soul energized but the multiplying cells had a unique energy of their own. Immediately her anger flared and Celeste brought her fist down. Nancy screamed, doubling over. Furious, Celeste jumped her, slapping her backward and stuffing the sheet into her mouth. Covering the younger woman with her own body, Celeste pinned her to the bed. Using the belts attached to the frame, she tied Nancy's arms to the bed frame. If

Dominic knew he had succeeded, he would take Nancy with them. She wouldn't allow that to happen. She was going to be the only woman in his life. Grasping Nancy's throat with one hand, she felt for the life force with the other. She'd take them both. Dominic would never know. Smiling, she found the flutter and turned to Nancy. "So you succeeded." Nancy tried spitting out the sheet. Celeste slapped her and shoved it further down her throat. Nancy gagged. Returning her attention to the multiplying cells, Celeste reached out. Long black strings flowed out of her fingertips. Nancy jumped as they penetrated her skin. Celeste tightened her grip on her throat. The strings found it. A soulless group of cells yet it pulsated with an energy of its own. The strings broke through the cell membranes and sucked them to empty shells. The energy rush was stronger than anything Celeste had experienced before. It tasted sweet, but was no more than a nibble. The strings radiated out, attacking the reproductive system and the other eggs waiting to ripen, then moved on to the other organs, working their way upward. The energy from the uterus and ovaries brought back flashes from her own fertile period as short as it had been. It drove her onward. She wanted more. The strings pierced and drained each organ they touched, making Celeste stronger. Reaching the heart, they attached themselves like suckling babes. Nancy arched her back in pain. Her heart beat wildly. Celeste felt the surge of power. Her heart fluttered. Nancy collapsed. Celeste took a deep breath. A gargling sound came from Nancy's throat like the last sips from a straw. Smiling, Celeste withdrew the strings and climbed off the empty shell.

Stretching to full height, she felt immortal. Nothing could stop her. Tomorrow after the ceremony, they would stop at the farm on the way out of town. She couldn't take the land with her, but everything else of value would be taken, leaving Cheyenne's empty husk of a corpse behind.

CHAPTER EIGHTEEN

Cheyenne awoke to the hundreds of tiny shooting pains on her face and arms. How long she had been asleep, she didn't know. Vaguely she remembered being awakened, sometimes just to talk, other times to eat. Once Lilith helped her to the bathroom. The bandages still covered her eyes. She reached up and touched them.

Out of the darkness, a hand gently encircled hers. "Shush." Jane whispered. "It's okay."

"Jane?" Startled, Cheyenne reached out with her other hand. "You're back already?"

"I'm sorry I wasn't here for you." Jane's voice quivered. "I'm never seem to be when you need me."

"It's not as bad as it looks." Cheyenne felt the mattress beside her sink under Jane's weight. "Did you find what you needed?"

Suddenly Jane burst into tears. "I'm sorry! It's all my fault! Cheyenne you have to forgive me."

Someone ran into the room. "Jane? You didn't tell her?" The voice was Lilith's.

"What's going on?" Cheyenne demanded, sitting up.

Jane snuffled, "She has to know."

"Tell me what?"

The mattress sank on the other side of her. "Cheyenne." Lilith took her free hand. "You have to try to stay calm. There was nothing we could do."

"Nothing—" Suddenly Cheyenne panicked. "Where's Mercury and Aries? Aries! Mercury! Come!" She tried to slap her leg, but both women held on to her hands. She struggled to free herself.

"Cheyenne stop!" Jane cried. "Aries is outside. He's fine"

Startled, Cheyenne stopped struggling. "Where's Mercury?"

Lilith rubbed the inside of her arm. "I'm sorry. His heart . . . his heart just stopped. It was in his sleep last night." She added quickly. "There wasn't any pain."

Cheyenne felt herself go cold from the inside out. Behind the bandages, the tears welled up and burned down her cheeks. The air wouldn't go into her lungs. She gasped for breath. The pressure increased. Her chest hurt.

"I'm going to take him to be cremated later this morning." Jane whispered. "We wanted to tell you first."

"I want to see him. Take the bandages off."

"But Lady Margaret said—"

Cheyenne cut Jane off. "Take them off!" She jerked down her hands, freeing them both and yanked at the front of the bandages, but only succeed in pulling her head forward.

"Okay. Okay," Lilith conceded, grabbing her hands. "I'll do it. Jane, go get Lady Margaret."

Jane jumped up and ran from the room.

On the left side, something was pulled free and the pressure around her head reduced as the bandage was unwound.

"Keep your eyes closed," Lilith ordered. "It's nearly off."

She felt the end of the bandage touch her shoulder and the pads on her eyes being removed. Ignoring Lilith's order, she opened her eyes. The brightness startled her and she closed them again. Without waiting for them to adjust, she flung back the blankets and felt for the edge of the bed. "Where is he?" Her eyes fluttered as they adjusted to the light. The pressure on her chest increased. She stood. The room spun around her. Her knees started to buckle beneath her. She didn't care. It was her fault. She should have been there for them.

"He's downstairs. Let me help you." Lilith pleaded. "It wasn't anybody's fault!"

"Yes it is!" Cheyenne screamed. "It's mine!"

Harshly Lilith grabbed her and spun her around. "No! Don't you even think that! It isn't your fault. It theirs—Celeste and Dominic's. They caused this to happen. Not you!"

Lilith's words were lost in a tornado of would-da, could-da, should-da—but didn't do. Snapshots of all the missed opportunities to prevent it—but she had listened with her heart to Celeste's promises when every other sense and intuition screamed against it. She had listened and Mercury paid with his life. He trusted and loved her; she failed him. Her knees folded; She landed on them with a thud. She didn't feel it. The pain in her chest outmatched it. She shivered. The room dimmed around her. Her hands and feet went numb.

Somewhere far away, Lilith yelled for Lady Margaret. Footsteps ran in her direction. There were voices; they called to her. It didn't matter. She had to find Mercury.

Suddenly something cold nuzzled her check and whined. Through the shifting haze, she saw Aries. He alternated between lying across her lap and nudging her in the face with his nose. She felt his fear. He licked her face. His tongue was warm on her skin.

The two realms overlapped. In the doorway, Mercury's spirit sat, watching them. His tail wagged. He crossed the

317

room, walking through Jane's legs, and joined with her. He was inside her and she could hear his thoughts. He told her how much he loved her and Aries. But it was his time to go, not hers. He begged her to stay. Aries still needed her. The others, who loved her, still needed her. He promised to come back. But now he had to go through processing. Whatever happened, he would always be grateful for the time they spent together and would be there to greet both of them when it was their turn to cross over. She tried to hold on to his spirit—to keep him inside her. He transformed from the dog into his true form of a loving soul of light. He kissed her forehead and released her. Backing away, he smiled and disappeared.

Cheyenne felt empty and alone, lost between the two worlds. Her body began to weaken from the stress. She saw the cord that kept her connected. It would be so easy to snap it. Aries whined. Without words, he asked why she wanted to leave him alone. Mercury had left. Didn't she love him too? Yes, she cried, dropping her own cord and wrapping her arms around him. Her whole body became hot then cold only to become hot again. She opened her eyes. The room was crystal clear again. There was something over her face. She tried to push it off.

"No. No," Lady Margaret whispered. "It's oxygen. Just breath. You'll be ok. We're going to take you to the hospital."

Unable to talk, Cheyenne shook her head. She reached out and found fur. Aries licked her hand and laid across her stomach.

"No. You have to go."

Aries growled, exposing his teeth. The hair raised on the back of his neck.

"Aries. Come." April reached for him.

He snapped, finding her forearm. She screamed. Jane pulled her back and wrapped her arm in a towel to stop the already dripping blood.

"Aries!" Lilith scolded. Just as quickly, her voice softened. "Aries. We just want to help your mommy. She is very sick. If you don't let us help her, she will go to Mercury."

Aries growled, refusing to give ground.

"Aries. Please. You know me." Jane knelt before him. "I love Cheyenne. Please let us help her. I can't be without her either."

"No. Wait." Gripping her injury with her free hand, April suddenly shook her head, her eyes blinking rapidly. "If she leaves the farm, they'll find her."

"Who—" Lilith answered her own question. "Celeste and Dominic?"

"No matter what happens. We all have to stay here."

"I can't." Lady Margaret knelt beside April and examined the bite. "I'm on call. Two women are due in the next couple of days. If I get a call, I go. April, you're going to need stitches. Not many. Two or three."

"Oh, great!"

"I can do them."

"Thanks." Jane looked at April. "You can't be serious. Lady Bridget, Shelly and I are due to meet some people from out west this afternoon."

April's voice took on a deadly serious tone. "If you leave the farm, I get the feeling you'll die."

"Okay. Okay." Lilith injected. "Everybody stays. What can we do for Cheyenne? We can't just leave her on the floor!"

Lady Margaret snorted. "Like now we have a choice?"

"Yes. We do." Lilith walked around and stood in Aries direct line of sight. "Aries. Help me get your mommy back to bed. She's staying. And so are all of us. But we need you to protect her. Understand?"

After a moment he relaxed his guard and shifted his weight off Cheyenne. Cautiously Lilith moved forward and lifted Cheyenne back into bed, covering her back with the sheet. Immediately, Aries jumped up and laid down beside her.

"Good boy." Lilith reached out and stroked his head.

He licked her palm and stretched out beside Cheyenne.

Feeling the warmth of his body next to her, Cheyenne relaxed. The pain in her chest ease but did not go away. Breathing became easier and deeper.

Lady Margaret brought a glass of water and a couple of gel capsules to her. "Take these. Its valerian root. You need to sleep."

Cheyenne pushed her hand away. "What about Mercury?" Her voice was a mere whisper.

Lady Margaret looked to the others.

"I'll make sure his body is taken to the vet. I know you want his ashes back." Jane stepped closer to the bed. "Before it leaves, I'll cut some of his hair for you."

"I want to see him."

Jane shook her head. "You don't have the strength to come down. I promise you. He was peaceful. There wasn't any pain for him."

Lilith sat down beside her and brushed her hair from her cheek. "Really, sweetie. I walked into the kitchen and started tea. I didn't even know he was gone until he didn't get up with Aries. It was too late to call the vet."

Cheyenne nodded and accepted the pills. Until the water touched her lips, she hadn't realized how thirsty she was. She drained the glass.

Lady Margaret took the empty glass from her. "More?"

"Yes. Please."

Moments later, the glass was refilled and returned to her. Before she finished drinking it, the herb had already begun to take effect. Her body relaxed into the mattress and her eyelids closed. The air mask shifted back into position. She drifted into the nothingness of the induced sleep. There were no dreams. No emotional confusion. Only the emptiness to surround her and keep her company.

Briefly she would rise to consciousness. Once a young woman, she didn't know, stood beside the bed. Her hair was long and dark; she smile was full of love. One of her hands rested above Cheyenne's heart; the other on her solar plexus. Her skin beneath her hands felt hot.

"Shush," the young woman whispered. "I'm Shelly. Jane's friend. Let me help restore you. It's a combination of Reiki techniques. Don't worry. You can't drain me. It's the universe's energy. I'm just directing it where you need it."

Cheyenne shifted in the bed. The air mask had been removed. Aries still lay beside her. She tried to thank her, but sleep once again drew her downward. Time was irrelevant. How long she slept she didn't know. In the distance, she heard the phone ring several times. She'd surface briefly, only to dive back under when it was answered. It seemed the phone was more active than normal. *It was an important piece of information*, Cheyenne wondered why . . . the thought was lost before it was completed.

The phone rang again, only this time she came fully to the surface. The last shadows of twilight stretched out across the bed. Within a few moments, they would fade into the darkness of night. Aries no longer lay beside her. For an instant she panicked, only to have her fears relieved with his familiar barking outside in the yard. Shelly giggled and called his name. Happily barking he answered. Cheyenne recognized the sounds of play; it brought a sad smile to her lips. She was grateful for Aries strength, yet sad that Mercury had gone beyond. It was all different. Nothing would ever be the same. There was emptiness in her heart where Mercury had lived. She remembered telling someone once that the emptiness would only remain as long as you mourned what you lost, instead of being grateful for what you had. *They were foolish and cruel words*, she thought; *what was I thinking?*

"It wasn't you." Came the immediate answer. *"It was me speaking though you to another child of light who needed comfort."* The voice was the one she heard when her hands touched the earth and when she asked for healing advice. *"So now I say to you. Cheyenne, child of my heart, you have lost nothing. The love and joy you shared remains within you. As always his spirit will never be far from you nor you from him. But his lessons were learned and it was time for him to move to his next task. If in hadn't been now, it would have been soon. But I will bring others to you who will need your love and wisdom. Do not let the pain you feel now deprive you and others of the bounty of love in your heart."*

"Mother Dragon." Cheyenne reached with her spirit. "I am grateful, yet—"

"I know child." No other words were said, yet the meaning was so clear. No matter what she felt, the endless supply of unconditional love would continue to flow to her and through her.

She sighed and tossed off the blankets. The cool air awakened her further. Stretching, she sat up. The room spun once, but immediately settled. Her feet touched the floor; it was still slightly warm from the sun. Stumbling and weaving, she made her way to the bathroom. Standing and washing her hands, she got a look at herself in the mirror. The sight shocked her. Her hair was damp with sweat. The dark circles made it look like she had two black eyes, which was made to look more extreme by the paleness of her skin. Her mouth had a pasty taste. Without thinking she reach for her toothbrush and paste. Quickly brushing, she turned on the shower, letting it run until steam seeped through the slightly open door. She stepped into the hot stream and closed the door. The water massaged her; it felt good. The steam filled the shower stall. She breathed in is as deeply as her sore chest would allow. She was no longer in pain, but the prolonged fight to breathe had left a dull ache behind. Shaking her head, she forced herself to think of other things. She couldn't get stuck.

Reaching for the shampoo, she quickly lathered. Pain shot through her scalp and face as the soap seeped into her cuts. For an instant, anger flared; *how could she have misjudged Celeste so much, for so long?* Stepping back, she rinsed and rubbed conditioner in the short strands. She wasn't sure who she was angrier with Celeste or herself. Picking up the soap, she lathered the sponge and gently washed herself. The texture of the natural sponge stimulated her senses, but it also irritated all the tiny cuts on her face and upper body. She focused on the pain, forcing it to awaken her endorphins. Breathing deep, she let the pain flow out of her with the water running down her body. She began to feel more like herself. She slowly rinsed and turned off the water.

Her skin tingled. Her stomach growled. It was time to get back to business. She opened the shower door and stumble on her way out. Rubbing her big toe, she smiled at herself, thinking so much for declaration of strength. She dried off and wrapped her hair in a towel. At least her hair no longer hung out and dripped, she consoled herself. She dressed and slowly walked downstairs. Hearing voices in the kitchen, she followed them. She turned the corner, but stopped out of sight. She didn't know why.

Jane and April sat at the table. Lilith leaned against the sink. A woman she didn't know paced between them; her hands moved as she talked. The voices were too low to understand their words, yet there was definite tension between them. The phone rang; Jane jumped up and answered before the second ring.

"No." Her voice rose in tone and pitch. "She isn't here. Did you try Rachael's? She likes to hide there."

Lisa? Something was wrong. Cheyenne stepped into full view. "What's wrong with Lisa?"

Startled, Jane nearly dropped the phone. "She's missing."

April stood. "You should be in bed."

"I've slept long enough. How long has she been missing?"

The voice on the other end, yelled for Jane. She returned her attention to the person at the other end. "Yes. She just came downstairs . . . I'll tell her . . . Yes. We'll look around . . . I will. You call too . . . Right. Bye." She hung up the receiver. "That was Carmen. They still can't find her. She went off with Melanie late this morning. No one has seen her since. I told Carmen, we'd look around the farm again."

"Okay." Lilith pushed off from counter. "Everybody but you." She pointed at Cheyenne. "You may be vertical and coherent, but you still look like death warmed over."

"Good. I'd hate to feel this bad and no one notice. I'm hungry. What's to eat that is fast and not eggs or pancakes?" Turning her attention to the newcomer, Cheyenne held out her hand. "Hi. I'm Cheyenne. Who are you?"

Smiling and clicking her tongue on her teeth, Bridget accepted her hand. "Bridget. We met earlier but you probably don't remember. Shelly and I took turns working on you."

"I vaguely remember Shelly."

Bridget nodded. "She said you chatted briefly. She's outside with Aries. He's a good dog. He only left your side when he really had to go."

Cheyenne nodded. "Where's Mercury's body?"

"At the vet," Bridget continued. "Shelly and I took him. We also did some shopping—."

"Why are you here?" Cheyenne cut her off.

"Cheyenne." Jane intervened. "She came with me."

"No." Lady Bridget motioned for her to be silent. "I understand." She turned back to Cheyenne. "I am here because you inherited a problem that we didn't take care of when we had the chance." She shifted her weight from one foot to another. "Shelly and I are here to help you take care of the problem you shouldn't have had."

Cheyenne met her gaze. "Our problem isn't all your responsibility. We had a problem," she glanced at Jane, "we just didn't know it."

Jane slowly nodded. "Only you saw it, but no one wanted to believe you."

Cheyenne realized she had a choice; she could dwell on all their mistakes, including her own, or she could forgive them both, and not waste their energy away on guilt. She already knew *Mercury still loved her; he did not hold her responsible. The Goddess didn't. Why should she? And if she wasn't, then neither was Jane.* She cleared her throat. "Jane, neither you nor I caused Mercury to die. It wasn't our fault. I don't blame you and neither does he."

Blinking rapidly tears filled Jane's eyes, quickly overflowing onto her cheeks. "I thought you would hate me."

Slowly Cheyenne shook her head.

"You'd have every reason to."

"No. If I hated you. I would have to hate myself."

"Why? You tried to stop them."

"But I didn't do enough."

"Because I stopped you."

"No!" Cheyenne snapped. "Listen. I am the sole owner of the farm. All the decisions were ultimately mine. I chose to listen and believe her as long as I did. From the very beginning I had bad feelings about him. But I didn't listen to them. If only—"

"If only," Lady Bridget cut it. "If, would have, should have . . . could have. If we get stuck second guessing—20-20 hindsight then we will make the same mistakes."

"Ok." April injected. "We need to focus on the problems at hand. Which is finding the little girl and feeding you," she pointed at Cheyenne

"And preparing for whatever they are going to pull next. Cause you know they aren't done." Jane added.

"Agreed," Lilith picked up the thought. "I'll send Aries back in to guard the walking wounded. April could you stay as well, you qualify. You're also the best cook. Feed the woman while the rest of us will have a look about the farm."

We'll need to have battle plan." Bridget nodded toward the door. "While we're looking for the girl we can start looking for weapons and a way to defend the house."

April encircled the bandaged part of her arm with her other hand. "What makes you think they'll come here? Wouldn't they be smarter just to leave town?"

Jane turned to face her. "We've done some research on him. When it get too hot, he always runs, but not before getting revenge."

"And the full moon." Bridget planned her hands on her hips. "He was always more active for the three days—one before, the night of and the day after." She quickly added. "This time we have the advantage. Actually several. He doesn't know Shelly and I are here. Plus," she smiled, "we brought more friends."

"Enlighten us." April opened the refrigerator; reaching in for the package of hamburger, she suddenly stopped in mid-movement. "Who are your friends?"

"No!" Jane suddenly cut in, staring at April. "We don't know for sure they're here or when they'll be. As a matter of fact, they may not come at all."

"Jane?" Bridget's eyebrow rose. "Do you know something I don't?"

Her head tilting slightly, Jane focused on the brown eyes. "Things changed."

They had a connection. Cheyenne felt it. For some reason, Jane was holding something back.

"Okay. We'll pair up in teams." Lady Bridget dropped the topic. "Lilith and Shelly. Jane and I. That way each team knows what we're looking for."

"I only saw her once," Lilith contradicted.

"More than me or Shelly." Bridget clapped her hands together. "Head'em up and move'em out."

Without waiting, Jane headed for the door, closely followed by Bridget. Lilith shrugged and followed. She opened the door and Aries came in; she scratched his head on the way out.

"Aries. Come to momma." Cheyenne sat at the table and patted her lap. He crossed the room and sat in front of her. Scratching his ears, she felt comforted. She looked up and smiled at April. "So what are you going to make?"

April's attention was focused on the closed door. She seemed different. Her appearance hadn't changed, yet there was something about her that had been altered.

"April?"

Slowly her head turned to look at Cheyenne. There was something about her eyes. The bright light of her spirit seemed dimmer than before.

Unexpectedly Cheyenne felt awkward. They had known each other only a short time and now the woman before seemed like a complete stranger. Instinctively she pulled Aries closer. "If you look in the freezer," she pointed to the pantry, "there are some bags of goulash. We always made extra and froze it in individual portions. They make good, quick meals." Her eyes made her uncomfortable, but she dare not look away. "You just put them in a pan with a little water and put a cover on it. The steam . . ." Suddenly she ran out of things to say.

Blinking rapidly, April open and closed her fist. Breathing in sharply she stood up. "I need to get some fresh air. I'll be right back." Without waiting for a reply, she ran out the back door, allowing it to slam shut behind her.

Aries licked her hand and whined.

"It's ok." She said it, but Cheyenne didn't believe it. She walked to the closed door; part of her wanted to lock it. It wasn't logical but it was the way she felt. She had learned to trust her feelings.

April paced in the middle of the backyard, angrily talking to herself. Her one hand alternated between massaging and scratching at her shoulder. She looked up; their eyes met. There were stress lines around them that hadn't been there moments before. "I can't stay." She screamed.

"Why?" Cheyenne asked, but still reached for the door lock and turned it.

"I just can't"

Lilith stepped out of the tack room. She was barely visible in the rapidly growing darkness. "What's going on?"

April spun around. "I have to go."

"Why!" Lilith demanded, marching across the distance between them. But she stopped short when she was close enough to see April's eyes. "What happened? Your eyes?" She reached out to touch her.

April stepped backward out of Lilith reach. "I don't feel alone. You were talking about the girl and I felt something ugly touch my shoulder. I couldn't make it go away. I came inside me. I could see her. I don't know her but I knew it was her. They have her. She is so afraid."

"Do you know where she is?

"I can see it."

"Can you describe it?" Lilith walked closer to the house and the sensors turned on the spotlights, illuminating the backyard.

April nodded.

"Shelly!" Lilith yelled. "Shelly!"

The young woman appeared in the corral doorway. "What? Did you find her?"

"Maybe. Get Jane and your mother!"

"Will do!" Shelly ran toward the storage sheds.

"It's so hard." April began to tremble. "It's so strong." She looked toward Cheyenne. "I had to leave. It wanted me to hurt you."

Let by Shelly, other women ran across the lawn and joined them the circles of light.

"We have a problem," Lilith began quickly.

"An understatement." April folded her arms across her chest, holding herself close.

"He's touched you!" Bridget cut in. "And his darkness got in. I can see it."

"I have control now." Tears welled up in April's eyes. "I don't know for how long."

"They have the child," Lilith continued. "She can see where."

"Celeste and Dominic? Why do they want her?" Jane stepped closer to April.

April again retreated. "They need her." Her teeth chattered. She dug her nails into her upper arms. "It's getting hard. They are gathering their energy." She spasmed and dropped to her knees. "He lost something that bound him to a blood oath. They are going to replace it." Sweat ran down her cheeks mixing with her tears. "It is a sacrificial knife."

"Lisa!" Jane shouted. "He wouldn't. She's his niece!"

"Not any more."

"Where are they?" Lilith cut in. "Tell us!"

"It's near a high energy source. Not a main lay line but the junction of two smaller ones."

"There are several." Cheyenne contributed from the house, still unwilling to join the circle outside. "There is a quarry, about twenty miles North of here. It was abandoned in the sixties when the water filled it faster than it could be pumped out. There's also a valley about five miles southwest. There are several springs, which combine to feed into the Manistee River. There is a small island where they flow into the river. The island is only about a half mile in diameter, but is a safe haven. It's been said a land bridge rises up to give safe passage to those who have a pure heart."

"And the spirit of the river will reach out and drag those who follow the dark path down into the mud." Jane interjected. "I remember hearing the story. It was part of an Ottawa burial ground, but now its part of Leonard Farm."

"There is another place. The last acres of old growth trees. In the center, there is a very powerful natural circle. You are either welcomed or the forest chases you away." Cheyenne continued. "It's here."

"That's how Cheyenne and I met." Lilith piped in. "I was driving through town and it called to me."

"But it refused Celeste and me." Jane stated bitterly. "After two attempts, I gave up. But Celeste kept trying until a tree nearly dropped on her."

"It was something she resented me for," Cheyenne added.

"Did she ever make it to the inner circle?" Bridget asked.

Jane and Cheyenne looked to each other. They shook their heads.

"They will go there. Celeste wants to make a point." April's voice quivered. "But not now. I see an old house. It was blue once but now the paint has flaked away. There are two sheds." Her body shook. "One was small. No paint. The larger was painted to match the house. But not good. It's also faded." Her hands dropped from her chest to the ground. "There is a windmill. It's rusted. There were three fields planted. The corn died." She gasped for breath.

"I know where that is!" Jane shouted. "It's the Leonard Farm."

"I can't stop them." April collapsed onto the ground. Her fingers dug through the grass into the dirt beneath. Her voice became a low unintelligible growl. Screaming, her back arched once, and she fell face down. Unconscious. Her body trembled. April still fought for control.

"April!" Lilith screamed and reach for her.

"Don't touch her!" Lady Bridget screamed and intercepted her. "She'll infect you!"

"We have to help her!" Lilith snapped back, reaching for April.

"No!" Bridget shoved her back. "There's nothing we can do. It's up to her. She'll fight and live or she'll lose and die. But it's up to her. If you touch her, they'll do the same to you, through her." She spun her around so their eyes met. "As long as she fights, they can't take over. But if they are able to reach you through her, you both will die."

"What about Lisa?" Jane snapped. "We have to save her!"

"Yes, Mother, please." Shelly stepped back into the light.

Slowly nodding, Bridget released Lilith. "You and I will get the others."

"You'll never find the farm." Jane stepped between them. "If you don't know the area it is very difficult to find."

Cheyenne opened the door and stepped out. "Jane, you can't leave."

"She right!" Lilith agreed.

"How much time does Lisa have?" Jane countered. "Could any of you sleep well knowing we didn't do anything? I'll call Sammy and take you to the farm. She'll meet us there."

"I'll—"

"Do nothing!" Jane cut Cheyenne off. "You can barely stand." She pointed at Lilith. "You have to protect Cheyenne," she hesitated, "and make sure they don't do any damage through her." She pointed at April. "We'll meet up with Sammy and the others."

"What others?" Lilith demanded.

"Never mind." Bridget matched her tone. "We'll take my car."

"Wait!" Lilith stepped in front of Jane. "What if the detective is like April? She was also touched during the attack."

A wry smile crossed Bridget's face. "I don't buy trouble in advance. Let's go."

Jane forced a smile. "Take care of her for me." She looked over her shoulder at Cheyenne. "I'll be back. Promise."

Cheyenne knew that was a promise she might not be able to keep. Blinking back the tears, she smiled and waved. "You better keep that promise."

The threesome disappeared into the darkness; car doors opened and closed. The engine started and they were gone.

"We can't leave her out here." Lilith walked up to Cheyenne.

Cheyenne shook her head. "She's your friend. You love her. But if she loses the battle . . ." She let her voice trail off, leaving the threat hanging in the air.

"What do you want to do?"

"We have to bind her—if they can't use her any more maybe they'll lose interest."

"How?"

"The old fashion way." Cheyenne nodded toward the fire ring. "There should be enough wood to make a circle around her big enough not to physically hurt her. The pile off to the left was just cut. It's green. But there is a stack of dry next to it. Go get it. You build the circle. I'll take care of everything else."

"What are you planning?"

"Any binding magic we use they can work around it. We need to set a physical barrier." Cheyenne looked at the prone woman. "It might be enough to help her fight them off."

Lilith hesitated, staring at her friend. "I wish I had known before.

"There are several things I wish I had known before." Cheyenne sighed. "So much would have been different." Cheyenne turned on her heels, but stopped short. "And bring a couple of shovels. We'll have to dig fast." She went into the house. Quickly she found the sea salt in the kitchen . By the time she returned to the backyard, Lilith was already returning with a second armload of wood. She spread the salt in a wide circle around April.

"Salt?"

"It's a purifier." Cheyenne nodded. "Put the wood out about here." She pointed to the area about five feet from April. "We need to dig a ditch for the water around the fire."

"A binding with the four elements? What are you going to use for air?"

"I have dried sage and cedar in the greenhouse."

"You might want to add some dragon's blood for extra power. Its purity will help cut off their darkness."

"Good idea."

April moaned. Her body had ceased twitching, yet it seemed to be in constant motion as the battle waged within her.

"Do you think she can hear us?"

Cheyenne finished the salt circle. "I don't know. But I'm afraid they can."

"I understand." Lilith returned to the fire pit for another armload.

Taking a deep breath, Cheyenne pushed down the pain. Aries whined from the kitchen door. Her mind raced for a safe place to hide him. *But where? Celeste knew every place. For right now, he'd stay in the kitchen. Once they had finished, she'd keep him close.* Her body protested. The pain in her arms radiated up her to shoulders. In spite of everything her stomach growled. *Fine time for it*, she thought, walking to the greenhouse. She grabbed to long strands of hanging sage, one of cedar, and a bag of dried dragon blood resin. On the way out, she picked up a shovel. By the time she got back, the wood circle was nearly completed. She dropped the herbs and started on the trench. It didn't have to be deep or wide just enough for the water to be able to pool with the help of the hose. Wordless they worked. The wood circle was finished. Cheyenne unrolled the hose and pulled it to the circle. She turned on the water. Slowly the water rolled around the trench. The dry ground greedily soaked it up. But the continuous supply kept the forward motion. The water came around and combined with itself.

"With this water, I purify this space. Creating a barrier that no evil may cross." Cheyenne began.

"With the salt of the earth, I purify this space and create a barrier that evil may not cross." Lilith continued, spreading a second circle of salt outside the trench.

Cheyenne picked up the herbs and divided them between the two of them. They spread them on top of the logs. "With these special herbs," Cheyenne felt the energy around them stir, "I purify this space with the power of air and create a barrier that no evil may cross."

They stepped back over the ditch and Lilith lit a match. "With fire I purify this space and create a barrier no evil may cross." She reached forward and brought the match to the wood. It didn't ignite. They looked at each other. Lilith lit another match. The flame died. "I call upon the Divine power of fire. The salamander of the elements to bless this circle. Create a barrier of your special power to protect my sister April from those who attack her." She struck another match. The flame was good and strong. "April, you can hear me. Fight them. You are an Amazon. A warrior. The daughter of warriors. Call upon the strength of the tribe." Lilith reached forward and lit a bundle of sage. "Upon the walls of caves of the Old Ones, it is written that no one shall interfere with another's free will to choose their path. Those who force their will on another shall only find themselves and their own ugliness staring back. Their reflection shall radiate so even the blind may see the ugliness within and without." She touched the flame to the log. It flickered then burst around the circle. Lilith jumped back. The flames spread and rose knee high.

Hoping for some kind of confirmation, Cheyenne watched the prone body. The movement of the flames gave her features dark shadows. It reminded Cheyenne of a death mask. She shuttered.

Lilith stepped beside her, encircling her arm around Cheyenne's waist. "Go inside. I'll watch her."

The warmth of her nearness helped still the growing fear within her. She shook her head. "Neither of us should be alone."

"Did you get a chance to eat?'

"Not yet."

"There is leftover stew in the frig. Go nuke it and then come back. I'll be fine for a few minutes. Besides," Lilith stepped back, "if something happens, you'll need to be as strong as you can be."

Cheyenne knew she was right. She nodded. "I'll be back in a few."

Lilith stepped closer to the circle. "It's not but I feel like it's my fault."

"I know that feeling." Cheyenne stepped back and returned to the house. Aries met her at the back door. Happily he tail wagged as he followed her around the kitchen. Frequently she reached down and scratched his ears. It was as much for her benefit as his. She just needed to touch him. Filling a bowl with the stew, she popped it into the microwave. Instinctively she checked their dishes. Aries was empty, but Mercury's was still full. She snuffled back the tears; he was gone. Licking her lips, she swallowed and picked up the dish. Aries sat at her feet, looking up at her. His brown eyes tried to comfort her. She was grateful for him and the others who held her. Intellectually she knew she would find a way to adapt. The grief would give way to other emotions.

But right now, she needed to feel it. Gently, Aries scratched at her leg. She poured the contents of Mercury's dish into the one on the floor and set the empty on the counter. She motioned and Aries immediately started to eat. Moments later, the microwave dinged and she opened the door. She ate without tasting. She emptied the bowl and rinsed it in the sink.

Through the window, she watched Lilith's silhouette highlighted by the flames; her stance was that of vigilance. Around her the darkness hid the rest of the world for good or bad. *Why did this have to happen to Lisa? Was it my fault?* Shaking her head, she tried to clear the thought from her head. Instead she focused on the now; the who, what and why's would wait until later when it was safe. She walked toward the door. Patting her thigh, Aries joined her. Together, they walked back to the circle.

"I'm back."

Lilith shook her head. "I need to gather more wood. At this rate it won't last long."

"It hasn't been that long."

"I know." Lilith's voice was filled with as much doubt as her own.

It had been almost an hour with no word. All the what-if's started to rise as her imagination took over. "When you get back, I'll get more herbs."

Lilith nodded and disappeared into the darkness, only to return a few minutes later with an armful of wood. "This is the last of the seasoned. If I use the green, it should give us another hour. Maybe more." Carefully she placed the logs next to the ones, which were the closest to becoming embers.

"It'll be enough." Cheyenne said it, but didn't believe one word. "I'll be right back with more herbs."

"Are you sure you want to go by yourself?"

"The greenhouse is the safest place." The thought just occurred to her. *Between the way it was built and the way she grounded it, it was the safest place on the farm.* The exterior was made of metal and glass; neither of which would burn easily. Originally she used the thickest panes available for insulation, but now it would be an additional line of defense. There was only one entrance. "Aries come. I'm going to leave him inside."

"Cheyenne, don't separate yourself from him."

"They want me not him."

"They want to hurt you." Lilith's voice was level and calm, yet there was an undercurrent of anxiety. "Think of everything Celeste has done and caused to happen. She won't stop at hurting you. She won't be happy until she has destroyed everything you build and hurt everyone you love. Hiding Aries away won't save him. They'll find him. What about the livestock—the horses, the goats—"

"Morgan and her pups!" She had forgotten, but Dominic wouldn't have. He would remember and find her.

"What about them?"

"She defended me from Dominic. He was very angry with her. He would have tried to kill her if Jasmine and Walter hadn't showed up."

"Jasmine and Walter?"

"Jerry's dogs. The five of them and sometimes Chester ran in a pack." The reality set in. "Jerry has aligned himself with Dominic. Goddess, please protect them. Did Carmen move in?"

"Yesterday."

"Is she home?"

"Not as far as I know. I saw her drive off midday." Lilith looked in the direction of the cabins. "I didn't see her dog with her. I think she was going to work. We need to call her."

Cheyenne's mind was racing. She didn't know what to do. She took a breath. "Ok. I'll get the herbs and you make the call. We'll meet back here and go from there."

Lilith nodded. "I'm also going to get my sword. I get the feeling we may need it." She looked over her shoulder at April. "Do you think she'll be safe?"

Cheyenne followed her gaze. Involuntarily she shuttered.

"What?"

Cheyenne shook the feeling off. "Be back." Without waiting, she walked as fast she could toward the greenhouse; Aries followed. She opened the door and turned the light on. It was quiet and peaceful. Nothing had changed. He sat at the door, waiting for her. Quickly she grabbed the remaining sage and cedar strings. Passing by her worktable, she instinctively grabbed her knife. It was used for trimming plants and cutting twine mostly. It wasn't large but it had a good edge. She hesitated. Unlike Lilith's sword, she didn't have a sheath to carry it. It wouldn't be safe to put it in her pocket or to slip it into the waistband of her shorts. Instead she cut a long length of twine; she looped it around the blade, just beneath the handle on the dull part, and tied the ends around her waist, allowing the blade to hang over her abdomen. It was makeshift and unstable. But it felt familiar.

Feeling like she was missing something, she looked around. Through the window, she saw the lights above the corral entrance come on. Morgan had walked out, triggering the sensor. Standing in the oval beams, she searched the field. Stretching her neck back, she gave a long howl. In the distance, two dogs answered her call. Aries replied in kind. In disbelief she watched him run across the yard and join Morgan at the barn. She followed him out as far as the corner of the greenhouse. Two more shapes jumped the corral fence and joined them in the doorway. It was Jasmine and Walter. They quickly greeted one another. The newcomers circled around, searching. Aries nuzzled them and they returned their attention to the pack. They still waited. Morgan called again. A muffled response was followed by the sound of breaking glass. From the darkness, Chester joined the group. They greeted him and together they walked inside. Moments later, the pack with the addition of the pups walked out of the back of the barn toward the open fields and the forest beyond.

Part of her was relieved. Any place she put them could just as easily be turned into a trap. All of them knew the land. She turned back toward the house. The nearly full moon was beginning to crest the treetops. Its light spilled across the field and on to the backyard. April stood in the center of the circle, staring at her. The back door opened and closed. Slowly April's head turned to watch Lilith walk toward her, buckling the sheath of her sword around her waist. Securing the buckle, she looked up and stopped short. Staring, she continued to the flaming circle. There were words spoken between them; Cheyenne couldn't hear the words but their body language was not of two friends. Warily she walked across the yard and joined them.

Angrily, April pointed the circle. "Maybe you can explain this." She demanded. "My friend," she emphasized the words, "doesn't seem to trust me enough to give me a straight answer."

Cheyenne looked to Lilith; she shook her head. Returning her attention to April, she instinctively rested her hand on her hip, bringing it closer to her knife. "It's a circle of protection."

"Against what?" April demanded, taking a step closer. The flames immediately flared, forcing her back to the center.

"It's a barrier." Lilith stared at her. "Nothing evil can cross it."

"You are naming me evil?" April's voice rose an octave. "How dare you!"

"No. The circle has named you so." Cheyenne cut in. "Otherwise you could easily step over the flames."

April pounded the vacant the air in front of her. "You can't do this to me."

Lilith responded by placing more wood around the circle.

"You can't!" April screamed. "I don't deserve this!"

"And we do?" Cheyenne countered. "You claim to be a Dragon. Yet the evil found a home in you so easily. Why is that?"

"I am not evil. I made mistakes. But I found my path again. I made up for them."

A car drove up the driveway and parked in front. The door opened and closed. All three became silent. Footsteps on the gravel approached the backyard. Stepping back into the shadows, Lilith pulled her sword from the sheath.

Cheyenne grabbed the handle of her knife. *Now what,* she thought. She pivoted and stepped back, creating the best view she could of April and the newcomer. The house and the garage remained dark. The sensor for the barn light had timed out and the light had shut itself off. The only light came from the rising moon and the glow of the flames. The footsteps stopped. For a few moments, Cheyenne only heard the crackle of the flames and the beating of her own heart. She reached out with her spiritual gifts; she was too injured to sense anything. The footsteps continued, only more cautiously. The crunch of the gravel alternated with the silence of a footsteps on grass. Cheyenne guestimated that whoever was on the side of the garage. Licking her lips, Cheyenne called out. "Who's there?"

Moments later Carmen appeared in the faint light of the moon. "Sorry. After Lilith's call. I didn't know what to expect."

Cheyenne exhaled. "You scared the—"

"Shit out of us." Lilith finished the thought, stepping out of the shadows and sheathing her sword. "I didn't expect you so fast."

"I was already on my way home." Carmen crossed the lawn. "Rachael called and had me close early. Something's up. I have never heard her afraid before."

"Something's up," Cheyenne confirmed. "And it isn't nice. Just so you know. The dogs, including Jasmine, Walter and Chester have packed with Morgan and Aries. They have taken the pups to the woods."

"How did he get out?"

"I heard glass breaking." Cheyenne met her part way. "I think they'll be safer out there. They know the turf."

"I don't like it."

"Neither do we, but we don't have a choice." Lilith stepped next to them. "We think Celeste and Dominic have

Lisa. Jane and a couple of new friends have gone to get her."

"They were briefly at the store with Rachael. Soon after Rachael left. She was strange all day. She wouldn't let anyone go into the back. Then suddenly she calls—tells me to clear the store and go home." Carmen pointed to the fire. "Ok. I'll ask. What and why?"

"They think I'm evil," April snapped back. "Get me out of here."

"What the hell is going on? Rachael calls in a panic—and Rachael never panics! She says we're not safe. I'm to go straight home—to run over anything that gets in my way?"

"Is she by herself?" Cheyenne remembered the grudge Dominic had against her. Rachael Franklin might not be at the top of his shit list, but she was definitely in the top five."

"No. Kevin's with her. When did you suddenly get so concerned?" Carmen planted her fists on her hips. "Ok, someone start explaining."

"You want an explanation." The flames around April flared, but she still smiled. "It's begun. Your rescuers have themselves become sacrifices. Nothing can stop them. They'll be here soon." She waved her hand over a section of the flames and they lowered. "Your petty magic won't save you."

"Shit!" Lilith shouted.

"Here." Cheyenne held out two of the strings of sage. "Spread them around."

Each of them took a strand, Stretching them to full-length, they tossed them on the logs. They smoldered threatening to put out the fire. Suddenly they burst into flame, pushing

April back toward the center. Led by Lilith, they added the green the circle.

April smiled, "How long will it last?" She quickly answered herself. "Not long and I'll be free."

The smoke pattern suddenly changed. Forming a cone, about five feet above the circle, an image appeared. It was Lisa, as they had known her. As she smiled down on them, the smoke elongated and the child was transformed into a grown woman with the eyes of their mother. Her braids revealed her rank as an elder and warrior.

Cheyenne knew her as their mother's sister. "Mesha?"

She nodded and turned to face off with April. "This far and no farther. The evil will end here."

April grabbed at the image only to find vacant air.

Mesha returned her attention to Cheyenne and Lilith. "Daughters of my sister, the evil is coming. I shall hold it back as long as I can. It is not safe for you here. Go to the forest. To sacred place. It is there you must meet them."

Frustrated, April screamed and grabbed at the apparition. "You can't stop us." She growled upward.

Mesha looked toward Cheyenne. "You have kept your honor and your oath to your clan. Know that no matter what happens, the darkness cannot touch you. It can harm you body, but will never be able to touch your soul."

"Is that why," Lilith pointed at April, "she lost the fight?"

"Yes," Mesha nodded. "The decisions and actions of the past betrayed herself and her clan. It is why the darkness was able to find a home in her heart."

"You don't know anything!" April screamed. "I changed!"

"I'm sorry April. If I had known . . ." Lilith's voice trailed off.

"It's your fault!" April pointed at Lilith. "You brought me here. You caused this to happen to me!"

"No." Mesha shook her head. "You brought yourself here. To test yourself. Again you lost you way." Her head turned slightly to make eye contact with Lilith. "You are a loving soul who gave her an opportunity. What she did with it is only her responsibility. Not yours on any level. Do you understand?"

Lilith nodded.

Mesha continued. "You must go."

"What about Jane and the others?" Cheyenne stepped closer to the ring. "They went to save you."

"They did their best," Mesha smiled. "I was grateful they tried." Suddenly her head snapped up and she looked off in one direction, but as quickly her gaze shifted to the opposite. "There is no more time! Run! I have awakened the other dragon." Her voice rose an octave.

"Rachael—" Carmen began.

"No! The other. That one is not safe either."

Cheyenne followed her gaze to the road. Car lights were coming down the road. For an instant, she stepped between time and space. She could see them miles down the road. Laughing at the conquests. Confident in the success. There were two cars. Celeste, Dominic and three others she didn't know were in the first. Jerry and four others were in the second; she knew they were going to Rachael's. In slow motion, the two sets of car lights bounced on the road They were about five miles away. There was very little time. She thought of using herself as bait so the others could find safety.

Lilith reached out and took her hand. "We all go."

Carmen took her other hand. "Agreed."

Time snapped back to normal and Cheyenne looked down the road. "They are in two cars. Jerry and others are going after Rachael. Celeste and Dominic have three others. They are about five miles away"

"How do you know?" Carmen released her hand and took several steps in the direction of Rachael's cottage. "Kevin is with her."

"He won't be able to save her." April reached out and waved her palm over the flames. They flared, but immediately started to burn themselves out. "Any more than you will be able to save yourselves or those you love."

Ignoring her, Cheyenne said an unstructured prayer for Jane and the two others. "This way."

The threesome quickly walked to the shadows. Cheyenne led the way down the path. The quickest way was off the path, through the forest. They reached the tree line and began threading their way through.

A movement in the shadows caught Cheyenne's attention. Before she could warn Lilith, the form separated from the shadows, becoming a large man, bare to the waist with some sort of animal skin covering from there to his knees. Startled, Cheyenne let out a shrill scream that faintly resembled Lilith's name.

Jumping backward, Lilith tried pulling her sword. It cleared its sheath only for it to be kicked from her hand. Angrily she lunged at him. Casually he avoided her attack and knocked her to the ground. She screamed.

The moonlight reached into the trees and she saw him more clearly. On top of his head were feathers. Yellow and white horns curved forward out of the sides of his head. His eyes were rimmed with white, as was the star on his left cheek and the crescent moon on the right. In the center of his face, a long toothed snout protruded. There was foliage around his neck, but the dimness and the distance hid what kind. His shoulders were painted yellow, but his arms and hands were painted white. She searched her memory. There was something. But it was so long ago. No name came, yet awe and fear flooded over her.

He bent down easily and picked up Lilith's sword off the ground. Only then did he release her. With one stroke, he buried the sword deeply into a stump. He motioned. Two more, dressed as he, separated themselves from the shadows. One reached for Cheyenne's knife and pulled it; the string easily broke and it joined Lilith's weapon.

Angrily, Lilith crawled out of his reach and stood, returning to her companions. "Why didn't you help me?" She snapped.

"How?" Carmen's tone matched Lilith's.

"Ahotes." The word sprang from Cheyenne's lips. It was from a vague memory from the time soon after Celeste found her. A mother, from the village, scolded her child, using the name Ahotes and the Restless One to frighten her son into being good. No one would explain the terms to her.

The men merged again with the shadows and were gone. Lilith moved toward her sword.

"Don't," Cheyenne warned.

"But—we need it!" Lilith protested.

Cheyenne shook her head. "We have to go on."

"What about—" Carmen pointed back toward the farm.

"No!" Cheyenne cut her off. "They'll protect us." Without waiting, she continued forward.

Wordlessly they followed. Carmen's inexperience echoed in every crunch of leaves and snap of every twig, telegraphing their position with each step she took. Part of Cheyenne wanted to leave her behind, but she knew it was wrong. They had to stay together. Carmen stumbled over a fallen branch. It snapped under her weight. Quickly she regained her balance. Over her shoulder, she saw Lilith flinch. After what seemed forever and three days to Cheyenne, they reached the outer ring of the sacred circle. She motioned for them to say within the safety of the trees, while she continued out on to the field. It was quiet. She expected a radical change, but there was none. She continued toward the center tree. Halfway there, it occurred to her she should have thrown up what little shield she had left. But it was too late. She sensed they were there and they had already seen her weakness.

Cheyenne was nearly beneath the canopy of the tree, when Celeste stepped into view. The width of the trunk had concealed her. Her hair was long and black. Dressed in a halter-top, jean shorts and mid-calf boots, she walked with the freedom and ease of a woman in her mid-twenties. Her eyes reflected the moonlight as she stepped from the shadows of the branches. "Nothing special about this place." She cruelly smiled. "Not any more. We didn't expect you. But no matter." She traced her finger down her shoulder to her hip. "Do you like?" She didn't wait for an answer. "No? Neither did Jane. You both flaunted your youth."

"Where is Jane?" Cheyenne sputtered. "Celeste, what did you do?"

She smirked. "You might as well tell your friends to come out. We know where they are."

"What did you do to Jane?" Cheyenne demanded.

"Come out! Come out, little ones!" she yelled toward Carmen and Lilith. "We won't hurt you." She lowered her voice. "At least not right away."

"Stop it!" Cheyenne screamed, pushing Celeste backward.

With a casual swing, Celeste sent her flying backward.

Cheyenne roughly landed on her back, sending dust up all around her. Blood oozed from her lip and nose. "Where's Jane?"

"You always did have spunk."

"I survived the desert and whatever put me there." She focused on her anger, allowing it to give her a new strength. Ignoring the pain and blood, Cheyenne lifted herself back up. "You're nothing."

Slowly Celeste pulled the dagger from her right boot. The blood had congealed from the tip to the handle. Triumphantly she held it up. "You gave Dominic's dagger to the police. You shouldn't have done that. It was very special. Consecrated by the blood of an innocent. She was a priestess's daughter. You made it necessary to make a new one. We couldn't find a priestess's daughter—at least not right away. But we found something better. A dragonet. By accepting, she forfeited her heritage."

"I know what you did," Cheyenne snapped. "Lisa told me."

For an instant, Celeste's confidence wavered. "Tell your friends to come out. I want to make them my friends too."

"Is that how you got your youth back?"

"It was easy," Celeste bragged, swinging her hair back over her shoulder. "The Dark One taught Dominic. Dominic taught me. Now I do what ever I want. Dom," she called, "would you invite the others to the party. I'm getting hungry."

Wolves howled from three directions.

"Run!" Cheyenne screamed.

"They won't get far," Celeste laughed.

"Neither will you." Cheyenne leaped.

Celeste easily stepped out of the way. Cheyenne landed face down in the dirt. Celeste stomped down on her back, holding her against the ground. "To think I once thought you were special. My mistake."

The pressure on her back made breathing difficult. The heels pushed directly against her spine; it would be very easy for her to snap her back. In the distance, the growling wolves converged on the area where she had left Lilith and Carmen and were quickly followed by screams of terror. Suddenly, the screams were cut short and there was silence.

"Oops!" Celeste chuckled. "I have to feed elsewhere. Like right here. I hear Mercury died. Oh, too bad. And that Aries deserted you. No matter. I found him. He was delicious."

The dirt in her eyes made mud from her tears. Cheyenne no longer had a reason to fight. It was over. Better to release her tenuous hold her spirit maintained on this body and set her spirit free than to allow them to feed off her. Suddenly there was a new presence—old, yet stronger. Cheyenne felt them approach through the vibrations in the ground. She remembered it from somewhere in her past; she knew it then to be of the light.

"The wind tells me you have two hearts, daughter." The female voice was elderly and unfamiliar.

The pressure on her back increased. Cheyenne fought for each breath.

"You have no right to judge me," Celeste snapped.

"I have every right," the old voice contracted.

"No!" Celeste's voice rose an octave. "Not even Grandmother and mother can judge me now. They are dead and I am free."

"Your grandmother. My mother." The woman's voice was calm and dignified, completely secure within herself. "I am your mother's sister. Now elder to our family."

"I never acknowledged you as my elder!"

"But I did." Another strange female voice spoke from behind Celeste. She too was older, but not as old as the first.

"And I." The third female voice was close to the second. She was much younger than the other two.

Cheyenne felt Celeste pivot on her back, pushing her heel deeper into her skin.

"As do my other children," the second voice continued. "Your nieces and nephew. As do their children."

"But me and mine do not!" Celeste screamed.

"We shall see," the elder woman stated.

A moment later, Celeste screamed and the pressure on Cheyenne's back was released. Cheyenne took a deep breath, replenishing her oxygen deprived lungs. She rolled onto her side. A hand appeared before her face. It was callused and wrinkled, and the thinning of the skin made the veins and arteries more prominent, yet the power and strength contained within the aging body made Cheyenne shrink back in awe.

"Take my hand child. Let me help you."

She accepted the offered hand and painfully stood to face the elderly woman. Tied back into a smooth braid, her hair was long and white. Although her skin was brown from the sun and from her heritage, it was almost translucent with age; as if the years she lived had slowly worn away all but the final layer of skin. In spite of her age, the wild girl of her youth still lived in the brown eyes. Her teeth had yellowed, with a chip in her right canine. But her smile was no less warm or loving. She was wearing a full ritual dress of a High Priestess. Cheyenne recognized it from the pictures of her Grandmother Celeste had shown her.

Celeste screamed profanities.

Cheyenne turned.

Two women held Celeste's arms behind her back. The older woman was about Celeste's natural age, but she was inches taller. Her hair was cut short and curled around her head. The younger woman was just as tall and mirrored the older woman's features, except her hair was worn long and loose. Celeste continued to struggle against them.

The elderly hand released hers and began to brush the dirt from Cheyenne's face. "I am called Elizabeth by the white man. My family and clan call me Naquamuysee. But you shall call me as your cousins do, Grandmother."

Panic crossed Celeste's face. "She's not of my blood."

"Are you not the child Celeste brought from the desert?"

"Yes." Nervously, Cheyenne tried calling her by her name, but it came out jumbled.

The old woman smiled. "Grandmother."

Cheyenne tried again, with no better success. She took a long deep breath. "Yes . . . Grandmother."

"No!" Celeste screamed.

Grandmother turned to the other newcomers. "Daughter," Grandmother began, "Celeste asked you to be the child's sponsor to the family."

"Yes," the elder one responded. "My sister came to me, crying. She wanted a child. But the Great Spirit had chosen not to bless her. She went on a spirit journey into the desert to find answers. She found a white child. Bloody body and broken spirit. No one thought she would live. The Elders wanted to return her to her own people. Celeste thought she was her only chance to be a mother."

"Was your blood mingled?" Grandmother continued.

"Yes." She quickly continued, "Grandmother said no. But when she was strong enough we took her out on the mesa and took the bonding oath. Celeste left with her the next morning. She didn't want Grandmother to know. But I told her after they left. She nodded and nothing more was ever said."

"I renounce her!" Celeste growled. "Cheyenne betrayed me. She betrayed our family."

"No." Cheyenne whispered. "I still have my honor. Celeste can't say the same."

"No!" Celeste pushed and shoved, trying to free herself.

Grandmother nodded. The women released Celeste and stepped back. She pointed toward the elder of the two. "This is Beverly. She is Celeste's elder sister. And her eldest daughter, Shane."

Celeste searched the ground until she found her knife. "I don't need you! Any of you!" In a fluid motion she grabbed it and leaped at Grandmother, bringing the blade to the elderly woman's throat.

Calmly the elderly woman continued. "Do you accept us as your family?"

Stunned, Cheyenne nodded.

"Shut up old woman," Celeste hissed. "Nothing you can do can make any difference."

"I accept you as spirit of my blood." Cheyenne knelt before the elderly woman.

Beverly and Shane echoed their acceptance and stepped on either side of Cheyenne. Beverly offered her hand to the younger woman and pulled her back to her feet.

"It doesn't matter!" Celeste slowly pulled the knife across the elderly woman's neck, cutting through the skin. Blood oozed from the thin line trailing behind it. Celeste laughed.

Shane and Cheyenne screamed.

With a quick flick of her wrist, Beverly made a sign in the air.

Out of the ground, a wolf sprung, leaping at Celeste. Grabbing her arm, it bit down.

Celeste screamed. "Dominic!" Her hand snapped open. The knife dropped.

Pulling backward, the wolf yanked its head, spinning Celeste away from Grandmother. It knocked her to the ground and circled around her. Stopping at her feet, it rose onto its hind legs and became the warrior who had taken Lilith's sword.

"Ahote!" Celeste squeaked, crawling backward. "Dominic! Help me!"

Beverly ran to Grandmother. Ripping a long strip from her shirt, she carefully wrapped it around the shallow cut. "It's not deep."

"I'll be fine." The older woman patted Beverly's hand, but allowed her to continue to put pressure on the cut.

"It's not my fault!" Celeste whined. "Dominic . . . I love him. I just wanted to love him."

"You knew," Cheyenne countered. "You had to know. He arrived and evil came with him."

"That's a lie!" Celeste sat up. "He isn't evil. He loves me!"

"Loves you?" The elder woman stared at her. "What kind of love prompts you to harm others? To steal property and their soul's energy."

"I never—"

Beverly stood and walked toward Celeste, the anger flaring in her eyes. "We have been here nearly two days, talking to people—asking questions. You have dishonored yourself, your family and your people." Her voice became deadly cold. "I disown you. You are no longer of my blood or my spirit." She picked up the knife. "This is appropriate. With the blood of your victims, I cut you forever from my life. As they are dead, so are you." She sliced a curl free and released it to the breeze.

Looking up at her sister, Celeste trembled. Her fingers digging into the soil. "I don't need you. I never needed you. You're weak." She pointed at Grandmother. "You always let them do your thinking! That's why you hate me."

"I didn't hate you," Beverly whispered. "I loved you."

"Help me." Celeste reached out to her. "I just wanted to be with the man I loved."

Beverly stepped backward. "You don't even know what that is." She dropped the knife and returned to Grandmother's side. "I'm ready."

The elderly woman nodded. With the two younger women's help, she stood. In a clear, strong voice she began to sing. The two other women harmonized with the chant.

Cheyenne recognized only a few words. They called the Chamahiye—Snake Chief of the underworld, and Kwanitaqa, the one horned God.

Celeste jumped to her feet and tried to run. Springing from the ground, the warriors grabbed her, forcing her to stay.

The words ran fluidly together. One chorus ended, another began, building in rhythm of words.

"I just loved a man!" Celeste screamed.

No one listened. The ions of the air charged, becoming as individual as ice crystals shimmering in the full moon. They snapped and crackled. Heat radiated up from the ground. It felt more like a sun-baked desert than a grassy field. Cheyenne wanted to run. She couldn't move. Even Celeste ceased to struggle. The wind calmed, yet the flashes danced around them in a circular pattern. Grandmother raised her arms, arcing them over her head. In one hand she held a pouch. At the zenith of the arc, ashes spilled from the bag, being caught up in the electrical cavalcade around them. The flashes became forms. Burning eyes peered at them. Faces with no distinct features drifted toward them. A face formed out of one of the shapes. It was an older woman. Slowly her image formed a distinctness of its own. Suddenly the chanting stopped.

"Mother," Grandmother began. "See into my heart. Know what I know." Their eyes met.

"Grandmother! It's a lie!" Celeste screamed, again struggling to free herself.

The apparition turned toward Celeste. "Daughter, why have you brought shame to our family?"

"I didn't Grandmother. I just wanted to be happy. Please Grandmother. Don't I deserve to be loved?"

"It is said you practice black magic. That you steal others' souls." The apparition's eye burned into Celeste. "My eyes see the truth that your words cannot deny. Your hair dark and your face untouched by time. The corn is planted from seed. The seed grows to become root and stalk. As the seeds mature, the hair darkens. When the corn is ripe, it has completed its cycle of life. The stalk dies and returns to the earth to replenish it for the new life to be planted." The apparition slowly pointed to Grandmother and Beverly. "They are preparing to join me in spirit." Her finger arched to the younger woman. "When last I saw this one, she was a child. Now she is a woman ready to bear children of her own." Her arm curled in and unfolded, pointing at Celeste. "Your hair is dark, you face untouched by time. Why daughter?"

"Grandmother—please!"

"Why daughter?" The apparition demanded.

"Dominic!" Celeste screamed.

"Why daughter?" she persisted.

"No!" Celeste growled. "You won't shame me. Not any more!" She reached out her hand. The knife sprang from the ground; its hilt landing neatly in her hand. Her fingers curled around the handle. With a backward lash, she cut the nearest warrior's shoulder, slashing upward to cut through his neck. With a flash of the already bloodied blade, Celeste spun around, cutting deeply into the stomach of the warrior on the right and back fisting the one on the left. Quickly the blade found the chest of the third warrior. She buried it to the hilt. With a snap, she freed it. He fell backward. "By the blood sacrifice, by the oath given and received—I summon Dominic and his shadow."

From beyond the oak tree, a wolf howled. Celeste smiled. "He is coming."

"You have condemned yourself child," the apparition spoke sadly.

"To what? Happiness. Love. To having my own child! He loves me. He'll protect me. You never did."

"You are no longer of my blood." The Apparition began. "I banish you from my heart and my soul. I release you forever to face your own deeds."

"Celeste." Grandmother spoke next. "You are no longer of my blood. I banish you from my heart and soul. I release you to your own deeds."

"Am I supposed to care?" Celeste laughed. "I have Dominic and all the power you denied me."

A growl, which became a laugh, cut her short. The wolf stepped out of the shadow, transforming into Dominic. He crossed the space between him and Celeste. He embraced her and stared at the apparition. "You see, old woman. I have won." With a wave of his open palm, the apparition disassembled and fell to the ground. The embers faded and disappeared. The warriors vanished back into the ground. "The dark path has always been stronger."

"See what all your chanting and prayer has got you. Nothing." Celeste gloated. "I'm strong and young. You are old and worn—"

"But what did it cost you?" Beverly protectively stepped between them and Grandmother.

"I didn't pay anything. I took their souls and they gave me life. They made me young again."

"As will you." He pointed at Shane. "I will make good use of you."

Undaunted, Shane squared her shoulder. "You cannot touch my spirit." Tilting her head, she faced off with Celeste. "I speak for all of my generation. You are no longer of our blood. I banish you from our hearts and our souls. I release you to the path you have chosen."

Cheyenne felt it was now her turn. "Celeste. I banish you forever from my heart and soul. I ask the powers of justice to stand between us. I give over to them the karma you owe me."

"I banish you. I banish you." Mockingly, Dominic waved his hand up and down in front of them. "Not real effective."

Grandmother gently pushed Beverly from her path and stepped closer to him. "As elder and priestess of the Bear Clan—"

"You are not my elder!" he growled.

"I speak for your blood family and sever all ties to you on all levels. You no longer have a clan. No ties of blood."

He backhanded her, knocking her to the ground. "Shut up old woman!'

Grandmother continued; her voice strong and confident. "I call forth the spirits of our ancestors to protect our journey. May the Bear spirit give us strength. May the Eagle spirit take our words to Sotuknang and his uncle, Taiowa. Let not the fourth world end for the deeds of these two; who have two hearts yet have love for none."

Shane quickly cut in. "The ties have been severed. These two shall face their crimes alone. None will stand by or for them. None will give them shelter." She reached into her pocket. "As it was arranged by others before, I call in the names of their spirits and stand for them as guardian." She threw three crystals on the ground between them and Dominic. "With these thrice blessed stones by the bonded three, in the name of the Maiden, Mother, Crone I call the Old Ones. Through the path weaved by the three faces of the Goddess travel from your realm to ours and manifest fully to create justice for all who have been harmed."

As the last word was spoken, the crystals burst into flame, setting the field aglow brighter than the noonday sun. A circle of fire surround and separated Celeste and Dominic from the rest. Wildly he waved his hands, trying to disburse them. His efforts only fed the flames. The ground rumbled and shook.

Simultaneously, the surface erupted as they burst forth, wings extended. Their scaled bodies reflected the full light of the moon. Their heads rose higher than the ancient oak, while their claws barely cleared the soil. Wing tip to wing tip, they hovered in a circle around them. Their eyes glowed with white light of the noonday sun. Lightning flashed in their pupils. Another being quickly followed. Hovering above them with no distinct shape or mass, the Mother Dragon watched. Her energy shimmered and crackled, charging the sky with her distinct presence. Her wings created gusts of wind. Her breath heated the air. Carefully watching, she waited without hinting of her intentions.

"We, the Sisters of Justice," they spoke in harmony, "have come to the seekers of justice."

Astonishment and fear appeared in Grandmother's and Beverly faces. Shane stood firm, extending her arms wide mirroring their wings. "I have called." She began slowly. "In the name of the others—Bridget, Jane and Shelly."

"Why do they not stand before us?"

Shane pointed at Celeste and Dominic.

The glowing eyes focused on the duo.

Celeste tried to hide in Dominic's arms. He shielded her with one; the other waved wildly above his head. He shouted; his words echoed off the beating wings, creating a feedback which left them jumbled and unintelligible.

Shane continued; whereas his voice echoed, hers drifted among them like a summer breeze. "They called you to bring justice. These two," she continued to point, "have broken the laws of man, the laws of spirit, and the laws of the universe in this lifetime and others. They have trapped us in a cycle of death and deceit, holding us back from the growth we have earned."

"We care nothing for the laws of man." They harmonized. "But we shall see the others. Open the book of yesterdays. Show us the paths these souls have traveled."

"You have no power over us." Dominic growled.

Their eyes first focused on Shane. Her back arched and her head tilted back. The wind from their wings lifted her up. Her arms dropped to her sides. She slowly spun around in midair. Just as quickly she was carefully deposited on her original place. Opening her eyes, she turned her head to look at Dominic and Celeste, the glow of the experience still burning in her eyes.

Grandmother was lifted next. For an instant, she fought, only to relax as she began to understand. The makeshift bandage slipped way to reveal the rapidly healing injury. Returning to the ground, she touched her throat and nodded her gratitude. Beverly followed. She immediately opened herself to them. A wide rage of emotion crossed her face. Tears streamed down her cheeks as she was returned to the earth.

Cheyenne felt their eyes fall on her. Wind rushed through her. She thought nothing more of her body as the kaleidoscope of images overtook her. Snapshots of places and people flashed, without time to remember the names. A prison camp of soldiers. A father with laughing eyes and a stern mother with a tender heart. The guillotine. The man whose betrayal of a trusted friend brought them both to death. The pages flipped like a kinescope only the images danced out of sequence. Barbarians raided from the north. Their valley invaded. A horse won for honor. Envy from one who thought her beauty was all she needed. Again betrayal. The images stopped. Time shot forward to a birth surrounded by anger and pain. A man who hated her existence. Beatings. Rage. Pain. The freezing cold of the desert followed by the unrelenting sun of the day. A coyote licking her face, his saliva wetting her lips bringing her back to awareness. Cool water given by a warm heart. Three women. The images became familiar. She was again standing on the field. Her eyes were drawn to the twosome. She could not turn away.

The flaming eyes directed their attention to Celeste. She would not release her hold on Dominic. Together they were lifted. Only it was not like the others. Faces appeared in the air around them, preventing the Beings of Justice from reaching them. Some of them Cheyenne knew. Maxie was among them. His face was contorted with pain and fear. Cheyenne felt no sympathy for him. There were at least two dozen others she could put a name to, yet there were others who seemed familiar only their facial features were masked by whatever bound them. The Being from the West reached out, unfurling her hand. The faces began to disappear as each soul was released until only Dominic and Celeste remained. Celeste cried out in pain. Dominic pulled her closer. They returned to the earth. Their bodies once again matched their ages. Celeste stumbled. Dominic caught her.

Above, three pairs of eyes focused on the Being in the North. Time slowed. The air heated. Dominic pulled Celeste toward the trees. The Being in the South tossed them back. Dominic landed face first. Celeste was not so lucky. She twisted in the air, hitting hard on her back and side. She didn't move. Dominic crawled to her. Brushing the hair from her face, he kissed her lips. Jumping to his feet, he lunged for freedom. Without effort, he was knocked back. Curling into a ball, he chanted in a language beyond words. His shape shifted into a large gray wolf. Snarling he sought a weakness. Finding none, his eyes shifted to Grandmother. He howled.

His call was immediately answered from several directions. As on cue, four other wolves stepped from the shadows of the trees and circled toward the group. They entered the circle, carefully avoiding the hovering talons, and joined with Dominic. Growling, they moved into attack posture.

"No!" Beverly screamed, stepping in front of the elderly woman.

"Who intervenes between these two souls?" They questioned in harmony.

"I do," Beverly's voice wavered.

Grandmother whispered, "I know what they want."

Dominic growled and circled around her. The other four moved in the opposite direction, separating her from the other women. She did nothing to defend herself.

"No!" Lilith screamed. Surrounded by Aries and his pack, plus two strange dogs, she limped out of the shadows, half carrying Carmen. "This will not happen!"

From above, a talon hand reached out and protected the elderly woman from her attackers. Frustrated, they sought another target, looking first at Beverly then at Shane. Beverly sought the shelter beside her aunt. Shane defiantly stared back.

Cheyenne was shocked by the their appearance. Aries coat was matted and blooded. There was an open and bleeding wound on his back haunch. She wanted to run to him. The other dogs had similar injuries. Chester dragged his left leg; the broken bone had ripped through his skin. Morgan and the pups trailed the group; one of the pups was missing. She didn't want to think about its fate.

Carmen had a deep bite on her left leg. Blood had streamed down, covering from her upper thigh to her ankle. Bruises and scratches covered most of her exposed skin, disappearing beneath her clothing. With each step, she grimaced.

The color of Lilith's skin hid her bruises, but the scratches on her arms and legs revealed she also fought hard. Blood had dripped from her cheek onto her shirt. Reaching the circle of talons, she helped Carmen sit beneath their protection and continued alone. The pack surround Carmen; the injured painfully lying down. "No. There are others who deserve justice." Walking deeper into the circle, she looked up. "I speak for those who have been injured or killed. What is between them can wait for another time and place. I had a friend who was turning her life back to the light. But now she is again lost in the darkness."

"All choose their own path," The Eastern Being spoke alone.

"She didn't choose!" Lilith countered, squaring off with her. "Neither did the others consent. He forced his way into their lives and souls."

"We know of this." The Western Being craned its neck downward, confronting Lilith with its fiery eyes. "What is it you ask?"

Without flinching, Lilith answered, "I wish him—all of them to receive full measure of justice."

"Would you face the same justice?" It immediately responded.

"I have not always been truthful. I have stolen. I have killed in battle. I have loved what was not mine and caused others pain." Lilith took a deep breath and quickly exhaled. "I have also loved unselfishly. I have brought life from my body to replace that which was taken. I have been a loyal friend."

"All this is true." The Eastern Being confirmed.

"I have made my mistakes." Lilith continued. "But I have learned from them. In the past, he betrayed me."

"You want vengeance!" The Western Being leaned forward, bringing her face within inches of Lilith's.

"No." Lilith stepped backward. "I want justice. No more. No less."

"Name its form." Gracefully it lifted its head up and backward, returning to the same posture as the others.

Lilith hesitated.

"No!" Cheyenne blurted out. Surprised by her own words, she found herself standing beside Lilith. "I too demand justice."

Immediately the eyes focused on her.

Cheyenne felt her stomach quiver, but not her resolve. "I too was betrayed by him. More than once. Each opportunity he was given to heal the wound between us, he chose to do more harm."

Dominic circled around toward her. The others trailed behind, watching and waiting.

"I speak now not only for myself but also for my sisters." Cheyenne continued.

"As so I," Lilith added.

"I, we, forgive and release the past in order to move on to the future."

Growling Dominic leaped at Cheyenne. A clawed hand reached from the south, catching him in midair. Bones snapped. Dominic's crushed body was dropped at their feet. The others ran into the darkness.

"Satisfied?" The owner of the talons asked. "Or do you wish the others to meet the same fate?"

For an instant, satisfaction washed over her, but she quickly checked it. "I am grateful my son Aries is alive. I am grateful my friends are alive and will heal." Tears overflowed her eyes. "I am satisfied that it is now over and that our paths will never cross again."

"What justice do you want dispensed on his soul?" It continued.

"It's time for us to go home and mend our wounds." Cheyenne looked to Grandmother.

She nodded and looped her arm through Beverly's. Together they slowly walked toward Cheyenne. Shane joined them as they walked past her. Cheyenne and Lilith also turned away from the center of the circle. A talon hand chopped down in front of them. They tried to walk around it. Again, Cheyenne's path was blocked, but Lilith's path was cleared.

"What do you want from me?" Cheyenne demanded.

"To see into you're true heart," they answered. "Why did you not call your Mother Dragon? You could have ended this at the beginning."

Cheyenne didn't have an answer. "I don't know." *Calling Mother Dragon had simply never occurred to her.*

"Did you stray from your path of honor as the other?" The Eastern one questioned. "Is that why you did not take action yourself?"

"No." Cheyenne looked up at her. "My honor is intact and clear." Without forethought, she continued. "She was my friend. She was my enemy. Then she was nothing. But I did not trust my motives to be truly objective. If I had interceded on my own behalf, justice would have been tilted out of balance. No one can judge that which they are a part of." She hesitated for a moment and continued. "I did not call the Mother of all Clans. I do not have a reason beyond I did not think it was proper."

"Child," A new voice gently spoke. "You never need a reason to call upon me. I am here for all the children of my soul. In your sadness and your joy, you may come to me. It is in me that all the clans get their strength. Your honor is indeed intact. With my blessing and love, you are released to follow your destiny to the end."

Cheyenne looked through the talons. The Ahote warriors again emerged from the earth, completely healed. One lifted Carmen into his arms and carried her toward the path home; the another carried Chester. The other dogs protectively followed their injured members. Grandmother and her family were behind them. Only Aries and Lilith waited for her. Inwardly smiling, she looked up at them. "What happens to them from now forward is none of my business."

"You have no doubt?" The Eastern One asked skeptically.

"None of my business," she repeated curtly.

"Or mine." Lilith echoed.

"You don't want to know what will happen to them?"

"No." Ignoring the sharp edges of the claws, Cheyenne reached out and pushed it out of the way. To her surprise, it gave freely. Without the thought of looking back, Cheyenne walked to Lilith. Their eyes met.

Lilith nodded.

Together they spun around and marched toward the path. Aries joined them and they entered the forest. Cheyenne focused on taking the next step and the one that followed. Once Lilith stumbled; she caught herself and kept going. There seemed to be no words, no complete thought, just a goal to reach. She didn't know what she would find, but she wanted to be home. Aries whined. She reached down and scratched his head. It was as comforting to her as it seemed to be to him. They couldn't stop. Not at that time. They had to leave it all behind. Cheyenne had a feeling if just one of them looked back, they would all be bound again in the same cycle of betrayal and violence. Behind them lay the past. The future waited ahead. Cries from behind echoed among the trees. It was beyond anything she had heard before. High-pitched, like metal on metal, yet it was not. Human, yet not. It radiated agony and terror—pain beyond words. With one hand she grabbed Aries collar; with the other, she found Lilith's hand. The screaming continued, louder than before; they hesitated. Cheyenne bit her lip. Lilith squeezed her hand, but they did not stop. The tree line was close. Cheyenne fought the instinct to run the rest of the way. Neither of them had the spare energy. From behind the wind blew past, pushing her hair into her face. It reeked of rotting flesh. Cheyenne gagged.

"Oh, my Goddess," Lilith groaned.

They broke through the trees and stepped onto the moon-lit field. Only then did they stop. The air was fresh and clean. Cheyenne released Lilith's hand and knelt beside Aries. The bite was deep, but nothing that wouldn't heal.

"How is he?"

Cheyenne stood. "He'll need stitches and a lot of TLC"

"Won't we all."

Cheyenne looked toward the farm. With the full moon, she could see the buildings clearly. They were dark and quiet. The brightness prevented her from seeing the light of the circle. If the fire still burned, they would not know until they reached the back yard.

'Let's do it." Without waiting, Lilith continued down the path.

Cheyenne and Aries followed a few steps behind. Reaching the crest of the hill. Lilith stopped and waited for them. They rounded the barn together. The fire circle was dead. April was gone. Was she one of the wolves, who joined Dominic or was she able to escape? At that moment, Cheyenne was too tired to count the number of her potential enemies. The spotlight came on as it sensed them approaching the back door.

Lilith opened the screen door. The creak seemed louder than usual. She pulled on the back door; it swung open. "Hey lady, ya think you should lock your door when youse go out."

The absurdity of the statement, made Cheyenne snort. "Who's going to get me out here? The boogie man?"

Lilith groaned and walked inside, but immediately stopped and pointed. Cheyenne looked past her at the light shining through the dining room archway from somewhere in the front of the house. Her heart sank. She stepped inside and motioned for Aries to stay. He couldn't defend himself but neither could either one of them. Quietly closing the door behind them, Cheyenne pulled two knifes from the block, handing one to Lilith. Her eyebrow arched at the size of it, but she said nothing.

Several people whispered from just beyond the archway. Their words weren't clear.

Cheyenne pointed. Lilith nodded. Passing through the kitchen, Cheyenne passed Lilith and took the lead. Of the two, she was the stronger, more able to defend against an attack. Suddenly the light turned on. Blinded by the brightness, Cheyenne involuntarily turned away, but just as quickly turned back, brandishing the knife in front of her.

"Cheyenne!" Jane screamed in delight. "Thank Goddess. We didn't know who . . ." Her voice trailed off.

"Jane?" Blinking rapidly, Cheyenne tried to focus. The light was turned off and Jane flipped another switch, turning on the light above the sink. Cheyenne's vision cleared. Jane stood a few feet from her. Even in the semi-darkness, she could see the welts and bruises on Jane's face and arms. Bridget and Shelly stood behind Jane; they faired no better. "I thought they killed you."

Tears streamed down, Jane's cheeks. "I thought the same thing about you."

"Celeste said—she said." Cheyenne stepped backward into Lilith, suddenly suspicious. "She said she killed you."

"They were going to." Bridget cut in. "But they saw the dragon spirit and lost interest in us."

"What happened?" Lilith stepped around Cheyenne. "Didn't Sammy help you?"

Jane shook her head. "We decided in the car not to involve her. With her knee in a cast, there wasn't anything she could do."

"She could have sent help," Lilith chided.

"Knowing her, she would have gotten out of her hospital bed and joined us.

"They tied us up and said they'd take care of us after they took care of you." Shelly stepped into the room. "They knew your body would be vulnerable."

"How do we know they aren't just using you? Like they did April." Cheyenne stepped forward, trying to appear more confident than she actually felt.

"What do you mean like April?" Bridget snapped.

"She lost the battle." Cheyenne matched her tone. "She became more than their eyes and ears. She became one of them."

"That's why they were waiting for us." Shelly voice reflected the rapid workings of her mind. "How were you able to take flight and protect your body? They were so sure you couldn't."

Bridget pushed past Jane and confronted Cheyenne. "We are not one of their pawns. Are you?"

Cheyenne shook her head. "No!"

"How were you able to take flight?" Bridget persisted.

"I didn't!" Cheyenne snapped back. "We had to run for our lives."

"Then who was the dragon?" Jane stepped between them.

"I don't know." Cheyenne shook her head. "Lisa—Mesha told us—"

"Mesha?" Bridge questioned.

"I know that name." Shelly's voice began as a whisper. "But I don't know why." She touched her mother's arm. "I know that name. Don't you?"

Bridget shook her head. "No!"

"She was our mother's sister before." Lilith explained. "In a valley where we lived together in peace."

"Until we were betrayed." Cheyenne cut in. "By one of our own."

"Like now." Jane picked up the thought.

"Did we finish the circle?" Shelly sounded disappointed. "I wanted to be part of the justice."

Lilith shook her head. "It has only begun."

"What are you talking about?" Angrily Bridget stepped away from them, spinning on her toes to face them. "You didn't answer my question. Who was the dragon?"

"I don't know!" Cheyenne matched her angry tone. "Lisa's spirit appeared in the smoke of the circle. She said she had wakened a dragon to protect us—you. But that's all she had time for."

"Have you seen April?" Lilith's hope shone in her brown eyes.

"No." Bridget dropped her defiant stance, concern filling her voice. "She wasn't here when we got back."

Lilith shook her head and walked from the dining room into the darkness of the kitchen. "I was hoping.." Her voice trailed off.

"After you left," Cheyenne began, "it was able to fully take over her. She fought the best that she could."

"But she was a dragon!" Shelly voice raised an octave. "Her honor would have protected her."

Cheyenne wanted to comfort Lilith, but there was nothing she could say or do to help her friend through her grief.

"Things she had done tarnished her honor." Bridget brushed her daughter's cheek. "It was before you knew her. She did things," quickly she added, "but we thought she had made up for them. She'd changed so much. Helped so many others who had started down the same path as she. We thought we restored her honor. I didn't see it. Maybe I could have—"

"She didn't know either." Following Lilith into the kitchen, Cheyenne reached out and massaged Lilith's hunched shoulders. "We didn't know. If we had . . ."

"What could we have done?" Lilith cut her off.

"I don't know." Cheyenne didn't have any answers. "Since the attack, the darkness lay dormant, hidden until they needed her. It wasn't her fault."

"I'm sorry." Jane began slowly. "We all lost good friends to him."

Shelly circled her arm around her mother's waist. "It wasn't your fault either."

Jane took Bridget's hand in her own. "It's time we all forgive ourselves for what we did do and didn't do." She extended her free hand to Cheyenne. Sliding her hand down, she found Cheyenne's hand and entwined their fingers. She became the link that brought them all together. Jane smiled. "Goddess, we have endured much pain and sorrow. We have lost friends and loved ones. We have questioned ourselves and our paths."

Breathing deeply, Cheyenne felt the energy rise among them; it flowed freely between them, cleansing and healing. Mercury's image appeared in her mind. Lisa walked beside him. For a moment, they stopped and looked back. Love and hope radiated back to her with the message that soon they would be back for the final battle. Together they turned and continued the journey, fading from her vision. Blinking rapidly, she felt a tear fall down her cheek. Lilith reached around and wiped it away.

"May your strength and wisdom continue to grow within us" Jane continued. "We are grateful for your protection and you guidance. Thank you for bringing us together so we may share our pain and be healed by each other."

Bridget cleared her throat. "Thank you Lisa for sending the dragon to protect us. I am sorry we could not have protected you." She drew Shelly closer. "We came to save you, but you saved us. May the Goddesses guide and protect you on your journey. May it be filled with peace."

"Protect and guide April," Lilith began slowly. "She-she really was doing her best. To me she was a loving, supportive friend. What she did—she-she . . ." Her voice trailed off.

"We ask that she be forgiven." Jane continued. "What was done, was done. We ask that she be protected and guided back to her path of light with grace and ease. As for us, we forgive her."

"I forgive her," Cheyenne echoed.

"May her clan find and reclaim her someday," Shelly added.

"Thank you." Lilith whispered. "Across time and space, I speak to you my sister. May your anger be healed. May your soul find peace. May you accept our forgiveness and my love. May you again find you way back to the path of light and wholeness so our paths may again join together."

"Dear friend," Bridget picked up the thought. "You brought joy and healing to so many lost souls. As you have healed others, may you find the healing and protection you need. I pray the strength and wisdom you gain through your many challenge guide you back to your true self. Until that time, each day I vow to light a candle in your honor to light your way with loving energy."

"So mote it be." Jane ended the prayer.

Aries scratched on the back door. Snuffling, Cheyenne smiled. "I'd better let him in." Giving Lilith a final hug, Cheyenne walked past her through the kitchen and opened the door. Aries limped in and immediately lied down at Cheyenne's feet. He looked up at Cheyenne. Nodding, she scratched his head. "I have to make a call." Stepping around Aries, she walked to the counter and opened the phone book, searching for the listing of the vet.

"Did the others come to the house?" Lilith wiped away her tears and turned around. "They left the field ahead of us."

"Others?" Jane questioned.

"Carmen, Beverly, Shane and Grandmother. They were at the field. Shane said she represented the three in calling the Bringers of Justice." Lilith answered.

Bridget shook her head. "They would go to Rachael's." Quickly she turned to Jane. "They were at the store. We gave her the crystals we charged. I was going to tell you but things got a little crazy."

"It was my idea." Shelly cut in. "The three of us could have called them. Shane would be able to use them and I wanted to make sure . . ." Her voice trailed off.

"I understand." Jane reached out and gently touched Shelly's shoulder.

"They must have taken Carmen with them. Lilith, how badly was she hurt?"

"Bad enough to go to the emergency room."

"Chester is definitely going to need a vet as well." Cheyenne picked up the receiver.

"What do you mean as well?" Jane ran into the kitchen. Seeing, Aries she stopped. "Ohmygod! Aries."

Questioning, he looked up at her.

"It looks worse than it is." Cheyenne dialed "I'll clean him up and take him in. He'll need stitches. But he'll be ok." Cheyenne reached down and scratched his ears. "We all need to assess the damage to ourselves. Lilith, it wouldn't hurt for you to see a doctor, too."

"I'll be fine."

"Sure you will. And you called me the walking wounded."

"Fine. What shall I tell them?"

Kneeling beside Aries, Jane gently stroked his head. "Good point. Someone should call Rachael's. There are going to be a lot of questions. We'd better get our stories straight."

DENOUEMENT

The early morning sun cast was still casting long shadows. The bird sang and flew on the light breeze. The horses had begun their trek to the back part of the pasture. The chickens clucked and scratched at the ground. They still needed to be fed.

Lilith closed her car door It was all packed and she was ready to go. She slowly walked to the hood of the car and stared at the field beyond the barn. Her eyes still held regret and pain. It was going to take a long time for the joy to return to them.

Cheyenne was going to miss her, but she had already stayed a week beyond what she'd planned. She walked up behind her. "I wish you could stay."

Lilith shook her head. "It's time for me to go."

"I know."

"When will Shelly be back?"

"A few weeks."

Bridget and Shelly had returned home a couple days after the investigation ended. Shelly was coming back. She would be living and working on the farm. Bridget wasn't happy, but she wouldn't stand in her daughter's way.

"She has some good ideas." Cheyenne continued, not saying what she really wanted to. "Her idea to build the ramp and dump the manure right in the spreader will save time."

Lilith nodded. "Have you been back yet?"

Reluctantly, Cheyenne followed her gaze. "I wish the police would have found their bodies. It would have answered their questions." The truth was she didn't know when she would go back. She didn't want to risk connecting herself to them again. By staying away and focusing on other things, she kept her mind off questions that were better never asked.

"Me either." Lilith shook her head. "It just would have caused more problems."

"I'm glad it's over."

Lilith turned to meet her gaze. "It's over between them and us. But it's not over."

"For now it is." Shrugging, Cheyenne leaned against the car. "Are you going to be able to go back the mundane life?"

"The boredom and routine will be good for me." Lilith smiled. "You going to focus on the harvest?"

"The farm and Dragon's Herb will take up most of my time from now on."

"You ever going to give this place a real name?" A glimmer of humor sparkled in the brown eyes.

"Funny you should mention it." Cheyenne tucked her fingers in her front pockets and smiled. "I had a dream last night about a valley. It was lush and peaceful. It was called Dur'ga. Land of—"

"Mother's garden." Tears appeared in Lilith's eyes. "Home."

"She wants us to become a family again. To face our betrayers as one." Cheyenne stood. "We will face them here. It's already in motion."

"When the time comes, I'll be back." Lilith reached out and rubbed Cheyenne's cheek. "I'm going to miss you little sister. But I need a break."

"We're all going to be quiet and mundane for a while." Cheyenne patted the back of the dark hand. "Me included. Did Jane tell you she went back to her old job?"

"The TV station." Lilith nodded. "She seemed excited about it."

"I'm happy for her." Cheyenne looked toward the cottages. "Sammy keeps trying to get her to help again. I'm glad she refuses."

"I was talking to Sammy this morning. She was just getting home. There was another murder last night."

"I know. They're looking in the wrong place."

Lilith eyebrow arched. "What do you know?"

"It's going to get worse before it's over." Cheyenne stood and hugged her. "It's time for me to go to work and you have a long drive ahead of you."

Lilith backed away. "Why am I getting the feeling, when I find out—I'm really not going to like it?"

Cheyenne smiled and backed away.

"Great!" Lilith opened the door and slipped behind the wheel, closing the door. The engine started easily. "Love you."

"Love you too." Cheyenne waved.

Slowly, the car backed up until it faced the driveway and started toward the road.

Cheyenne stared after it long after the dust had begun to settle. For the first time in a long time she felt safe and back on her path. In the past few days, it had occurred to her how different her life could have been if she hadn't convinced Celeste to stay with her. So much pain could have been prevented, yet she would have missed out on the joy as well. Slowly she turned and walked toward the barn. It was the yin and yang of life. Joys and sorrows. People come and people leave. She stopped and looked at the cabins. Only two were empty now. Hearing that Jerry had disappeared, Selene had called her and asked to move back. She didn't want her and her girls to live in their old cabin. Cheyenne had understood and gave her the one Dominic had lived in. Jerry's dogs were happy to be back with Selene. Cheyenne shook her head. Lisa was dead. Melanie was missing, presumed dead. So much pain for one family. She continued to the tack room and opened the door. Cally raced to get inside before she closed it. A strange tan and brown tabby sat on the counter. Seeing Cally it hissed and growled. Cally responded in kind.

"Hey!" Cheyenne yelled. "Newbie's don't have territory rights. You want to stay here—you behave."

It purred but still glared down at Cally. There was something strange about the cat. It made all the other animals nervous and seemed to find its way into places the other cats couldn't. Filling the cat dishes, she watched it jump down and start eating from the dish furthest from Cally. There was something different about it. Watching the tabby, Cheyenne crossed her arms and leaned back against the counter. It looked up. Their eyes met. They looked familiar. Shaking her head, she smiled at herself for being silly. "Ok. I'm going to work. No fighting or I'll pull both your tails." Walking into the barn, she started planning the rest of her morning.